05-02-14

05-03-14

A HASIDIC TALE

A rabbi asks his students, "How can we tell when night has passed?"

One student says, "When it is possible to tell a dog from a wolf."

Another suggests, "When it is possible to identify the fruit on the tree."

As each student responds, the rabbi shakes his head, no.

Finally, one student cries out in frustration, "Then you tell us!"

The rabbi smiles and says, "It is when you can look on the face of any man or woman and see it as your brother or sister.

"If you cannot see this, it is still night."

SNOW
RISING

MATT BALDWIN

SHADOW
MOUNTAIN

Visit us at ShadowMountain.com

Library of Congress Cataloging-in-Publication Data
Baldwin, Matt.
   Snow rising / Matt Baldwin.
      p. cm.
   Includes bibliographical references.
   Summary: Jason Snow signs up for a mountain climbing expedition in hopes of finding some meaning in life. Coached by mountain guide Clara Schroeder, Jason Snow finds a new, more authentic way of living.
   ISBN 978-1-60641-658-7 (hardbound : alk. paper)
   1. Mountaineering—Fiction. I. Title.
   PS3602.A59544S66 2010
   813'.6—dc22   2010011544

Printed in the United States of America
Publishers Printing

10 9 8 7 6 5 4 3 2 1

For Val, Nick, and Lauren, with a prayer for a peaceful future

CONTENTS

CONTENTS

PROLOGUE

No one wakes up in the morning hoping to suffer all day. The human endeavor, regardless of race, culture, or class, is founded on a deep and profound desire for well-being, happiness, joy, contentment, or peace. If such virtues will determine the quality of every instant of our lives, shouldn't we know what they are?

Discovering these virtues is difficult. We live on a seething planet that provokes conflict: of bullets and bombs, of philosophies, cultures, and opinions, and of words. We're increasingly polarized: The right moves further right, the left moves further left, and the center is stretched thin. Husbands and wives drift into separate worlds while children isolate themselves with technology. Inner cities and suburbs live in dramatically different cultures, and perverted, radicalized ideology finds ears for its rhetoric in the poor, illiterate, and disenfranchised. A generation ago, politics and religion could be thoughtfully and intelligently discussed among diverse people; the chasm between us is now too wide for most to straddle reasonably.

How does the world cultivate sustainable peace when we're more culturally and philosophically divided than ever?

What if the great human virtues all have a common ancestor? What if these virtues are merely consequences of a cause so fundamental that our happiness is inextricably entwined in understanding it?

What if most of the values we call core are not core at all? What if the values we're instilling in our children, our families, and our organizations won't hold up in the furnace of challenge, competition, aggression, and conflict? What if today's roots of leadership and influence are being grown in soil that Western culture has sterilized for over fifty years?

Those are difficult questions. There are some who say that violent conflict is inevitable, given our pressurized human condition. They have given up on peace. For others, it's unclear whether any one person can make a difference anymore. What *is* clear to everyone is that the world is getting smaller, much smaller. Media sources flash the news within seconds of event impact. Counterattacks are planned not weeks or months from provocation, after tempers cool and thoughtful heads prevail, but within minutes or hours, when adrenaline, anger, and hate are sharp. Weapons, whether military, social, or emotional, are sophisticated and destructive. Far too often, war is a marketplace in which death is exchanged for money or pride—or both.

Fueling the conflict is a widening gulf between the wealthy and the poor. Those without advocacy are regressing and have very little to lose. Paradoxically, and despite recent economic downturns, the developed world is enjoying a standard of living unparalleled in human history. However, happiness has never been so elusive, joy so difficult to find. At home, the breakup of marriages and families is on a sprinting pace, with no letup in sight. Love and fulfillment are considered in self-centered terms: Whom can I attach myself to who will give me what I want? How can I earn more, buy more, and have more? Happiness is perceived as a product of status, wealth, social acceptance, appearance, fame, and leisure. Business runs just in front of a wave of investor impatience and discontent, and vision extends barely beyond the next quarterly report. Government corruption is rampant, our moral compass demagnetized by money. Stress is on the rise, the cause of more heart attacks than heredity, poor nutrition, and lack of exercise combined.

Under these influences, personal peace is swept away in favor of grabbing a piece of the pie. We're selling our soul. We've become an outside-in culture: What can I *acquire* that will provide me *inner* satisfaction?

Sustainable peace within our families, throughout our communities, and between cultures and nations will come only when we begin to resolve the internal discord that plagues us individually. If, as seems likely, the degree of aggressive contention a person expresses on the outside is a direct reflection of the personal turmoil experienced on the inside, peace can only grow one person at a time. Perhaps it's time we stepped forward, individually, to declare peace with ourselves, our families, and our communities. Peace works from the inside out, not from the outside in.

More than at any other time in human history, peace, both personal and social, must be considered with new vigor, new vision, and new determination. Peace must be pursued through a realistic framework, one that outlives the usually temporary effects of changing circumstances, compromises, and treaties. Individuals, families, organizations, and nations all struggle with problems that may appear process- or policy-oriented, but that are actually deeply rooted in a wholly inadequate model of self-fulfillment and power. We are so focused on symptoms that we've become blind to the cause. We must move ourselves beyond the processes and policies and sincerely examine the principles that form their foundation.

Beyond basic necessities, material possession has nothing

whatsoever to do with happiness. In fact, those born, raised, and folded into affluent cultures may well be at a disadvantage in finding contentment. Wealth is a distraction few can overcome. Those who build their life on "things" are programmed to fail. When the "things" disappear, as they generally do, the false foundations their owners have constructed their lives on are swept to sea in a wave of challenge. No one would knowingly build a home on lowlands susceptible to flooding during high tide, yet we construct our happiness on possession and position.

My aim is to illuminate an alternative way to look at the world—one person at a time. Certainly I do not have all the answers. There is nothing new about my ideas; the sustainable values discussed within these pages only serve as reminders of what has proven true before. I believe their harmony is undeniable, even eternal, and will be proven true again by anyone who seeks to live with a peaceful heart and a curious mind. I invite you to join me, and leave you with two questions: one, can you be an advocate for the changes you desire to see in yourself and in the world around you; and two, do you have the audacity to find out?

Matt Baldwin
Wasatch Mountains, Utah

Chapter 1

MISSING

The night began as many others. He pulled the big SUV off
US 26 east of Zigzag, down a short graveled roadway, and right
into the driveway of their rustic, cedar-clad cabin just west of
the mountain. Bringing the truck to a stop next to Anna's black Volvo
wagon, he got out to stretch and breathed his first gulp of mountain
air: thin, crisp, and clean. He could hear the Sandy River rushing in
the distance, gravity and rock defining its course. Tomorrow he'd be
up early; get unloaded; grab the waders, vest, fly rod, and tackle; leave
the family to their own devices; and head for the river.

Jason stepped quietly into the old cabin, said a cursory hello to
Anna, Brian, and Jesse, made his way upstairs, and settled comfortably
at his old heirloom desk. There was peace in this place, even with the
undertow of unrest. The soothing smells of cedar, leather, and crackling fire wafted through the cabin as he casually leafed through the
materials he'd received from Cascade Mountain Guides: packing list,
itinerary, orientation information. Had he covered everything? Was he
ready for this?

The truth was, he'd been dead bored and miserable for months. He wanted to do something new and challenging, something to wake up a life anesthetized by material success and emotional isolation. Most of all, he wanted to escape the pounding of an unrelenting conscience. When he'd seen the poster in a downtown window, he'd decided that a climb up 11,240 feet of slumbering volcano was just the ticket. He'd contacted Cascade in July of last year, having been advised by a good friend and experienced climber to ask for a highly sought-after guide known as Merlin. Booked for the remainder of the climbing year, Merlin had spots available the next May. Jason signed up and used the date as motivation to get his sedentary physique back in shape during the dripping Oregon winter.

It wasn't until several weeks ago, when talking with Lance Kennedy, a former mountain guide and business acquaintance, that he learned who "Merlin" was: Clara Schroeder, a fiftyish, retired chemical engineer who was, according to Lance, an institution on the mountain. She'd been tagged with the nickname years ago for her route-finding skills, an uncanny nose for the whereabouts of lost climbers, and a reputation for the heady discussions she would mediate during summit climbs. Discussions that, Lance said, had affected him and others he knew for years after.

"She's been through it," Lance emphasized. "She knows what she's talking about. Listen to her."

Clara was reportedly a delightful combination of guide, philosopher, historian, chemist, teacher, motivator, geologist, and athlete. And she was tough. "Pioneer tough," Lance said. He clearly thought the world of Clara.

He'd met her in 1973 on his first ascent of Rainier. Lance and his team of climbers had been fighting miserable weather for nearly thirty-six hours, were still 800 feet below the summit in forty-mile-per-hour winds, and were seriously considering abandoning any attempt at the top. Three climbers, two young men and, he remembered, a lanky young woman who showed strength, grace, and ease in the face of a cold wrath, appeared out of the howling blizzard above them. They'd been to the summit and taken some photos, said it was wonderful, wished them well, and continued their descent like a stroll in the park. Thank you, Clara Schroeder.

After his descent of Rainier, Lance tracked Clara down and began a friendship that had survived calm, turbulence, and the twists and turns that define the course of a life's existence. She was just that kind of person: a force that raised the tide of all she touched.

All this made Jason wince a bit. He worried that someone like Clara would look straight through him, see him for what he was: lost, alone, and void of substance. He'd naturally been a little nervous about the climb anyway. Now he was unnaturally anxious about meeting Clara. He regularly did business with heavy hitters, CEOs and CFOs, and had no uneasiness in holding his own in the rocky geology of executive strata. Why this sudden distress over meeting a mountain guide? Kennedy's description of Clara excavated old bones long buried, and he didn't know why.

He had suspicions, however. Had he really become uncomfortable with . . . what? Authenticity? Had it come to that? Clara represented, by description at least, something he had once thought he would certainly become, a lover of life and of people. Someone who had an influence on others, made them see things in themselves they never saw before. Someone who enthusiastically grabbed the proverbial bull by the horns and didn't let go until they'd had the ride of their life. He wondered if it was still possible for him to be that person. Jason didn't know, but he had his doubts.

Knowing that his wife and two teenage kids were flopped in the great room downstairs, it occurred to him that he should probably make an appearance. A fleeting thought. He knew Anna would read it for what it was: obligation rather than desire. And he knew, from repeated experience, what would come next: a whispered but pointed "conversation" about him becoming more involved with the family. Same stuff, different time and place. Jason played the images in his mind and heard the audio, all of which summoned the usual throbbing of the head, not because he felt bad for his lack of participation, but because he knew that nothing but an argument would come from the interrogation. Avoidance was the better option, and he had that down cold.

Time with his family had slowly eroded over the past several years. Like a shallow lake drying up during the peak of summer heat, it didn't happen all at once, but slowly and at an undeniable pace.

He found himself missing more games, activities, and family outings. Lately he'd missed a variety of social engagements with Anna due to "important" work at the office. He couldn't admit to her that it wasn't the work that kept him there but the tension between them that kept him away. Jason disliked himself for not having the guts to confront the problem, to take a weekend away with this wonderful woman he had once loved so much, to see if they might work things out. To begin again. He suspected the thought of spending an entire weekend alone with him was more than she could bear.

He'd forgotten Anna's birthday last year, and although she hadn't appeared outwardly upset, Jason knew he'd hurt her and told her he was sorry. She'd kindly accepted his apology, but she couldn't mask the disappointment abundant in her deep brown eyes. Anna couldn't have cared less about gifts. What did mean a great deal to her was consideration. A gift was a symbol of time spent, of the fact that Jason had invested effort in thinking about her and what he might do to make her happy. It had taken him years to figure that out—that it wasn't the gift per se, but the thinking and behavior behind the gift that was the treasure for Anna.

That knowledge had finally struck him some years ago when he was looking through a family album. Anna had written captions under the various photos, cards, and drawings that the kids had given her over the years. Included were six poems written on colored craft paper and stapled together, poems that Brian, nine years old and in fourth grade at the time, had collected for her as a Mother's Day present. Handwritten on the front cover was a note: "Dear Mom, Happy Mother's Day. I got these poems at school with the help of Mrs. Thompson. She's nice. They remind me of you. Thanks for being my Mom. I love you, Brian." Anna's caption underneath said simply, "The finest gift I've ever received from my wonderful son Brian." Upon reading this, Jason considered that perhaps she'd written her inscription for Brian's benefit, that it was an acknowledgment to him that she understood. Further thought made him realize that Anna's caption was a mother's honesty. It *was* one of the finest things she'd ever received—from anyone. A gift of scrap paper, felt marker, and time, and priceless to her.

He thought it ironic that once he began to understand what made her tick, they began to drift further apart. Was it because Anna felt he knew how to make her happy and yet chose not to give her those simple things? His time? His consideration? His thoughts? Himself? Perhaps that was the sharp wedge driven between them. Maybe ignorance *was* bliss, he thought. Knowledge carried the weight of responsibility and expectation.

He slipped the climbing brochures and equipment list back into his briefcase. Remaining upstairs, he moved to the comfortable old brown leather sofa, stretched out, opened the cover of *Angels and Demons,* and promptly fell asleep.

Chapter 2

FISHING

He awoke early Saturday morning as light filtered by tall timber was forming. The rest of the family was still asleep. He rubbed the stiffness out of his bones and stretched, put on a pot of coffee, and grabbed a granola bar. Rifling through his duffel bag for waders and jeans, he changed, grabbed vest, fly rod, and tackle, and quietly slipped out the back, careful to not let the screen door slap against the door frame.

Jason headed upriver along a narrow path that skirted the eastern stream bank. He'd thought he should encourage Brian to come along, but his selfish desire for solitude defied his conscience. After all, Brian was old enough to make the decision himself—if he wanted to fish, he would fish. He was eighteen, and Jason shouldn't have to drag him along. Jesse, fifteen, was simply not interested—at all. She had once commented that she loved the whole idea of fishing, except for the cold, the hassle with the equipment, the discomfort of being wet for most of a day, the slimy feel of fish, the taste, and the bones. Other than that, fishing was just great. When Jesse did join him, she spent more time picking flies out of streamside Oregon Grape than catching trout. Anna, a capable fly fisherman in her own right, wasn't inclined lately to join him and ruin a perfectly good day for both of them. Throwing barbs at each other was not what either considered relaxing recreation.

After twenty minutes of dipping and dodging blackberry, rocks, and old-growth snags, Jason stopped at a spot he'd fished many times. Here, the Sandy widened some, creating room for a small counterclockwise eddy near the opposite bank, a perfect location for rainbows and browns to glide against the swift current. A forty-foot cast would land a fly just upstream of the eddy; then he'd float it dry right over the top of the hungry trout. Jason studied the river, careful to notice which insects the fish were surfacing for. He'd never considered himself much of a fly fisherman. He was a clumsy mechanic in an artist's world. Some on the river could tell you every species of flying critter, how it correlated with the calendar, water temperature, and the feeding habits of local fish species. He didn't tie his own flies and couldn't perform a roll cast to save his life. But he was, finally, marginally competent at the basics, enough at least to catch a fish every so often and to enjoy this ancient river with its peaceful sights, mossy smells, and eternally soothing sound of water in motion. Jason had always considered moving water a fundamental sound, nature's bloodstream coursing through arteries of rock.

Lately, however, even his enjoyment of the Sandy had waned. He fished alone. In previous years the solitude had provided a soothing relief from the turmoil of modern living and allowed him to reconnect: to think, consider, and clarify. Recent days on the river were less enjoyable. His conscience was a voice he couldn't avoid, not even out here. It spoke clearly and seemed a constant companion. As a result, the solitude mocked him, declaring his life a disappointment, reminding him that it hadn't gone the way he'd hoped. Oh, he was "successful," but success came at a price that had proven too significant.

His father was what Jason called a truth seeker, a spiritual man. Although Dad never claimed affiliation to a particular religion, he was fond of the notion that it was easy to gain the world and lose your own soul. How painfully correct his father had been. Why hadn't he listened? Was it a typical generational disconnect, or was it something else?

Prepping his leader and fly, Jason tried to find a word that was an appropriate reflection of how he felt. Frustrated? Troubled? Angry? Bitter? Misunderstood? Disappointed? Discouraged? Perhaps that last one was it. The others had no required connection to discouragement. Discouragement was a disease all its own, as different from disappointment and frustration as a head cold was from cancer.

Wading knee-deep into the cold, swift current, he braced himself and began letting out line. Ten o'clock. Two o'clock. Ten o'clock. Two o'clock. The patient rhythm took time to develop. He was always too quick, too abrupt.

Slow it down, he thought.

Rainbows and browns were two things left in his life that didn't jump when he demanded, a fact that left him less willing to enjoy a stream bank. He was not born with a fly rod in his hand.

Growing up, Jason remembered spending a couple of days a year fishing with his father, who always seemed politely amused by his son's ability to whip any patch of water within casting range into a frothy, fishless mire. Jason didn't stalk the rainbows and browns with technique or cunning so much as he drove them to other locations through noise and disruption. It wasn't until he'd reached his late teens that it finally occurred to him why father always waited for son to select a stretch of river to fish before heading upstream or down a safe distance. Jason drove the fish like cattle. Dad simply had to open the gate and collect them.

Once Jason had settled in, his thoughts wandered to things other than fishing.

He'd spent nearly his entire career at Northwest Design and Engineering and had certainly brought in the revenue. His team was talented, but they walked carefully around him, and he suspected he knew why. His autocratic and sternly authoritative leadership had brought the group success; you'd think they'd be grateful. They weren't. They performed out of a fear of his authority and the possible loss of their jobs rather than out of respect, trust, self-motivation, or innovative drive.

Jason was discouraged that it always fell to him to lead out on new projects, that the team held back until he pointed the way despite an impressive level of competence. They seemed hesitant to communicate their ideas openly, especially if those ideas appeared to differ from his. He had canned his share of underperformers in his day, replacing them with better talent. Yet the overall effectiveness of the organization never seemed to change substantially. So, Jason pushed them harder. Demanded more. As years went on, he became less sympathetic and more dictatorial, less concerned for the problems of people on his staff, more concerned about the problems the staff created.

In recent years, the firm had become what Jason had always sworn he would never work for, a turn-em-and-burn-em shop. Hire them, demand their allegiance, scare them silly when necessary, work them to death until all energy and enthusiasm were spent, then see them resign out of a survival instinct or terminate them for someone new, someone ignorant of the environment they were entering. Turn-em-and-burn-em. This was not the system that was touted during NDE job interviews, training, or staff meetings, and it was not what Jason wanted. It was simply how it was. It wasn't his fault upper management had created a turn-em-and-burn-em shop. He was working to keep his job as much as his team members were.

If his staff thought he was tough, they ought to try walking in his shoes; try explaining an underperforming quarter to C. J. Sampson without getting skinned and rotisseried. He couldn't allow a breakdown in results or the entire team would suffer, starting with him. Of course, if he had a choice, he would do it differently, but he was senior management, and the expectation was that he'd pull hard on the party line.

The firm had on several occasions attempted to stem the tide of mistrust and staff turnover. Consultants had been hired. Mission statements were produced. Organizations were realigned. New philosophies adopted. New processes instituted. Ultimately, effectiveness regressed.

So much for consultants.

Jason was convinced that a mission statement did more harm than good. Why hang some declaratory statement on a wall for everyone to see, only to have management prove its incapacity to meet its own standard? Mission statements caused expectations to rise, and management would hammer those expectations with actions inconsistent with the written values. Integrity, trust, loyalty, and any drive for creative communication were all casualties of such a process. Big staff problems always followed, requiring management to respond with more formalized controls and mandatory procedures, a descending spiral difficult to stop once started and responsible, perhaps, for more business failures than a lack of good ideas or capital.

Jason knew well that in many cases it was *his* actions that had violated staff expectations, not to mention his own sense of right and wrong. But business is business—follow the money and get over it. And, as a rainmaker, Jason had built layers of insulation he hoped would defend him from the consequences of violating corporate dogma. However, no amount of insulation could protect him from his own conscience, which was eating him alive from the inside out after years of purposeful betrayal.

A big rainbow broke the surface and momentarily bit on the fly. His line went straight and the graphite rod tip quivered. Jason, lost in thought, was startled at the movement. The trout was long gone before he'd even considered setting the hook. Typical. Good thing there was plenty of food in the cabin. A dependence on his skill with a fly rod was what Anna called the Snow Diet. No fish.

The forty-four-year-old father of two slipped back into his own head.

I have nearly everything I ever wanted, yet I wake up each morning feeling like I'm nothing. I'm married, have great kids and good friends, and feel like I'm alone in the world. I'm successful by just about every worldly standard, but unhappy. I'm generally respected within the community, yet feel like I'm faking it, like I've somehow fooled everyone around me.

These were not pleasant thoughts, especially since they appeared without any apparent resolution. Jason wondered whether he would be able to resolve his circumstance even if he possessed answers. He was who he was, and he knew the adage about teaching old dogs new tricks. Change was hard. The proliferation of twelve-step programs was testament to that. But his problem was not an addiction, was it?

He shook that thought out of his mind. Why would someone *choose* unhappiness? Why would someone choose to act in a way that got him the opposite of what he wanted? Why would anyone do that? It made absolutely no sense, none whatsoever, and Jason wasn't going to waste any more energy thinking through that little nugget.

Another strike, a brown this time. Jason didn't attempt a response. Time to pack this party up and go home. He'd been on the river about four hours, lost a favorite fly in submerged snags, and was fishless to boot. Not an uncommon haul.

He stepped carefully through the flashing current to the riverbank, gathered his soggy tackle, and headed back to the cabin.

Chapter 3
THE BROKEN BOY

Jason Snow worked for a leading architectural and engineering firm in Portland, Oregon, the head of a promising, innovative team of architects, designers, and financiers who specialized in institutional projects: schools, churches, hospitals, and government buildings. Although it wasn't his firm, he knew that C. J. Sampson, founder and CEO, was well aware Jason was a rainmaker, and he was compensated accordingly. He'd invested considerable time cultivating both talent and contacts, the latter with the knowledge that business was still driven by who you know more than what you know, a characteristic that irked him. That is, until he fought his way into the circle.

He was plugged into the old-boys network: Multnomah Athletic Club, Portland Golf Club, neither of which he frequented more than a couple times a year. Still, he understood how deals were done and was willing to do what it took to thrive in an environment of competition and aggression. He'd managed to survive in an industry known as much for being cutthroat as cutting edge. And his company, though socially friendly and politically correct, operated on a centuries-old system of patriarchal hierarchy and alpha-male leadership.

Jason thought often about the paradox that he lived in a liberal town, in a liberal age, and worked in an industry that, from the outside, appeared socially conscious, even enlightened—yet within, the old fabric of "crush your enemies and kill their children" was still worn with unspoken pride. It frustrated him that what seemed to work at the office failed so miserably at home. He felt the need to remind his family continually that he deserved the respect and admiration he'd earned in his profession. The disparity was a vise that crushed Jason and killed his relationship with Anna and their children.

He wasn't blaming the business for his unhappiness. He knew that by most standards he was a success, which had gotten him . . . well, nowhere. It was this disconnect that plagued him, the dissonance between the values that worked at the office and those that were required of him at home. He was lost. Jason felt like he was living a perpetual coin toss at the start of a football game: Which goal did he attack and which did he protect? Offense or defense? Home or away? He had to admit to himself that he knew when he was failing at home. His conscience was damaged, not dead. But how could he be expected to make the mental shift between the selfish considerations of survival in a work environment and the selfless considerations of a father and husband? He'd been losing this game for years and didn't see a turnaround in the making. He felt lost, angry, unappreciated, and alone.

What angered him as much as anything was the recognition that he had let his father down. He'd done things he wasn't proud of, and he was old-fashioned enough to have a profound desire to someday look his deceased father in the eye, if only figuratively, and report that he'd done his best, that his time on earth had been well spent, that it had mattered to someone other than himself.

Dad was not a demanding man. Jason considered him enriched with characteristics from another time and place. Smart yet uncomplicated, his father had an unspoken expectation that people should do the right thing for the right reason, whatever the circumstance. Jason wondered seriously about the number of people left on the planet who thought about the world in that way. He considered it an "old-time" view, one stoked in the furnace of a severe test, and thought it unlikely that those traits could be developed in a modern world of convenience, wealth, and plenty—Jason's world.

Jason had once considered his father's perspective naïve, simplistic, and unrelated to a world of "eat or be eaten." Recent years had brought hard lessons learned through experience, and with them a creeping accommodation that perhaps Dad's perspective was the result of willful mental exertion. Jason was only beginning to acknowledge that such exertion required a toughness he could hardly comprehend.

He genuinely wondered about his ability to apply a template that seemed so out of touch with the modern requirements of survival. And yet, his father had awakened every morning to the same sun he did. Somehow, he had chosen to see and act differently. Dad had learned to look through the lens of adversity and see clearly the blessings of the test, seeming grateful even for the pokes and potholes life threw at him. Jason couldn't remember his father ever acting in behalf of someone else with an expectation of receiving anything in return. Dad had been selfless and happy about it, a virtue that aggravated Jason in his inability to grasp the concept.

Jason, in a memory that seemed only days old, not decades, vividly remembered an incident that cast deepening shadows over the rest of his life.

❋   ❋   ❋

He'd entered the University of Oregon in the fall of 1980, pledged Beta Theta Pi, and moved into the frat house on Patterson and Eleventh, having left home on the heels of the Iranian hostage crisis, the eruption of Mount St. Helens, Reagan's trouncing of Carter, *The Empire Strikes Back*, the buzz over "The Miracle on Ice" at Lake Placid, and the shooting death of Lennon at the Dakota. Friends consisted mostly of frat buddies who were as disconnected from academic excellence as he was. They spent their days concocting means of entertainment and chaos, each party or prank an escalation of the one before, superb confirmation of the theory that with each additional college frat boy added to the mix, the collective IQ divides in half. Serious injury and hilarity were the general outcomes.

A couple of months had passed since he'd skipped his first class, and the fun was heating up. There was spirited competition within his house for bragging rights over the best prank: late teens and twenty-somethings wrestling for single-digit emotional maturity. Even Jason found the constant barrage of adolescent activity a little much, but he didn't say anything for fear of being cast off into outer freshmandom by upperclassmen.

His father had allowed him use of the family pickup for college, a red 1964 International with an iron brush guard, torn seats, and rusted bed. The vehicle was referred to affectionately by his frat mates as "The Piece."

It began harmlessly enough: a week prior to Thanksgiving break, past midnight, a long stretch of unlit sidewalk bordered by thick juniper bushes that connected the library to men's on-campus housing, living accommodations for male nobodies too socially backward to get accepted into Greek society and too poor to afford a decent apartment. The nerds. Perfect. The combination proved far too enticing for Jason and some Beta inmates.

They called the setup "flash and grab" and had—quite successfully, they thought—executed the strategy on several Jack-Daniel's-induced occasions. They'd laughed themselves sick for hours afterward.

Things were coming together as Jason waited in The Piece just beyond the wash of the lone streetlight. A young man—thin, tan cords, maroon Members Only jacket, calculator clipped to his pants pocket, glasses—exited the library and walked a little too briskly toward home and, Jason imagined, a hot date with a new computer game, Pac-Man or something.

A smile grown by anticipation creased Jason's face. "Come on, dude, come on," he whispered. "Just a little farther. That's it, that's my boy. Come to papa."

A marked car. Campus security. Really bad timing. Although, Jason wondered, how seriously can you take two guys riding in a white Chrysler Newport with a green and yellow duck mascot stenciled on the door? Not very.

Jason blinked the headlights to warn his co-conspirators. No response. Slipping the International into gear, he released the clutch and accelerated down the side street to stop the charade and avoid a lashing. Too late. Four Betas wearing gorilla masks jumped from the bushes screaming. Two of them pantsed the kid while the other two snatched his backpack. Terrified, mouth wide open in silent shock, and with pants down around his knees, the young man stumbled backward and lost his balance as his ankle twisted over the edge of the concrete curb. Jason watched as this strange spectacle fell in the street directly in his path. He mashed the brakes and gripped the steering wheel while the front tires jumped over what felt like a speed bump.

Jason got stopped and closed his eyes in horror for a second or two, then jumped from the cab, not wanting to look under the heavy truck. Silence. The four gorillas stood frozen in place. He ran to the front and saw bloodstains on the brush guard just in front of the right front wheel. Just behind the wheel was a leg with a new joint broken between knee and ankle. Jason's stomach flopped over. The rest of the body lay limp under the International.

He spun to see the security car resting at a nearby intersection. They'd apparently not seen the accident.

"Grab the leg," he ordered in a hiss. "Pull him out."

"Pull him out?" one of the gorillas responded. "Are you kidding? We'll pull his leg right off. You pull him out."

Jason swore, quickly moving to the exposed leg. "Do I have to do everything myself? You guys are idiots."

Reaching underneath the truck as far as possible, he grabbed the young man above the knee and pulled him from under the truck and up onto the sidewalk. It was not a pretty sight. The boy was unconscious. Blood smattered his face, his glasses were gone, he had abrasions everywhere, but the leg was the thing. Jason winced at the unnatural angle of the break.

"Jump in, now, let's get outta here," Jason yelled as he ran back around to the driver's side and leapt in the cab.

"Let's get outta here? Man, you *are* nuts." An odd-sounding statement from a guy in a gorilla mask. "This guy needs help. You can run if you want, Jason, but I'm staying."

Jason jumped again from the cab and ran back around to the four Betas, swearing a steady stream. "You get in the truck now or I'll kick your butts, you hear me. Now get in!"

There was a craziness in Jason's eyes that none of them were willing to test. The four jumped into the bed while Jason again raced around to the driver's door and dove in. The student's small blue backpack was heaved through the open passenger side window and into the cab. He turned the starter, jammed the truck in gear, let loose of the clutch, and slammed the door in one motion.

Thinking he'd made a clean escape, Jason sped off down the dark street, only to see flashing lights jump to life on top of the campus security vehicle. Something took him over and he felt his right foot stomp the accelerator. He heard shouts and bodies bouncing in the bed behind him. For a split second Jason considered the odds of an old International outrunning security, but he didn't like his chances. He gave up the escape and began to pull over, only to see the security car stop well behind him, lights still flashing. Two officers jumped out to tend to the broken boy.

"That's it, Jason," one of the gorillas said, "I'm getting out."

"Not quite yet," he yelled through his side window.

Back in gear, he popped the clutch and sped into the blackness of the old brick and ivy campus, four gorillas desperately clinging to the truck bed behind him.

Two days went by before campus security rapped on the front door of Beta Theta Pi.

"You fellas have a Jason Snow living here?" they asked without introduction, dead serious.

"Yeah."

"We'd like to see him. Now."

Jason spent the next hour at the offices of campus security before being driven to the Eugene Police Department. He tried to keep his eighteen-year-old cool while his heart blasted out of his chest and fear strangled every breath.

"You drive an International?"

"Yes. It's my dad's."

"We know. We called him."

He literally felt his peripheral vision narrow. The statement had the effect of g-forces he couldn't counteract, a punch to the stomach. Not that he was afraid of his father. Just the opposite. He couldn't remember his father ever lifting his voice or hand to him, and it was that understanding that sickened him. Could he have done anything more to disappoint a man whose title of gentleman fit like well-worn work gloves?

"You called my father?"

No response.

Dad, he thought. They had called Dad. All the idiotic college pranks suddenly flooded him with an unexpected anxiety that bordered on a nervous breakdown.

Jason closed his eyes and saw his graduation gown stripped off, cap and tassel removed as if in a court-martial, and his college degree torched in the course of one stupid evening of fun—a hinge in a life swinging wildly out of control.

"Was it your truck that hit that boy?"

Jason opened his eyes, looked at his questioner, and knew what he had to do.

"What boy, sir?" he responded. "I don't know anything about hitting a boy."

"You sayin' you and your International weren't involved in running over a young man outside the library two nights ago?"

"That was not me, officer. I'm telling you, ask my Beta Theta Pi brothers. I haven't been near the library since I came to school in September."

"You think this is funny?" the officer asked, leaning forward.

Jason considered his flippant remark and toned it down. "There's nothing funny about some guy getting run over. But I'm telling you, it wasn't me."

"We'll see. We're going to impound the truck and have a little chat with your fraternity brothers."

Jason winced inwardly but managed a response. "Feel free."

"Lock him up," an officer said. "We've got twenty-four hours to shove this lie down his throat."

Jason winced again, but he kept his mouth shut as he was ushered to a cell. He could still remember the sound of the tumblers moving and the clank of the iron latch.

Around eight p.m. his father arrived and was escorted back to Jason's cell. His eyes were deep set, face ashen, lifeless as dead flowers. Jason could hardly bring himself to look at him.

"Why didn't you call me, son?" his father asked.

"I didn't want to bother you with this, Dad."

"Bother me? You're in jail. You're accused of running a young man over in our truck. Bother me? You should have called."

His father gripped the bars and looked down at his shoes for a moment, then raised his head slowly.

"Son, I love you. Always have. Always will. I love you because you are my son, not because you're perfect. I had some time to think on my way down here tonight. I remember when you were born. Our first. Your mother was so excited. I was a nervous wreck. Your birth meant I had to grow up, and quick. No more 'me.' It was 'us' from then on, and I wouldn't go back and change a thing. You were so small, so tiny. I remember holding you the first time, the most innocent thing I've ever held in my trembling hands. I asked God that day for the wisdom a father needs to raise a son. Prayed harder than I can remember before or since. Your arrival in our home turned a boy into a man. It didn't take long for me to realize I was as much the student as the teacher. Jason, you have been a blessing to me every day of your short life. I have learned more by being your father than any university could possibly teach. I'm so grateful. We've had a good time, you and I."

Jason looked away, not wanting his father to see the shame spilling down his face.

"I want you to know," his father continued, "without any reservation, that although there's a set of bars separating us, my love for you is no less today than yesterday. Do you understand that, son?"

Jason tried to compose himself. "Yes, Dad, I do."

"We all make mistakes, some bigger than others. I make mistakes every day. I just hope they're not the same ones I made yesterday. It won't ever matter what you do, Jason. You will always be my son and I'll love you."

His father tensed, and Jason knew what was coming.

"Son, did you hit that boy?"

There are moments that come and go quickly but, like big

meteors falling to earth, have a devastating impact. Moments with consequences that ripple long after the initial event has passed.

"No, Dad, I didn't hit the boy. It wasn't me."

Dad paused and breathed deep. "I believe you, son. No reason not to."

His father asked for a chair so he could sit in the hall outside Jason's cell. He stayed in sight for hours.

Three officers returned about 11:30 p.m. and guided them into a small room with tile floor, steel chairs and table, blank yellow walls, no windows. Jason had been in custody for over nine hours.

"I'm Sergeant Daniels. This is Officer Rhodes, and Detective Sawyer." Daniels extended a hand to Jason's father. "You must be Mr. Snow. You're welcome to stay or go. Whatever you want to do."

"Officer," his father nodded. "I'll stay."

"Suit yourself. I'll just ask you to remain quiet while we ask some questions. You okay with that?"

"Fine," Dad responded.

"Jason, you have anything you'd like to say before we begin?" Daniels asked. "Things will be a lot better for you, kid, if you confess before we start this process. If you make us prove our case, you're going to jail. College will be a distant memory. You'll be snuggling with Bubba. Understand?"

Jason watched his father sit forward, quiet but clearly uncomfortable.

Daniels was not a big guy, as cops go. Five-ten, eleven, maybe. Lean. Clean shaven. Short brown hair parted. Black shoes spit-shined. Marine. Ramrod straight and lacking any apparent sense of humor. He was wearing a deep blue short-sleeved uniform shirt that exposed a small star tattoo on his ripped right forearm. His right index finger was gone past the big knuckle, and Jason considered Daniels capable of having bitten it off himself if the need had arisen. This was not a guy to mess with.

Jason quickly ran the last two days through his head. He'd thoroughly cleaned the brush guard with Grey Goose. It had taken three expensive bottles of the vodka to do the job. He'd stashed the blue backpack in the crawl space at Theta Pi and carefully wiped down the grill and hood of the red International. He was convinced there was no evidence on the truck, and his four buddies had discarded the gorilla masks in a dumpster at Autzen Stadium. Still, he was sitting in a room with three teed off police officers who had probably spent hours combing the truck and, Jason worried, perhaps identified and interrogated the gorillas.

Jason drew a breath.

"Look, Officer Daniels," he began. "I have not hit anyone with my truck. Whatever happened, I was not involved. Not me. Not my truck. I don't know what else to say."

"Where were you two nights ago?"

"Running on the Prefontaine."

U of O has an extensive network of bark dust trails named for Steve Prefontaine, the Oregon distance runner of the early 1970s who nearly single-handedly started the running revolution.

"I'm on the cross-country team. I was training."

"After midnight?"

"All the time," Jason responded.

"Isn't that a bit odd, running that late?" Daniels asked.

"This is U of O, Officer. I think you can appreciate that stuff happens at every hour of every day. I ran for an hour or so that night."

"Anyone with you? Teammate? Frat buddy? Girlfriend?"

"Just me."

"What do you know about some guys in gorilla masks?"

Jason knew the officer was watching his every nuance: every move, every breath, every eye movement.

"Don't know anything about gorilla masks."

"That seems odd," Daniels responded.

"Why's that?"

"Betas are infamous for late-night raids in gorilla masks. I'd have thought you'd have heard about that. No?"

"Betas and every other fraternity on campus, and most of the sororities, know that gig. But I know nothing about gorilla masks two nights ago."

"How many Internationals do you think are on campus?" Daniels asked pointedly.

That was the question Jason had been dreading. Internationals were rare, so rare he couldn't recall ever seeing another one on campus. He was sure they were going to begin pinning him in a corner that had no escape. His father turned and looked at him squarely.

"Don't have any idea," Jason responded, as casually as he could summon.

"Seventeen."

The acknowledgment was like a Christmas present in November. Jason breathed without force for the first time in twenty minutes.

"Really. Seventeen."

Jason's confidence was building. He pulled himself up from a slouch.

Daniels stared at him with lasers.

"Why was your brush guard wiped down with alcohol?" Daniels asked.

"Wiped down? I had six frat buddies sitting on the hood a few nights ago, all drinkin' like fish. They spilled more than they drank."

"I suppose you know nothing about a blue backpack?"

"Blue backpack?" Jason echoed.

"The young man who was hit was carrying a blue backpack," Daniels responded. "It was taken. But you wouldn't know anything about that?"

"No, sir."

"Thought so," Daniels responded, his voice thick with sarcasm.

He pushed himself back from the table. "Look, kid, we think you're the guy. Sooner or later we're going to nail you. You sure you want to walk out of here knowing you've got an entire police department watching your every move? Wouldn't it be easier on everyone if you just came clean?"

Jason's father sat back in his chair and crossed his arms but held to his promise. He said nothing.

Jason was too far down the road to turn back. Worse, he couldn't imagine what it would do to his dad to hear him confess.

"I'm really sorry some kid got hit. Really. But I didn't do it."

"Okay, son, if that's your story. We haven't found what we need yet, but we will. We will."

Daniels stopped and glared at Jason with a gaze that would set a forest on fire.

"You want to play? We'll play. Let's get him out of here. Mr. Snow, you're free to take your son home, but there's a condition."

"Thank you," Jason's father responded. "What's the condition?"

Daniels stared straight at Jason and pointed an amputated finger at his face. "I want you to go back to your frat house, lay your head on that pillow each night, and before you nod off, think about the fact that a young man is lying on a hospital bed in intensive care with a leg so busted up it's likely he'll not have it much longer. I want you to think about that every night. I want you to live with it, breathe it, dream it, and eat it. You hear me?"

"That's about enough," his father responded, standing up.

"I think you're absolutely right, Mr. Snow," Daniels said. "Get the kid out of my sight."

Father and son left the station and drove to the impound yard to retrieve the red International. Nothing was said. Jason felt relieved that he had escaped getting thrown in jail, although a cloud had formed in the upper atmosphere of his conscience. He'd hit the boy and gotten away with it, but the slow, low-grade grinding in his stomach didn't feel like vindication. It was a different kind of jail, an emotional confinement that made his reflection a disgusting shadow to look at.

"Okay, son, I'm headed home. I'll call Mom. She was pretty twisted up."

"Thanks for coming down, Dad," Jason responded. "I'm sorry to have bothered you with this. Could you believe those guys? I didn't think they'd ever believe me or let me out of there."

"They still don't believe you, and you need to remember that. You get caught with a parking violation, and they'll make it difficult for you. I suppose I'd do the same if I thought a guilty boy was walking free." His father paused. "We'll see you in a couple of days for Thanksgiving. You coming up Wednesday?"

"I'll drive up Tuesday night. No classes on Wednesday," Jason responded.

"Good. See you then." Another pause. "I love you. Take care of yourself. My light's always on for you, son."

Jason smiled ruefully.

With that, Dad drove away to catch the 5 and a two-hour drive north to Portland and home. Jason returned to the frat house with less zeal than before. He knew there was something tearing at his father; he could see it in his eyes, hear it in his voice.

Dad's words caught in his mind. He considered that perhaps a real man would have stepped forward and confessed the thing, taken his lumps for a poor decision, gotten it behind him, and moved on with a slate that wasn't perhaps entirely clean but at least was livable. He weighed the pain of living with the indiscretion against the pain of confession and determined the former a less painful road to walk. After all, disclosure was not going to heal the broken leg.

The day after his release, Jason rolled silently out of bed and in the stillness before a misty sunrise pried open the cover to the dank crawl space. He retrieved the blue backpack, wrapped it tightly in a black plastic garbage bag, duct taped it shut, then carefully exited through the back door of Beta Theta Pi out to the truck, walking briskly through thick wet grass. He shoved the wrapping under the bench seat, making room by rearranging the two axes, maul, wedges, and shovel his father perpetually stored there, just in case. After making sure it was entirely concealed, he began considering a good place to rid himself of the last piece of evidence tying him to the hit-and-run.

He was already planning to move out of the frat house after Christmas break and sever contact with the four gorillas and the inevitable memories. The five had quickly come to an uneasy understanding: If one of them went down for the incident, they'd all go down. An agreement, Jason knew, designed to assure that five cocky frat boys would keep their mouths shut.

❉   ❉   ❉

Jason grimaced at the stark and painful memories of the event. Even given the twenty-plus years that had passed, he could still view the event in his mind's eye as if he were sitting in a theater watching on a big screen. However, as vivid as the pictures were thus far, it was the feeling in his gut that was inescapable. The worst was yet to come.

❉   ❉   ❉

He drove the red International home on the Tuesday evening before Thanksgiving, just as he said he would. He was greeted with a mother's care and concern, hugs, "have you lost weight," and food. It was not so much Thanksgiving around his home as it was Thanksgivings. Each day was a new feast. Jason went to bed that Tuesday evening feeling secure for the first time in days. He was home, relieved that Daniels was nowhere near.

He slept late, well into the middle of Wednesday morning, and came down to find sausage, bacon, ham, fresh fruit, hash browns, orange juice, bagels, cream cheese . . . and his mother waiting to whip up a fresh batch of blueberry pancakes. *How good is this?* he thought. It beat the heck out of stale Cheerios and expired milk.

"There he is. There he is," his mom said with a delight only a mother could get away with. "How'd you sleep?"

"Just great, Mom, really good, thanks."

"You're the last to eat, so clean it up. Your dad's been gone for a couple of hours. I tried to keep breakfast fresh, but no guarantees."

"It looks great, Mom, thanks again."

He loaded his plate heaping full and was still waiting for pancakes when the bomb hit.

"What's Dad up to?" he asked.

"Oh, you know Dad. Janet Salisbury, the single gal who lives across from Hidekis, needed some help. She has this stump in her front yard, all that's left of the big Doug fir that fell in the storm in early October. What a shame. Beautiful tree. Dad thought it was time the stump came out. He took Red over there with the chain saw and winch. Should be done by now, I'd think."

Jason's stomach wrenched and he suddenly lost any notion of appetite.

"He took the International?"

"Sure. Why? Did you need it this morning?"

"Uh—yes. No."

"You a little sleepy yet, Jason?"

"I'll be back, Mom."

Jason jumped up from the kitchen table and moved quickly toward the utility room.

"Hey, where you going?" she asked. "These pancakes will be done in just a minute. Get back here!"

Rushing out the utility room door and into the garage, Jason found no sign of the truck. He ran through the garage and out the side door onto the concrete path that led to the backyard and Dad's old shop. Not there. Mind racing, he tried to calm himself. If Dad had found anything, you could bet he'd be back here. He considered his options and concluded that his best alternative was to head over to the Salisbury place and "help" with the stump.

Jason ran back around to the front of the house and into the garage through the main door, still open from his father's exit earlier in the morning. Old wooden workbenches were built in wherever space allowed, with clean tools hanging neatly above them on the wall.

It was then that he heard the unmistakable hum of the old four-cylinder International coming up the street. His father pulled in, carefully parked the truck in the driveway, and set the brake. He'd apparently not noticed Jason standing at the back of the garage next to the table saw. Dad got out, stepped to the back of the truck, lifted an axe in one hand and the big wooden-handled maul in the other, and started into the garage.

"Hey, Dad, what's up?" Jason said, stepping forward tentatively.

"Morning, son," his father responded.

Two words; that was all it took. His father's tone was one he hadn't heard in some years. He tried hard to piece together the circumstances of a previous conversation with Dad that had frightened him to this extent, but couldn't place it. He knew, however, that it had cut a swath through him before, and the short exchange they'd just had severed the stitches and reopened the wound.

Dad walked to the back of the garage next to where he was standing and set the axe and maul on the concrete floor, sad eyes never looking up as he pulled aside a grey blanket laid out over the worn wooden bench. Jason's heart planted itself in his throat. He couldn't breathe, couldn't think, couldn't move, his pulse beating hard in his fingertips.

Black plastic, duct tape, and a blue backpack.

Chapter 4

QUALITY TIME

I t was just after noon when Jason reached the cabin. The sun was bright in a cloudless sky, somewhat unusual for Oregon in May. Heavy ancient forest surrounded the place and kept it fleece cool on days like this. Jason stowed his gear, removed his waders and hung them on an iron hook to dry, and went inside. Plates with remnants of lunch were left on the blue tile counter next to the stainless-steel sink. They'd already eaten, he thought, with no expectation of trout for lunch. Imagine that.

"Hey, Dad," Brian greeted him from the kitchen table.

"Brian," he responded.

Jesse was poured into the couch in front of the satellite TV. Anna, sitting in an old stuffed chair by the fire, her back against one arm and feet draped over the other, said nothing and continued reading.

"What have you been up to? Sleep in?" Jason asked.

"Just working on some homework before Mom and I go for a hike," Brian answered. "Jesse is too girly to muddy her retro Nikes in the great outdoors. I think she's writing love letters to Danny Boy."

With that, Brian broke into a painfully poor melody. "Oh, Danny Boy, the pipes, the pipes are calling," he sang, "from glen to glen . . . hey, Jesse, who's this Glen guy? Are you two-timing ol' Danny Boy?"

"Just shut it," Jesse retorted. "Whatever!"

"Where you going hiking?" Jason asked.

"Ramona Falls," answered Anna from the chair, sparing no time to look up from her book. "The two of us are leaving as soon as Brian finishes his homework. Might be nice if you and Jesse hung out together for once."

Jason bristled. *Give me a break*, he thought. He was sure Jesse didn't want to spend time with him any more than he wanted to spend time with her. Theirs was a mutually agreed-upon separation— a demilitarized zone guarded on both sides with assault weapons. He couldn't help but notice Anna's preemptive decision to exclude him from the hike. He'd have joined them, but the coolness in her declaration was enough to convince him he should keep his distance.

Ramona Falls was a spectacular hike, well-known in northwest Oregon. It meandered a short distance up the Sandy River valley to its headwaters, then off on Ramona Creek. The gradual incline made it an easy climb. However, the point of the hike was not exertion, it was the falls: a sprawling wall of water that took you by surprise as it tumbled over a cascade of rounded rock, glimmering and winking in finely textured sunlight. Really dazzling stuff. It was a great hike for conversation, since few who undertook it would be out of breath, but clearly Jason was not invited.

"Jesse," he offered with forced enthusiasm, "how about we hang out today? Anything you'd like to do?"

"Dad, I really need to go somewhere within cell range. I can't believe Mom drug me up here this weekend when I have so much to do. I've got tons of people to talk to."

"Tons of people? You mean darling Danny?" Brian piped up.

"Don't you have homework or something?"

"Jesse, we'll have to see," Jason broke in. "I'm not going to run around all afternoon and play 'can you hear me now.'"

Entering the remodeled kitchen, he heated some minestrone, broke off a piece of sourdough, poured a glass of milk, and headed to the loft overlooking the back porch. He put the tray down on the heavy oak desk that sat directly in front of the window he had installed last summer. Jason had enjoyed the project immensely. Just himself, a little lumber, nails, a circular and chop saw, shingles, siding, and the window. He'd ripped off the old cedar shakes and cut roof rafters back far enough to frame in a small dormer. The entire thing was nearly complete in just two weeks. *Nearly:* a word well understood by anyone who has ever owned an old cabin.

It was here that nature passed before him, right across the frame of his new window. He loved the view: the nearly perfect scale of a tall fir tree; the random yet remarkable mural of bark that covered and protected it; the commitment the tree had to reproduction, dropping cones to the forest floor each year. Jason wondered about the organic energy required annually to produce the cones, and whether such an effort would continue if the tree could think and feel and understand how many thousands of seeds would be required to produce one tree. The chances of success were spectacularly remote. Yet, he considered, even with those odds, he was looking out at an old-growth forest that was already 200 years old when Meriwether Lewis, William Clark, and the Corps of Discovery had passed this way in 1805. The pattern of nature had obviously worked.

He finished lunch alone and returned downstairs to the kitchen. Anna and Brian were filling their day packs with water, energy bars, and insect repellent—always insect repellent. (There were bugs in these woods that you'd swear had aluminum propellers and could carry off a robust kindergartner.) The two of them would be gone until dinnertime.

"Jesse, let's you and I take off too," he said. "I need to get a couple of things for the climb."

"Great, I'm ready to get outta here, for sure," she answered.

Jason put on a white "Ski Sun Valley" baseball hat as he and Jesse exited the front door, loaded into the Suburban, and headed to town.

"So," he said, trying to make conversation with a teenage daughter whose world he knew precious little about, "what did you guys do yesterday after you got here?" he asked.

"Well, Mom and Brian and I aired out all the bedding. Smelled like mice poop. Just the most disgusting thing ever. Totally yuk!"

"Everybody needs a place to live, Jesse."

"Let me help you with this, Dad: They're mice! Hello? Outside! Anyway, we finally got all the beds made and brought wood in. We had to unpack all the food and stuff. Oh, Brian whipped Mom at Scrabble!"

"No way!" Jason responded, considering her statement.

When had Brian grown up enough to beat Anna at Scrabble? She was a formidable player, not just because of her terrific vocabulary but also because of her superb grasp of the tactical nature of the game. She had the irritating ability to place one letter on the board that would complete three words and gain her forty-three points. Anna had a facility with language that was enviable, and for Brian to beat her at her game had to be considered a rite of passage. He was sure, however, that Anna was more delighted than Brian at the feat.

When they reached town, Jason pulled into the small parking lot that served a grocery store and local coffeehouse. Jesse popped open her cell phone, scrolled down to Danny's number, jumped out of the truck, and began walking across the lot.

"Take your time, Dad," she shouted back over her shoulder.

Jason shook his head as he stepped down and pressed the security button on his ignition key. "Quality time," he whispered sarcastically. He had met Danny Brickley and liked him, unfortunately. He was a fairly accomplished young man, responsible, and he seemed to genuinely like Jesse. But he was a teenage boy, and that brought with it perils Jason could barely allow himself to consider.

His instinct was to lock his daughter in a closet for her own protection.

Anna's wisdom had prevailed, and he had actually agreed to allow Jesse out of the house until ten on weeknights—after homework, of course—and eleven-thirty on weekends. He trusted her, he really did. But he'd been young once, and he was reasonably sure he knew what Danny Brickley was thinking. He knew that the weight of peer pressure and hormones could entice even the most thoughtful teenager to be foolish. His beautiful daughter always occupied a large, though unspoken, place in his heart.

Jason entered the small grocery store. As usual, it seemed a little musty and dim. How long had that can of cream of mushroom soup been on the shelf?

Whole Foods it wasn't. Even the grocery carts seemed sub-sized, as if people on the mountain ate less or something. Knowing that their trade was with recreational visitors, the owners jacked up their prices to where they bordered on laughable. Jason grabbed four rib eyes and six potatoes and put them in the cart.

Jesse is not going to be happy that I'm done already, he thought.

Absentmindedly, Jason snatched a *Redbook* off the magazine rack and flipped it open, praying that no one would enter the small market and see him perusing a recipe for vegetarian soufflé. Wouldn't be good. The teenage boy behind the worn Formica checkout stand, who wore a baseball cap cocked low to the side and sported enough piercings to make Jason wonder whether he'd fallen face-first into a tackle box, eyed him suspiciously.

"Just waiting for my daughter," he said defensively.

"Sure thing, Mister. Knock yourself out."

Jason cringed, knowing this kid had probably heard every excuse in the book.

After checking out, he walked back to the truck with his bag of groceries. Jesse, twirling her hair around her index finger like twine on a stick, was giggling into her phone. He twitched his head toward the car.

"Hey, Jesse, let's go."

She continued to chat, walking ever so slowly toward the Suburban. Jason placed the groceries in the back and got in while Jesse stood outside, still talking.

Jason leaned over and knocked on the passenger window, "Hey, you. In!"

She flipped the cell phone closed and got in. "A little grouchy, are we, Father?" she commented.

"Not to worry. You can call him back. I need to head over to the outfitters' to get a piece of equipment for the climb."

Jesse's face lit up.

Jason couldn't help but smile. Jesse was one of the few people who saw through his gruff exterior and called him on it regularly. She'd even taken to calling him "Bark," as in "all bark and no bite." The tactic worked well for him, keeping people at a comfortable distance so they couldn't get a good look.

"So, Jess, what is it you like about this Danny guy?"

"He's cool."

"Okay, I understand cool, but why do you like him?"

"I don't know—he makes me laugh. He talks to me. You know, seems interested."

"Those are great things to have," he responded awkwardly.

And there the conversation ended. Jason pulled into the Gear & Go lot and parked. They both jumped out, bound for their own errands, and parted ways once again.

Jason bought two additional plastic water bottles and some lens defogger he hoped would keep his goggles from steaming up on the climb. He exited Gear & Go with a small paper bag, collected Jesse—who was still talking with ol' Danny Boy on a cell phone that by now, he thought, certainly had grafted itself to the left side of her head—and made the quiet and uneventful drive back to the cabin.

Jesse ran from the truck to the front door, only to find it locked. "Dad, I need the key," she yelled back.

"Coming," Jason answered.

Anna and Brian had not yet returned from the falls, but he was hungry and determined to start the barbecue. A steak and foil-wrapped baked potato would hit the spot.

Once inside, Jason put away the groceries and climbed the wooden stairs to the loft. Setting the water bottles and defogger on top of his pack, he returned downstairs and to the deck outside to fire up the Weber and listen to the song of the river. He would cook two steaks now and wait until the hikers returned before starting the others.

Jason threw on the foil-covered potatoes and let them bake at high heat for some time before starting the steaks.

"Jesse," he called through the screen door, "you want yours blow-torched, right?"

"Real funny, Dad. I want mine *done*—not bloodred and still snorting."

Having finished cooking the steaks and potatoes while enjoying the tweak of cold left in the high spring air, Jason called through the screen door: "Jesse, we're about done out here. You want to eat outside on the deck, or inside?"

"Inside," she hollered back. "I'm watching *Ocean's Twelve* and can't peel my eyes off of Brad Pitt."

"That's just great, Jesse. What is he, about ninety-eight years old?"

"He's thirty-something," she countered, "and he's got an attitude. Did I say he's hot?"

Brad Pitt was not the only one inside the cabin with an attitude. Jason turned off the barbecue and shut the valve on top of the steel propane canister. He fought his way through the screen door, a plate of red meat and potatoes in one hand, greasy cooking utensils in the other. Jesse was oblivious to the commotion.

"Thanks for the help," he said.

No response.

"Jesse," he nearly hollered.

"What? Criminy, Dad. You don't have to yell."

Jason smiled. "You want me to plate your steak and potato?"

"No," she responded, "just leave it there. I'll get it."

Jason forked a rare steak onto his plate and quickly transferred the ball of hot foil. He cut the potato open and dashed it with salt and pepper, then picked up the plate and moved to the fridge, where he opened the butter container without removing it from the shelf, raked a knife across the surface, and plopped the contents inside the potato. Sealing the lid, he repeated the process with sour cream, careful to cover his tracks by removing any butter residue from the white substance. Anna hated him doing that. He considered taking a swig from the milk carton but thought better of it.

Jason pulled loose a Diet Coke before closing the fridge door, then fetched a fork and steak knife and headed upstairs to his loft, which on this day served as a refuge from Jesse, Brad Pitt, and rampaging teenage biochemistry. *Heaven help me,* he thought.

Chapter 5

PEN AND PAPER

He awoke early Sunday morning, startled that he'd lost track of time. The place was pitch-dark and silent as deep space. A sliver of guilt slid under his skin that he had spent virtually no time with his family since arriving. *No worries. They're not going to miss me,* Jason thought.

Jason stood in groggy blackness and fumbled for the cast-iron lamp on the table to his right, its outline silhouetted by the window behind. The forest outside the cabin was lit in moonlight that cast thick blankets of shadows. Jason turned on the lamp, and his view of the forest vanished in a bombardment of light. Shielding his eyes from the intensity, he reached for the lamp again, this time to turn it off. It took some time for his eyes to adjust, but slowly the world outside began to reappear.

He padded quietly down the narrow wooden stairway in stocking feet, pulled on boots and a fleece jacket hanging by the door, unlocked the deadbolt, and slipped outside for some fresh air. He pulled gloves from a pocket—with them, a note dropped to the moist ground. He bent bare-handed to pick it up. Angling the small piece of paper toward the moonlight, Jason could easily make out the writing. It was from Jesse.

"Dad," it said, "I hope you find what you're looking for on top of that mountain. We all do. I'll be thinking of you. Love, Jesse."

His heart swelled. *Simple things,* he thought.

He stashed the note back in his pocket and continued on around the cabin on the gravel path that led to the front porch, walking gently to keep from waking the family. Rounding the corner, Jason stopped. Something was wrong. In the drive sat his Suburban. Next to it, where Anna's black Volvo had been . . . nothing. The car was gone.

What the devil? he said to himself.

He walked back to the detached garage and peered through the side window, wondering if she'd put the car inside for the night. Nothing. He walked, briskly now, to the cabin's front door. Locked. Jason bounded off the front porch and back around the cabin to the rear door he'd just exited.

Entering the cabin, he first checked the kids' beds in the bunk-room, knowing that no amount of commotion would disturb them from their unconsciousness. Neither bunk had been slept in. No bags strewn around the room. No clothes piled in the corner. No socks on the floor. Confused now, Jason moved to their bedroom, diagonally across the downstairs great room, and lifted the black iron latch. The door opened. The bed was empty. Anna was gone. Brian and Jesse were gone with her. On the old patchwork blanket sat an envelope.

Jason swallowed hard. His life with Anna flashed before him. Thoughts rushed his mind like white-water. Had he blown his marriage? Of course he'd blown his marriage. What he was really wondering was whether Anna had at last reached the end of her patience with him and walked out without an argument. No fight. No war of words. Just a quiet recognition that she could no longer tolerate his emotional absence and the hole he'd dug in her heart.

Jason reached for the note, lifted the flap of the envelope, and removed the small paper inside. At least it was short. No essay about his many shortcomings and the destruction he'd caused her. Just a few simple sentences.

Jason,

The thought of being alone in the world is frightening at this point in my life. However, alone and single is not nearly as devastating as alone and married. We live under the same roof, yet we've become strangers, roommates at best. It must be hard for you too. It's time we made some decisions, maybe time we moved on. You're not the person I married. I'm sure you feel the same about me. Life seems to have beaten both of us. I have no fight left. The kids and I have gone back home so you can have the space you seem to need. We'll talk when you return from your climb. Good luck. Please be careful.

Anna

Darkness descended on Jason as if the only door to a sealed room had been slammed shut. He put the note down and sank slowly to the bed, elbows rested on knees, fingers clasped together. Minutes passed. Time spun to no recognizable value. What had he done? Had it really come to this? How could Anna say she was alone? He was there—mostly.

No he wasn't, he recognized. He'd been gone for some time, lost in his disappointment in himself. He'd dishonored himself in small choices, each of which, he knew now, had ripped a piece out of him and, quite literally, crippled him from the inside out. Oh, he hadn't made the big mistakes. There was no affair, no uncontrollable addiction, no physical abuse. But his desire to withdraw from himself because he disliked what he'd become also meant he'd withdrawn from other relationships, from those who mattered most. From Anna.

Jason sat alone in quiet desperation, disturbed by the brutal emotional pain he'd caused his wife, who was wholly undeserving of such treatment. Anna was not perfect. Certainly she had her faults. But the beautiful girl he'd married on that June day nearly twenty-one years ago was still there: curious, wonderful with people, trusting, gentle. He would get glimpses of her innocence now and then. What had he done? It occurred to him that many of her problems resulted from his treatment, from the influence he had on her. She had defended herself as best she could with the few weapons she had, a force that paled when compared with the arsenal Jason had crafted during years of warfare with himself and others. Now she was tired. What had he done to Anna? What had he done to himself?

Jason wandered outside. He had to clear his head, to get a grip. Dawn was breaking bright to the east, backlighting the mountain. A white summit cloud had formed, obscuring the peak. What a paradox: nature's simple magnificence and life's overwhelming humiliation. He couldn't remember ever being quite so grateful for his family while so frightened of losing them. He wondered about the conversation that must have ensued between Anna, Brian, and Jesse before they had left for home last evening while he slept upstairs.

Jesse's note flooded back to him: "I hope you find what you're looking for on top of that mountain. We all do. I'll be thinking of you. Love, Jesse."

He felt disgusted at the thought that his kids were suffering because of choices he'd made and actions he'd taken. Nausea began to grip the back of his throat. He took several quick steps away from the cabin and, bending from the waist with his right hand clenched hard against his abdomen, lost the contents of his stomach.

Hunched and sick, he staggered slowly to the back deck, sat down, closed his eyes, and, for the first time in years, wept.

Chapter 6

CHARLIE MURPHY

He didn't know how long he'd been sitting on the porch that Sunday morning, back propped against a railing post, legs outstretched on the old wooden deck, his mouth still acidic and bitter. He briefly considered canceling the climb out of some notion of marital responsibility, but the fact was that he and Anna had been emotionally divorced for some time. Besides, canceling would amount to an admission that he'd done something wrong, an admission of fault, and he wasn't about to open that door. This was probably just another ploy by Anna to get more attention, an emotional maneuver he wasn't going to fall for. The physical separation wasn't that big a deal. However, he made a mental note to call his attorney when he returned home, just in case he needed aggressive representation. His material assets were all he had left, and he wasn't about to see them liquidated by a spouse who thoroughly misunderstood his motivations.

Jason thought it odd, given the circumstances, that Anna was not who he was really thinking of. Instead, it was his father and his career.

Dad had been a moral compass, true north. Given life's complications, Jason suspected that at some weak moment along the way his father *must* have chosen poorly, made a wrong decision, or misjudged someone. But Jason could not remember witnessing any such event. Not one. Dad was a rock in the face of trouble, not easily rattled. He seemed to have a well, a reserve deep inside him that he could summon in the face of challenge and difficulty. He wielded his strength not as a weapon, as Jason had so skillfully practiced, but as a shield that warded off any hint of discouragement. Dad had lived a life of quiet integrity, and Jason was only beginning to understand its value. But Dad was gone now. He had died of heart failure twenty-five years ago, less than a month after Jason's hit-and-run accident. Although the autopsy had been inconclusive, Jason still carried the weight of responsibility. From the moment he had received that unimaginable phone call from Mom, he had fought the hemorrhaging realization that he was the cause of an enlightened life's having been lost much too soon. Beyond the guilt, he missed his father deeply, a solid rock in Jason's life of sand.

Nearly two decades ago, Jason remembered, just a couple of years after graduation, another shattering event occurred that still made him cringe.

He'd gone to work for Flegger Norman Company, a large architectural firm where a college degree qualified you to run coffee and replace broken protractors, not exactly what he'd had in mind after six years of costly university education. Impatient, he was counseled to keep his wits about him, wait for an opening, and then be prepared to perform when his number was called. The opportunity came in the form of a project in Scottsdale, Arizona.

Jason was to lead a team responsible for designing and managing the installation of the communications infrastructure for a large, sixty-million-dollar mixed-use development. Jason jumped at the opportunity and quickly immersed himself in long hours, technical details, and meetings with engineers and installers. Virtually all his design work was underground: routing, cabling and conduit for existing services, and building capacity within the system to handle future upgrades. Charlie Murphy, who'd been recruited to Flegger Norman the same year as Jason, was also chosen for the Scottsdale project.

Charlie and Jason became quick friends and began to spend time together socially. Charlie had a cocky personality that everyone took with a grain of salt. However, he was reliable and he was bright, and more than once he preserved the integrity of their project by recognizing design flaws or discovering component irregularities. And he got along great with the contractors.

The infrastructure was completed on time and within the developer's budget, and all systems worked like a charm. Jason had a major project success under his belt and was on his way up, and he took Charlie with him. That is, until two and a half years later, when Flegger Norman Company was contacted by the Scottsdale developer over concerns about their inability to locate the conduit necessary for a fiber-optic upgrade.

Jason and Charlie flew out together to resolve the issue on-site, sure that the missing conduit was there. After they spent two days climbing down every manhole and peering into numerous communications vaults trying to resolve inconsistencies between construction drawings, "as-builts," and what had actually been installed, it became horrifyingly clear that the conduit was *not* there. The answer to the design flaw required strips of pavement, concrete sidewalk, and landscaping to be dug up for installation of new conduit. Traffic flow and pedestrian access were disrupted and a major tenant occupancy was set back for several months, all at a cost of hundreds of thousands of dollars. For almost four months, this beautifully manicured center looked as though a mole the size of a VW Bug had rampaged through it. Jason wasn't sure who had made the mistake, but he knew he was the lead, and the oversight could cost him his job.

The mistake quickly escalated into legal threats, leading to binding arbitration. During a statement in front of an arbitrator and legal counsel representing the two parties, Jason found himself testifying that the mistake could be traced to Charlie Murphy, who, he offered, had done substandard work throughout the project and whose activities he'd had to watch carefully and often correct. The statement was far from true, of course, but Jason's career was on the line and he knew he had built enough credibility within the firm by then that his opinion carried more weight than Charlie's.

Word never got back to Charlie about what had happened; Jason saw to that. He was simply informed by a senior VP that he was no longer an employee of Flegger Norman due to the "problem" in Scottsdale. Jason breathed a sigh of relief at having sidestepped the disaster. He'd gotten away with the charade without anyone knowing better. But *he* knew. He would always know.

Jason had weathered the fallout of the "Scottsdale Bomb," as it became known, but left the firm less than a year later due to the rock that had formed in the pit of his stomach—a rock he was sure wouldn't go away until he was divorced from the constant reminders of his unscrupulous actions.

A new environment would heal his conscience, he remembered thinking.

It had taken Charlie Murphy months to find a new job; he'd finally had to move his family out of state. Jason would see Charlie now and again at professional conferences, and it was all he could do to look Charlie in the eye and say hello.

The rock in his stomach never left him.

Interspersed in a career of successes was a string of discrepancies similar to the one in Scottsdale, though less spectacular—experiences Jason had learned to spin, irregularities he had maneuvered to throw a bright light on his accomplishments and a dim light on his failures and even on his colleagues when necessary. He had become a master at subtle manipulation, acting benevolent when it was in his best interests to do so, being nice when "nice" played to his advantage. Most of his indiscretions were not by themselves formidable, but taken together they formed habitual patterns that, he had begun to suspect, could have significant consequences both personally and professionally. Ironically, his career had never been in better shape. However, the day of personal reckoning had arrived, and it numbed him to the bone. His choices had hit the fan.

He wondered what the course of his life would have been if he'd told the truth about the Scottsdale project, or even if he'd somehow been found out. Perhaps a lesson learned at that young age wouldn't have carved as wide a swath through his life as his actions now were doing. Back then, he'd had much less to lose, much less to protect. Now, the accumulation of misdeeds was proving a bill too large to pay. What started as raindrops had indeed become a raging river, and it appeared that his marriage was going under as a result.

Thoughts of his father brought back an old poem that Jason remembered Dad reciting occasionally:

> *In the furnace God may prove thee,*
> *Thence to bring thee forth more bright,*
> *But can never cease to love thee;*
> *Thou art precious in his sight.*
> *God is with thee, God is with thee;*
> *Thou shalt triumph in his might.*

For a moment Jason considered how world politics and events had been turned upside down to the point that his father's poem could easily be used as the mantra of a suicide bomber in Kandahar. However, his father always used the recitation as a way to connect with the good that comes from bad, with the learning that comes from suffering, with the humility that comes from humiliation—never as a justification for doing harm to others.

His father's definition of optimism differed from any he'd ever heard: "Optimism is not seeing the world through rose-colored lenses, or practicing positive mental attitude. These are distortions, not reflections, of a real worldview. Optimism is a recognition that the greater the problem, the greater the learning, and it's up to us to uncover the learning."

Jason couldn't imagine how he was going to talk his way out of this furnace to come forth more bright. No amount of clever manipulation was going to satisfy Anna. Was it possible to find optimism in a life distorted? Incineration was more likely.

Where were the values that his father had instilled in him and his mother had lived? Were they gone and forgotten, or just buried under piles of justification? What had caused him to trample the values he knew deep down would bring him happiness? Was the draw of instant gratification, status, and pleasure that compelling? Apparently. Jason was up to his eyeballs in success.

He had all but forgotten what it meant to listen to his conscience and act accordingly. He was hearing it now. Ultimately, he knew he had to resolve his internal conflicts before any sense of peace would come to him and to the rest of his relationships, both personal and professional. The question that remained was this: After all these years, could he break free of the web he had woven and earn back his family's trust and his joy for living? At this moment, it felt as if his life depended on it. And it did.

Recalling another bit of wisdom his father had once offered, Jason winced at the truth of it: "Son, as soon as suffering and sorrow become painful enough, one moves forward." Jason was going forward into the unknown, unsure of what he would find.

❋   ❋   ❋

He spent the rest of Sunday packing for the climb, hoping that the next two days would bring new experiences but, more than that, new insight. Heaven knew he needed new insight. He remembered being flabbergasted at the equipment list he'd received from the guide service, three dozen items that, in total, cost as much as a home theater system and required a recreational vehicle to transport.

He wasn't sure he could get everything in the back of the Suburban with the seats folded down, to say nothing of hauling it up 11,240 feet on his back. The required equipment list, to put it mildly, seemed overly substantial, reminding him of contracts his firm signed at the initiation of services. A battery of attorneys had obviously investigated every possible problem and committed the possibility, however remote, to language so oppressive in length and obscure in meaning as to be unintelligible to anyone but themselves. Job security. Jason wondered how important a foil heat blanket was really going to be. *We're not camping on the far side of the moon, are we?*

As if by mirrors and a miracle, all equipment and extra clothing, when packed carefully—that is, jammed—fit into his backpack. He was a little hesitant about the first time he'd have to loosen the top cinch cord of the pack, wondering if the contents would explode out like confetti from a noisemaker at a New Year's Eve party.

Chapter 7

DEAR JESSE

Cascade Mountain Guides ran a disciplined program of climbing instruction and rescue techniques for new climbers. The south face of Mount Hood was known as a "walk up" by experienced mountaineers; however, it was also the source of a surprising number of accidents, tragedy, and death. Scores of climbing mishaps over the years had resulted from a variety of causes.

In 1986, a high school climbing group from Oregon Episcopal School was caught in a freak May storm. The party included fifteen students, one parent, two teachers, and two expert consultants. Seven died of hypothermia, and several lost limbs to severe frostbite.

In 2000, an accident occurred involving a well-known climber who, after summiting and unroping from her team to enjoy the spectacular vista from the top of Hood, was literally blown off the north cornice right in front of her climbing buddies. A rescue team finally located her body 2,500 feet below the summit at the 8,700-foot level, atop Eliot Glacier.

In 2002, on a spectacular spring day, a local television station was broadcasting a mountain rescue live. There were three dead and six injured climbers from three different rope teams who had all been swept into the Bergschrund Crevasse at 10,700 feet. An Air Force Reserve Pave Hawk helicopter lost its rotor traction in the thin air and abruptly crashed, rolling down a steep section of mountain with crew and critically injured climbers on board, spewing helicopter parts and bodies like shrapnel. It could have been much worse. No one died as a result of the accident. However, five crew members were injured, one seriously.

Given such events, the guide service spent a day teaching climbing techniques, first aid, survival, and crevasse rescue before turning anyone loose for the summit. Monday would be spent under the watchful eye of Clara Schroeder, who, Jason had been told, was meticulous in her preparation and known to take nothing for granted. Only after satisfying Clara would anyone assigned to her team be cleared for a Tuesday ascent.

Jason poured himself a bowl of Froot Loops for dinner, a pathetic commentary on a successful, career-driven, well-educated boomer. He cleaned up, finished prepping his gear, filled water bottles, set his pack and equipment next to the front door, and turned in early. The silence was piercing. Jason had long sought a sense of quiet solitude. At age forty-four, he had it now—no conversation, no children to nudge or lovingly irritate, no playful giggling, no card game that somehow had become a Snow tradition, perhaps no marriage. Awful. Just awful.

For the better part of two hours Jason lay in bed, eyes open, listening to crickets, the river, and the creaking of tall timber in a light breeze, willing himself to sleep. It wasn't working. Never had.

Unlike earlier in the day, when his thoughts had been dominated by his father and his work, now they turned to his family—more specifically, to Jesse. The note she'd written to him rested on the bedside table.

Her sixteenth birthday was fast approaching; he couldn't imagine how that had happened so quickly. It seemed to Jason that she was five just yesterday, and she adored him. They both had changed. The last couple of years had proven difficult for the two of them, Jesse trying to find her way and Jason trying not to lose his. He'd given her just about every gift a teenage girl could want—counterfeit currency in a market whose gold standard was time. They'd grown apart, and it was Jesse who seemed the one more willing to reach out, more desperate for a connection. Afraid of what she might see up close, he had withdrawn into his career and the status that went along with it, hoping to find some sense of personal honor.

He recalled an event that had helped carve the bedrock of their relationship.

Jesse had begun her sophomore year in high school the previous fall. She was full of brains but lacked the wisdom that would come with experience. She was outwardly confident, but he and Anna knew that the self-assurance she showed on the outside was a cover, camouflage for a teenager unsure of who she was on the inside. She was trying to find her place in the world, holding fast to her parents with one hand while pushing them away with the other. Anna knew the drill and handled it well. He, on the other hand, felt as though he were living in a foreign land with obscure customs and a language he didn't recognize. Like every couple, they hoped and prayed they could show their daughter the way before someone else pointed her in the direction of disaster.

Parenting was tough work. Jason always fought with himself over how much rope to give his two kids. Anna's theory prevailed. Better, she thought, to let them make minor mistakes while still at home and under a parent's watchful care than to shelter them from all of life's mistakes and disappointments, only to set them free in a mysterious and complicated world to make their first big mistakes just out of the nest. Let them get a flavor for choices, good and bad, while she and Jason were there to pull them up when necessary. Still, he found it

extremely difficult to allow his children to make poor choices and suffer the consequences, especially when he saw that train coming from
the far distance with plenty of time to change direction.

Jesse had come to him in late November to ask about going to
a party after a football game. She was fifteen at the time, but Jason
looked through a father's eye and saw an innocent child. He'd been to
those parties himself years ago and was entirely too familiar with the
unseemly possibilities. He had forbidden her to go.

"Too young, Jesse," he said. "Nothing good happens that late. You
can go to the game with friends and grab an ice cream or something
after, then come home."

Jason remembered Jesse's response: "Daaaaad! What am I, eight?"

"When was the last time complaining got you what you wanted?"
he asked her.

"You can be such a dork," she responded.

"Bingo. I'm a dork. That's my job," he said, smiling, which only
irritated her more. "Football game? Absolutely. Party after? Absolutely
not."

Jesse left the house in a huff, aware that her dad loved her, albeit
in a pain-in-the-butt sort of way. It was a dance with two steps Jason
was learning on the fly: father, friend, father, friend. He knew he was
constantly stepping on her feet, offbeat and a little ragged.

Confronted with a choice by friends anxious to prove their popularity, Jesse went to the party, justifying her choice in the fact that it
was either ride to the postgame celebration or walk home.

Greg was a nice enough guy. Cute. Good smile. A senior, which
provided a young sophomore with instant credentials. She was inside
the in crowd and loving it. The party was typical: high school kids
pretending to enjoy the awful taste of beer, the choking burn of their
first cigarette, and music played at a decibel level capable of shifting a
large house off its foundation. And kids, lots of kids.

They danced for over an hour and tried to talk over the pounding of the CD player. Greg finally motioned with his hand toward his ear and shook his head. He couldn't hear.

"Follow me," he screamed in her ear.

He grabbed her hand and led her downstairs into a back bedroom. Jesse knew immediately she had entered a space not right, not . . . *appropriate,* a word she heard in her head but spoken in her mother's voice. She and Anna had had the discussions that mothers and daughters have, discussions that now flooded her mind wishfully.

Greg was aggressive and she soon found herself fighting him off, running from the basement back up a dark set of stairs crowded with bodies and out the front door to the cold street outside. A light November rain was falling, visible through the wash of the streetlight and more comfortable than the warm basement filled with choices she was not yet ready to make.

It hit her that her friends, and thus her ride, were somewhere back there in the maze of kids and music and consequences. Should she go inside and find them? No way. Should she call home and suffer that humiliation? Not good. Should she walk home? Try to find another ride? How had this happened? Her dorky father suddenly appeared much less dorky. She didn't know what to do.

Greg stepped out the front door and her heart stopped.

He walked quickly toward her. "Hey, Jesse, what's going on?" he asked. "We have this great time going and then you bolt?"

"Look, Greg. You're great. I just need to get home, that's all."

He looked at her with shocked expression. "So, your game is to act the part, look the part, but when it comes to having the guts to take the next step, you chicken out? Is that it?" He grabbed her wrist. "I think you need to come back inside with me."

Panic overcame her and she shook him off. "Leave me alone, Greg. Just leave it. I'm going home."

"Run back to Mama," he said, forcing a laugh while watching Jesse walk away.

Jason could still remember her sobbing voice on the cell phone.

"Dad, I need help. I'm so sorry. Can you come get me, Dad? I'm sorry. I'm so sorry."

He grabbed his keys and shot from the house, glad she'd had the courage to call but angry she had acted against his direction. It proved a paradox that defined their relationship. He asked only one question on the way home: "Are you okay?" Her simple "yes" was the end of the conversation. Jesse understood she'd screwed up, and Jason was smart enough to know she didn't need her father to remind her. After all, he regretfully considered, his daughter was riding home with a man who had done far worse.

That had been six months ago, and they'd drawn a tentative truce. They loved each other, but each was wary of the other.

Recognizing that he'd lost his battle for sleep, Jason rolled out of bed and slipped a navy blue fleece over his head, zipped it to the neck, and once again headed upstairs to the loft and his window. He sat at his desk in the dark for some time and looked out into the night. Wisps of moss clung to the north side of tall firs. Blackberry, huckleberry, vine maple, Oregon grape, fern, and other growth he couldn't identify fought for space on the forest floor. The Sandy ran quietly in the distance. What to do for Jesse? he thought. What could he possibly give her for her birthday that would make any kind of difference now? It occurred to him that he could still give her his heart, something he hadn't shared for much too long. He wondered if he even knew how.

It had been years, possibly since the advent of e-mail, since Jason had penned a handwritten letter to anyone. He pulled a clean sheet of white paper from the printer, dug out his father's old fountain pen from the top drawer of the desk, and began.

Dear Jesse,

   With your sixteenth birthday soon upon us, you and I are miles apart, and I realize now that the source of our separation is me, not you. Certainly not you. So, for your birthday, I offer you some simple words from the heart of a lost man.

   First, I want to thank you. You have been the finest daughter any father could ever hope to have. In fact, in some real sense, you were not sent to me as much as you were sent _for_ me. You have had more impact on me than I have had on you. You have been a joy, and I'm so proud of who you are and what you are becoming. I'm so proud of you for taking your own path, for your desire to see what's out there in the world, and yet in all of this, for your courage in staying true to yourself and who you are.

   Second, I wish for you to find joy and happiness in life. There are many miserable people. Believe me, I know this. Some are miserable through their awful circumstances. Most of us are miserable simply as a result of our own stupid choices. You have been given much. In all your blessings I think you can find purpose—first, to find and understand the true sources of joy; and second, to try to alleviate the suffering of those who have not found those sources. I wish that this path had come to me earlier in life, but I'm only now beginning to see. You are developing a character that is a builder of people. You have a great influence on your friends and family around you, perhaps more than you can imagine. This influence will get larger as time goes by, but only if you are able to see life for what it really is, and that is not an easy thing. I can only tell you what life isn't. It isn't the accumulation of things or the status of a blind world.

Third, I can hardly believe you are turning sixteen! It just doesn't seem possible. Many people told me when you were small that I should enjoy you while you were very young. Soon, they said, you'd get older and become someone that I wouldn't enjoy as much. I've never once had that inclination about you. I can't imagine thinking more highly of you next year than I do this moment, but somehow it seems to always happen that way.

Soon, Jesse, you'll be old enough to make many of your own decisions. I wish for you joy in finding humility in the stars and supreme confidence in your heart. It is there, I've seen it. You have shown it to me. You are all I ever hoped having children would be.

Happy birthday. I'll love you always.

Dad

Jason slipped the letter into a plain white envelope, folded the flap inside, and addressed it simply, "To Jesse." Replacing the silver cap on the old fountain pen, he laid it beside the envelope, on the desk this time, not in the drawer. He would pick the envelope up on the way home on Tuesday or Wednesday. He reached for the lamp, clicked it off, and made his way in the dark back downstairs to bed. Seeing her note still on the bedside table, he placed his hand over it as if to absorb its warmth, and he thought of his beautiful daughter. Perhaps she was still his girl.

He wondered if Anna would ever be again.

In just a few hours he would be on the mountain. He had to get some sleep.

Chapter 8

HOMELESS

Up until about seventy million years ago, Oregon was covered by warm seas. Then land began to appear from the tropical waters, and volcanoes dominated the skyline. The Cascades began emerging in fits and starts about forty million years ago, and by seventeen million years ago they had grown to such an extent that their influence affected the climate by blocking moisture carried east by winds from the Pacific Ocean.

Volcanoes and plate tectonics drove the water out of Oregon. Land was on the rise. A landscape emerged that was warm and moist. Palms, walnuts, avocados, and pecans grew, and along with them lived the early four-toed horses and rhinos. Crocodiles ruled huge swamps. Later, the fossil record reveals that saber-toothed cats, tiny camels, and enormous pigs roamed freely.

About seventeen million years ago something changed. Volcanic activity began sending huge floods of lava, which we know as the Columbia River Basalts, across the landscape east of the Cascades. This continued for five million years: Flood after flood of flowing lava buried everything in its path. All plants and animals were killed and entombed. There were some periods of quiet—long enough for life to reestablish itself, only to suffer the same fate as its predecessors.

After the growth of the Cascades, the blocking of moisture from the west, and a decline in enormous lava flows, tropical plants were replaced by the vegetation we see today. Animals of an earlier time were never to be seen here again. Instead, antelope, deer, bears, modern horses, and mastodons roamed the landscape.

Many of what are now known as the High Cascades, the big peaks, began their rise eight million years ago during the Pliocene. They ascended to dominate their surroundings for a hundred miles or more, producing environments and cultures like nothing in the world. To the west grew dense maritime forests of Douglas fir, western hemlock, and red alder; to the east, a much drier climate produced stands of ponderosa pine, with western larch at the higher elevations.

Native Americans inhabited the area for thousands of years and developed deeply held legends about the Cascades. The Barlow Trail, which veered southwest from the Columbia River at Hood River, wandered along the south side of Mount Hood through Government Camp, ending in Oregon City. It was the first established land path for settlers through the Cascades in 1845 and formed the final link for the Oregon Trail.

All known historic eruptions in the contiguous United States have come from Cascade volcanoes. The most recent, Mount St. Helens, produced a catastrophic eruption in 1980. Seven thousand big game animals, twelve million chinook and coho salmon, and millions of birds and small mammals are believed to have died in the eruption. Fifty-seven people perished, with twenty-one bodies never recovered.

In all, St. Helens lost approximately twenty-three square miles of rock in an explosion five hundred times more powerful than "Little Boy," the hydrogen bomb dropped on Hiroshima, Japan, in 1945. The event took 1,314 feet off the top of the mountain and deposited it into the upper atmosphere. Within a couple of hours, air currents were dumping inches of the gritty material all over Washington and Oregon. Three days later, ash began falling in the eastern United States.

Jason, just days from high school graduation, recalled watching from the street in front of his home along with many of his neighbors as the plume of ash reached 80,000 feet, ascending at a mile a minute. It was the first time in his life he could recall feeling an overwhelming sense of awe, graphically delivered by the massive power of nature. He remembered not knowing whether to run toward it for a better view or away from it for cover. It was humbling to realize that man was definitely not in control.

Not even close.

Having grown up in Oregon, Jason had come to love the High Cascades, all of which he had known since middle school by their locations north to south: Garibaldi in southern British Columbia; Baker, Glacier Peak, Rainier (the tallest of the Cascades at 14,411 feet), St. Helens, and Adams, all in Washington State; Hood, Jefferson, Three Fingered Jack, Washington, the Three Sisters, Broken Top, Newberry Volcano and Caldera, Bachelor, Bailey, Thielsen, Mazama (Crater Lake), and McLoughlin, the Oregon volcanoes; and Medicine Lake, Shasta, and Lassen Peak of northern California. All received heavy winter snowfall and had extensive glaciers, which offered arguably the best ice and snow climbing in the lower forty-eight states.

Jason remembered his father suggesting that if he were ever lost in Portland or its surroundings, he should find Mount Hood and use it as a guidepost, knowing that it rose from a plateau sixty miles due east of the city. Today, as then, Mount Hood offered Jason some possibility of direction. And so those mountains, especially Mount Hood, had served as monuments to nature's power and wonder, beacons of stability and direction. They were as much a symbol of northwesterners as they were of the Northwest: rugged, independent, diverse, beautiful, ever changing and yet always remaining the same.

Anna and he had jumped at the chance to own a small cabin in the dense woodland west of the mountain. A part of Mount Hood National Forest, the ground under the cabin was leased from the Forest Service under a 100-year agreement. They'd purchased the cabin outright and over the last sixteen years spent well over their original purchase price to improve, upgrade, and maintain their quiet sanctuary. It was the best money they'd ever spent.

The cabin now represented memories more than location: Thanksgiving, Christmas, spring breaks, regular winter ski trips, and weeks here and there during summer and fall—experiences attached to the structure as surely as windows and cedar shakes. It was a place of family and tradition, despite the current estrangement, and would, in Jason's mind, always be.

Up at 4:30 a.m., Jason showered, dressed in medium-weight polypropylene thermals, light fleece T-neck, dry-fit socks, Gore-Tex bibs, an outer Polartec jacket of waterproof and breathable synthetic, and a fleece hat that warmed his head and ears. He remembered coming to the mountain years ago to ski dressed like the Michelin Man with goggles; it was nice that these days he could wear half the clothing weight and be twice as warm.

He prepped a breakfast of hot chocolate, Cliff bars, a banana, and a small box of raisins, and checked his equipment one last time. Then he walked to the bedroom, carefully folded Jesse's note, and zipped it into an inside pocket. Placing six additional energy bars in an outside compartment of his pack, he slipped on running shoes and gloves, hoisted his equipment, and headed to the Suburban.

After loading his gear, Jason went back to lock up the cabin. He remembered some years back, during a cold February, a homeless man had gotten into their cabin after he'd left the back porch door unlocked. Jason still wondered how in the world that man had found his way to a cabin on Mount Hood in the dead of winter.

He remembered it looked as though the man had been there the better part of a week when Jason and Anna found him one Friday night: lights out, feet propped on the ottoman, nice fire going, a glass of milk and a package of Chips Ahoy sitting beside him, sound asleep.

Anna screamed when she walked in on the man, startling him awake and bolt upright, eyes the size of dinner plates, cobwebs still clouding his perspective. Jason hit the lights and lunged for a wooden relic of a ski pole they had displayed in the corner by the door. He pointed it at the intruder, the old webbed leather basket hanging limp in front of him. The man grabbed the cookies from the leather chair and clutched the bag to his chest with both hands like they were all he had in the world.

"I'm sorry, I'm sorry, I'll go," he said.

"Darn right you will, in the back of the sheriff's patrol car!" Jason fired back.

"No, please no, I'll just go," he said.

The man was dressed in a worn-out pair of brown Red Wing work shoes, the style Jason's father was so fond of. Unlike his father, though, this man had no socks, and his black pants were cut off and frayed at mid-ankle, exposing a couple of inches of bare leg. An old collared shirt peeked out the top of an insulated, waist-length cotton jacket that had seen many winters. Jason remembered thinking it odd that this fellow was sitting there in a warm cabin, asleep, but clothed like he was expecting to be put out into the cold at any moment. The man seemed more frightened of them than they were of him. Jason quickly scanned the cabin for signs of theft or damage, but none was visible.

"Anna, call 911, then take a look around and see what's missing, and find out how he got in. Look for cracked doorjambs and broken windows."

He turned to the uninvited guest, waving the ski pole. "And you, old man, you just stay right there and shut up."

"Nothin's gone," the man said quietly. "Look, I've slept here on my bedroll in front of the fire for a couple of nights, that's all. Just trying to warm up before movin' on. I'm real sorry that I've upset you, but I've taken nothin' and I've been awful careful to clean up. Please just let me go. I'll leave you some money for any food I ate. Please, sir, I don't want no trouble."

Jason could still remember the look in Anna's eyes. Having found nothing amiss upstairs or down, she walked back to Jason's side and pulled on his upper arm. He looked at her and knew exactly what she was thinking.

"No, absolutely not," he shot back before she'd even said a word. "We are not just letting him go, Anna. He'll wind up harassing a neighbor if we do, or worse. He broke into our cabin—our cabin!"

"I didn't break in, sir," the man said softly. "The back door was unlocked. Look, there's no damage done, there's nothin' . . ."

Jason immediately realized he'd left the door unlocked.

Both he and Anna looked at the door.

"Anna, any sign of a break-in anywhere?" Jason asked, knowing the answer.

"None," she replied. "You're right, Jason. I don't think we can just let him go."

Jason nodded agreement. A pale concern came over the old man's face as he recognized he had apparently lost his only advocate.

"I think we need to give him a decent pair of socks, some food, maybe some money, and at least drive him back to the main highway. He's going to freeze walking out of here dressed like that."

"What?" Jason looked at her dumbfounded.

"I think there's a big old coat in the garage none of us has put on in years. At least it's warmer than what he's got on now. Let's give it to him, Jason, we're not going to use it."

Jason felt the anger start to well up from deep in him. "You are *not* serious?" he yelled. "Have you lost your mind?"

He could clearly remember that she suddenly looked as fearful as their homeless guest.

He'd had enough. "This is your lucky day, old man. Get your stuff, now, get it."

Jason flung open the back door. The man bent quickly to pull his bedroll and a white plastic sack from the floor. Jason was on him. Throwing the ski pole aside, Jason grabbed a fistful of jacket collar in his left hand, the visitor's leather belt in his right. Yanking the man across the floor, he heaved him out the door with a force that carried him off the end of the deck and hard onto his right side in the snow beyond, bedroll and plastic sack skittering past him.

"You come near here again," Jason seethed, "and next time you'll land in a six-foot hole dug just for you, you understand me, old man? Now, pick up your stuff and go. Right now. I don't want any of your crap left around here."

When Jason turned to walk inside, he saw a look in Anna's eyes that was no longer fear. It was something else. She was crying, hands over her mouth and nose. He stepped in and closed the door, satisfied that he'd taken care of the situation. Watching him, Anna moved backward into the small kitchen.

"What is wrong with you?" she blurted out between sobs. "He'll freeze out there. He's got nothing. Look at him. What's he supposed to do, Jason?"

"He's supposed to get out of my sight and off my property, that would be a good start," Jason shouted. Now angrier, "He broke into my cabin, Anna! My cabin! Ate my food, slept on my floor, and who knows what else. Who does he think he is? Who do *you* think he is? For heaven's sake, Anna, what are you blubbering about? Wake up, the guy's a nobody."

Anna, almost inaudibly, asked him to take her home. They stayed long enough to ensure the old man was gone, climbed in the truck, which hadn't been unpacked, and headed back. She was silent for most of the trip.

Finally, Jason could stand it no longer. "What's the problem, Anna? Why are you so upset over some homeless guy? I don't get it."

Anna sat quietly for what seemed like minutes. Finally she said, "I'm not crying for the old man, Jason. I'm crying for you. It's you I feel sorry for."

That was it. That was all she said. The moment proved a fold in the canvas of their marriage. Things were different afterward.

Jason remembered it all again as he checked the front and back porch doors, made sure the windows were secure and the garage was locked tight, climbed into the big SUV, and backed out of the driveway, cold gravel crunching under tires. Up the slight hill and right, and right again onto US 26, Jason headed for Timberline and a date with Merlin and a sleeping giant.

Chapter 9

MEETING A MOUNTAIN

Mount Hood National Forest consists of 1.2 million acres, has four designated wilderness areas, and boasts more than 1,200 miles of hiking trails. Hood is second only to Mount Fuji in the number of climbers reaching the summit. And it is spectacular. With five ski areas, including the only one in North America open twelve months a year, the region is both a summer and a winter recreation area that is precious to residents and visitors alike. The views and vistas are breathtaking, although Jason was less occupied with the sights before him than the voices in his head.

Timberline Lodge, a mountain retreat at 6,000 feet on the southern flank of Mount Hood, was declared a National Historic Landmark in 1978. The Palmer Glacier, uphill from the lodge at the 8,000-foot level, has served as summer home for the U.S. Ski Team. Built between 1936 and 1938 as a Works Progress Administration project during the Great Depression, the lodge was constructed using native timber and local stone, all cut, hauled, and assembled by remarkably talented workers who were unemployed until hired by the federal WPA. The building was crafted entirely by hand, inside and out, and stands as a tribute to a government's response not only to the physical needs of people during a desperate time but also to the needs of their spirits. The lodge has pride stamped all over it.

Jason remembered coming up here as a kid. His first memories were before he entered school, and were filled with sledding at Government Camp and Snowbunny Lodge, snowball fights with Dad, Mom threatening them both with dismemberment if she were ever hit, which, to her delight, she always was. And, he found, she could pitch a mean snowball. He even remembered those trips around the east side of the mountain and into Hood River for apples and cider in the fall. "The best on earth," his mom would say. These thoughts always brought a smile to his face. Those had been simple times, before life got so complicated. Today, Hood River was known less for its apples than for its role as the center of the windsurfing universe, with boarders riding powerful west winds funneled up the gorge and colliding with the hydrologic force of the massive Columbia rushing toward the Pacific.

The twenty-minute drive to Timberline was a visual feast, through the ancient forest, east toward Government Camp, then north up the access road to the lodge, with the south side of Mount Hood thick in his windshield. Lift towers became visible, like thin black candles stuck in a straight line on a white birthday cake, with chairs suspended between them by cables so small at this distance as to be wisps of fine silk. Snow still covered the entire bulk of the mountain and it glistened in the thin morning air, the sky above beginning to wake up in a purple blue. What a sight it was.

Jason had always been a mountain man, not in the sense that he wore buckskin and hunted grizzly, but because he'd always felt a connection to something outside himself at high elevations. Anna was a beach person. She preferred casual walks along the sand, watching the surf by day and listening by night, hunting sand dollars and gazing out at a fading horizon. He liked the beach and the thought of what was "out there" in that vast ocean. But the mountains—there was something fundamental, perhaps essential, about the mountains, and even in his current state of confusion he could appreciate the ancient belief that mountains were temples, sacred places close to God.

Jason remembered going flying with his dad when he was very young. A friend owned a small private plane and invited the two of them to go along one Saturday morning. Up to that moment, Jason's concept of the world had been two-dimensional. He had dashed childishly about the landscape, unaware of its dynamic nature, moving left and right, forward and back, happy in this world and entirely ignorant of its possibilities.

The three of them climbed aboard and buckled up, and the friend yelled "clear" and fired the motor. The prop spun to life. They taxied out to a narrow strip of asphalt, turned into the wind, and accelerated down the runway. Jason even remembered the uneasy feeling in the pit of his stomach as the plane left the ground, staggered for a moment in near weightlessness, then rose up, the force of it pushing him back into the seat.

Wow! He recalled his young eyes plastered to the outside window, seeing a world new to him in all its diversity. He saw for the first time how things connected. Small streams flowed to rivers. Roads fed to highways. Towns connected to towns through a now-obvious set of arteries that gracefully followed the lay of the land. Large buildings were located on large streets, smaller buildings and homes on smaller streets. Rural hills were less populated than valley floors. Why hadn't anyone told him about this? His two-dimensional world disappeared that day, shattered into a three-dimensional perspective, and he was never to see his environment the same way again.

Looking down at earth from 8,000 feet, with nothing between him and disaster but an overblown pop can with wings, driven by the whirl of a propeller he hoped was still there but couldn't see, he was both frightened and thrilled. But the view—the view! Flying north from the Willamette Valley, Jason could look left and see the coast range with the Pacific just beyond; slightly right of straight ahead was Mount Adams, Rainier barely looming hazy in the far distance. Off the right diagonal was St. Helens, then still a massive cone with its top intact, and out the right window was Mount Hood, just seventy or so miles due east—all of this in a short turn of his head. He sat stunned. What a world this was.

Even at that young age, sitting spellbound in the backseat of the small Cessna, he had been overcome. Elevation had brought wonder—and it still did. It seemed now to be the only thing that really humbled him, the only thing that could get past the façade of pride, arrogance, and self-importance. Jason had loved the mountains all his life, and skied as much for the view and the wonder as for the rush. That sense of awe was one of the few constants in his life of uncertainty. Perhaps it was why he now wanted to stand atop this mountain he loved so much, to see things from as high as possible.

Maybe, just maybe, there were answers up there.

He steered the big Suburban into the lot below the lodge and parked, remembering not to set the emergency brake up here. Just about every skier and climber makes that mistake just once: coming off the mountain after a cold day, usually at night, usually in the wind, tired and anxious to get home, only to find the brake pads frozen solid to the rotors, welded there in immobility.

Slightly inconvenient.

He'd been given directions to meet his climbing party, including Clara Schroeder, in a small building just south of the main complex. Nervous anticipation swept him like a broom. Jason left his gear in the SUV and made his way uphill for the rendezvous.

Entering the hut, he first encountered a woman sitting behind a desk marked "Cascade Mountain Guides Summit Climb Check-In."

"Hello," she said, "and welcome. Your name?"

"Hi, Jason Snow," he said, extending a hand. "I'm looking for Clara Schroeder."

The woman stood and gripped his hand firmly, "I'm Clara Schroeder. Pleasure to meet you, Jason. I'm so looking forward to climbing with you."

Jason's stomach jumped to the back of his throat.

Clara Schroeder was tall, about five-foot-ten, with tanned face, high cheekbones, and clear brown eyes. Her black hair was now singed gray and carefully braided to mid-back. She had a pearly smile and a gaze that was piercing, just as Jason had feared.

Clara's face glowed with character and color, the kind produced only by a life exposed to wind, sun, and challenge. A pair of glacier glasses hung suspended from her neck, the cause of the "raccoon lines" around her eyes. She smiled, and wonderful creases aside her eyes and mouth formed more visibly. Makeup and hair coloring were obviously strangers to her lifestyle; lip balm, sunscreen, and zinc oxide were the only necessary enhancements. *Pioneer tough,* Jason thought. Put this woman in a cocktail dress and heels, with makeup and hair done, and she would be runway stunning. He also sensed that she would kill him with an ice axe and hang his body from a lift tower for even considering the possibility.

"Follow me," Clara said. "I'll introduce you to a fellow climber." With that, she was off in a gait that was swift and natural, like fast-flowing lava. Lanky, with a hurdler's body, she moved with long strides and a boldness more common in young athletes than in fifty-six-year-old retired chemists.

What have I gotten myself into? Jason thought.

Jason was the second of four to arrive, fifteen minutes ahead of scheduled check-in. He followed Clara to a far corner, where a very proper-appearing Japanese man stood at her approach.

"Jason Snow," she announced, "I'd like you to meet one of your best friends for the next two days, Aaron Nakashima. Jeff Glendale and Sophie Frederickson are yet to arrive. Please get to know each other. I'll be back in a few minutes." With that, she was off again.

The two of them stood in uncomfortable silence until Aaron broke the ice: "Very nice to meet you."

They shook hands and began a conversation.

Aaron Nakashima was a serious, fifty-two-year-old biotech executive from Bend, Oregon, who looked five years younger than Jason. *Analytic* didn't begin to describe the devotion he focused on relatively mundane considerations. Divorced, with one grown son, Aaron ran, mountain biked, fly-fished, and kayaked in the beautiful high desert of central Oregon during the summer months and skied during the winter at Mount Bachelor, a favorite yet lesser-known mountain that produced impeccable powder.

Doesn't anyone work anymore? Jason thought.

Aaron was not a big man, five-foot-eight at a stretch, but wiry strong, with a determined countenance.

A sparkplug of a young woman came through the door carrying equipment that looked as though it weighed as much as she did. The tops of her ski poles, which were vertically strapped to her backpack, slapped against the top of the door frame with a clank. She ducked.

"Sorry," she said sheepishly. Approaching the two men, she asked, "Are you two climbing with Clara?"

"We are," Aaron intoned, a little too formally, given the circumstances.

"Great. I'm Sophie Frederickson."

"Nice meeting you."

Sophie smiled. She joined the group but did not take off any of the equipment that massed against her back. Instead, she flitted from one foot to the other. She was ready to go climbing, having already dressed, with mountaineering boots laced tight and zinc oxide applied. Jason looked her over and thought that with the addition of crampons, she could summit without any additional equipment. *Rope me to her*, he thought.

Aaron continued his introduction. He said he'd done some climbing earlier in his life but had been away from it for years now. Having never been up Hood, Aaron considered his photo history of Oregon adventures incomplete without a shot from the top of the state's tallest peak. An avid photographer, he was hoping the weather would cooperate and provide an unobstructed view southeast to Jefferson, the Three Sisters, and Bachelor, five white beacons known well by residents and visitors in Deschutes County.

"You've all climbed before, I presume?" Aaron asked.

Sophie and Jason shook their heads no.

"Not at all," Sophie replied.

Aaron's cringe did not go unnoticed.

Another commotion sounded at the front entrance. The three of them watched as a painfully underdressed man carrying a disheveled load of equipment in his arms lumbered toward them, bumping chairs and tables like an icebreaker.

"Hi, I'm Jeff Glendale. Hope I'm not late."

In a hasty release, he dumped all his equipment to the floor, sounding like rocks hitting snare drums. Aaron, Sophie, and Jason flinched.

"Are you the other three idiots who volunteered for this abuse?"

Nods all around. Aaron looked perturbed.

Jeff Glendale was a little on the heavy side, with a Marlboro hanging from his lips. He was married with three small daughters, all of whom, he said, were currently terrorizing lodge staff while his wife, Cheryl, sorted through photographs in the visitors' center. Jeff sat down at their table and pulled a sack from the mound of rubble at his feet. The bulging paper bag was stenciled with the logo of a local mom-and-pop restaurant, an impressive find at 6:45 in the morning.

"I talked 'em into grillin' me a burger. Little bacon. Little cheese.

Dash of Tabasco. Now we're talkin'. Do I look like an omelet guy to you? Not bad, huh?" he said with a grin. The filter of the cigarette was all that was left smoldering in a glass ashtray.

"You must be kidding," Jason said.

"Breakfast of champions," Jeff shot back.

Aaron Nakashima looked thoroughly disgusted.

Jeff's wife, Cheryl, not a small woman in her own right, appeared through the front entrance.

"Hey, honey," she yelled over to Jeff while waving a postcard, "thought I'd pick you up a little token of the top. Might be the only way you'll see it." She giggled.

"Really amusing," he quipped.

Jeff was wearing painters pants cut off mid-thigh and a black T-shirt with "Happy 30th Stud . . ." printed on the front and "Muffin" printed on the back. The shirt was recklessly short, threatening with every movement to expose body parts that no one wanted to see. Neon yellow flip-flops decorated with a rainbow of paint drippings rounded out the ensemble, certainly a unique way to make a special first impression. It was twenty-nine degrees out.

Should be an interesting couple of days, Jason thought.

Having lived in the shadows of Mount Hood most of his life, Jeff had finally determined that this was the year to climb it. After all, if he waited, he would only be another year older and, if history was any indication, a few pounds heavier. Watching Jeff devour the double-decker burger, fried onion rings, and blackberry shake, Jason wondered to himself how in the world the man would make it to the top of the mountain alive.

Clara appeared out of nowhere and wasted no time in getting to the point. "You're Jeff Glendale?" she asked.

"In the flesh," he responded.

"Pleasure to meet you, Jeff. Now, please put that thing out," she ordered. "You've heard of the smoking ban? High elevation and nicotine are not good company. And that's your last burger until you're out of my responsibility. Tonight, carbs are king."

Jeff was wise enough not to respond verbally, but the smugly perplexed look on his face told the story: *Who died and made you Queen for a Day?* Jeff admitted to being a novice climber and, not surprisingly, mostly physically passive except for the aerobic effects of screaming at the television during *Monday Night Football*. Listening to him, Jason thought, *He's in for a real cardiovascular treat.*

Sophie Frederickson, they learned, was a twenty-two-year-old psychology undergrad at University of Oregon. At about five-foot-two, she looked like she weighed maybe a buck twenty, with tightly curling brown hair hanging to her shoulders. Watching her bound around the hut, Jason wondered if she might just run all the way up the mountain. Sophie was a former ski racer from Jackson Hole, Wyoming. A bad fall in a downhill, resulting in a terribly dislocated shoulder and her third concussion in two years, had ended her competitive career at University of Colorado. Having transferred to Eugene, mostly to get away from a skiing program that still ran hot in her veins and to focus on school, she now skied just for fun. But the intensity was still there, still present in those huge blue eyes, and she was looking for new challenges.

A friend had suggested that climbing up a mountain might be as much of a rush as racing down one, so Sophie had immediately registered with the guide service. She was lit up about the climb, her first alpine experience, and ready to go.

Clara, with a grin that betrayed her delight, sternly remarked, "She'll drag us all to the top if we don't tie her in behind us. Find her something heavy to carry—one of Jeff's burgers will work. I don't want her shooting all her summit film until I get up there too."

Sophie beamed.

After meeting his climbing team, Jason excused himself and walked quickly back to the Suburban for his gear. He considered calling Anna to let her know that he was there and ready to go, then thought better of it. *Why should I cave to her?* he said quietly to himself. *She should be calling me.* He hoisted the pack to a shoulder, grabbed his boots, closed up the SUV, and headed back up the hill to the climbing hut, anxious to get up the mountain.

Chapter 10

ARMOR IN THE CHINKS

T he team spent Monday learning the basics of alpine climbing: clothing, equipment, ropes, knots, carabiners, belaying, rappelling, snow and glacier travel, crevasse rescue, first aid and injury precautions, avalanche survival and the use of avalanche beacons, alpine rescue, teamwork, weather changes—all of these taught with an assortment of personal stories and the wisdom of Clara Schroeder.

She was adamant that if you spent enough time in the high mountains, you were going to encounter trouble. Count on it. Even if your planning and technique were impeccable, the odds of a freak accident or fast-moving weather were weighted in favor of fate, and you'd better be ready, because trouble was likely to rear its head at the most inconvenient times and places.

She told a number of stories about accidents occurring at various elevations and on a variety of mountains, all of which would have been relatively benign just a hundred feet above or below the actual fall zone, but which caused critical injuries or death given the

climbers' specific location at the time. Fate, it seemed, was always a
climbing partner.

Most unsettling of all was Clara's lesson about crevasses, those
gaping chasms of indeterminate depth that populate glaciers. Clara
called them fascinating mountain features. Jason saw them more as
icy graves. Sometimes visible, sometimes hidden, these things seemed
prone to form in the least opportune places: at the tops of glaciers,
at a change in pitch attitude where the slope angle increased, at the
outside of glacial turns, or at any other unsuspecting locale of nature's
unpredictable choosing. To say that Clara's comments were troubling
didn't begin to describe Jason's anxiety.

"My job as guide," she said, "is to find a safe route up this mountain. However, once we're on the glacier, all of us must keep an eye out
for sagging trenches in the snow. And you may not notice an actual
depression. You may just notice that a particular patch of snow has a
different sheen, a strange texture, or a slight color variation. These are
the signatures of a hidden crevasse, places where gravity has pulled
down the snow, covering the mouth of a monster."

Just great, Jason thought. If her desire was to scare them, she was
succeeding.

"Alpine climbing is a continual game of 'Find the Crevasse,' and
where there's one, there are probably others. You must remember, just
because you can't see them doesn't mean they aren't there. The most
serene-looking snowfield can in fact be a minefield ready to swallow
any unsuspecting or distracted climber. And the vertical force of a free
fall into a crevasse, especially if ropes are slack, almost always results
in others in the party being dragged in before the fall can be stopped
and anchored.

"It is absolutely essential," she continued, "that you follow my
path up this mountain and back down, without wavering, unless I
direct you otherwise. Everyone clear on that?"

Jason considered checking Clara's boot print against his, but pride prevailed, and he stopped before making a fool of himself in front of the others.

"Got it," Jason answered.

From that point forward, he discovered snow inconsistencies in every step and was careful about wandering outside Clara's tracks.

During their day-long training, a concern arose as a result of Jeff's inability to "self-arrest," a technique used to stop one's own slide down a steep slope after a slip or fall. Self-arrest is a series of moves that ultimately puts the person in a facedown, feet-first slide, with the climber applying body weight to the pick end of his or her ice axe and driving it hard into the snow, braking the slide to a stop. Countless times, Jason watched Jeff slide a hundred feet or more down their training slope before coming to a stop in a depression at the bottom. The more Jeff practiced, the worse he got, perhaps due to the exhaustion that quickly set in from marching back up the hill and trying again, and perhaps due to his concentration on perfect technique.

"Jeff, fast is better than pretty," Clara would holler at him.

Although it was painful to watch Jeff's struggle to get stopped, Clara's determination to help him was remarkable. After she was satisfied that Aaron, Sophie, and Jason had the basic technique down cold, she instructed them to keep practicing by attempting the arrest starting in a variety of positions: headfirst on your back; headfirst on your stomach; feet first; tumbling; ice axe dragging behind as if you'd lost grip on it during a fall; and so on.

"Use your imagination," she instructed. "Ask yourself what could go wrong up there, and how you would get stopped if it did."

Then she turned her attention to Jeff, sliding right beside him down the steep slope, talking him through each step of the sequence and demonstrating the steps as they slid along, then hiking back up with him side by side, discussing possible modifications and offering encouragement all the way. Up and down they went.

Jason couldn't watch her dedication to helping Jeff without

feeling a sense of connection to this woman. It was clear that she was not performing this exercise merely as a result of her responsibility as a guide. The smiles, giggles, arm pumps, and even the stern corrections that emanated from her were genuine, and Jeff seemed determined to learn the technique more out of a desire to please Clara than out of concern for his own safety. In his struggle to understand and perform the arrest and her resolve to help and to keep discouragement at bay, Jeff and Clara seemed to develop a relationship that appeared as trusting as any Jason had experienced outside his immediate family, all in the course of an hour or so. Clara was a magician, physically and emotionally, and Jason was entirely unfamiliar with the alchemy she practiced.

Aaron, on the other hand, seemed to watch the proceedings with an indignant sense of disgust.

"Shouldn't she be spending a little less time with Michelangelo and little more time with the rest of us?" he said to Sophie and Jason during a water break. "He's getting his money's worth, while we're here playing in the snow like a bunch of grade-school tobogganers."

"Why does that bother you so much?" Sophie asked.

"It bothers me because Jeff has no business being up here, and he should know that. Look at him. If he has a heart attack up there tomorrow, who do you think is going to have to carry him down? Who do you think is going to miss a chance at the summit because of his lack of preparation? Wake up and smell the coffee: He's the anchor in a group of speedboats. She should cut him loose and let the rest of us enjoy the climb at a decent pace."

Sophie nearly jumped at him. "I don't agree. Jeff's got a lot of heart, and I'll take heart over brains any day. Besides, he's a kick in the pants. I think he'll do fine."

Aaron, more indignant now than before, answered, "Forgive me when I tell you that your twenty-two-year-old opinion doesn't cut it. You've got a lot to learn, young lady, not the least of which is respect for someone who knows a lot more about the problem than you do. I've been around the block a time or two. You'll see tomorrow how right I am, and then you'll wish that Clara had done what I've suggested. Trust me."

The conversation ended, but Jason stiffened at Aaron's last comment. How many times at work and at home had he himself tried to make his case by stating his authority? It suddenly occurred to Jason, after hearing his own words come out of Aaron's mouth, that anyone who must state his or her authority, whether in order to win an argument or to motivate, had none.

Still, Jason wondered about the physics of stopping a falling body the size of Jeff's—considering the fact that they would all be roped together—and whether his mass and potential velocity would yank the rest of them off the mountain. Jason could imagine the chaos of five climbers, all roped together, sliding and tumbling down a mountain, gaining momentum by the second while trying to self-arrest for the sake of themselves and their fellow mountaineers. It was a chilling thought.

Jason's concern was confirmed when Clara, near the end of Monday's training, announced the climbing order.

"I'll be first, then Aaron, Jason, and Sophie. Jeff will be last. I think Jeff will be the slowest of us, so the rope between Sophie and Jeff is probably going to be reasonably tight, with little or no slack, which is exactly the way I want it. If Jeff slips and falls, I want the four of us to anchor him immediately, before he picks up speed. If any of the rest of us take a tumble, I want Jeff to fall on that axe of his and secure our team, along with anyone else not involved in the slide. Jeff, you okay with that?"

"Good with it, boss," he replied.

Jason only wished that were true. *I've got Mr. Cholesterol with questionable skills covering my rear end. Just perfect*, he thought.

Their other problem came in the form of a very sore shoulder on Sophie Frederickson, the shoulder she had dislocated just a few months before, damaging the rotator cuff. A thirty-pound pack on the back of anyone not accustomed to carrying weight can cause pain over time. Put that weight on a bad shoulder that is prone to further injury, add altitude and a steep slope, and you're asking for trouble. One thing was clear: Sophie Frederickson was one tough girl. She wasn't about to admit that she hurt, but the occasional grimace on her face gave her away. At one point during a break in training, Jeff and Jason caught her taping a chemical heating packet to her shoulder blade.

"You going to be okay, sparky?" Jeff asked.

"I'm good, thanks."

Clara asked at least twice if she was all right, and each time Sophie's response was the same, "I'm fine, stop asking."

Clara finally pulled her aside at the end of the day. The rest of them overheard the conversation.

"Sophie, are you going to be able to deal with the pain of that shoulder? I know how much something like that can hurt. I'm going to tell you now, if you get in trouble up there tomorrow, you've got to let me know. Look at me, Sophie. I'll have no hesitation at all with stripping that pack off your back and carrying it myself to the top of this mountain and back down if necessary."

Aaron, Jeff, and Jason looked at each other wide-eyed. They knew that Clara, as the guide, was already carrying extra equipment, and Sophie's pack would put her load in the seventy-pound range, big weight on a fifty-six-year-old woman plowing a path through snow and up a steep mountain at 11,000 feet. Was she serious?

"I've carried more weight than that," Clara continued. "I want you to have fun tomorrow, to enjoy the experience, not turn it into a death march. Are we clear on that?"

"Clara," Sophie said, "I can't let you carry my stuff, no way."

"Listen. A climber in big pain is a dangerous climber, one prone to mistakes. When you start thinking about a sore shoulder, you stop thinking about placing that next step correctly, you stop concentrating on your axe placement. You stop looking for trouble. Things happen too quickly up here. I want you to promise me that you'll let me carry your gear if you're hurting, or I won't be able to take you along tomorrow. That's my condition. Yes or no?"

Sophie just looked at her. "You're the most bullheaded woman I've ever met."

"Thank you. That would be a yes, I presume?"

Sophie nodded.

The three men shook their heads at one another.

"Two tough broads," Jeff remarked.

"I'll second that," Aaron said, "but I'm not so sure she should be going tomorrow. She could be a hazard to us all. I'm here to get to the top of this mountain, not to carry someone else's load or be held up."

"Thankfully, it's not your call," Jeff shot back with a touch of defensiveness. "You may be a big shot in Bend, but you're just a grunt up here. Just like the rest of us."

"At least this grunt can stop his own fall," Aaron countered.

Jeff grinned the same grin Ali had before he'd knocked Foreman cold.

"Look," Jason chimed in, "I think Aaron has a point. Sophie adds risk to all of us. Maybe she should—"

"Gentlemen." Clara was suddenly beside them. "Anyone have something important to say?"

No one said a word.

She moved closer. "Put yourself in her shoes," Clara whispered. "She's out of competitive ski racing. She's still got smoke coming out her ears and is ripe for a challenge, and she's got a heart the size of this mountain—you saw her today. She'll probably lap us all. As long as I think she's okay, I'm taking her up top. I'd do the same for any one of you."

She paused for effect.

"Let's go up this mountain tomorrow together. I'll be looking after each of you. I'd die before I saw any of you hurt. However, any one of you can decide to withdraw if you don't feel safe. I'll make sure you get a full refund, no questions asked. I'll pay you out of my own pocket if necessary."

She looked right through each of them.

"I'm in, big-time," Jeff responded.

Jason and Aaron nodded their heads. "Me too," they said in unison.

"Good," Clara said. "Now, let's get our equipment picked up and go have some dinner. Anyone hungry? Jeff, for instance?"

"Right behind ya, sister," Jeff said enthusiastically.

"Sister? Really? My mother," she said, "would not be pleased to hear you say that."

They all chuckled. Somehow, in a matter of seconds, Clara had thawed their little spat.

Chapter 11

EXPECTATIONS

S ilcox Hut is located at 7,000 feet, a mile hike from Timberline
Lodge, at the top of the Magic Mile chairlift. Used by climbers,
skiers, and partiers looking for a private hideaway, Silcox provides cozy accommodations for twenty-five to thirty overnight guests
and a jump on early-morning summit attempts. The team, careful to
stomp the snow off their boots before entering, walked into a rustic
paradise where a strong fire was burning in a large fireplace and hand-
carved tables and chairs invited people to gather. It was wonderful:
the smoky smell of fir and pine mixed with the aroma of pasta and
fresh-baked bread, the view south down the mountain to the main
lodge and valley beyond, and the distant Cascades to the southeast
illuminated by a low-setting western sun.

This was Jason's kind of place.

Manned by Phil Chambers, full-time host, cook, and caretaker,
trained in CPR and other vital first-aid techniques, the hut offered
conveniences unexpected at a place this remote: running water, heat,
light, and indoor plumbing. Communication was maintained with

the main lodge by radio, and a snowcat delivered nonclimbers and supplies daily.

After storing his equipment and getting out of his boots, Jason wandered over to the expanse of windows and admired the majesty outside. Clara slipped up quietly behind him, surprising him.

Folding her arms and looking out, she said, "This view is worth the entire trip, don't you think?"

"It's spectacular," he said.

"I've looked out this window hundreds of times," she said, "and it's never failed to bring me peace. It always puts my small problems into a proper perspective. And when I say small, I don't mean petty."

"I could use a dose of peace right about now."

Clara turned to look at him carefully and smiled. Both stood for a moment in silence. She appeared as though she wanted to say something but was hesitant.

"Jason, I feel like I need to share something with you that's personal, but I would never want to make you feel uncomfortable."

"Please, Clara," he responded. "You are not going to make me feel uncomfortable. I'm willing to listen to anything you have to say."

She looked up, as if she were gathering a story from some high place, then began.

"I was diagnosed with breast cancer six years ago, and after I spent some time feeling sorry for myself, I came up here, looked out at the world from this very spot, and realized I was a lucky girl. I was so darn grateful for all I'd been given and for what I had experienced. I'm a chemist, Jason, but I'm here to tell you, chemistry doesn't cure cancer. It does help the body fight it, that's certainly true, but ultimately it's the mind and body and its marvelous immune system that kills the cancer. I began fighting my cancer that day, and my weapon was gratitude. It took the fear away. After I got my perspective straight, I never again experienced the sheer terror that came to my mind and heart when the doctor first said the 'C word.' It occurred to me, standing right here, that I should see the cancer as another mountain, one of many that I've climbed, and I was determined to learn something from the experience. In fact, part of my ability to be grateful for the experience came with the realization that I would discover things about myself and about others that I would not have known had I not had cancer.

"It may sound strange to you, but cancer became my favorite summit. It shone new light on all the other mountaintops I've stood on. So, it's easy for me to stand here and realize how lucky I am to be alive, how wonderful life really is. We live in a beautiful place, Jason. I wish more people could see this, experience this. Maybe it would do for them what it does for me."

Phil Chambers bounded up. "Clara! Great to see you."

"Phil, you're looking so darn good. If I wasn't a happily married woman . . ."

Phil beamed.

Clara turned to Jason and said, "Phil, meet Jason Snow, part of our wonderful group of climbers going up tomorrow."

"Great to meet you, Jason," Phil said. "I hope you know you're climbing with one of the finest people I've ever had the pleasure to call my friend."

"I'm quickly realizing how true that is," Jason responded.

Clara winced. "That's about enough of that. What's for dinner? I'm hoping it's that lasagna you're so famous for."

Phil laughed. "And the only meal we serve up here."

Off to the kitchen they went, arm in arm.

Jason was left wondering how someone who'd had cancer could possibly consider herself lucky. He stood at the window gazing out for several minutes.

It took the fear away. Clara's statement echoed in his head.

He didn't know about gratitude, but the view did fill him with a sense of how small he really was. Looking back to the west, he knew that Anna was out there somewhere and that she was hurting, mostly because of him. It started as a small notion and began to grow. He wanted to talk with Anna, to tell her how sorry he was for his selfish behavior. *Great time to have my conscience come alive,* he thought. *Seven thousand feet up on the side of a volcano with no cell phone.*

❄ ❄ ❄

After dinner, Clara called them together.

"Could I talk with the four of you for just a moment?" Clara asked in a tone that caused a serious demeanor to come upon the group. Leaning forward now, her eyes intent, she said: "Thank you so much for allowing me to enjoy a couple of days with all of you and for your confidence, which I have yet to earn. I want you to know that tomorrow you'll have a thrilling experience. You'll see Mother Nature as never before, and she is a grand dame to be sure. The views from up there are beyond my description. You may have seen photographs from the summit of Hood, but a picture cannot convey the awe. A picture cannot convey the raw emotion of standing on something so big and feeling so small. It is a view, a vision really, that will remain in your mind long after any photo has faded dull. It never gets old for me. You may find yourself feeling a level of humility that evades your daily routine, yet at the very same moment feeling stronger, more alive, than ever before. It's that inherent strength that I want you to see in yourself, or perhaps to find for the first time in years. That strength is latent in every one of us.

"The most important discovery you'll make on this climb," she emphasized, "is the discovery of yourself and what you're made of. I want you to enjoy the journey, not just the destination. I want you to cherish every step, every view, and every emotion. By registering for this climb, you've purchased my hands and back and brain. It's yet to be determined whether I'll win your heart, mind, and spirit. But that's my intention. That is what will make this climb either something you'll always remember or something you'll want to forget."

Pointing west toward Portland with its cosmopolitan population of more than two million people, she continued softly: "I want to share with you something very personal, something about why alpine climbing has meant so much to me during the course of my life. Let me be as clear as I can. Whatever you think life is down there, up here things are different. There can be no competition, no win-or-lose mentality, no adversarial relationships, no hate, no envy, no selfishness, no dishonesty, no disloyalty, no backstabbing, no protecting your own turf at the expense of others, no posturing, no sucking up, no politics. Please understand, up here those are not just inconvenient personal characteristics—they can be death sentences, and the death may turn out to be your own."

She had their attention.

"What is mine is yours while we're on this mountain. Whatever I've got with me: food, clothing, medicine, equipment, experience even, I've brought not for me but for you, and, at the risk of sounding like a musketeer, you for me. If one of us gets hurt, we all get hurt. Damage to one person means damage to the collective group, since each person makes a contribution to the strength of the team. A success for one, however small, is a success for all of us. The rope that tethers us together for safety is also a symbol of our commitment to one another. If one of us requires medical attention to the point that he or she must come off the mountain, we come off together. We will not split up or leave anyone behind. Do you understand? This is a determination you must make now, right now, because when you get up there, you'll be enticed by the summit like a pirate to gold. Climbers much more skilled and experienced than you have lost their lives by going for a summit that exceeded their capability, was beyond the strength of their collective team, or was well outside their own safety commitments. So, instill it in your heart and soul now. Whatever we do, we do as a group, and we will not risk the health of any one of us just to put someone on top."

Jason smiled nervously, and Clara noticed. She smiled a wise smile back, but it was not an expression of happiness. He detected that her subtle response was one of understanding, that she saw his unhappiness and somehow, in that small moment, understood him. *Merlin*, he thought.

"A couple of final thoughts," Clara remarked. "We all show up with unique talents and gifts. But we also bring our own narrow perspective of life and how things should be. We are all prejudiced: We all 'pre-judge.' We observe a person we don't know and immediately begin to fit him or her into a box we're comfortable with. Those boxes consist of things like ethnicity, race, intelligence, social stature, and gender, stuff that satisfies our previous experience. Even things like body size, the way we dress, posture, and eye contact will color a person's character before you ever really know that individual. It is the nature of the beast. I want you to hear me carefully: Our differences, when combined with common values, give us enormous leverage. Two ideas are better than one. Five are significantly better than two. That diversity just may be what saves us. But if we lack those common values, diversity will only produce conflict and intolerance. It may be what destroys us.

"It's your choice."

Clara stopped to look at each of them squarely.

"Our purpose, our shared value, is to have a deep experience and get everyone off this mountain alive. We've got to work together. But more than that, we've got to come together, or someone's going to get hurt. I've lived with death and injury on this mountain by avalanche, fall, weather, and crevasse. But, I will not live with death due to our inability to look out for one another. That catastrophe I am not willing to accept, and neither should any of you.

"And finally," she said, "some of the most remarkable climbs of my life have come on those days when the summit was out of reach. Maybe it was weather, equipment failure, or the health of a fellow climber. Once or twice it was simply a feeling that I was compelled to trust. I've made my share of mistakes up here. However, I absolutely believe that the measure of a human being is not in whether we make mistakes. We all make mistakes. The measure is in how we act in relation to those mistakes; it is calculated in the character we respond with. Now, I know that an admission like that may not be what you expected from a mountain guide you're about to follow up an eleven-thousand-foot volcano. However, as you can readily observe, I'm human. You'll get all this human has to give. I want you to know that getting you to the summit is important to me, but not as important as getting you down safely and back to your family and friends. If circumstances require me to turn us around and descend, I'll try to make that judgment through the eyes of the people closest to you, those who want you home safe and healthy. The summit has no value if its price is injury—or worse."

If she only knew, Jason thought.

"The summit should not be your only measure of success. Don't spend so much time focused on results. Instead, relish the process; pay attention to what you learn. What will you discover? Will you make new friends? Will you find someone or something residing inside you that was unknown or long forgotten? Maybe all you'll do is find the kid in you again, that long-lost ability to laugh and find joy in simple things. If that's all you find, it's more than enough for me to count this climb as remarkable. It may be that someone at this table tonight will help you find that kid, long buried under a big pile of status, title, pride, responsibility, stress, or discouragement. Stranger things have happened. And if there is something I can do for you that will make this climb more enjoyable, I hope you'll trust me enough to let me help you. It would be my great privilege."

Clara sat back quietly. No one spoke. All eyes were riveted on this woman who'd just opened a portion of her soul to a group of people she barely knew. She was either foolish in her disclosure or profoundly trusting, and this was not a foolish woman, which confused Jason. Vulnerability and personal disclosure as strong character traits presented a leadership paradox he couldn't begin to get his arms around. Clearly, Clara functioned on a set of principles that were beyond him. There was something in her demeanor, in the way she spoke, that stirred something in him. He didn't know what it was specifically, couldn't define it or quantify it. All he knew was that she had him, as cynical and thick-skinned as he'd become, and he found himself strangely uncomfortable with the comfort he found with her. He sat stunned, studying this remarkable woman, wondering what gave her that inner strength of character. He'd observed her briefly in action and knew her by word and reputation, and that was enough for now.

Jason would gladly follow her up this or any other mountain.

Finally, Jeff broke the silence. "My wife will tell you I've been a kid all my life. I think I can help you all with this one."

Clara laughed out loud with the rest of them and clapped her hands in delight. "Now, that's what I'm talking about," she giggled.

Jason just smiled quietly and observed her. *A human magnet*, he thought.

With that, Clara jumped up from the table and began clearing dishes. Plates, utensils, and glasses clanked in the grasp of what appeared to be an experienced kitchen hand. The climbers objected to their guide cleaning up after them, but she was adamant.

"I love doing this. Gives me a chance to annoy the heck out of Phil in the kitchen. I'm up here all the time. You folks go enjoy the view."

There was no use arguing. Clara was already gone with the first load.

Aaron, Jeff, and Sophie made their way to a couch by the fire. Jason thought of joining them, then changed his mind.

"I'll catch up to you guys in a little while. I'm going to head outside and watch the sun go down."

"Enjoy," Sophie said. "Just don't be heading to the summit without us."

"Even if he left now," remarked Jeff to Aaron, "Sophie would still beat him to the top."

"Ain't that the truth," said Jason.

Chapter 12

QUESTIONS, NOT ANSWERS

J ason pulled on boots, jacket, and gloves, opened the heavy door, and slipped out into the dusk. The air was cold, and a breeze bit the tops of his ears and face. Dry snow crunched like Styrofoam under heavy, Vibram-soled boots. The bench sat facing south and gave him a 180-degree view: ocean, coast range, and Portland to his right; the Willamette Valley front right; central Oregon and the Cascades just off his left, and eastern Oregon at far left. He estimated his viewing range to be two hundred miles, although it was hard to really tell. Whatever it was, it was big. This was a beautiful state, diverse in climate and lifestyle.

West of the Cascades the environment was temperate, green, and wet and included the stunning Pacific coastline. This was the Oregon most nonresidents identified with. The east side was high desert: dry, hot in the summer, snowy cold in winter, more like a Colorado or Utah climate. The state was a paradox: the high-tech Silicon Forest in the west, ranches in the east; dense populations in the west, rural in the east; liberal politics in the west, conservative in the east;

thick Douglas fir forests covered in moss and fern in the west, tough ponderosa pine forests with juniper and sagebrush in the east; urban sophisticates in the west, rural outdoor lovers in the east. Those were vague generalities, Jason knew, but they painted a reasonably true picture of a state that was divided politically, economically, socially, environmentally, and philosophically. Perhaps it was due to this vast diversity and the ideas it leveraged that Oregon seemed always on the cutting edge of social thinking: the bottle bill, the Oregon Health Plan, and physician-assisted suicide were prime examples. This was a state in which it was illegal to cut down a tree without a satchel of permits but entirely legal for a doctor to help a patient cut short a life.

All of this made for a most interesting place to live. From his home, Jason could travel an hour west to the Pacific Ocean or an hour east to Mount Hood. He sat contemplating all this while watching the sun lower itself onto the western horizon. The door to the hut opened, and out trudged Clara carrying a large bag.

"They said I'd find you out here. Mind if I join you?" she asked.

"Not at all," Jason replied. He slid over and made room. Clara stashed the bag behind the bench and sat down, drinking in the view.

"Tell me about yourself," she finally said. "You born and raised here or transplanted?"

"Born and raised," Jason replied.

"How is it that someone who seems to appreciate the outdoors as much as you has waited until now to climb this mountain?" she asked.

"I guess I never had a reason before. I was content with living nearby, skiing it regularly, using its hiking trails, fishing. Never really had a desire to climb it. Don't really know why."

"So what's changed, what's your reason now?" she asked with a tone of genuine interest.

"I don't know." He paused, then said, "I guess I'm looking for answers."

Clara smiled. "You think you'll find answers up there in the thin air of the summit?"

"I hope so," he said, chuckling. "You of all people should know. Are there answers up there?"

"Depends on what you're looking for, I suppose. I hate to break it to you, but I find many more questions up there than answers. But that's just me. I love questions—much more than answers."

"That sounds like it comes from someone content with her life," he said. "Me, I have no answers. I'm drowning in questions. The last thing I need is more questions. What is it about questions that's so darned interesting?"

She smiled again. "I'll tell you why I like them. Our Western culture values answers, but questions are really much more interesting."

"How do you mean?" he asked.

"Let me give you an example. Imagine that every person is a box. Everything we know is inside that box, and everything we don't know is outside that box. In fact, there are many more things outside the box that we don't even *know* we don't know."

Jason realized this was true and was surprised he'd never thought of it before.

"Now," she continued, "let's suppose I ask you a question. If you know the answer, it's going to come from inside your box. If you don't know the answer, that knowledge lies outside your box. However, if I am patient, and I provide fertile soil for you to explore and discover, if I haven't made you feel stupid but have your trust, you may just ask a question, and that question is going to come from the *boundary* of your box, that narrow edge between what you know and what you don't know. The question becomes much more interesting than your answer because it defines the boundary of your box and begins to give me a glimpse of your personal reality, how you see and experience the world, how you think. But I must listen very carefully. I must learn to nudge you along and encourage a searching that stretches your boundaries without being too quick to provide answers. It is this kind of environment that builds curiosity and a joy of discovery. Understand?"

"Yes, I think so," he responded.

"Let's assume that you learn something new, something that was previously outside your box. You've drawn a new boundary, a new box, larger than the first, to take in this new knowledge. What's happened? The boundary of the box, the boundary between what you know and what you don't know, just got bigger. It may be true that you know more today than you did yesterday, but with this new knowledge, you've become aware of many new questions. You've gained one new answer and ten new questions, and it's now your responsibility—your joy, really—to explore the possible answers to these new questions.

"This is a fundamental truth: New knowledge enhances an ever-increasing sense of our own ignorance. The more we know, the more we know we don't know. Feynman called it 'the expanding frontier of ignorance.' Ask anyone over the age of fifty whose wisdom you appreciate, and they will confirm this truth.

"Think of it another way. Who is the most ignorant person you know?"

Jason knew lots of ignorant people. He shrugged his shoulders.

"I believe," Clara continued, "it's the person who thinks he or she knows everything, or at least behaves that way. 'Know-it-all' has never been a term of endearment. It's an attitude that may stem from some people's inflated view of themselves. But more probably, they're lacking in personal esteem, or they may be looking for social validation. This much is certain: There's no such thing as a know-it-all. Accepting our own inevitable ignorance requires a real sense of humility. It requires us to admit to others and ourselves that there is much beyond our small understanding, that we can learn all kinds of stunningly remarkable things from the most unexpected people and circumstances if we'll just give them a chance."

Jason sat thinking. "So," he asked, "with ten new questions for every new answer, when do we catch up?"

"Never," Clara said with a smile the size of the view in front of them. "And isn't that great! That means that life will always carry a sense of discovery. It'll always be an exploration to see what's around the next bend in the river or on top of the next summit. I look at people like Aaron, Jeff, Sophie, and you and ask myself, What do I get to learn from these people, whose life experience is unique? What can I learn from them that I couldn't learn from anyone else on earth? Every day brings a series of complex questions, and with them some remarkable answers."

They sat silent for a minute or two before Clara began to stand. "I've bothered you enough. I'll let you enjoy the view."

"No, please stay," Jason said, pausing out of some embarrassment for being so quick with the request. "Look, I've really enjoyed your company. Seems like a long time since I've talked with anyone about something other than work. Heaven knows, Anna is tired of that. And frankly, so am I."

Clara sat back down. "Are you sure? Sometimes answers require independent contemplation."

"I'm sure," he replied. "Independent contemplation is painful these days."

Clara reached behind the bench and pulled up the heavy nylon bag filled with supplies. "Would you help me prep some gear?" she asked.

"Sure," Jason responded.

She pulled out a new climbing rope that had been wound into a tight circle. "This needs to be coiled and packed. If you would, be careful not to stand on it. Bind it in the top when you're done and use the Velcro straps to secure it into the bag. Have you done this before?"

"Never," he said.

"Good, I'll get to show you."

It was a small thing. Just a brief comment. *Good, I'll get to show you.*

All the same, the expression jolted him. He'd spent most of his life trying to hide his ignorance, trying to fake his way past it, and here was a woman who seemed happy about it, joyful in the opportunity to see him learn, however small or inconsequential the learning appeared. It was as if a weight had been lifted off his mind. Was it possible for him to simply be who he was and still be . . . worthwhile? He shook himself back into the moment.

Jason began to unroll the rope and coil it as Clara had showed him. She pulled out a stack of first-aid items and a neoprene bag and began packing the gauze, scissors, ointments, bandages, and other items in the bag, arranging them carefully. They worked in silence for a while as Jason considered how much of himself to disclose, something he virtually never did anymore, even to Anna.

Finally, he just started. "Clara, you seem so sure of things, so centered in your life and your direction. How did you find that in yourself?"

Again he considered how much to reveal, then pressed on.

"Everyone thinks I'm so successful. Some of the younger guys in the firm have even asked me about how I got to where I am. If they only knew. My wife's on the verge of leaving me and it's my fault. I've done things I'm not proud of, and the misery that comes with bad decisions stays a long time, well beyond any sense of triumph or success. I'd like to pull the guys at work aside and tell them they really don't want to go where I've been. But then pride always gets in the way, and I slap them on the back and tell them to work hard and look for opportunities to differentiate themselves—like that's some kind of revelation. I don't know, Clara. I guess I thought I'd have things figured out by this point in my life, but I'm further away now than when I started."

Clara was silent for a moment. Then she turned to him and smiled.

"You know, Jason, I love to run. I run to stay in shape for climbing. Most people who live in my neighborhood have seen me out pounding the pavement on the roads near our home. I've run the area for years now. What if you lived in my neighborhood and one morning, while leaving for work, you spotted me lying in the street next to the curb, about a mile from my home? Anxiously, you stop your car, get out, and rush over. You find me there unconscious. I have contusions and abrasions on my forehead and the right side of my face. My right wrist and forearm are broken, and I have severe scrapes on my knees and anklebones. Now, remember, I'm unconscious. However, if by some strange miracle you were able to ask me questions so you could help, what questions would you ask?"

"Well," he began, "the first thing I'd do is call 911 and get someone there as soon as possible. I think it's pretty obvious what happened, so I'd probably ask who hit you. Then I'd call the police and report a hit-and-run."

Even as it came from his own mouth, Jason winced at the phrase that brought back haunting memories of awful choices.

"You've assumed lots of things," she commented.

"Yea, I suppose I have, but what are the options? You're pretty beat up, Clara."

"What if I told you that no one hit me?"

"I'd be curious about how you got so banged up. Did you trip? Were you run off the road? How could a runner go down in the street and do that much damage? It doesn't make sense."

"No," she said, "it doesn't. Anything else you want to know?"

"I don't think so," he said. "I'd probably wait there with you until the ambulance arrived."

"What if the ambulance doesn't come? What then?"

"You always have this kind of luck, Clara?" he asked.

"Never," she said, smiling.

He continued: "I'd probably make sure that your neck was supported and not moved around. I'd try to get some help from someone nearby. Maybe try to put a splint on your arm and wrist, clean up the cuts and scrapes and bandage them as best I could."

"What if I told you my neck was fine, no breaks, no problems. What would you do then?"

"I think I'd wait until you came to, maybe get you something to drink, and then carefully help you into the car and get you to the ER."

"Okay, I'll buy that. You've treated me pretty well, and I appreciate it, believe me. But you've missed something big. You see, Jason, I had a heart attack while running and it dropped me in my tracks. I was incapacitated before I hit the ground. You've done what you thought you could. You treated my arm, my wrist, my cuts and abrasions; you attempted to give me water and make me comfortable; but I'm D.O.A. because you were treating the symptoms and missed the cause. You were fixing the obvious, distracted by the injuries on display, and missed the real problem, much less evident but much more fatal.

"Finding answers to our problems is a lot like that. We've got to find a way to strip out the clutter and discover the real cause. Only then will we find the answers."

"How do you get to the real cause?" he asked.

"It's not easy." She paused, as if considering what might resonate with Jason.

"Have you ever been in an avalanche?" she asked at last.

"Not a big one, thank goodness. Just small slides that were caused by a skier's disruption, but nothing I could legitimately call an avalanche. You?"

"I've been in and around a couple," she said, "one on Rainier, another on a miserable climb up McKinley. Talk about helpless. They are just plain scary. Both of them went in slabs. I'll never in my life forget the sound, Jason, never. It's seared into my memory. There was a distinct *pop* when the slab broke free, like nothing I've ever heard in the mountains that is naturally occurring. A hollow, echoing *bang* followed by the roar of a freight train."

Jason's anxiety increased as he considered what the following day might bring.

"I remember as a little girl watching my father fell trees. I would stand well back out of the way, but I could still hear the sound of his axe striking hard against the tree trunk, wood chips flying, like I was three feet from him. Bang!" she yelled, clapping her hands and startling Jason. "That hollow axe-against-tree sound is as close to an avalanche fracture as I know, like a gunshot. It's more than a little unnerving to hear that loud pop. Instinctively you know, deep in your gut, even if you've never heard it before, that nothing good can come from a sound like that up here. Panic begins to grip you in the split second before you look up, and when you do, you see that the mountain has broken loose above you in one huge sheet. And if fate has put you in the avalanche's path, escape is nearly impossible. It just moves too fast. If you're in a climbing party, about the only thing you can do is scream a warning to the others, turn your back to the white explosion coming at you, and brace yourself, praying it doesn't hurt too much when it hits. In the chaos that follows, you desperately swim and kick and claw your way toward the surface before the snow stops moving, because when it does, it will set in around you like concrete."

"Were you hurt in either one?" Jason asked.

"Yes. My heart was broken both times. Two good friends gone on McKinley, one on Rainier. It took us two and a half days to find the second climber on McKinley, even with the help of mountain rescue. We were not going to leave him behind. He left a young wife and three of the cutest little girls you'll ever see. I knew I'd never be able to look her in the eye not having brought her something to bury. People need something to bury. Those three climbers and their families go with me to the top of every mountain I climb. I miss them still."

"With losses like that," Jason asked, "how do you keep climbing? Why would you want to continue doing this, given the risk?"

"It seems foolish, I know," she responded, "but in some fundamental way I'd feel like I was squandering a horribly expensive education if I quit. Each experience, good or bad—but especially the bad—brings knowledge. I'm a better climber today, certainly a better guide, and I hope a better person, for having gone through those awful events. I'm much more alive down there," she pointed to the valley below, "when I spend some time up here."

She paused, a memory forming.

"Some people paint to find tranquillity; others play music, or cook, or garden. I climb mountains. It's part of who I am. I'm married to a marvelous man who understands. I know he worries about me on every climb, though less now than he did years ago when our children were young and I was climbing more difficult routes. But the hug we get from each other when I return is precious in its understanding. Climbing, by virtue of its inherent risk, degrades a person's ability to take life for granted. Compassion, humility, and gratitude are the result. I'm not suggesting the effect is universal, but for me, climbing mountains takes a black-and-white world and turns it to color." Clara paused for a moment. "What turns it to color for you?" she asked.

He thought hard. It was a disappointing exercise. He couldn't think of a thing, really. He kicked the snow at the base of the bench. "Not much anymore, sorry to say."

"Pretty common," Clara responded.

"I'm open to suggestions."

Her smile was gentle. "Jason, I couldn't begin to offer you advice. I'm just a mountain guide."

And Yoda, Jason thought, *was just a short, bald guy with a cane.*

She continued, "I know what works for me. I'm not sure it applies to anyone else."

"Try me," he said.

"You sure?"

"I'm sure. Both barrels."

"Okay." She paused, considering. "I've spent my life in the sciences, a chemist by education and profession. I learned early on that if you wanted to accomplish anything worthwhile in chemistry, there was a set of fundamental principles—I called them axioms—that had to be followed. Innovation came when someone developed a deeper understanding of the underlying axioms and applied them in a way no one had considered before. They didn't invent the axiom. They discovered it. And the invention, the innovation, came when they figured out how to use the axiom to make something extraordinary occur.

"To make a breakthrough in chemistry requires the chemist to understand the language of axioms better than his or her native tongue, and then to create chemical actions that are congruent with those axioms. The better you know the fundamental principles and techniques of element combination, the better you are at predicting outcomes. Everything has a sequence, Jason, nano to micro to macro. From the most minute, intelligent elements within a human nerve cell to the operations of an entire civilization, order emerges from disorder according to the same fundamental principles. You must follow natural law. There is no way around that fact. Anytime a scientist attempts, knowingly or unknowingly, to violate natural law, failure is the sure result. A seed planted in dark soil grows to the light.

"Intellect is no match for truth."

Chapter 13

SYMPTOMS DON'T KILL YOU

onsider that avalanche we just talked about," Clara offered. "If I asked you to describe an avalanche, how would you do it?"

Jason thought carefully about her question. "Well, I guess I'd say that an avalanche is a powerful movement of snow down a mountain that leaves debris in its path."

"Not bad," Clara responded. "However, what you've described, the things you've observed, are *consequences*. And the really interesting question is, consequences of what? Snow moving down a mountain leaving debris in its path—that's a consequence of something much more fundamental. Some axioms were combined with a specific set of circumstances and an action, caused by either internal or external forces. Axioms, circumstances, and a single point of action cause the avalanche. We can learn much more about an avalanche and how to stop it, or how to protect ourselves from it, by understanding the basic axioms that produce the event. Once those elements combine in just the right way and that first 'boom' is heard, once the fracture occurs and the slab is unleashed, the devastation that results is a consequence.

"The pictures we see on the nightly news of people buried, trees down, homes wrecked, cars engulfed, rescuers in a frantic search—those are all consequences. And trying to solve a problem by focusing on consequences is hopeless. It goes against natural law. Why? Because we have no control over consequences; we have no choice. Consequences are controlled by axioms."

"So what do we do?" Jason asked.

"Well, we try to really understand the axioms," Clara answered. "In an avalanche, those basics are found in slopes from thirty to forty-five degrees. Slopes less than thirty degrees are too shallow for large fractures; slopes more than forty-five degrees are too steep for large snow accumulation. What we're looking for is a situation in which the snow on top is heavier than the snow under it. Next, we look for deep stresses that can occur at the top, sides, or bottom of the slope. And we look for an abundance of possible triggers: snow chunks falling from trees, cornices that can break off, anything that can cause an initial disruption. Those are the axioms governing avalanches: huge forces stored in the form of potential energy, waiting for action, waiting for static stresses to be released into kinetic monsters. By understanding them, we can control them, at least to some extent. We fire mortar shells into slopes that meet our critical avalanche criteria before significant snow can accumulate, intentionally causing small avalanches and avoiding the big ones. Ski patrollers break off cornices, eliminating triggers. These systems are much better than constructing protections such as avalanche fences that are intended to stop or slow down a major slide. We've found that if we work *with* natural law, we are much more successful than if we work *against* it. Do you understand what I'm saying here?"

"Yes, I think so," he said. "You are saying that there is a small set of principles—you call them 'axioms,' also known as truth or natural law—which are fundamental to the way something is going to behave. In your example, an avalanche. And if we can understand those axioms and their characteristics, we can solve problems much more effectively than we can by focusing on consequences, which is where our eye is drawn because that's where all the action is. Am I close?"

"Very good," Clara said with a grin. "So, how does all this apply to you and me?" She looked at him, waiting for an answer.

Jason thought for a moment. He was being pushed intellectually and liked the exercise. "Well, I'm pretty sure it means that we need to look for the cause of the problem and stop responding merely to the symptoms. But I have to say that navigating through problems to find their source is not simple. I mean, in theory, it's easy enough, but figuring out the real cause of problems is not some trivial task. Remember how well I did at determining why you were lying on the side of the road bleeding. I think you said D.O.A."

"Precisely," she grinned.

Jason sat in silence, digesting this.

After a few moments, Clara plunged in deeper. "Mind if I just talk through some thoughts I have, Jason? They may sound a bit strange at first."

"Please. Not at all."

"I've always found it fascinating to contemplate that if you took four people, from the four quarters of the earth, and synthesized them down to their basic physical elements, they'd all look exactly the same. No difference. It doesn't matter what their gender is, what race they are, what their circumstances are, how their DNA is sequenced, whether they can read or write, whether they're rich or poor—none of that matters. They synthesize to carbon, hydrogen, oxygen, and nitrogen. All of them. Just four elements. Humbling in a way, isn't it?"

"Yeah, it is."

"We are all physically the same, from her highness to the homeless."

106

He watched as she seemed to be choosing her next words carefully.

"I want you to think about another possibility: What if, embedded in the emotional life of nearly every human being on earth, there is a small set of axioms—basic, fundamental truths—that cultural analysis has shown to exist in every sustainable civilization, race, and gender; axioms that have been duplicated and considered legitimate in every society; axioms that would appear as basic elements if human beings could be synthesized emotionally. Axioms that, when witnessed in their purest form, we naturally respond to, even gravitate to, regardless of circumstance. Axioms that can be described as truth."

"Sounds a little preachy," Jason observed. "Looking for a convert? You may have the wrong guy."

Clara smiled. "I do happen to believe that we all have a spiritual nature, but what if I told you that these few axioms are independent of any particular philosophy of life? They exist as fundamental components of all the world's major religions, but they are equally revered by people who possess no hint of religious inclination. What if I told you that the consequences of your life, your happiness and misery, are bound up in either your adherence to or your violation of these axioms? Whether you believe in these axioms or not has no effect whatsoever on their existence. You can choose to not believe in gravity and, at your own peril, suffer the consequences."

Jason's head was spinning. "Where do you come up with this stuff?"

"The sequence follows natural law," Clara said, her eyes bright with excitement. "Human behavior is an avalanche, subject to the same sequence that governs all of nature. We choose what we believe, and we choose our actions. Everything else is a consequence. Life is a sequence that begins in choice and ends in consequence."

They both sat and thought for a moment.

"Life is a sequence that begins in choice and ends in consequence? I'm still not sure how it applies to me," he acknowledged.

"Well, let's construct something concrete," she offered, "something that will allow us to visualize all of this."

Clara walked over to the woodpile next to the door and pulled a random stick from the stack. Returning, she began to draw something in the snow.

"Let's assume," she continued, "that axioms are the most basic virtue, the first virtue. These are things that are true, self-evident. Natural law is an example. Axioms come first."

"Stop a minute, Clara. Can you give me another example?"

"Okay." She thought for a moment. "Let's suppose that your child comes down with the flu. She has some symptoms: fever and nausea. As an informed parent, you know that fever and nausea are evidence of sickness, not the sickness itself. The key to her sickness lies below these symptoms. She might have a viral infection, for instance, and axioms teach us that her immune system is responding by creating a symptom called 'fever.' The actual cause may be any number of things: She might have stomach flu, she might have food poisoning, or she might be under huge stress, which, we now know, can cause all kinds of nasty biochemical responses.

"As a parent, you make the effort to find the natural law, the core cause of her illness. Perhaps you get her to a doctor, someone who has enough knowledge and experience to find the core issue, someone who won't dance around the symptoms."

Clara wrote the word *Axioms* in the snow.

"Axioms," she emphasized.

"Next, our beliefs and values are our convictions about life and what we think is true. They are desirable characteristics that serve as principled guideposts in our lives."

"How is an axiom different from a belief or value?" he asked.

"Good question. With your sick daughter, you have some beliefs and values about how to heal her. If you learn that she has a viral infection, you'll call on those beliefs and values to determine what action you might take. Here's a news flash for you: Your beliefs and values do not represent truth. They represent what you *think* is true.

"Equally responsible parents may have vastly different beliefs about how to treat a child with these symptoms. Some may believe they should take their daughter to a doctor right away. Others believe in homeopathic approaches. Some have religious beliefs that preclude medical care. Some believe that the more she has to fight the disease without aid of medication, the stronger her immune system will become. Some believe they should starve a cold and feed a fever.

"There are many beliefs and values for any one circumstance, a variety of which may be legitimate. Each of us must struggle with our beliefs and values, holding them up to the light of the axioms underneath. For example, if the cause of your daughter's symptoms is stress, a prescription for penicillin may not be very productive in the long term. Understand?"

"I understand," Jason nodded.

"Now, I want you to notice that axioms contain the truth. Absolute. Remember, whether I *believe* in gravity or not is my choice. However, my belief or lack of it has nothing at all to do with the existence of gravity, or, for that matter, the consequences should I choose to defy it. If I don't appreciate the proven effects of gravity, I may jump off a roof and suffer severe consequences. Or perhaps I do believe in the principle of gravity but feel defiant toward it—maybe I jump off the roof anyway. Same consequence. Beliefs don't change axioms.

"So, in axioms lies the truth, and in my beliefs and values lies what I *think* is true. I have no influence, no choice, in the axioms. I don't determine truth. Conversely, I have complete influence and choice over what I believe to be true. *Therefore, the strength of my beliefs and values, the power of my convictions, is defined by how closely what I believe to be true mirrors the axioms, or what is actually true.*

"What if I told you," Clara continued, "that you have only two choices in life? You can choose what you believe in, what you value, what your convictions are—that's the first choice. The second choice is this: You can choose your actions, how you behave. Everything else in life is a consequence of those two choices.

"What if I told you that your search for personal integrity, your desire for personal esteem—to feel better about who and what you are—is a consequence?

"What if I told you your learning and wisdom and your accountability are consequences?

"What if the trust you develop with people around you, your ability to communicate openly and honestly, and your ability to innovate and create are consequences?

"And finally, what if the degree of influence for good you have on people around you—spouse, children, friends, coworkers, everyone—and your ability to be a peacemaker in your relationships and within your community are all consequences?

"What if all of the things I've mentioned are consequences of the choices you've made: what you believe and value, and how you act in relation to your beliefs and values?"

Jason considered his ability to change his beliefs and values—or anyone else's, for that matter.

"I can tell you this," Clara continued. "My experience is that the closer my beliefs and values are to what is really true, the happier I am. And the further away my convictions get from truth, the more miserable I am. Don't get me wrong: That doesn't mean life is easy when my values reflect the truth, but it usually does mean that I'm at peace with myself, that I have a sense that I'm on the right road. Life isn't necessarily easier when I believe gravity to be a true principle, but it is a lot less dangerous. So, first: axioms; and second: beliefs and values. You with me so far?"

"I think so," he managed.

Both Clara and Jason jumped when the door to the hut suddenly flung open. It was Jeff, of course, dressed down again in cutoff painter's pants and the "Stud . . . Muffin" T-shirt.

"Good gosh, Jeff," Clara said. "You about scared me to death!"

"All right, listen up, you two ice sculptures. I've been sent by Phil, our head cook and chief bottle washer, to thaw your bones. We understand that Jason is a remedial student in desperate need of more help than the rest of us, but I don't want to have to come out here in the middle of the blasted night to pry your hardened corpses off this bench. Besides, it'll be darned hard to strap you to a sled when you're frozen in the sitting position."

"What a nice picture that is," Clara remarked.

"Phil has made up the finest pot of hot chocolate west of Vienna," Jeff continued, "and he's not letting any of us partake till we get you two inside. Now, as far as I'm concerned, you could stay out here till hell freezes over, but now that you're getting between me and Phil's chocolate, well, I'm prepared to take drastic measures if I have to. You'll both accompany me inside. Now. I mean right now!"

"I didn't know you cared, Jeff," Clara giggled.

"Perfect timing," Jason said. "All this has been really fascinating, but I can no longer feel my feet."

They followed Jeff back into the great room, where a black iron pot of hot chocolate sat on a lacquered wooden table, steam billowing up into the vaulted pine ceiling. A red ceramic bowl of marshmallows sat beside it, accompanied by a plate of chocolate chip cookies. Jason removed his gloves and rubbed his hands over the warm pot while Clara stood in front of the crackling fire, removing her jacket.

"Isn't this the way it's supposed to be," declared Clara. "What a perfect night."

"What in the world are you two talking about out there, a cure for cancer?" Jeff asked.

"Well," Clara responded, "funny you should say that, because, in a way, that's exactly what we're doing."

"Yeah," Jason said, "however, she's doing it by cutting a hole in the top of my head, pulling out all my brains, examining the little that's there, and stuffing them back in."

"Sounds rather painful," Aaron said. "I think I'll stick to the in-hut conversation."

"Me too," Jeff chimed in. "We were in the middle of prying information out of Sophie. She told us about some of her ski-racing adventures. You probably didn't know her college ski team ranked in the top five nationally her freshman year. She made the junior Olympic team and was headed to Colorado Springs for training until she busted her noggin."

"Listen," Sophie countered, "it really isn't that big a deal."

"Your injury must have been disappointing," Clara replied.

Sophie shrugged.

"I spent about six months having a pity party, but I'm over it. Stuff happens. You move on. My mom finally got through to me one day. She said it isn't so much what happens to a person that defines them, it's how they respond to what happens to them that defines them. She told me not to kid myself: Bad stuff happens to everyone. Some have the backbone, she said, to turn it into something constructive.

"My mom's a pretty tough woman. She might as well have hit me with a hammer. I'm not sure why it affected me to the extent that it did. Maybe it was the right time. Maybe it was because I trust my mom. So I sucked it up, applied to U of O, and left the 'why me?' attitude in Colorado. Time to go find something else to get totally jazzed about. Just think, if I hadn't been injured, I never would have met the four of you. I wouldn't be climbing this beautiful mountain, sitting in this hut, or enjoying Phil's world-class hot chocolate.

"Sometimes I think things happen for reasons we never learn about until years later. Maybe the injury was a fork in the road that pushed me in a new direction, one that, in the long run, will prove much more interesting than the one ski racing would have taken me down. Who knows? Who really knows? But here's the thing: I'm sure going to do everything I can to find out."

"Smart girl," Clara said. "I'd very much like to meet your mom sometime."

Sophie laughed. "The two of you together would be frightening."

The banter continued as they warmed their bodies and spirits inside the small community of climbers. With hands cupped around mugs of hot chocolate, they turned their talk to tomorrow's climb.

"We want to be climbing by 2 a.m. tomorrow," Clara announced. Wake-up is 1:15 a.m. I'd advise a prompt reaction to the alarm. Phil has a juvenile sense of humor. Need I say more? Given that, I'd like each of you to check your equipment against the equipment list before bed tonight. Unpack if you have to. Make sure everything is there. If you're missing something, no problem. Come see me. Phil and I will get you what you need. In fact, let's get that done right now. That okay with everyone?"

"Sure," Aaron said. The rest nodded.

The climbers hoisted themselves from the table and started upstairs. Jason started to follow the other three out of the room, but when he reached the doorway, he turned to Clara. "Clara, I've been wondering. Am I required to subscribe to some specific philosophy or theology in order to benefit from what we were talking about tonight? Is there an ideology behind all this?"

Clara smiled. "No. In fact, it is independent of any particular philosophy or theology. However, any belief system that is dispossessed of these fundamental axioms is a false belief system and will ultimately bring sorrow to the individual and dis-integration to the organization."

"So, if we're not talking about a specific philosophical system,"

Jason replied, "then we're talking about truths so fundamental that they include all sustainable belief systems. Is that true?"

"True. People get wrapped up in trying to prove that what they believe to be true really is, even when the outcomes from their beliefs and values cause consistent emotional misery for themselves and others. The key is to get wrapped up in finding *truth*."

"Then why don't we?" Jason asked.

Clara smiled. "The people who get stuck are those whose personal convictions are planted in fear, pride, hate, and arrogance. It takes courage and rigorous honesty to look for truth, a willingness not to be afraid of an honest inquiry. By the way, Jason, an honest inquiry can be eye-opening, even painful."

She reached for another cookie.

"Now, let's get your equipment checked."

Jason left the room and went up to his bunk. He lifted his gear out of his pack and laid it on the fleece blanket. While unpacking, he considered his earlier conversation with Clara. It reminded him of a time some years back when his young son had become ill. Brian had an escalating fever and nausea, just as Clara had described. Both he and Anna were reasonably confident in their ability to handle childhood illnesses. They gave him ibuprofen to bring down his fever, made sure he had cool, wet cloths for his head, gave him liquids to drink every hour, and tried to make him comfortable. Jason had considered it a run-of-the-mill flu.

At about one in the morning, Anna's concern began escalating. Brian was complaining of stomach cramps, and his fever had risen a degree. She wanted to take Brian to emergency, but Jason hesitated, wondering if she was overreacting. He had an important early meeting and the loss of sleep was not going to help his effectiveness or concentration, although he kept that concern to himself, knowing such a disclosure would expose his motivations and anger Anna. Especially since he feared that she might be right in her concerns.

Still, his argument prevailed, which meant Anna spent the night in a chair by Brian's bed.

Anna, frantic over Brian's lack of rest and increasing stomach pain, rustled Jason awake early. It was five a.m. when they finally bundled their son into the car and hurried to the hospital. It took the doctor only a moment to diagnose appendicitis. Brian was quickly wheeled into surgery, and Anna and Jason began a long vigil in the waiting room.

The surgery proved successful—however, the doctor spoke to them afterward about how close Brian had been to a burst appendix. "Minutes," he'd said.

Jason still flinched at the incident. He recalled that long evening in light of the conversation he and Clara had just had. He remembered his guilt and failure at not having followed Anna's instincts to take Brian to the hospital hours earlier. Now he understood that he and Anna had been functioning on different beliefs and values—and, he acknowledged, perhaps he'd betrayed some of his own. And since his agenda had prevailed, his son had suffered as a consequence.

He finished checking his gear and carefully repacked the equipment, wondering, as he worked, how many tragedies he'd created because he was too busy being right about the symptoms while ignorant of the cause.

Chapter 14

CONSEQUENCES

Returning downstairs, Jason found himself again peering through the south windows, transfixed by the view. Timberline Lodge glistened in haloed yellow light nearly a mile below. As he stood taking in the simple grandeur of the mountain and the sights it provided, his thoughts returned to his conversation with Clara, who was now sitting peacefully alone next to a crackling fire Phil had stoked minutes before. He considered how many times he'd done wrong and tried feeling right about it. Often. Too often. No amount of justification, he knew, repaired a punctured conscience. He wandered over and sat opposite Clara.

"What is it you're thinking about?" she asked.

"Where do I start?"

He sat forward and rubbed his head with both hands, itchy from a day in a fleece cap.

"I'm beginning to see how misguided beliefs and values can lead to misery. I've experienced that many times, although I didn't know the sequence. I just never realized that there was some standard of truth—axioms—that I needed to reckon with."

"There's more to the sequence, actually, but only one more item we have real control over," Clara said.

"And what is it?" he asked.

"Remember when I told you about the only two choices we have in life? The first thing we choose is our beliefs, our values. Can you remember the second?"

Jason thought for a minute, then finally shrugged. "It's left me," he confessed.

"The other thing we choose is our actions. And so, the third virtue in our diagram is *action*."

"Action? As in, how I behave, how I act?" Jason asked.

"Exactly. There is a space between what happens to us and how we react, stimulus and response. For some of us, the space is small indeed, but there is space. To a degree, your actions reflect what you believe to be true, what you value. However, we all do things that are contrary to our beliefs, things that betray our conscience, things we feel terrible about. Your conscience is an early warning system, telling you usually one of two things. One, your conscience may prod you to recognize an opportunity to take action that is congruent, or integrated, with your beliefs and values. Or two, your conscience may warn you that you are considering acting in a manner that is incongruent, inconsistent, or in violation of your beliefs and values. One is a green flag, the other, red. One is 'I ought' and the other is 'I ought not.' Don't you think most of us know when we are making a poor choice? When we're looking for the easy way out? When we're betraying our conscience?"

"Yeah, probably," Jason had to admit, although begrudgingly.

"People spend millions of dollars every year to have psychiatrists and psychologists lead them out of problems they knew would result when they chose to act. How did they know? Their conscience was screaming at them before they acted. It had erected a roadblock and was waving a red flag the size of a billboard, and they chose to drive right on through. Their problem isn't that they failed to hear the voice or see the flag, it's that they chose to ignore it. They betrayed themselves. They had control of the situation until they chose how they were going to behave. A man cheats on his wife. A woman gossips. A man erupts in anger at his children. A mother starts drinking at noon every day. A husband and father gets lost in pornography. An employee steals from an employer. A boss promises a promotion but never follows through. Once action is taken, consequences follow. To our great regret, we have no control over consequences. Consequences are a product of axioms, or truth."

"I'm not sure I buy that," he chimed in confidently. "I know lots of people who have done some pretty lousy things, everything from marital infidelity to corporate scandals. Stuff you couldn't imagine. Many of them have pretty much avoided any of these consequences you talk about. Their spouses have no clue. Business associates are completely unaware of any impropriety. You name it; people have gotten away with it. If consequences were based in axioms, or truth, then consequences would appear as part of every bad decision. And clearly they don't. Look around you. Good things seem to happen to bad people all the time."

Clara smiled again, and Jason was beginning to recognize the expression as an acknowledgment that he had missed something big—again.

"What makes you think," she asked, "that there aren't consequences?"

"Well, because they haven't been caught," he said, immediately seeing the weakness in his own argument.

That smile again. "So," she asked, "you believe that getting caught is the only consequence?"

Jason wished he hadn't been so stupid. As he sat there on the couch, with this Cascadian view out the south window, his life flashed before him. He was, in fact, on this mountain at this moment because he was looking for a way to feel better about the lousy choices he'd made, most of which were actions only he would ever be privy to.

"No, Clara, I don't believe that. I wish it were true, but I know it's not."

"How do you know?" she asked.

"Because," he answered, "I've done all kinds of lousy things I've not been held publicly accountable for, but that hasn't kept me from feeling disgusted with myself. For me to sit here and say there haven't been consequences is a denial of what actually happened."

"And what happened?" Clara asked.

"You missed your calling, my friend. I feel like you've taken the top of my head right off and have an unobstructed view of the mess inside. Are you working for my wife? Maybe my employer?"

They both chuckled.

"I'm working for you," she said.

That, he knew, was true.

"What happened?" Jason continued. "I'll tell you what happened. Each time I made a lousy move, one that I absolutely knew was going to be lousy before I acted—which, by the way, is how it always happens for me—I ripped something out of my insides. I reached in and tore something out. Bad choice. Rip. Bad decision. Rip. Betray my conscience. Rip. Behave against what I believe to be true. Rip. Act against what I value. Rip, rip, rip. I'm wondering if there's anything left inside. After all this time, I think maybe I've become deaf to the voice of my conscience."

They both sat quietly, each feeling the weight of Jason's words. He considered what he'd just said. For the first time in his life he had acknowledged that his misery was his own doing, not someone else's fault. Not Anna's, not Brian's, not Jesse's, not even Flegger Norman's or Northwest Design and Engineering's. The taste was bitter. He was his own problem. He'd also come to believe what Clara had so carefully outlined: Every choice has a consequence. Some good. Some bad. And the fact that a poor choice may happen independently and without public revelation does not in any way diminish its personal impact. In fact, he considered, it might even make it worse, because the result is that you end up living a double life. In some strange way, being caught would be a catharsis. As humiliating as it might be, it would present a chance to get the awful thing behind you, to move on. The fact that you've never been found out simply means you're still carrying all that baggage, and over the years it becomes an unbearable load. Shame grows in the dark.

"So, you've experienced the pain that accompanies misalignment between your values and your actions," Clara commented. "You've defied your conscience. What follows are guilt and justifications. It's a psychological welfare state. When we receive an increase without an investment, we may think we've found nirvana, but ultimately it leads to a feeling of self-loathing and personal contempt. There's no such thing as a victimless crime. Our conscience is unavoidable. However, once on this path, it's hard to get off. Psychological welfare."

Jason considered the fact that misalignment of actions with values, or values with truth, would cause misery. It seemed true. He certainly had enough experience by now to feel the weight of acting as though it weren't true. He winced when he recalled the shortcuts and throat-cuts he'd made in his life and couldn't pretend he had avoided the consequences of defying his own value system. His joyless life, his peril of losing his family, bore witness to the truth of what Clara was saying.

Jason felt the stirrings of learning something new, something unique. Clara was mentally twisting him into seeing the world from different perspectives. But with new knowledge would come an expectation of change. A woman like Clara would demand that. Talk was cheap, and she was anything but an armchair philosopher. She might never say it out loud, but Jason knew in his heart that learning without execution was unacceptable to her.

"Gandhi," she offered, "said something very interesting that applies to our conversation. He said, 'A man cannot do right in one department of life whilst he is occupied in doing wrong in any other department. Life is one indivisible whole.' In other words, there is nowhere to hide. One hole in the hull of our convictions eventually sinks the whole ship. There is a sequence, Jason, undisclosed to most of us. But consider: no trees without seeds, no roof without walls."

She allowed this to settle in a moment before continuing.

"The components of any decision are sewn together. You cannot damage one without causing problems for the rest. For example, misalignment is the result of your actions being inconsistent with your values and beliefs. As soon as that happens, you are in conflict. You've betrayed your conscience and you know it. There is no escaping that fact. It is, as you so artfully described it, a 'rip' in your emotional fabric. And what happens? You begin to justify your actions. You begin to blame. You begin to find fault in others. You become irritable. You stop trusting yourself. Perhaps you stop trusting others. You stop communicating. You begin to get angry at people and events that hadn't bothered you previously. You begin to see the world as a place in which your glass will always be half empty."

Another pause. She was a patient mentor.

"And then, tragedy strikes," Clara said. "You begin to look outside yourself for your happiness. You begin to crave social validation, realizing that integrity, character, and personal esteem cannot come from within so long as your behavior is in conflict with who you believe you are. So, rather than change your behavior or your values, you begin to look for social acceptance. And, unfortunately, there is always someone out there who will tell you that your behavior is perfectly acceptable, which leads you further away from the path. Over time, perhaps your belief in who you are begins to darken.

"There is no peace in this process. No peace. Once a person goes outside himself or herself to find happiness, misery is a sure result. No amount of money, fame, success, popularity, social acceptance, title, power, or even self-medication will satisfy your appetite for peace. Your conscience is the one thing in this world that will never give up on you, not ever. All of us stand condemned, not by some external notion of right or wrong, but by our own beliefs and values, our own conscience.

"We may spend our entire life running from the voice inside us, but it will always beat us to the finish line. It knows who we are. More important, it knows who and what we can become.

"Forcing peace from the outside in will always prove a temporary solution, Jason. Ultimately, there must be a change of heart. The soul of the person must transform first before long-term interpersonal peace has any chance at a foothold. Maybe some questions need to be considered: How can I alleviate suffering? What is there to learn? What am I grateful for? What is my conscience telling me to do?

"A man at war with the world was at war with himself first. Peace begins on the inside and works out."

Chapter 15

INTEGRATION

J ason sat stunned at her comments, letting the concepts flow into
his mind like water.

*Going outside yourself to find peace produces misery. A man at war
with the world was at war with himself first. Peace starts on the inside and
works out.*

He wasn't at all sure he understood the ramifications of those
ideas, but they rang as true as anything he'd heard in years. They
reached inside and grabbed his gut. More than anything, something
whispered to him that they were true.

Clara sat back, watching him process her words.

"What we've been saying so far, simply, is that there are laws that
govern our existence. What is behind the law? That's the great question. But the law itself is inescapable. Avalanches don't slide uphill.
My heart rate does not decline during exercise. Molecules do not become less active when heat is applied. I may not know the genius
behind turning liquid water to a snowflake whose crystal structure

is unique in all the world, but I do know that the snowflake, once created, will not violate natural law. That I can count on.

"Baby steps, Jason. I don't need to know the source of natural law to recognize its truth. After all, science and religion have been fighting over that since Descartes, Galileo, Aristotle, and before, with no apparent progress. In fact, it appears that both parties to the conversation are more polarized than ever, with little room for a third alternative or a desire to understand one another.

"Remember, people get wrapped up in trying to prove that what they believe to be true really is, instead of getting wrapped up in finding truth. If science is good, it doesn't mean that things that are not science are bad. It just means they are not science. Likewise, if religion is good, it doesn't mean that things that are not religion are bad. It just means they are not religion.

"You and I may disagree on the ultimate source of gravity, but to deny gravity itself because the source is in question proves disastrous. That kind of thinking must become unacceptable to us, Jason.

"Let me ask you a question. When you act in a way that is consistent with your beliefs and values and those values are consistent with true axioms, what is the result? What kind of person is the product of such a pattern of action?"

"Well," Jason responded, "I'm not sure. I guess I feel . . ." he paused.

"Don't make this harder than it is," Clara said. "Who is the person you think about when you think of someone who acts consistently with a set of beliefs and values that are aligned to truth?"

Jason did not have to think hard. "My father," he replied quietly.

"And how would you describe him?"

Jason pondered the question, then smiled. "He was . . . solid. He was a man of integrity."

They were silent for a moment.

"And you," she said, "who are you when you act consistent with your values?"

"Like my father, a man of integrity. I feel better about myself," he said quietly, half hoping Clara hadn't heard the admission.

She looked serious.

Sitting straight and turning directly toward him, she said, "You are saying that you feel better about yourself when you act with integrity, which often means giving up something that you really want. For example, you might forego some personal accolades by acting in a way that shines a light on the accomplishments of someone else rather than your own. Is that what you really mean? If it is, that is exactly the opposite of how many of us behave. How do you explain that?"

Jason was surprised by how strongly he felt about the truth of this argument. He also knew, without doubt, that in the few instances in his life when he had followed this kind of sequence, he had felt a satisfaction that was wholly unavailable in his usual self-serving course of action. In those instances, he had found himself standing a little taller, trusting himself more. He had, indeed, felt better about himself, and he couldn't deny it.

"Look, all I know is how I felt inside when I was able to do what I thought was right."

She smiled again, like a mother teaching her child. "Why do you believe this so strongly, when, as you said, you follow it so seldom?"

This was getting more than a little painful for Jason.

"Let me take some heat off you," she said. "I believe you advocate it because it is buried in you, just like it's buried in me and in just about every person who walks the planet. Life is a sequence that begins in choice and ends in consequence. The whole process is governed by self-evident axioms that, when witnessed, stir something in us that we call 'truth.' You seek integrity because it's in harmony with natural law, and you know it."

"You know," he said, "something happens in your soul. I'm not sure what. But there's no feeling like it in the world. Whatever it was, whatever loomed just a minute before as a sacrifice, as a denial of immediate gratification, becomes a gift larger than the sacrifice, but only after the sacrifice is made. Integrity. I've heard it said of faith that first we jump, and then we grow wings. Integrity is like that too, I think. That's what you have to gain. The sacrifice turns into a gift that is priceless."

Clara smiled, stood, and reached for the poker to stoke the fire.

"There are," she said, sitting now on the hearth, "some things you must understand. First, integrity is a personal virtue with enormous social implications. It has to do with you and you alone. It does not involve other people. Some mistakenly believe that integrity is an interpersonal characteristic, some character trait that either succeeds or fails only when two or more people are interacting. But integrity, first and foremost, is personal. Integrity is born when your beliefs and values come together and are consistent with your actions, and it dies when they are not.

"The virtues that produce integrity are also capable of healing the rips created in your emotional fabric when you betray your conscience. In fact, they are the only things that will heal such an injury. We talked earlier about all the various methods we try instead: wealth, power, fame, status, social acceptance, pleasure. Those are all counterfeit methods, devoid of the power to heal and transform. All of them are very enticing. None of them are effective. Personal integrity, simply put, is the act of listening to and following your conscience, as long as your conscience is in harmony with the axioms.

"Second," Clara continued, "sacrifice is a component of integrity. In every good thing there is sacrifice. Integrity is learning that what is right *by you* may be different from what is *right*. You described it perfectly: The sacrifice turns into a gift that is priceless.

"And third, accountability coexists with integrity. The good news is, for the person of integrity, accountability is welcome. Imagine living a life that had no fear of scrutiny."

Jason gazed down at his boots. He didn't want to look that closely at his own life. Imagine how terrifying it would be to open it up for others to see in. But he allowed himself the consideration. What would it be like if he lived a life so consistent with truth that he never feared scrutiny? To him that seemed difficult, nearly impossible. But underneath the doubt, he felt a glimmer of something alive. He couldn't name it yet, or figure out how to get his hands on it, but he identified it as the nearly unrecognizable face of a lost friend.

Chapter 16

A FIVE HIRES A THREE

I t's getting late and I've rushed this to a spectacular degree, but
do you understand?" Clara asked. "Or, have I made a mess of all
this?"

"No. No mess," Jason responded. "What's fascinating to me is
how easily it fits together. It appears obvious, so simple. Not that that
makes it any easier to execute. But I've never heard it explained this
way. It feels dynamic."

"Good," responded Clara. "Let's refresh: First, *axioms*—truths that
are self-evident.

"Second," she said, "*beliefs and values*—or, if you prefer, convictions. Remember, axioms are things that are true. They are absolute.
Beliefs and values, our convictions, are what we think is true. There is
one truth that explains human existence, but there are scores of beliefs and values. There is a world of difference between the two.

"Third, *action or behavior*—what we do, how we respond.

"And forth, *integrity*—with its twin, accountability. Each leads to
the next. A sequence. You with me?"

Jason nodded. "Running as fast as I can, Clara."

"Good. We'll talk briefly about the next virtue, and then we need to hit the sack. It'll be an early morning. That okay?"

"Sounds good," he said.

She paused for a moment, then launched in.

"Let me ask you another question. If you lived a life of integrity, if you remained true to your conscience, true to your values and beliefs—in other words, if you walked your talk—what would be the result? What would the product be of this behavior? How would you feel about yourself? And, interestingly, would it change how you feel about others?"

Immediately, his experience with the homeless man who had stayed a few nights in his cabin exploded through his memory and stabbed him in the heart.

Would it change how you feel about others? In his mind's eye, he could see his horribly hostile reaction to the old man and the contempt he'd shown him: pitching him out and threatening him with harm. Jason pondered this while wondering if his reaction had had less to do with the old man than with how badly he had been feeling about himself.

He remembered the old man telling him that the door had been left unlocked. In a surge of panic stoked by what he now knew was a real sense of personal loathing, Jason had realized that the intrusion was partly his own fault. This simple act of negligence had allowed an intruder to breach his doorstep. His response to his own shortcoming was to blame the transient.

He could hardly admit it, but when he had witnessed Anna's altruism, he had become enraged out of, what, jealousy? Looking back, it seemed so ridiculous now. What was it that he could possibly be jealous of? The guy was homeless, for heaven's sake.

Then it occurred to him: compassion. It was her *compassion*—compassion from which he felt he had disqualified himself. The homeless man was outside the inside of society. Anna, even through the layers of dirt and years of disrespect, saw his humanity. Somehow she was able to synthesize him on the spot and see him as an equal who just happened to have some challenges, challenges that were not better or worse than her own, just different.

Anna's response to the old man had been to alleviate his suffering. Jason's had been to increase it in an attempt to exorcise his own guilt and disgust. Jason had known in his heart, even then, that his actions, the way he was living his life, had disqualified him from receiving her compassion and generosity, and that killed him. He hadn't been angry at the old man; he had been angry at himself. He had been furious at his inability to act in a way that was worthy of Anna's respect—which, as pathetic as it sounded, was what he wanted more than anything.

"Clara," he offered, "I'm afraid I've done some incredibly stupid things. Horrible things. The answer to your question is—yes. I think I would see other people differently. Is it common for people who don't respect themselves to disrespect others? Is it common for a person who has trashed his own character to willfully conspire to trash the character of others, thus elevating himself in his own eyes by diminishing everyone else? Is it possible for me to hate someone fundamentally because I see a part of him or her that I despise in myself? If I feel unworthy of love, acceptance, or admiration, do I lose my ability to feel those things for others? Is that possible? The implications of behavior based on feelings of inadequacy and fear seem enormous. Is that what you're saying?"

"What do you think?" she asked.

"I don't know," he answered, shaken by the possibility. "I . . . I don't know."

"Know this: If the answer to your question is 'yes,' it could lead to some painfully critical assumptions about why we seek power, or fortune, or fame, or any number of things that we think we want. Is it possible that what we are really trying to do is repair and rebuild the structure within us that has been ripped out, piece by piece, by our own choices? By actions that are incompatible with what we value? We go seeking materials for the required repair on the outside. We attempt to rebuild the structure from the outside in—however, it can't be constructed that way. We try because it presents itself as the path of least resistance. It appears to be the easy way out, but this road never leads out. It is a counterfeit. It is trickery in the worst form.

"Always remember, Jason, the way that appears easy is never the easy way. And the result? Look around you. There are people everywhere who appear to have everything a person could ask for: money, status, titles, social acceptance, fame, you name it. They are up to their neck in 'things,' and yet are so miserable that they can hardly look in a mirror each morning."

She sat forward.

"The repair is not available outside ourselves. The repair we are talking about must come from inside. Aligning what we do with what we believe—that is how we produce the material for the repair. That's the only way."

Jason was squirming. "Okay, okay, let's stop there," he said. "Are you saying that anyone who aspires to have money, or tries to build a successful business, or wants anything that could be described as a 'thing,' is motivated because he or she is broken on the inside? I have a real hard time with that. Sometimes I want something because it's the reward I promised myself I could have if I reached a goal. Or maybe I want something because I know it will make Anna happy, or my kids, or it's what my father would have done. There doesn't appear to be anything ominous about that. No frightening psychological undertones. Are you really saying that any material desire or accomplishment is the product of trying to fix a broken character?"

"I don't know," she responded. "Is that what we're saying?"

"You're playing with me," he said.

"I'm trying to get you to think beyond yourself."

"Look," Jason said, "there are times when I desire something out of an honest drive to move forward, to accomplish something, to someday be able to say to my kids, 'Your dad did that.' You know, that innate feeling of building upward on the foundation left by the previous generation. I think that drive is completely legitimate. However, I know of other times when I desired something, materially or in the form of status or title, because I wanted others to see me as someone who was important. You know, that feeling that if I drive a fancy car or have a fancy title, people will think I'm someone I know I'm not. Or maybe I wanted to see myself as someone who was important because I was unsure of my value. I guess what I'm saying is that it can work both ways. Am I wrong?"

Clara was already grinning.

"I think you said it very well," she said. "Certainly it works both ways. You must simply realize and admit that there are times, perhaps even the majority of times for some of us, when we desire things solely out of a need to make ourselves feel better about our lousy behavior. My gosh, Jason, that is a grand discovery. The question we should be asking ourselves is, does this desire for something material, or some perceived upgrade in social status, or whatever it might be, align with the axioms? If it does, put your heart and soul behind it. It will produce joy. If it doesn't, reject the desire—it will produce misery."

She paused, her eyes cast upwards.

"Again, life is a sequence that begins in choice and ends in consequence. Natural law cannot be avoided. We have no control over consequences. They are driven solely by axioms, by truth.

"What we're talking about," she continued, "this fifth virtue, is sometimes called self-esteem, although I like the term *personal esteem* better. Personal esteem is the reputation you acquire with yourself. Sometimes I think of it in terms of personal honor. It's how *you* feel about *you*. I want you to understand something here. But we need to reconstruct our model first."

Clara got up from her seat and walked to a small oak table near the door. She removed a pad of paper from the drawer, returned to her chair, and pulled a pencil from her vest pocket.

"Here's what we have so far," she said, and began drawing the diagram on the small pad. On the bottom she wrote, "Axioms." Above that, "Beliefs and Values," then "Actions," "Integrity," and finally, "Personal Esteem."

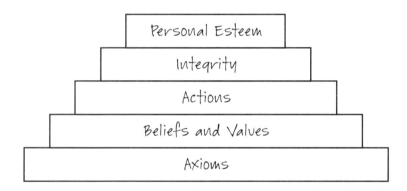

"Okay," she said, "now, this is something you need to understand: The answers to any problem are found on a level lower than the level on which the problem occurred. For example, the answers for a person struggling with integrity are found on a level lower than that. An issue of integrity is not resolved by working on personal esteem. Integrity *leads* to personal esteem, not the other way around."

Jason considered how terribly often he'd gotten that backward.

"I'm not going to gain integrity by trying to feel better about myself," Clara continued. "Integrity is gained by resolving conflicts between behaviors and beliefs. And issues of personal esteem," she tapped the top of the diagram, "are resolved by working on integrity," she moved the pencil down the steps, "or behavior, or aligning beliefs and values with axioms. Understand? Many people attempt to solve problems by making adjustments above the level of their problem, and, in so doing, they violate the natural sequence. In the end, such a course proves fruitless and delays resolution."

"What you've said makes sense," Jason said, "but it feels a little anticlimactic. Is all of this conversation just about developing personal esteem? This seems a little overdone. I can't pick up a magazine without it touting some 'secret to self-esteem.' Like if we just feel good about ourselves, all of our problems go away."

"Maybe it's because of the word *personal*," Clara said. "We usually think of personal esteem in terms of how it affects us individually. In practice, however, the social implications are huge."

"Isn't my self-esteem something that impacts just me?" he asked. "Hence, the word *self.*"

"Absolutely not," she answered. She paused to think, then continued, "Let me offer an opinion. I can't quantify it. There's no science behind my opinion that I'm aware of. But I absolutely believe it to be true, now more than ever. It involves the power of personal esteem.

"I worked in the corporate world for thirty years as a chemist. In that time, I experienced good managers and bad, good work teams and bad, good CEOs and bad, even good companies and bad. May I ask you another question?"

"By all means, please."

"Let's assume," she said, "you are a manager responsible for making decisions about hiring and firing within your group. Let's also assume that you are struggling with your personal esteem. On a simple one-to-ten scale, with one being 'very low' and ten being 'very high,' let's say you'd peg your personal esteem at a five. Midpoint. Understand?"

Jason nodded.

"Good. You are in the process of interviewing candidates for a position within your group, choosing someone with whom you'll work very closely, someone you'll manage. Let's assume that your interview process whittles down the candidates to two. Both are equally qualified. However, instinctively you know that one individual has a quiet inner confidence that exudes personal esteem. I'm not talking about someone possessed with a false sense of himself or herself, but rather someone who is comfortable with who he or she is. Let's assume, for our little example, that our first candidate is an eight on our one-to-ten scale. The other candidate—remember, equally qualified—exhibits tendencies that point toward a person who has less personal esteem than the first, someone who is a three on our scale. Now, the question: As the manager of that group, whom would you hire?"

Jason was beginning to see Clara's questions coming, which did nothing but increase his anxiety over how to respond.

"I'd like," he said a bit sheepishly, "to say that I'd hire the person who was best for the job, someone who sees the world like I do."

"Would you like me to ask the question again?" she asked.

"Not necessary," he said, recognizing that his diversion had failed miserably. "I'd probably wind up hiring the poor schmuck who was a three because I would be uncomfortable with the eight."

"Why?" she asked.

"I think there's something about the quiet confidence of people who have their act together that is—what's the word?—unnerving to someone who is struggling. I'm afraid I'd be a little intimidated."

"I think you probably would," she responded. "I've observed that people with high personal esteem tend to be better leaders than people who struggle with who and what they are. They seem to make better decisions. Certainly they seem to be more altruistic—perhaps out of a sense that there is plenty for everyone. There's a lot less 'I' and a lot more 'we' in their daily interaction. There's less 'how is this going to make me look' or 'what will this get me' when they consider courses of action. If I'm a five hiring the eight, I'm worried that the eight might someday put my job in jeopardy. The eight might outshine me. The eight might inject too much competition into future job opportunities I'd be interested in applying for. I guess I'd probably pass on the eight out of fear of what hiring that person might mean for me down the road. I might even be uncomfortable hiring the eight due to relationships I have within my group. I might prefer to see long-standing coworkers receive future promotions instead of the new hire—a corporate form of nepotism: I'll scratch your back, you scratch mine. Doesn't sound very professional, does it?"

"No, it doesn't," Jason said, "but I can tell you it's absolutely the way it happens."

"And," Clara went on, "here's the rub: Multiply that one hiring decision by the number of times it happens within every organization in corporate America every year, and it's my opinion that the dollar loss in hiring the wrong person due to a 'soft' little thing like personal esteem exceeds the combined total of all corporate profits and all corporate taxes paid each year. It is, without a doubt, the largest non-balance-sheet expense any company suffers. Yet we pay next to no attention to it because we don't know how. Oh, we say things like 'our people are number one,' but we don't really understand what that means.

"We have few ideas about how to foster an environment that rewards and produces high personal esteem. In fact, many organizations require employees to violate their personal values in order to keep their jobs. In so doing, they exacerbate the problem."

"How," he asked, "could an employer require employees to violate their values? How is that possible?"

"Well, imagine you're a physician. You are employed by a large health-care provider who, through a recent policy modification, is going to require you to begin making treatment decisions based less on patient need and more on cost/benefit analysis. Each time you meet with patients, you must look them in the eye and lie a little. You're going to recommend a program of treatment that the patient thinks you've developed solely out of your desire to help, but you know that's not true. You know there might be a half dozen other avenues of treatment or prevention that would provide better results, perhaps even significantly better results for the patient, but those alternatives are unacceptable to the financial model. How would that make you feel?"

Jason just shook his head.

"Or," she continued, "let's say you're a salesman for XYZ Company, which produces some sort of widget. The company knows there are flaws in design and manufacturing. You know there are flaws. Further, you know that once a customer has purchased the widget and experiences the inevitable problems that occur as a result of a flawed process, the company's commitment to customer service is virtually nonexistent. Yet, to keep your job, you're required to go into the marketplace and misrepresent the quality of the product and the support available after purchase. And when this whole thing goes sideways, as it surely will, whom is the client going to call with legitimately irate complaints? You!"

Now he was nodding.

"These kinds of work environments," Clara continued, "usually result in several consequences. First, the employees begin to resent the company for coercing them into betraying their consciences. Employee loyalty and trust are plowed under, and innovation, creativity, and commitment are sacrificed.

"Second, employees begin to get discouraged because, in violating their values, they begin to suffer personally. Their personal esteem is compromised, perhaps causing problematic issues to develop both at work and at home. They feel as though they've been backed into a corner. In order to support their families financially, they're required to trample their integrity. How effective do you believe a person is going to be in this environment?"

"I can't imagine it producing much of anything except hostility," Jason responded.

"And what is the end result?" She paused. "One: they may remain at the company with substantially compromised productivity and may even begin to bad-mouth company executives and procedures, causing a cascade of internal problems. Two: they may resign out of frustration and contempt. Or three: they may be terminated for lack of cooperation or production. The latter two require the company to absorb the costs of severance, hiring, training, and so on, and the whole process begins again. This is a loop that is unproductive, personally destructive to the employee, and remarkably expensive and inefficient for the company."

Jason whistled softly.

"This same principle stands true in personal choices as well," she continued. "If your son has low personal esteem, will he choose a spouse who has more or less esteem than himself?"

Jason felt a rock in his stomach as he pictured Brian. "Less," he replied with resignation. "Probably less."

Clara continued, "I think it is seldom that two people with significantly different personal esteems wind up together in a long-term relationship. Short-term flings, perhaps. But not in a mutually fulfilling courtship that is lasting. This is one circumstance in which opposites absolutely do not attract. And the difference that kind of decision could make in the life of your son—just think of it."

A shudder ran down Jason's back. He wondered what kind of impact he'd had on his children's sense of value. Had his influence been productive or destructive? Had he been a good father, one who instilled in them a sense of their own remarkable potential, or had he, by words and actions, caused them to feel lacking in personal worth?

"So you see," Clara continued, "what impact this soft little thing we call personal esteem can have in the lives of individuals. It will affect who they work with. It will affect who they marry. It will define who their friends will be and how they'll act toward others. It is monumental in its scope and influence. And it is a *consequence*. Remember, you choose what you believe in, what you value, and how you act and respond to life. However, once the avalanche starts, choices are no longer part of the equation."

She allowed him a moment to process what she'd said.

"Perhaps you have some personal experience with organizations like we've described. These may be reasonably profitable organizations as long as a very authoritarian leader is at the helm, but once that person moves on, trouble moves in because nobody else has been allowed to make mistakes. Worse, love and unity can't flourish in the acidic soil of aggressive authoritarianism. This leadership style becomes a disaster at home."

Disaster, Jason knew from experience, was as good a word as any.

Chapter 17

THE GOD QUESTION

N orthwest Design and Engineering," Jason said.

"What is Northwest Design and Engineering?" Clara asked.

"You've just described my work environment—and worse, I'm the one coercing my team in ways I know will require the betrayal of conscience you've described. But isn't that kind of circumstance impossible to avoid while building a business and fighting for market share? It's 'eat or be eaten' out there."

Clara smiled. "You know you're wrong when you come to believe you have only one option. How much more effective would employees be if they knew that their employer aligned with their values and would never ask them to betray those values? What kind of loyalty would that inspire? What productivity increases might employers see if their staff couldn't wait to get to work in the morning because the environment was creative, innovative, honest, engaging, trusting, and personally fulfilling? There are always alternatives to misrepresentation and coercion.

"If there is any fear-based leadership in the workplace—or in the home, for that matter—it will destroy the creativity and innovation of the employees and the ability of the leader to influence them in a sustainable way. If an employee feels like his production is scrutinized but his contributions are ignored, he will work in fear. If a father is afraid that his community will disrespect him if his children misbehave, he will wield an iron fist, and he and the rest of his family will live in fear. Fear is a dynamic emotion, and it drives executive decisions as much as it drives decisions made in the home. Any decision made in fear will ultimately prove deficient because it is reactionary, narrow in its perspective, and backward-looking, not forward-looking."

He felt her comments a little close to home.

"Think of it this way, Jason. The predator rarely feels fear. Only the prey. The predator is motivated by something other than fear: survival, confidence, hunger, responsibility, strength—something. The predator is focused and responsive. The prey is erratic and changes course constantly, not out of a desire to get anywhere in particular, only out of a need to get away from the predator. The prey is scattered and searching, looking at a hundred possible avenues—the predator, one. The prey, prior to attack, is tense and unsure. The predator is tactical and plans ahead. No young impala ever left its mother's side one African morning with the thought that it was now prepared to go looking for a predator: 'Let's go find that lion.' But that is precisely what a lion does with regard to its prey.

"The top of the food chain does not operate on fear, and the bottom of the chain is too oblivious to care. It's the middle members that dash about in fits and starts, hoping they'll taste another meal before something makes a tasty meal out of them."

The *middle*, he considered. Managers, VPs, fathers. Him!

"Don't misunderstand me, Jason. I'm not suggesting that we become raging carnivores and devour our competition. I am merely pointing out that the top of the food chain does not operate on fear. Likewise, a person who is operating at the top of his or her potential does not operate on fear, whether it's as a spouse, a mother or father, a student, an athlete, a teacher, a physician, or a businessperson. Ultimately, someone who is struggling personally will struggle professionally. If you require people to violate their values, their personal esteem is going to suffer, and when that happens, consistent, long-term effectiveness goes down the tube. They become the prey.

"I'd like to go back to something you mentioned just a moment ago," she added. "You said something like, 'I'd like to think I'd hire the person who sees the world like I do.' Do you remember that?"

"I remember," said Jason.

"I think that's a big problem."

He thought for a moment. "How could that be a problem?"

"Well, if I'm a manager and I hire people who see the world from the same perspective I do, why did I need the hire in the first place? Am I simply looking for a body to complete a task exactly the way I would? Let's face it, even in our enlightened age, some people are still uncomfortable about hiring someone who doesn't look like them, talk like them, or live their lifestyle.

"Redundancy. Congratulations, now I have two of me, and one was plenty. A person with a unique perspective is going to challenge the manager because they see the world from different points of view. They may be looking at the same problem, but one is going to see green, the other, purple.

"It takes a manager who is comfortable in his or her own skin to thrive in that kind of environment, someone with a strong sense of personal esteem, someone who enjoys being pushed by new and sometimes uncomfortable ideas. Someone who is not so attached to a position that, when the position goes down, his or her ego goes down with it."

Jason considered Clara's thoughts carefully. Many of her ideas seemed right on target. However, something was bothering him.

"Okay, I understand that personal esteem is a consequence, and that people who are struggling with their own sense of value probably are 'misaligned,' using your vernacular. Their actions, their behavior, are not consistent with their values. I understand that if, using an extreme example, you value marital fidelity and have taken vows to that effect, and at the same time you're involved in an extramarital affair, you are going to be destroying yourself from the inside out. That's one mistake I've not made, but I've known friends who got caught up in that whirlwind. Initially, it appeared to me that new life had been breathed into their souls. The excitement of the affair was intoxicating. But, as you've said, consequences always follow. Sometimes, their spouses never found out, but that didn't diminish the disgust they later felt for their behavior. Their lives became a train wreck. A conscience can be a weapon of mass destruction."

She nodded her agreement, then prodded him a little. "So?"

Jason was struggling to put his thoughts in order. "So, I'm thinking of Anna. She really is a wonderful woman, as unselfish as anyone I've ever known. Over the years she's been plagued with a feeling of inadequacy. She's had times when her personal esteem has been really low. This is a woman who will run herself ragged in service to others. To me, to Brian and Jesse, to friends, to anyone she perceives needs help. I can't imagine her actions being any more benevolent without the result being physical and emotional exhaustion. How does your framework stand up to Anna's circumstance? She's doing everything a human being could possibly be expected to do. There are no more hours in the day. She lives in integrity. There must be something more to personal esteem—something that would explain her struggle."

"Great observation, Jason. I've known some people who have suffered like Anna. Their misalignment is less obvious, but it can be just as destructive. Let's remember that we have *two* choices. What are they?"

Jason nodded. "I can choose my beliefs and values and I can choose my actions. Outside of those two, if I understand you correctly, everything else is a form of consequence. So how does that apply to Anna?"

"Until now," she said, "we've been talking about people who have solid beliefs and values, but who fail to act consistently with them. We've agreed that this creates misery. But remember, we have two choices."

"Are you suggesting," he said, "that low personal esteem could also be the product of poorly founded beliefs and values?"

"As long as we have the ability to choose," Clara explained, "joy or misery can result. Freedom always has jeopardy as its companion. What we choose to believe and value can create enormous problems and conflict. It's obvious when those conflicts show up in interpersonal or intercultural conflict. You're liberal, I'm conservative; you're wealthy, I'm poor; you're white, I'm black; you're religious, I'm atheist; you're American, I'm French; you're Christian, I'm Muslim; and so on. These affiliations can create powerful values that drive our behavior. However, misdirected beliefs and values can cause destruction on a personal level just as easily as they cause cultural conflict in politics and religion."

"Again, what does any of that have to do with Anna?"

"Her predicament," Clara responded, "is what I've come to know as the Great Discrepancy. Some of us evolve a set of beliefs and values so unrealistically elevated that no human being could live up to them. No matter how hard or how long those people work, no matter how much good they do in behalf of others, they will never feel good about who they are because they expect something from themselves that is unreachable. Maybe they expect perfection. Some people form these beliefs in an attempt to fill an emotional hole left by abuse, or abandonment, or divorce. Maybe they're forever trying to earn a deceased parent's acceptance. Maybe they live in a religious, environmental, monetary, or social culture in which their perception of what is expected far exceeds their ability to perform.

"I want to make clear that these expectations are usually built by the person, not by institutions. There may be many others in the same culture, religion, or social group who have no problem building a solid sense of personal esteem based on integrating beliefs and values with behavior. But someone like Anna will never be happy with herself until she gets a grip on her personal expectations."

"You've just described Anna to a tee," he offered.

"There are many people, women and men, just like Anna. Seems like somehow she has developed a stratospheric sense of expectation. It might be the result of observing others who appear on the outside to be perfect. Or perhaps it's embedded in a misunderstood cultural concept. Whatever the source, unattainable values are as much a contributor to misery as lousy behavior is."

Jason's brow furrowed. "What do you mean? What is a misunderstood cultural concept?"

Clara sat forward. "We're swimming in them. Say you were born into a very wealthy family. You may grow up with the flawed idea that a financial statement defines your value. Maybe you were born into a poor family and think likewise. Or you may be very religious, perhaps Christian, a religion in which it is sometimes taught that a person should aspire to become perfect. You may develop the mistaken notion that perfection is required *before* self-value is realized. Maybe your parents put a high value on education and have always been greatly disappointed in your decision to not finish school, regardless of your level of success, and you feel that you are somehow a lesser person because you don't possess a degree. Perhaps you're born into a culture that universally rejects divorce, and you've separated from your abusive spouse. Perhaps you were abused as a child, and you've developed the idea that somehow you deserved the treatment, or that because you were abused, you'll never be 'clean' or worthy of the love of another. You may harbor a belief that if someone does love you under these circumstances, they must be blemished themselves and are unworthy of your love. You may even harbor the expectation that virtually all people are abusive and, therefore, you may shy away from any serious relationship.

"I think most people would agree that those are unreasonable, maybe even false beliefs and values. They are misunderstood cultural concepts, and they cause untold emotional carnage. All of these folks have been sold a false bill of goods. They all believe that in order to be loved, they must produce value, when the opposite is true. They have value because they are loved."

"I'm not sure I know what you mean by that," he said.

"There are those who withhold love hoping to motivate someone to produce or to change behavior. That tactic may work in the short run, but the long-term impact will be troubling, perhaps very troubling."

"How is that troubling?" he asked, considering his habitual patterns at home and work.

"Because it makes people feel valueless unless they are performing equal to some esoteric standard. That strategy is destructive to everyone, but especially to kids searching for their identity and place in the world.

"It's akin to ranking the quality of the relationship you have with your kids based on the monetary value of the gifts they give you. 'Sally, $100, I like her best. Jimmy, $25, not so much.' Sounds ridiculous, doesn't it?"

"Yes, it does," he agreed.

"But the effect is the same as love portioned out based on performance."

"So," Jason asked, "does that mean you reward your kids for poor performance?"

"No. It just means that withholding *love* is not a part of the pattern. Withhold car privileges, television, whatever you think reasonable. But do not, under any circumstances, withhold love."

"Is that true for spouses too?" he asked.

"Sure it is. Some spouses withhold love, or intimacy, out of a desire to drive their spouses to change behavior. 'You've done something I don't like. You're an idiot. So, I'll punish you by withholding something I think you want.' Adults are not much different from kids. Again, that strategy may work in the short run—it may change behavior initially—but resentment soon finds a way in. It will wreck the person, and perhaps the relationship, in the long run."

"Then what *do* you do?"

"Gee, I don't know. Communicate, maybe?" she said, smiling. "Tell your spouse what it is that's troubling you. Tell her you're disappointed because of something she did. Tell her why. Talk it out. Give her an option for a more effective way to behave. But do not withhold love. Please don't do that. Trust me. It will not turn out well."

"So," he echoed, "when we're digging for the source of low personal esteem, we have to look at both our beliefs and our actions. Is that right?"

"Yes, that's right."

"But, who's to determine whether someone's beliefs and values are false or misplaced? Who has that kind of wisdom?"

"Ah, now you're getting to the heart of the matter, Jason. Truth is truth, is it not?"

"Yea, I suppose it is. I guess."

"Now, there's a strong position," she said, smiling.

"Truth is tricky, Clara. Sometimes it seems that my truth might be entirely different from yours."

"Perhaps, for now," she responded. "Truth has its own

gravity. It may take some time, but truth will draw us all in eventually. Ultimately, I believe we'll all come to the same understanding. We may be in vastly different places when reality finally dawns on us, but truth will win out in the end."

He paused, gathering courage. Typically, Jason dreaded this kind of discussion because the fight always ended in a bloody draw, with both sides looking like idiots with acorns for brains. However, Clara was perhaps the most open-minded person he'd ever encountered. He trusted her. And he knew they could disagree severely without sinking the ship. If ever there were an opportunity for a sincere shot at the God question, this was it. For once in his life he was sure he wouldn't be sorry he asked.

"What do you think is out there, Clara?"

She studied him carefully to determine the true nature of his question.

"I will answer only if you are comfortable hearing about spiritual things, Jason."

The fact that she asked made him a little more comfortable.

"I can't honestly say I'm comfortable with spiritual things," he answered. "Spiritual things are ghosts on fast horses during dark, rainy nights. You think you felt something pass, like a warm breath, but could you describe it? Not on your life. And no one would believe you even if you could. But I am comfortable with you. That's enough for now."

Clara turned to look him in the eye with nothing awkward in her directness.

She began, "I believe the source of truth is God. Perhaps you believe truth comes from a different place. Perhaps you are unsure. That's okay, my friend. Keep searching. Keep pushing. Each of us, after significant personal reflection that may take us to the very edge of our intellectual and spiritual capacity, must arrive at our own conclusion. God or no God? It is *the* question of questions. Either He is or He isn't. Know this, Jason: Given our limited ability to prove either position, both take large measures of faith."

"True enough," he agreed.

"I know world-renowned astronomers who believe the heavens above are the signature of God. They point radio telescopes at the vastness of space and observe the handiwork of the Lord of creation. And I know other equally renowned astronomers who see and do the exact same thing and cannot bring themselves to speak of a God. What could possibly cause such a gulf between two groups of remarkably competent scientists whose eyes observe the same phenomena but whose hearts speak languages incomprehensible to each other?"

"Obviously, we see and interpret things differently," he said.

"I think you're right, Jason. Our search for the source of truth is colored by personal and cultural motivations and opinions. As much as we despise admitting it, we all have a preconceived agenda. Once we've taken ownership of our prejudices, it's extremely difficult to give them up. Difficult, but not impossible."

"Do you think science will eventually uncover God?" he asked.

"My personal experience is that a creator will not be revealed in a new science, but only in the deep recesses of a single, solitary soul. In the doing is the learning. I look at the night sky and the sweetest of voices whispers to me of the reality of a creator. I cannot deny the sheer power of such a soft expression. I looked cancer in the eye and the voice was the same. Believe me, there are times when I think it would be so much easier if the voice would speak less adamantly. Sometimes it can be hard to find God in the awful events that define human existence. However, it is equally difficult not to find Him there. I believe it is during those times of sheer human horror that God is the first to weep."

"You're suggesting," Jason responded, "that although really bad things happen to good people, God still exists, and He may not be the author of these horrible wrongs? Despite the fact that He knows what's coming, He lets them happen anyway?"

"I'm suggesting that God is a God of laws. The freedom to choose is a truth God granted us. Some choose well. Some choose poorly. The consequences of those choices inevitably affect others. I believe that the loving God I know views our actions and is saddened by how we treat each other, but hopeful that our experiences, good and bad, will bring wisdom."

"Let's hope that happens sooner rather than later," Jason said.

"That is my sincere desire. Our perception of the source of truth does not change the truth, Jason. The laws of the galaxies are irrevocable and have been proven by observation and experimentation. The axioms are equally universal and also may be proven through similar means. I acknowledge a difference. One may be proven by the common mathematical language of the universe. The other must be proven by common, everyday people who are, by definition, subjective and prone to error. The truth is left for six billion people to uncover, each one for the first time. You are your own laboratory, your life a grand experiment."

He shook his head. "I just can't find enough answers to come to a conclusion. I guess what I'm looking for is something solid, something I can get a grip on."

"Do you love your daughter?" Clara asked.

"Of course I do."

"Prove it."

"So," he remarked, "we're back to the old clichés?"

"I'm simpleminded."

"Yeah, right! That's been my impression of you," he teased.

"You don't like the question," she continued, "because only you know what it means for Jason Snow to love Jesse Snow. Only I know what it means for Clara to love David. Not even Anna knows completely the kind of love you and Jesse share. Certainly there are common elements in loving relationships, but who's to say that each person's experience isn't remarkably unique? You can't prove it, but is there any doubt in your mind of the love that bonds you to your daughter?"

"None," he responded firmly. "Absolutely no doubt."

"So, if representatives from an alien planet landed on Earth tomorrow, beings who had absolutely no notion of love, could you convince them of its existence if they were void of the capacity to experience the emotion?" she asked. "You could sacrifice for Jesse, even die for her, but as impressive as your actions would be, they wouldn't begin to explain what love feels like, unless . . ."

"Unless . . . ?" he prompted.

"Unless you could get them to experience the miracle of love for themselves. Am I wrong? Have I missed something?"

"When was the last time you missed something, Clara?"

"Look, Jason, there are some things we just can't prove through the scientific method. There are things of the intellect, and there are things of the heart. Sometimes they work together; sometimes they appear to work in separate worlds. I've found a grand truth in that. Others find confusion. Many find nothing at all.

"But there is one thing of which I am certain: Perfect science and perfect religion are exactly the same thing."

Chapter 18

THE LIST

J ason thought carefully about Clara's comments. He'd never considered that science and religion could possibly have anything to
do with one another. Another idea, he realized, that turned his
boxed-in world upside down and forced him to think differently.

Clara concluded, "The only way for us to know if we are defying the axioms, what is true, is by examining the results of our lives.
If we're not happy, not feeling fulfilled, we need to look at the two
sources of choice." She stopped, looking at him expectantly.

"Beliefs and actions," he recited.

"Right. And that is where the work of our lives is found. Right
there. Beliefs or values and action are like two train tracks. When one
goes askew from the other, we get in trouble, we get derailed, and no
amount of power in the engine room is going to help until the tracks
are parallel again."

"A bold statement," Jason said.

"Has there ever been a time when boldness was needed more? I'm
claiming that there is a small set of truths that apply to all cultures.

There are axioms that ring true to all people and go right to the heart of the human experience, regardless of culture, race, circumstance, or philosophical preference. Truths that are greater than ourselves. Truths that transcend individual inclinations."

"That's huge," he said. "People have been fighting over that for centuries. We get so married to our various positions that we forget the point—to find the truth. I can't imagine mankind ever agreeing on any particular truth, even if it is true. It's never been done."

"Ah, that's not so," she protested. "It's done every day by good people across the earth. It's the claim that's difficult to swallow, not its manifestations."

"*That's* hard to swallow."

"Are you happy? Are you feeling happy about where your life has taken you?"

"Heavens no. But continuing to live a lie seems easier than rejecting my view of the world and starting over. That is a daunting task indeed. Big-time."

Clara was nodding again. "So, you've determined that you'll live with the disease rather than seek treatment—out of fear that the treatment will be worse than the cause?"

"That sounds pathetic. But yes, I guess I have."

Jason saw Clara tilt her head to the side and squint. It occurred to him that his answer was probably as shallow as it was unacceptable. Her eyes were suddenly sad.

"You've given up, then," she said, her words nearly as painful as Anna's letter. "You don't appear to be the kind of person who's going to walk away from the things in life that mean the most, at least not without a fight. You're in trouble, Jason. Discouragement is a product of fear. It is pure justification. Discouragement likes to whisper in your ear things like 'You can't change, it's too hard.' 'You're in too deep.' 'You've tried to change before and it hasn't worked. No sense in trying again. Why beat yourself up? Just accept your lot in life as miserable and frustrated and move on. That's just the way life is. Life is hard, then you die.' Sound familiar?"

A long moment of quiet ensued.

"A little too familiar, I'm afraid." He looked closely at her. "What's worked for you? How do you pry yourself out of lousy behaviors?"

A new spark returned to her eyes. "I willfully apply the axioms. It must begin with the way you think. The axioms always produce a third alternative, something beyond 'fight or flight,' something completely unexpected. Sometimes they produce alternatives that are so far away from what my logic conjures up that I have to force myself to go with them. And believe me, they are not always convenient. But they are always right. Always. Hindsight has proven their value over and over again. It's not too late for you.

"Most of us can change in a blink of an eye, as quickly as you can say, 'I'll change,' and mean it. There are some who struggle with unbalanced chemistry or structural challenges within the brain—clinical depression or bipolar disorder, for example—but those diagnoses are certainly in the vast minority, and there is wonderful help available for them, too."

Jason felt his throat constricting at the thought that he really could change. He considered his current situation.

"Look, I love Anna and my two kids more than I can say, but I'm standing on the threshold of losing them. I have a successful career that is so miserable I can hardly drag myself to work each morning."

She touched his shoulder. "The axioms can change all that. People will see a difference in you. More important, you'll see a difference in yourself. These truths, these axioms, stand tall enough to look over all the barriers that people have erected to separate themselves from others. These truths are so fundamental that they have the power to bring the entire human family together—not to mention your family, your marriage, even your career—because they are common to all people, races, and cultures.

"So, when you hear someone say, 'Well, the answer to this problem is to fight, to conquer, to have them submit to our power because
we have nothing in common with these people,' that kind of thinking
is simply wrong. It is the easy way out. The axioms determine whether
we use power or power uses us. Do you understand what I'm saying?"

"Maybe," he said.

"To answer your question about who can determine the propriety
of beliefs and values . . . truth has that kind of wisdom, I think. The
axioms are the standard. Do you recall what I said about people being physically the same the world over—carbon, hydrogen, oxygen,
and nitrogen? It's the same with the axioms. They are basic truths
embedded in the emotional life of all people; cross-cultural analysis has shown them to exist in virtually every human population.
Remember?"

"I remember," Jason said. "I believe you said that your life wasn't
necessarily easy when you were living within the axioms, but you
were at peace with yourself."

Clara nodded. "Look inside yourself. What's in there? What gets
to you?" She stood. "There's something I want you to see, and I think
Phil has it. Wait here. I'll be right back."

Jason shrugged, "Where am I going to go? We're at seven thousand feet on the side of a mountain."

Clara giggled. "Nothing like a captive audience."

She swept across the great room and through the kitchen door.
Jason smiled to himself. She clearly enjoyed this. She seemed to have
a passion and curiosity about anything she did that bordered on
childlike. He also noticed that it was just about dark, and at this elevation, without the disruption of city lights, the stars seemed so clear
and abundant that he thought he could step from one to the next.

She returned a moment later with what appeared to be a sheet of
folded notebook paper.

"Phil and I and many others have had this conversation many

times up here. Each time it's different. Isn't that great? And each time I learn something new, just as I am now. Phil is responsible for writing down more than the rest of us. He takes notes like I breathe. I knew he'd have a copy."

Clara handed Jason the paper.

"Look over the words on the paper. Take a minute and review them. You'll find an alphabetized list of about sixty-five characteristics that any person could adopt, any of which could be adapted into a value. There are many more like them that could be added, but these will do for now."

Jason unfolded the paper and began to read Phil's handwritten list.

Accomplished	Dedicated	Honest	Productive
Achieving	Deliberate	Industrious	Qualified
Ambitious	Dependable	Influential	Resolute
Articulate	Devoted	Inquisitive	Resourceful
Assertive	Disciplined	Inspiring	Responsible
Brave	Driven	Intuitive	Revolutionary
Brilliant	Educated	Magnetic	Self-assured
Capable	Eloquent	Motivated	Skillful
Charismatic	Enterprising	Organized	Smart
Charming	Enthusiastic	Passionate	Sociable
Committed	Fearless	Patriotic	Strategic
Competitive	Flexible	Perceptive	Strong
Confident	Focused	Persistent	Successful
Courageous	Gifted	Persuasive	Tenacious
Curious	Goal-oriented	Powerful	Vigorous
Decisive	Hardworking	Prepared	Visionary

"Pretty good list," he said, smiling.

"It is. Now, I want you to consider something. If your son or daughter came to you and said they wanted to marry a person with all of these characteristics or values in spades, a person who possessed every attribute in significant amounts, what would you think of that? Would you give them your blessing?"

Jason scanned the list again.

"I think I absolutely would, yes. That isn't a pretty good list—it's a remarkable list."

"I agree. Another question," she said. "Would you go into a business partnership with this person? Would you elect them to public office? Would you like to see them on your local school board? If you were an employer, would you hire this person if they applied for a job with your company?"

Jason considered her questions.

"Certainly I'd hire them," he said. "I'd like about thirty of them if possible."

"So," she continued, "can we agree that this list represents a strong set of characteristics, each of which could become a value? Do you agree?"

"Absolutely."

"Good," she said. "Now, I want you to consider the list in a new context. You're going to have to make some value judgments, some assumptions about people you may not know well. I want you to select someone who represents all that's good in the world, whatever that means to you. This is going to be someone who is remarkable in his or her influence. Perhaps it's someone you know, or it may be someone you've read about, or someone from history about whom you know something. Understand?"

Jason needed to think for only a moment. "My father," he said. "It would be my father."

"Nice. What a great compliment to your father. However, because you are so close to him, this may be a difficult exercise to complete objectively. Let's try it anyway. You'll need to be as honest and forthcoming as you can about his proven characteristics. Okay?"

Jason nodded.

"I want you to go back through this list of characteristics and determine whether your father had them or not. Was he accomplished? Was he a high achiever? And so on. Get it?"

"Got it," he responded.

Jason began at the top of the list again, this time considering each characteristic as a reflection of his father. It took him some time, perhaps because he was being overly sensitive to ensure objectivity. In the end, he felt he'd answered as honestly as he could; if anything, perhaps he'd been overly cautious. However, his careful consideration didn't seem to affect the outcome. His father possessed every one of the attributes, some more than others, but certainly all were present in this remarkable man.

"He has every characteristic listed here, and I've tried to be brutally honest. Is that realistic, that one man could have all these things?"

"Certainly it's realistic," she said. "This is the person you've chosen to represent all that's good in the world. I'm not surprised at all. Are you?"

"I suppose not," he said.

"Next," she said, "I want you to select someone who, unlike your father, is a person who represents all that is evil in the world—again, whatever that means to you. Can you do that?"

"I think so," he said. "But give me a minute."

Jason again thought about the possibilities. There were many people he didn't like, some he felt very strongly about. But coming up with someone who embodied evil was more difficult than he thought. Serial killers? Rapists? Corrupt businessmen? Crooked politicians? Abusive religious leaders? Who? He found himself going back in time, recalling all the real villains he'd known about. Suddenly, a name floated to the surface. It was obvious to the point of being shallow, but he couldn't think of anyone else he knew as much about or who had managed to dispense pain and horror as skillfully.

"Hitler," he said. "Adolf Hitler. Or is he just too obvious?"

"Not at all," Clara said. "He'll work just fine for our example. You're about to compare Hitler with your father, probably not an exercise you've done before or even contemplated doing. So, you know the drill. I want you to go back through the list of attributes and determine which of these characteristics Hitler possessed, if any. Again, consider each very carefully. Any questions?"

"Nope," he said.

He began at the top of the list for the third time, confident of the outcome. After ten or twelve characteristics, however, he stopped and glanced up at Clara, who was watching him carefully.

"Is there a problem?" she asked.

"Maybe," Jason said. "This isn't going like I'd expected."

"How's that?"

"Well, I'm ten or fifteen attributes down the list, and so far Hitler has all of them."

Clara smiled again. "Why don't you go through the rest of the list and try to find a characteristic that Hitler didn't have? Again, you're going to have to make some deep assumptions about his character and personality, but it's just an exercise, so do the best you can."

Jason scanned the rest of the list.

"The only characteristics that seem suspect are 'Honest' and 'Courageous,' and I suppose you could make a pretty strong argument for even those. He's everything on the list. How is that possible? Obviously, Hitler was nothing like my father."

Her nod was telling.

"It's possible," she said, "because these characteristics, or attributes, or values, whatever you choose to call them, although they are important and desirable, are not foundational. *They are not axioms.* The fact that two people as behaviorally disparate as Hitler and your

159

father—two people who stand on opposite sides of good and evil—can both have all these characteristics in common leads to only one conclusion. There must be something else, something much more fundamental in influencing beliefs and determining action."

Another moment of silence filled the room.

"I want you to remember the decisions you were prepared to make just a short time ago based on nothing but a confirmation that the person in question possessed these characteristics. Congratulations, Jason: You have no idea who your son or daughter married, who you elected, or who you hired. Yet, it is these kinds of characteristics, these attributes and values, that we go looking for when dating, voting, and hiring. Very few corporate interviews go beyond these basic behavioral tendencies. Why? Because the axioms are difficult to uncover. They require a new line of questioning, new thinking, and new interview skills. Some institutions and organizations like to call the values written here 'Core Values,' but without the axioms behind them, they are capable of producing almost anything. Therefore, these are not 'core' at all. How could they be core and foster such a diversity of action and results?

"This leads us to the axioms. It's why they are so infinitely important. My hunch is, when you learn the axioms and understand them, you'll see they are deeply embedded in your father's character and sorely lacking in Hitler's."

Chapter 19

FOUNDATIONS

Y ou're killing me here," Jason said. "What are the axioms? Based on what you've said about their impact, I'm assuming it's a long list."

Clara took a deep breath, shaking her head. "Not even close. Remember, your physical body, in all of its magnificence, in its ability to heal itself, to think, to feel, to reproduce, to grow, to move, to nourish, to live, all of this and much more, synthesizes to four basic elements."

He nodded, eyebrows raised, ready to listen.

"Likewise," she continued, "the axioms, as marvelous as they are, consist of just four components. These elements sound simple, but I've spent years trying to understand them. Each time I think I'm seeing the whole picture, I learn something that forces me in new directions. So, while they may appear simple, it's also evident that anything that carries the influence they generate will take a lifetime to understand. Which, may I add, is no excuse for failing to integrate them immediately into your life. We should be doing the best we can with what we have."

Jason made a T with his hands.

"Time-out," he managed. "Why didn't you just tell me what the axioms were when you started?" Pointing to the bottom of Clara's diagram, he added, "Axioms are the first virtue."

"I wanted to give you a vision of their impact. These four axioms are the foundation of all that occurs after them. They form the basis of strong beliefs and values, they direct behavior, they help secure personal integrity and a sense of self-value. All of it."

She paused a moment, looking down at the sheet of paper with the list of characteristics.

"If you are a victim of abuse, neglect, dishonesty, selfishness, and so on, you may look at all people as sources of pain. Further, what you believe you will receive at the hands of others is what human nature tends to give or reflect back. Thus, the belief becomes self-fulfilling. This is a perpetual feedback loop. Once you're on it, it is hard to get off. You've got to ask yourself a question: What defines the difference in thought and behavior between your father and Hitler?"

"Why thought?" he asked. "Why is that so important? I do what I do."

"You do what you do *after* you think what you think. Your mind is the architect of behavior. What you build inside that head of yours is your choice. Know this, Jason: life is played out in the five-inch space between your ears. Your capacity for doing good is colored by your willingness to carefully consider and then apply the axioms. The axioms have an alchemistic influence. Is it possible to go from mistrust to trust? Is it possible to go from a basic belief that people are inherently bad and evil and self-interested, to valuing every individual because each one is inherently good?"

"I hope it is," Jason said. "Just don't ask me how."

"The answer," she said, "is up to you. It is, always has been, and always will be your choice. And whatever you choose, your experience will justify your belief. So, are you happy? Do you find a sense of joy and wonder and curiosity in life? If not, why not? You cannot adopt the four axioms without feeling their impact in everything you do. They are the first virtue, and their adoption is required to yield the influence of the last, or eighth virtue, which may be the most powerful force known to man. You cannot have one without the other."

"Now you have my attention," Jason said. "What is the eighth virtue, this force so powerful?"

"Ah, patience, my friend. You want the power, the influence, without understanding its source. All things in good time. Let's discover the axioms first. But, I think we've had enough for today. Let's herd everyone to bed. We'll talk more tomorrow."

"You must be kidding," Jason whined. "What is this, some kind of junkie deal or something? Give a person enough information to get them hooked, and then abandon them? I'm not going anywhere until you tell me what the axioms are. You want money? I'll give you money."

Clara laughed out loud. "The axioms are priceless, but you already knew that," she said. "I guess I'll find you sitting right here early in the morning. Would you like me to bring you a blanket? It might get a little chilly."

"You're terrible, just terrible," he said. "I won't sleep a wink, and you know it."

"Oh, I think you'll sleep just fine. Exercise and altitude are known to knock just about anyone out."

Chapter 20

THE FALL

It was midmorning. The sun was bright in the sky and the climbing had been exhilarating, although more difficult than Jason had expected. The views he had witnessed were beyond anything he'd imagined. It was as if someone had turned up the intensity over the entire spectrum of visible color. Looking ahead, he could see Aaron, and beyond him, confidently cutting steps with her axe, Clara. It was then that Clara turned and announced they would rest for five minutes.

"Be very careful," she said sternly. "Bad things happen when you get careless. It's a very long way down from here."

Jason could feel Sophie tugging on the rope behind him. He turned to check on her, but the elevation hit him first. The mountain dropped away sharply for what appeared to be thousands of feet. It occurred to him that one mistake, one slip, one misstep, brought with it the real possibility of death. His legs tensed. Fear began to grip him. Just sitting down became a perilous undertaking.

"Use your axe," Clara said. "Dig out a flat spot to sit in. Take some weight off your legs for a minute or two. However, do not release the bite on both your crampons at the same time. Always keep one planted firmly."

Jason finally willed himself into control. He released the buckle of his helmet and tried to relax, tried to breathe.

"You okay, Sophie?" he asked. "How's the shoulder?"

"I'm fine," she said.

He hadn't expected to hear her admit anything other than that.

"Though if I didn't have to drag Jeff up this mountain," she said a little louder, "things would be better. I take a step, drag Jeff. Take another step, drag Jeff. Makes for a long day, you know? Men!"

Below her, Jeff howled at her comments.

"Listen, dude," Jeff shouted to Jason, "if I wasn't holding back this racehorse, she'd have plowed right over the top of you two thousand feet back. I'm here just trying to keep her from running footprints up and down your spine."

Sophie grinned from ear to ear as they stood for a moment and took in the landscape. Mount Jefferson stood immediately in front of them to the south, a hulk of a mountain from this vantage point.

"Hey, Jason," said Sophie, "sorry to bother you, but I could use a hand getting this pack off my back."

"Be right there," he shot back.

Jason took a step toward Sophie and felt the rope tethering him and Aaron tug at his climbing harness.

"Hang on, Sophie. I need to unrope."

He planted his ice axe in the snow beside him, then removed his heavy expedition gloves and stuffed them in the pockets of his coat. He unclipped the carabiner that attached his harness to the rope.

Clara watched with concern. "You be careful," she said. "I don't want anyone else unroping."

Jason began the short descent to Sophie, making sure his

crampons bit hard into the ice beneath him. *Halfway there,* he said to himself.

It began as a small thing. Jason's left boot broke through the surface of the icy crust, disappearing into a hole a foot deep. He tipped left, pack and equipment shifting along with him, putting that much more weight and momentum on an already over-weighted left boot. He panicked and tried to pull the boot out of the hole too quickly, and in so doing, lost his balance. He fell hard on his left side, the force of the impact pitching his helmet off and smacking his head on the ice. Immediately, he began sliding toward Sophie, his bare hands clawing for a hold.

"Jason!" Sophie screamed.

From above, he heard Clara. "Jeff, down on your axe, now! Now!"

Sophie had been looking up the mountain, watching Jason descend toward her step-by-step, crampons set hard as Clara had instructed. Jason's fall had happened so quickly that Sophie had no chance to avoid the inevitable collision. Sophie's crampons held their grip at impact, resulting in Jason knocking her straight over backward. She landed hard on the back of her head and shoulders as Jason pounded over the top of her. A muffled cry issued from Sophie, and Jason knew instantly his mistake had injured her. Fear tore through him. How could she self-arrest if she'd dislocated her bad shoulder? He reached out and tried to grab her.

Help her, help her, he thought to himself.

They were tangled in rope and equipment, accelerating toward Jeff.

Jason watched, almost as an observer, as tragedy played out in slow motion. He saw his axe planted vertically in the snow above him, safety cord dangling. He saw Clara screaming instructions, though now he couldn't hear them. He was aware he had neither gloves nor helmet. He saw the sheer panic in Sophie's eyes, and a deep, diagonal, cheek-to-chin gash, severing both upper and lower lips on her beautiful young face. He'd sliced her open with razor-sharp crampons as he bowled over her, beauty lost in a fraction of a second.

Her left arm reached out as they slid down the mountain, her right arm dragging lifelessly behind. And he saw Jeff below them, frozen in horror and disbelief, coming up fast.

The impact with Sophie had spun Jason around. Both of them were now sliding headfirst toward Jeff. Instead of following Clara's direction, Jeff started to move sideways on the mountain, trying to maneuver out of their path. Jason saw Jeff dive to their right, barely avoiding him. Sophie wasn't as lucky. She slammed into Jeff headfirst. He lost hold of his axe and started down the steep slope, arms and legs flailing and digging, crampons slicing at the ice like knives on granite. Jason could hear him grunting with exertion as he attempted to arrest.

But it was too late.

Thoughts of death and the loss of family and friends swept through Jason as all three now accelerated down an icy slope that surely would prove devastating. Above all, he knew with no uncertainty that he was responsible for this. Whatever occurred in the next few seconds, it was on him. Worse, he had been unprepared when called upon to help. At the moment they had needed him most, he was caught without the safety gear that might have saved their lives. He had willingly put aside axe, helmet, and gloves, essential equipment for any climber, out of an irrational notion that he would be all right without them, that all the mountaineering wisdom of the ages somehow didn't apply to him.

Clara had been prophetic: The worst had happened at the most inconvenient and seemingly innocent of moments. But thoughts of his own peril didn't haunt him as much as the pain he'd caused Sophie. And Jeff, his wife and two daughters waiting at the lodge for his successful return, didn't deserve to go like this. When friends needed him most, he had failed them. His stupidity was about to devastate the lives of countless people.

They were accelerating now at a startling pace. Any small dip or bulge on the mountain launched them into midair. Ice and rock formations swept by like the landscape from a speeding car. Each of the climbers, one by one, had given up any hope of stopping their descent. Gravity and their own mass were their remaining enemies. Only a wait for the end remained.

Jason saw the edge well before they reached it, a massive cornice eight hundred feet wide with nothing visible below. The three of them were still bunched together. He looked to the side, hoping that Sophie and Jeff had, by now, been knocked mercifully unconscious.

Please, he begged, *don't let them have to experience this. They've suffered enough.*

What he saw jolted Jason far worse than the edge they were about to go over. There were now three bodies besides his own, not two, all sliding on their sides and facing away from him. Sheer panic gripped him. Was it Aaron? Or Clara? Please, not Clara. Had she tried to save the three of them and sacrificed herself in the ordeal? His mind reeled. It had to be Clara. It was what she would do. It was what she would be driven to do, the good captain going down with the ship. He couldn't stand the thought that he had done this to her.

Before going over the edge, the three people beside him rolled and faced him, eyes wide open. Jason couldn't contain the scream that erupted from his throat. Next to him, all tethered together, were Anna, Brian, and Jesse.

Anna tried to scream out, and though he couldn't hear her voice above the sounds of death, her words were clear enough: "I love you, Jason."

Then she was gone. They were all gone, weightless in a plunge toward rock and the unknown.

Chapter 21

MORNING AFTER

H ey, Jason. Jason!"
He was jolted by a voice calling his name. Instinctively, he reached out for his family, only to find a wooden bunk. Panic seized him, although slowly he recognized that it was dark and his family was not there. Finally, his senses lifted their unconscious disguise. He had dreamed it. Dreamed the whole thing. Sweat soaked his bedding. He was both elated that it had been all in his mind and stunned that his mind could construct such a story. And he was exhausted. He placed both hands over his face and rubbed his eyes with trembling fingertips.

"You okay there, guy?" Jeff asked.

Jason stared at him from another dimension.

The night had sprinted past him at a pace that turned hours to minutes. Could it possibly be tomorrow already? He held up his watch: 1:20 a.m. He thought about staying in bed for a few minutes—until the memory of Clara's warning about Phil's wake-up call exploded to the surface like a balloon from deep water.

He rolled out of his bunk and hit the cold wooden floor with a thump. Jeff was already up and dressed. Jason had never thought the sight of Jeff would bring such relief.

"Morning, partner. You okay?" Jeff asked.

"Morning. Slept just wonderful. Great. The longest and shortest night of my life," he groggily offered.

Jeff grinned. "Ain't it grand! I don't know where you were, but it wasn't good."

What an understatement, Jason thought.

Sophie was stretching at the foot of her bunk.

"You okay, Sophie?" he asked, recognizing the moment it left his lips how odd the question might sound.

She looked at him quizzically. "You bet, Jason. You?"

"I'm good, thanks," he said. "Never better."

Jason rubbed his face, hoping his senses would take hold and his heart rate would return to normal.

What a night.

Aaron, still breathing heavily, seemed unconscious and oblivious to the activity around him. Jason could hear the clanking of thick ceramic plates and cast-iron skillets in the kitchen. Clara and Phil were already at it. The smell of bacon, sausage, scrambled eggs, pancakes, warm maple syrup, and sliced oranges wafted by his nostrils and watered his taste buds.

He sat still at the edge of the bed, trying to secure his head to his shoulders. Clara came up the stairs.

"Good morning, all. You ready for one of the finest days of your life? Weather looks perfect and the forecast is for more of the same."

"We're ready," Jeff said, clapping with exaggerated enthusiasm.

As she went by Jason, Clara stopped, eyebrows raised. "You always look like this when you roll out of bed?"

Jeff and Sophie giggled.

"Just hilarious," Jason responded. "And one fine mornin' to you, too."

She laughed while making her way down the small loft to Aaron's bunk. Nudging his shoulder, she said gently, "Aaron. Aaron. It's time to get to the top of this thing. You coming with us?"

Unexpectedly, her words sent a shiver up Jason's spine.

Aaron shot up from his bunk.

"What time is it? Am I late?"

"You're fine," she said, "but in grave danger of experiencing Phil's unusual sense of humor if you don't get up now."

"I'm up, I'm up," Aaron responded, sounding like a teenager late for school.

Chapter 22

A HIGH SHELF

The four climbers stood in the snow outside Silcox, cocooned by layers of clothing, darkness, and their own thoughts. Above them the mountain seemed to self-illuminate, white snow reflecting any starlight thrown through the atmosphere. Sophie reached for her helmet, found the headlamp switch, and turned it on. Each followed her lead. The summit disappeared as the ice and snow around them jumped with light.

True to form, Clara exited the hut at 1:55 a.m.

"Okay, everyone good to go? Lamps are working, I see. Phil has fed you well, has he not?"

"Nothing but a pleasure," he said, standing in the hut doorway. "I'll be right here when you return. All I ask is that you take good care of Clara."

"Thanks, Phil," Clara said. "We'll be fine. This is a strong group."

She turned back to her team.

"Axes? Crampons? Sunglasses and goggles?" Clara's eyes fixed on each of them one by one. "Water? Snacks? First aid? Jason, you've got the extra rope?"

"Got it," he said.

"Good, good." She gave a strong yank on each of their harnesses.

"Sunscreen should be in an outside pocket. You'll need it before you know it. Sophie, this is your first test. How's the shoulder?"

"A little sore, but not bad, about a three."

"Excellent. Let's just keep that number right there. You let me know what's going on."

"Got it," Sophie replied.

"I'm just dandy too, by the way," Jeff chimed in. "And thanks for asking. Legs are stiff as boards and hurt like heck. Can't lift either arm above shoulder level. And my neck moves only twenty degrees to either side. I'm about an eight."

"Wimp," Clara offered.

Smiles all around.

Jeff shrugged in mock disbelief. "You know, I've noticed a touch of inequality in how certain people—me, for instance—are treated."

"Your point?" Clara asked. "Sophie, I've got one of those internally spiked dog collars in my pack, the one that tightens with tension. If Jeff tugs on the rope a little too often, we'll just install that little device and move the rope from his harness to the collar. That should keep him moving."

"And quiet," Sophie added.

Jeff laughed, "That'd be a first, but if it works, no one better tell my daughters. 'Hey, happy Father's Day, Dad, look what we got for you.'"

Their laughter soon quieted to introspection and thoughts of the mountain and the climb.

After a little while, Clara's face cleared. "Okay, gang. Would you turn your lamps off for just a moment."

Each flicked the switch at the top of the lamp housing. The space around them went dark. Clara waited for their eyes to adjust.

"From this location you can't see the top, but it's right there," she said, pointing a gloved hand four thousand vertical feet above them. "That's our direction. But remember, the joy of the adventure is in the journey, not the destination. That's the first rule. Learn to enjoy every step, every breath, every sight, and every sound.

"The second rule is this: Never underestimate this mountain. It rises over two miles high from the valley floor. It's an ancient volcano. It is nature's expression of power and wonder. And it will bite you hard if you're unprepared. It's very climbable, especially on a grand day like this. But do not let its beauty dissolve your concentration.

"And the last rule: Until we all stand back at this location in twelve or so hours, we work as one. If the five of us work under the premise that the safety of all our teammates is more important than our own, we'll always have four people looking out for us. If you choose to reject that notion and assume selfishly that you are responsible for only yourself, you now have only one person looking out for you. I like the odds of the first much better than the second. Are you with me on that? That is my expectation of you. I'll accept nothing less."

She looked each of them in the eye, silently securing their agreement. Then she smiled and added, "Now, let's go find that little kid in you."

Clara checked to make sure each climber was clipped securely into the rope.

"Headlamps back on, please," she requested.

The landscape before them lit up once again.

Flicking the rope clear, they began a slow ascent up the face of the Palmer Snowfield. Each of them followed in turn, fifteen feet apart.

Jason was giddy, and for the first hour or so he had to consciously slow himself down. To climb Hood was something he had thought about doing most of his life. It seemed surreal that he'd finally acted on the desire. Why had he waited so long? He could feel his heart racing, not so much from the exertion or elevation as from the excitement of a goal within reach. Still, he was trying to practice Clara's advice—enjoy each moment. Clara, on the other hand, was a machine. Her steps were slow but solid. No wasted motion. No wasted energy. Methodical in her technique, she seemed never off balance or out of sorts. The five of them formed a train, step for step, with Clara leading the way.

Jason soon became lost in the repetitive meditation of the climb, soothing in its march. They'd made their way past the 8,000-foot level and the top of the Palmer Snowfield. Above Palmer, the route steepened toward the base of Crater Rock. A breeze was picking up from the east, twenty, maybe twenty-five miles per hour. Not strong enough to be dangerous, but enough to keep his attention. It was still dark, and Jason watched as snow and ice blew through the light of his headlamp right to left.

His thoughts turned to that miserable dream of the previous evening, the worst he'd had in years that he could remember. What kind of mind could conceive of an accident that resulted in killing his family? He understood the subconscious message. He had the tools to repair his marriage; he'd simply chosen not to use them. He had put them aside when Anna and the kids needed them most. She'd had her tools and was prepared to use them—that is, until he'd run her over emotionally, hurting her in countless ways, scarring her deeply. And the result was clear: He was losing his family. What chilled him more than the freezing temperatures outside or the stiff east wind, however, was the knowledge that he was *choosing* to lose them.

Taking responsibility for causing an accident was one thing. This was quite another. As painful as it was to recognize, there was nothing accidental about purposefully constructing a barrier that shut out the people he cared about most, then shooting arrows at them from the top of the wall when he felt bad enough about himself. Why would he do something like that? Why act in a way that he knew would bring sorrow and discouragement? Why spread the stupidity of his poor choices all over Anna and anyone else who happened to wander by at the wrong time? If Clara's ideas harbored any truth, it was because he was "misaligned," a word that was sorely lacking in communicating the pain it caused.

When Jason had broken his leg some years back, the ER doctor hadn't returned with the X-rays and said, "Oh, dear, your leg is misaligned." Not hardly. Instead, he said, "You've broken your leg, fractured it completely. We'll need to reset it, which is going to hurt like heck, and then cast it so it can heal straight."

Considering his current emotional state, that kind of behavioral diagnosis was not far off. The brutal fact was that his actions had broken away from what he believed to be true, what he valued. He'd fractured his conscience. The pain of realignment might prove substantial, and the time necessary for healing lengthy, but both paled in comparison to the devastation of spending the rest of his life emotionally broken. Perhaps it was time he summoned the courage to do what was necessary.

It was time to reset his thinking and how he chose to act. But how? He wasn't sure. He did know this much: Anna would be with him all the way if, and it was a big if, he wanted her back enough to change.

It was his choice. It had always been his choice.

In a memory he had long ago set on a high shelf nearly out of reach, Jason recalled Anna and their early years together. He'd loved her from the moment he met her, a bond so strong he'd thought such a thing possible only within the pages of fairy tales and love stories. Until Anna. He'd met her one afternoon on a blind date and had mentally married her by dinnertime. When he'd found her, he had found himself.

Looking back, he realized it was the small things that made all the difference: the soft texture of her long auburn hair against his face; her warm hand in his; his arm in hers; long walks in a sweet stillness they both longed for; a park on a warm summer Saturday with a blanket, a good book, his head resting on her lap as if it were always meant to be; lying in the soft grass on a clear night and contemplating together what might be out there.

Jason considered with wonder the precious nature of these little moments. None could be bought or sold. All were priceless and of indeterminable value. How had he gotten so far off track, so far away from home? It was those times with Anna and the places they'd shared that gave life depth and breadth, and he'd given them up for mud in shallow water.

Anna had a quiet charm about her, even when young, that seemed stately but invitingly approachable. She was as close to a renaissance woman as Jason had ever known well, a gift from the past living in the present. She wore jewelry in elegant simplicity, her wedding ring the only adornment on her perfect hands—something Jason always considered an unspoken symbol that nothing would infringe on her vows.

Anna was comfortable with anyone. Her acceptance of people cast a broad net across all classes and cultures, a characteristic that allowed her to thrive in a world of diversity and complex ideas. Her eyes came alive when witnessing joy in others, and were burdened when confronted with sorrow and pain.

Beautiful in a nontraditional way, Anna carried herself well. Her carriage and countenance were strong, head held high. Her clothes were beautiful but relatively inexpensive. Jason couldn't remember her ever looking anything but right. Even in workout gear, she was unavoidably attractive.

Jason recalled a sense of anxiety he'd felt in the early years of their marriage that came with climbing out of bed each morning to prepare for work, knowing he would not see anything as perfect as Anna's sleeping face for the remainder of the day. The soft words she spoke each day before he left the house he still remembered as if they'd been offered this very morning: "Jason, I'm so proud of you. Thank you for having me as your wife. I love you. See you tonight." Initially, he'd thought her repeated recitation of this simple phrase a little strange; however, it didn't take long before it became poetry.

He couldn't remember when she'd stopped her recitation, but it had been some years since he'd heard those words. Looking back, he wondered why Anna's withholding hadn't jolted him back to reality, hadn't gripped him with some sense of fear of losing her. It finally dawned on him.

He'd been lost in losing himself.

Chapter 23

BLIND

W e'll stop here for a break," Clara said, her statement dislodging his concentration. Light was spilling over the eastern horizon, although the sun was not yet visible. "We're not up high enough to be concerned about crevasses or rockfall, so please feel free to unrope and wander a bit, take some pictures. The light is beautiful this time of morning. The view to the southeast is spectacular. Jefferson first, about forty-five miles out, the Three Sisters, Broken Top on the left, approximately eighty-five miles out. Bachelor, Washington, Newberry, and others are out there too. These volcanoes, more than any other environmental feature, are responsible for shaping the geography and climate of Oregon. They've thrown astounding amounts of ash into the atmosphere over the last few millions of years and put down more lava than you can imagine.

"I like to sit here on the south side of Hood, looking at all these marvelous peaks, and imagine what it must have been like to have been here when they were going off. What a view that would have been! This whole landscape was once tropical—that is, until the volcanoes got hold of it. Can you fathom that? Fantastic. Just fantastic. Planet building in action. And Mount Jefferson is my personal favorite. What a stunning hunk of rock, the only Cascade mountain to be named by Lewis and Clark, and in honor of their sponsor and patron, Thomas Jefferson, a hero of mine and certainly the finest and most curious mind to ever occupy the White House. So, please enjoy. Take some water and a snack. Plan on being ready to go in an hour. Remember, it's the journey, not the destination. Stop rushing. Relax awhile. Think."

Jason, hesitantly at first, planted his axe in the snow and removed his expedition gloves. He reached for the camera stowed in a pocket in one of his shoulder straps and scanned the horizon for potential photographs. The view was indeed impressive and brought a dose of humility. Glaciered peaks dotted the landscape looking south, concrete evidence of the ring of fire. He focused his attention and camera on Jefferson, one of the most photographed mountains in North America. After a few pictures, he noticed Clara was kneeling, camera in hand, shooting pictures of a small rock-and-ice formation just east of their climbing route.

He wandered over to her.

"What is so enchanting?" he asked.

She looked up and smiled. "Isn't this fantastic? Look for yourself."

Jason bent over, resting hands on knees, and focused on the area Clara was so interested in. There was nothing to see.

"Very . . . interesting," he said slowly.

"You don't see it, do you?"

"How does a person know what he doesn't see?"

"Good point. Look here, just below the lip of this small rock. It's tucked back in, so you have to look carefully. Do you see anything?"

He knelt down next to Clara, lowered his head, and looked under the small outcropping, finally seeing what it was that had riveted Clara. He looked up at her and smiled.

"How in the world did you find this, Clara?"

"It's easy to see greatness and majesty in big things, big mountains," she said. "They have big views, but majesty resides in equal measure in small things, too. I've been coming to this spot for over a year now. Anymore, this means as much as the summit to me.

"Life is not about big things: big careers, big homes, big cars, big bank accounts, big egos. Life is about small things. Seedlings. Do the small things, enjoy the little things. The big things may or may not follow, but peace will always be a partner."

"But our culture is built on big things," he commented. "We are a consumer society. It's what makes us tick. You can't go a day without someone making a strong case that you need stuff to be happy."

"Yes, for now. However, isn't that more about trying to convince you that you need stuff to make *them* happy? What happens when that clock stops ticking? What then? What might happen, how might we be different, if we believed that *not* getting what we want, in a material sense, would make us just as happy as getting it? What would happen if we all came to realize that we don't need all this stuff? That once our basic needs are met and we have some semblance of security, stuff has nothing whatsoever to do with happiness? Life is about the small things, Jason. Do the small things."

Clara's words brought back his memories of Anna.

"Do the small things. What does that mean to you, Clara?" he asked.

"It means that when you come to the end of your life and look back, a slow walk with your daughter will mean more than your account balance. It means that flowers and a note for your wife for no particular occasion, only because you adore her, will mean more than diamonds on an anniversary. It means that showing gratitude to a friend for absolutely no specific reason will have more impact than picking up a lifetime of dinner checks.

"And, surprisingly enough, a sincere compliment about the quality of a colleague's work will probably mean more than an annual raise. Don't get me wrong—they want the raise. But the reason they'll stay with the company has much less to do with pure monetary compensation than you might imagine. They will be loyal to the company if someone is doing the small things. On the other hand, it usually doesn't matter how much they are getting paid if they feel unappreciated. They'll be gone before you realize what happened.

"Resources such as monetary compensation are the means, not the end. Don't confuse resources for the end. When money is confused for the end, people get lost. Life is all about small things. You know this is true. Give your wife everything she wants materially, and ignore her emotionally. Make sure she's underappreciated. How long will the marriage last?"

Jason turned away, not wanting her to see that the portrait she'd painted was his.

Here, on the side of a massive volcano, with a view beyond the mountain that was glorious in every direction, Clara's attention was focused on the smallest of seedlings, an evergreen of a species unknown to Jason that stood not four inches tall, surrounded by ice, leaning to the west and void of needles on the east.

Clara pointed at the seedling.

"Life clinging to life," she said. "Look how the wind has already defined its shape. In fifty years, when we're both dead and gone, this little guy will maybe reach fifteen feet, and be tough as nails. We're at absolute timberline, Jason. Nothing will grow any higher than this. Its chances for survival are small, but the protection offered by this outcropping may allow it to root deeply before it gets big enough to be directly exposed to severe weather. It has a chance."

Jason noticed a chill that had nothing to do with the mountain.

Clara unbuckled the waist belt and chest harness on her backpack, swung it around, and set the pack down in front of her. She removed a small sprig of needled evergreen, approximately ten inches long and smaller than the circumference of a pencil, which was tied to her top pocket by a piece of twine. She took out a razor blade from her first aid kit, carefully measured the height of the growing seedling, and cut the sprig she'd brought with her to the seedling's exact size. Then she put away the blade, zipped the pack, and retied the small sprig to her pack.

"I'll measure its growth a couple of times a year and check on it each time I climb this route. Nature, big or small, is tenacious in its dedication to growth. We should be so inspired."

They both stood and turned to look out over the expanse eight thousand feet below them.

"I noticed you taking some photographs of Jefferson. Quite a mountain, isn't it?"

"Beautiful," he said, allowing a moment to pass. "I'm curious, Clara; you've been on this mountain many times, seen this view every time up. When you look at Jefferson, what do you see?"

"I see the obvious: jagged rock and ice, an almost perfect proportion and scale; I see a tree line that wraps the mountain in a clothing of evergreens like a comfortable sweater. But, there is something else."

"What else?" he asked, eyes fixed on Mount Jefferson.

"Two things. First, notice the mountain itself. Is there anything unusual about the structure? Something obvious but hidden by the fact that when we look at an object so often the obvious becomes obscure?"

"I have no idea what you might be talking about, Clara."

She placed her left hand on his shoulder and pointed toward Jefferson with her right.

"Look carefully. The flanks and shoulders of the mountain are covered in a variety of vegetation: Doug fir, ponderosa and lodgepole pine, some cedar, even huckleberry and rhododendron. But as you move higher, vegetation begins to thin; it transitions to mountain hemlock and subalpine fir. Soon the tree line appears. Above it, nothing organic. Not a tree to be seen. Just rock and ice. As we approach the top, the mountain coalesces around a single summit. Vast masses of rock at lower elevations thin to a point as we go higher. What does that teach us?"

"What does that teach us? I have no idea. Look, Clara, like I said, you've lost me."

She smiled and squeezed his shoulder. "Simplicity and clarity increase with elevation. Think about that."

She might as well have hit him with a shovel. Before he could digest the whole truth, she was moving again.

"Second, I see a sequence. Pacific Ocean water evaporates to cloud formations. Air and cloud are blown inland on swift oceanic breezes, where the water is cooled. Liquid water freezes to remarkable crystal structures and falls as snow on the upper reaches of the mountain. Snowfall creates snowfields. Over time, snowfields compress into glaciers. Warm summer temperatures melt the glaciers back to liquid water. Gravity pulls the water into the path of least resistance. On Jefferson, water is dropped into tributaries and rivers such as Russell, Whitewater, Metolius, and others. Metolius runs to the Deschutes; Deschutes to Columbia; Columbia to the great Pacific, where the sequence begins again. Wouldn't it be fascinating to somehow isolate one small molecule of water and watch it revolve through this cycle?"

Now it was Clara who allowed a moment to pass.

"Human behavior runs a very similar sequence, I think," she finally added.

"How have I missed this stuff all my life? It was right in front of me."

"You look," she answered, "but you don't see. There are lessons everywhere in the form of symbols. Symbols teach powerful truths, Jason, but only if you understand the symbol."

"What does that mean? Symbols? Give me an example," he asked.

She considered for a moment, then lifted a clear plastic water container from an outside pocket of her pack.

"Describe for me," she said, "what is inside this container and what its characteristics are."

"Uh, it's water," he said a little sheepishly.

"No. I want you to describe what you see, not tell me what you think it is," Clara responded.

"Well, it's a liquid. I can see it sloshing around. And it's clear. I can see through it." He thought for a moment. "And it will conform to the shape of whatever container it's in."

"That's pretty good," she said with a smile. "Is that it?"

"That's about it."

Clara bent over and drew something in the snow, then went back over it with her finger to deepen the impression.

"H_2O?" he asked.

"Yes. H_2O. Everything there is to understand about earth's most abundant molecule is contained within the symbol for water. We know a single molecule of water has two hydrogen atoms bonded to one oxygen atom; we know it can be a liquid, solid, or gas, and the temperature range for each. We learn all kinds of fabulous stuff. The symbol for water, H_2O, conveys a level of knowledge far deeper than what we may learn from simple observation, but only if we understand the symbol."

Jason grinned. "Sounds like the chemist in you, Clara. Makes me feel like I've sat in a classroom for years and paid little attention to the instructor."

She looked at him through clear eyes. "You've lived your life blind to the lessons all around you—blind to the simple yet obscure vision of nature's quiet revelations. It's time you woke up, Jason. You've seen through a looking glass darkly, when all around was light."

Clara turned again toward Jefferson and smiled.

"Pure light."

Chapter 24

ALLEVIATE SUFFERING

H e didn't know how to bring it up. Twenty minutes of the allotted hour's rest had passed.

"Tell me about the axioms," he managed.

"Come sit," she said.

They sat side by side in the snow, heels dug into the slope.

"You know," Clara began, "human beings have an embedded desire for complication. If we don't understand something, we assume it's because the system or sequence underlying that thing must be blisteringly complicated. So, we give it lots of parts and pieces, many more than it actually has, and then lose ourselves in the mechanics. However, natural systems tend to be much simpler than our intuition suggests. Usually, they are beautifully elegant in their simplicity. Einstein's theory, $E=MC^2$. Even if you have no idea what it means, you can understand the simplicity of it, can't you?"

"Yes, I suppose," he responded.

"Empedocles, a Greek philosopher who lived in Sicily and was influenced by the great mathematician Pythagoras, put forth the idea that all matter is composed of four roots or elements: earth, air, fire, and water. Hippocrates subscribed to the idea of the four elements, however, he viewed them as elements of the body. In his day, Aristotle was influenced by these principles and expanded on them. Over time, these fundamental ideas were applied to mental thought and behavior."

Jason wondered if Einstein, Hippocrates, and Aristotle had anything for him.

"Carl Jung studied these ideas thoroughly and conceptualized the four elements of personality as intuition, sensation, thinking, and feeling—clearly derivatives of the work of Empedocles. Today, corporations and organizations the world over test potential employees for compatibility using the four personality variables of Myers-Briggs typology: Extrovert/Introvert, Sensing/Intuiting, Thinking/Feeling, and Judging/Perceiving. The Keirsey Temperaments—Artisan, Guardian, Idealist, and Rational—are also popular. There are others, too, each a direct result of the work of Empedocles.

"If you apply for a new job tomorrow, in computer technology, construction, or counseling, whether you're hired or rejected might depend on answers that highlight principles first put forth by a philosopher who lived twenty-five hundred years ago. It boggles my mind. Everything changes while everything remains the same.

"Four elements—earth, air, fire, and water. Or carbon, hydrogen, oxygen, and nitrogen. Or intuition, sensation, thinking, and feeling. We search the world over for the complicated truth, and all the while it hides behind our simple minds. John Foster Dulles said, 'The problem is not that we have problems; the problem is that they are the same problems we had last year.' Axioms will break us out of the habitual pattern of revisiting our problems and looping through them time after time."

Clara stopped and looked directly at Jason.

"So, what are these axioms, these four simple elements that

combine to set us on a path of truth? Four axioms that, when over-lapped with the values and characteristics we discussed previously, produce your father, and when overlooked, have the potential to produce awful, destructive behavior? These axioms are the earth, air, fire, and water of human activity. They reduce the toll of violence. They are the foundation of an influence for good."

She had his attention.

"The first axiom, Jason, is *compassion*."

"Compassion?" he asked.

Clara nodded.

"It is the ability to identify with the suffering of others and a drive to alleviate that suffering. Specifically, it's a desire to alleviate *any* suffering, which is different from wanting to resolve *all* suffering. To say that I'm responsible for the alleviation of *all* suffering is overwhelming. The job is too big to know where to begin. However, the alleviation of *any* suffering means that I'll commit to helping anyone, not just family, friends, or people who think or act like me. 'Any' reaches out to all people, even (and perhaps especially) those who do not fall within my 'socially acceptable' box. Maybe this person thinks differently from me, believes differently from me, acts differently from me, and sees the world differently from me. Don't misunderstand. I'm not suggesting that you adopt the person's beliefs or lifestyle. That is not being compassionate. That is being a chameleon.

"Compassion requires that we get out of ourselves, out of our own way. It focuses our attention outward. It requires us to experience suffering through the eyes of the sufferer—not just to see it but to feel it, to be vulnerable to it.

"In compassion, we remove ourselves from the throne at the center of our world and put another person there. The last person I want making judgments is someone with little or no compassion."

He wondered how compassion would fit into a work environment that was cutthroat and highly competitive.

"Compassion is love in action," Clara continued. "It is proactive. It is fearless. It is usually inconvenient. It is not always friendly, or soft, or charming. It contains the great elements of love, forgiveness, unity, empathy, sympathy, altruism, charity, tolerance, inclusiveness, caring, equality, freedom, and benevolence. There is a very close association between my feeling of compassion and my willingness to forgive. Compassion's antonyms are hate, enmity, and selfishness. Hate will never yield good. Hate grows out of fear; we usually fear something first and hate it later. Compassion distills selfishness into empathy, opposite ends of the same line.

"Listen up, because I want you to hear me. I believe the whole of humanity is interconnected. If one man gains, the whole of man gains. If one man falls, the whole of man falls. There is a great synergy in this interconnectedness, in this unity of man."

Jason ran his hand through his hair and took a deep breath. "I think I have a pretty good notion of compassion. I watch the news; I see horrible things happen to undeserving people. Good people just trying to get by day to day. My heart goes out to them. I've witnessed various forms of ruin—people who have made what they thought were good choices that led to disaster for themselves and their families. I get it, Clara."

"No, you don't. Not even close," she responded.

"Excuse me," he offered, shocked by her directness.

"You get sympathy, maybe even empathy, but you don't get compassion. Big difference. You watch events unfold that severely impact people and you feel sorry for those people. Perhaps you empathize with them, maybe because you can imagine putting yourself in their place. Compassion is beyond empathy. Empathy is a feeling. Compassion is an act. Compassion demands a rescue. Empathy simply considers the possibility."

A dry pit was forming in his stomach. Memories. During a lifetime of justifications he'd repeatedly thought about extending himself, lifting someone who'd been pulled down, who needed a boost beyond their own ability to break the crushing centrifugal orbit of discouragement, failure, or loss. It was, however, painful to come face-to-face with the fact that rarely did he act; rarely did he take the time or go to the trouble to reach out and be constructive. He was willing to admit that his inaction was partly the result of not wanting to help and partly because, in some cases, he didn't know how to help. He didn't have access to the secret formula for lessening the pain of loss, so, instead of acting poorly, maybe even improperly, he did nothing instead.

He remembered, painfully, an instance some years ago when a neighbor had lost a young son in an auto accident. He didn't consider the family to be close friends, but close enough for him to attend the funeral, which was all he could think to do. What do you say or give to a mother and father suffering over the death of a young son? Children are not supposed to die before parents, and when they do, the guts of a generational clock are ripped out, never to be the same again. Do you show up at the door with sub sandwiches and Dr. Pepper? Yes, he learned later, when he saw another neighbor do exactly that.

It occurred to him that perhaps there was no "secret formula," no mysterious elixir that would cast a spell of contentment over a household in crisis. Perhaps, he remembered thinking at the time, it was just the act of doing that contained all the value. He later convinced himself it couldn't be that simple.

Still, something was bothering him.

"You know, Clara," he said, "it occurs to me that I have a hard time feeling much compassion for a person who I perceive is responsible for *causing* a negative outcome or event. I feel much less compassion and am much less willing to forgive. What I really am, I suppose, is angry and resentful. If compassion is an all-encompassing truth, how does it play into that kind of experience?"

She pursed her lips, considering her answer. "Good stimulus, good response. Bad stimulus, bad response. Do you remember the problem with that process?"

"I do. Our happiness is taken hostage by whatever stimulus comes around. We divorce ourselves from being responsible for our own sense of joy. And most of our happiness is not found in the stimulus, but in the response. So? How does this apply to compassion?"

"Well," she said, "for whom are you causing problems when you live in a state of anger and resentment? You, maybe? You described this process. Anger—rip. Resentment—rip. We become our own worst enemy."

She looked at him closely, seeming to sense that she'd just touched him.

"Will you do something for me, Jason?"

"Of course."

"Is there a person in your life for whom you harbor a significant pool of hate and resentment? Someone you'd like to tear limb from limb if the consequences weren't quite so inconvenient?"

He thought for a moment. "Yeah, I suppose so. One or two."

"Good," she said. "I'm that person. I'm sitting here next to you. If that were true, how would you feel?"

He took a deep breath and pulled back his outstretched legs, clenching his lips and tightening his fists.

"Look at you," she said, grinning. "You went from relaxed to tense. Just thinking about that person brought stress and conflict. You're ready to fight, right? Knock-down, drag-out."

"I'm ready to fight. I owe them a shot or two."

"I understand. What you need to understand, though, is that holding onto resentment is like taking poison and expecting someone else to die. Anger destroys the person who is angry just as hatred destroys the person who hates. It is a form of suicide that kills just as surely as guns or pills. It does us no good. Do you know that stress causes more heart attacks than genetics, poor nutrition, and a lack of exercise combined?"

"Yes, I believe I've heard that," he admitted.

"Your choice to be unforgiving, angry, hateful, or resentful of someone you perceive has harmed you translates into far more problems for you than it does for that person. And to make matters worse, you may very well be dead wrong about the person and what you perceive he or she did. Sometimes what seems obvious is not so simple. Give it up, Jason. Spend your resources some other way. Perhaps compassion is the first step in reducing your anger and resentment. Try to see what happened through the other person's eyes, realizing that your own view may be distorted."

"Sounds good, but how does that work in real life?"

"Let's use something specific. My daughter, Rachel, is up to her elbows in a very tough problem. Did you know that on any given day, within the hospitals of our major metropolitan cities, ten to fifteen young people will be admitted with multiple gunshot wounds? Weaponry is different from what it was twenty years ago. The revolver is gone. We now have nine-millimeter semiautomatic pistols in the hands of kids with attitudes; put those kids in at-risk environments, and we get death and destruction."

A visual image played in both of their minds.

"Rachel is a trauma surgeon in one of those hospitals. Do you know that many foreign countries—Japan, Australia, and especially the Scandinavian countries—prior to sending surgical teams into war-torn regions, send them first to the major inner cities of the United States for triage training? The medical term used to describe this kind of treatment is 'damage control.' Why here? Because they are likely to see as many multiple gunshot wounds in a month in a hospital in the U.S. as they'd see in a career back home. It's great combat surgical training. Not much of a commentary for the world's leading industrialized nation, is it?"

"I had no idea. That's awful."

"It is awful," she agreed. "I remember Rachel struggling with the responsibility of removing a bullet from the arm of a youngster who was too young to receive a license to drive a car, yet had just gunned down several kids his own age. Beautiful young lives cut short in the blink of an eye. Talk about anger and resentment. She admitted to me that it was all she could do to treat the wound. What she really wanted to do was punish the person responsible for the carnage, to take a life for the lives he'd taken. After all, those deaths were not caused by cancer or some long-term illness, but by selfish and self-serving decisions."

"To put it mildly," he remarked.

"It came as a spontaneous thought that she could choose to see the deaths from the perspective of this young teen. He became a young teen rather than a gunman as soon as she offered him the compassion to consider the possibility that there was a core of humanity in him. It wasn't until she began looking at what was happening through the eyes of this youth that she began to understand that his circumstance was, in fact, its own kind of corrosive disease—a cancer embedded in the very heart of our society."

Unexpectedly, a wave of emotion lodged in Jason's throat. What was happening to him?

"As she and her colleagues looked deeper," Clara continued, "they found a triad: at-risk kids, at-risk environments, and semiautomatic weapons. They sequenced the problem. They found that if they could disrupt any one of the three, they could disrupt the rate of killing. It wasn't until compassion entered her mind-set that she was able to look beyond her immediate outrage and see the real problems. Then she could begin to form adequate responses, or at least responses that could help reduce the epidemic. Her hypothesis was so compelling that she began to volunteer in inner-city youth organizations, offering her experience and perspectives to kids.

"Simplistically, I guess what I'm saying is that compassion allows you to take a bad stimulus and turn it into a good response. Hate will never do that. Anger will never do that. Fear will never do that. Resentment, jealousy, and all the rest produce bad responses, which in turn become bad stimuli for the recipient. Who will have the guts to step forward and stop this spiral into hell? Gandhi said it well, 'An eye for an eye makes the whole world blind.'"

Jason shifted his weight. "What caused your daughter to make the shift away from anger and toward compassion?" he asked.

"I suppose it was her own pain," Clara said somewhat wistfully, "which came in the form of having to look in the faces of young parents and tell them that their children, their hope for the future, had died on the operating table, that she didn't have the skills to save them. That kind of pain will either drive you forward with determination to find an answer or it will drive you backward with determination to exact revenge, or maybe to just curl up and disappear.

"To this day she can hardly speak of these experiences; the pain is that great. But she used that emotion as fuel for positive change. These are not easy problems, but compassion is a foothold on the path upward."

"Your daughter sounds pretty amazing."

"She is. So is the power of compassion. It can be brutally honest and understanding in the same moment. It is never enabling of poor choices. It has no litmus test. It bonds a person to the rest of humanity. It doesn't worry that it may not have all the answers or know what to say or do. It is simply committed to doing something, anything. It is color-blind, belief-blind, behavior-blind, and hate-blind.

"Compassion, like love, is the commitment to the growth of another person, which defies our Western notion of love and companionship as a commitment to find a person I can attach myself to who will give me what I want. There is no love or compassion in that, only selfishness.

"Perhaps the ultimate expression of compassion is to befriend someone who considers you their enemy, and to alleviate their suffering. That kind of behavior makes friends of enemies and turns hate to understanding, perhaps even love. And it is sorely needed in a world whipped into a frenzy of violence and revenge."

"You sound a little like a bleeding heart, Clara."

"Maybe. But if we had more bleeding hearts and fewer weapons, what might this world be like? History's greatest teachers have all advocated for softened hearts. Perhaps only a soft heart can bleed. Your choice, Jason. You choose your own path."

He nodded, chewing on his lower lip. Then he spoke softly. "I've got a question. How do compassion and justice coexist? I've heard it said that compassion is no substitute for justice. How do you reconcile the two?"

"They are not mutually exclusive, not at all. An axiom will never exclude good. Injustice is the enemy of compassion. But justice without compassion is just plain scary. Justice without compassion is revenge and punishment, nothing more. That kind of justice produces more of the same—more revenge, more anger, more resentment, more frustration, more hate. Justice *with* compassion is accountability and responsibility, and perhaps progress. If both parties, the one harmed and the one responsible for causing the harm, are held accountable and are humble, good will come of bad. I would not want to live in a place where justice was meted out without compassion. It's been done, and the results are unacceptable."

He considered his usual behavior, then cringed.

Chapter 25

BASEBALL

A gust of wind slapped at them.

"Do you understand the first axiom, Jason?" she asked. "You must understand the first, compassion, before we move to the second."

"I think I understand it in big strokes," Jason responded, "but the more I think about it and consider its implications, the more complicated it gets."

"Welcome to the axioms," Clara responded. "Shall we move on?"

"Please."

"The second axiom," she continued, "is *humility*. It is the recognition that we are a small part of a large whole. In addition, and perhaps most important, it's a commitment to new learning. Remember our conversation yesterday about the box? New learning is outside your box. Humility provides a broad context and creates a sense that there's much more 'out there' than we ever imagined. It allows us to admit freely that we don't really know much. Humility teaches us that what we are becoming is more important than what we are doing."

"Humility isn't my strong suit," he offered apologetically.

"Guess I've seen a different side of you," Clara responded. "Isn't it fascinating that the most famous image ever taken by NASA was the Apollo 8 'Earthrise' photo that Bill Anders shot in 1968? It wasn't a photo of the moon, or the sun, or the solar system. We had to go to the moon to get a sense of ourselves. I remember seeing that photograph for the first time and thinking, 'My gosh, we're small—maybe we should start working together.' What we perceive as national, cultural, ethnic, and social boundaries down here were indistinguishable up there. We were simply one small planet in a vast universe of unimaginable phenomena.

"Got me thinking. The deep oceans are perhaps the most powerful physical force on the planet. Why? Because they stay low, they are humble compared to the dazzling mountaintops, yet all things flow into them. Humility is sometimes realized through our capacity to be awestruck, either by something we see, something we hear, or something we experience. It is the sense of excitement that accompanies a sense of wonder.

"Humility is an ever-expanding awareness of our own ignorance. The more we know, the more we know we don't know. People respond with two fundamental fears—the fear of not *having* enough, and the fear of not *being* enough. Humility allows us the privilege of realizing that more than enough is more than enough."

That one hit home for Jason. Enough had never been enough, until now.

"Humility won't let your ego get so close to your position that when your position goes down, your ego goes with it. Humility is inclusive, never exclusive. Humility looks hard for flaws in your own argument instead of in others."

Again, he was rocked by the truth.

"Humility is the overlooked and underestimated power behind cooperation and teamwork because it reduces or eliminates blame.

Humility is an acknowledgment that we've all made mistakes. Blame is not a component of improvement. Accountability, yes. Blame, no."

"I'm not sure I understand the difference between accountability and blame," Jason said. "I think people use them to mean the same thing, or at least I do. How is accountability a component of improvement and blame not? How are they different?"

"You work for an architectural and engineering firm, right?"

"Afraid so."

"Are you responsible for managing budgets?"

"I am for my group, yes."

"If your boss wanted to bring an accounting firm into your business, your group, to get a better understanding of where the money is going, how it's being spent, where the revenue is coming from, what areas are growing, what areas are regressing, how you could manage your assets better to accomplish the mutual objectives of the company, perhaps to get an idea of where you could reduce staff if that should become necessary, would that be a positive move as far as you were concerned?"

"Sure it would," he answered.

"What would the accounting firm do? How would they go about their business?"

"I suppose they'd first look at the books. They'd want to understand the profit and loss statement, the balance sheet, you know, credits and debits, assets and liabilities. After they understood the basics, they'd probably begin to audit the data to determine what's going well and what's not, and so on."

"Excellent. So, under your definition, *an accounting is an understanding of the whole picture,* where we're strong and where we're weak. Do I understand you correctly?"

"Yes, I think so."

"Could we say that being accountable includes a consideration of the whole, not just the assets, not just the liabilities, but both? Not just some small sliver of information that happens to justify a particular desired action? Could we say there is no 'spin' in accountability, no manipulating a couple of data points to the exclusion of a hundred others just to make your point?"

"Yeah, I'd agree with that."

"Now, let's make a shift. Your boss walks into your office and says something like: 'Your group is not meeting expectations, Snow, and I want to know who's responsible. I want some heads to roll. I want two termination suggestions from you on my desk by morning. Someone will be cleaning out their desk by tomorrow afternoon. I want to send a message. You understand me, Snow?' Would that be a positive move, in your opinion?"

"I see your point. Of course it wouldn't. He's looking for someone to blame. He's not really interested in understanding the problem. He's interested in finding someone to point a finger at, to say, 'There's the guy to blame for this mess.' And he's trying to motivate the rest of us through fear."

"Ah, good, good. And why does he want to point a finger? Why does he want to identify someone to blame?"

"Well, I'd guess he believes that if he finds a person he can stick with the problem, the problem doesn't get stuck on him."

"Excellent. Remind you of anyone you know? Your boss, perhaps? How about your kids, teachers, coworkers, politicians, anyone? You, perhaps?"

"It reminds me of a lot of people."

"Blame grows out of fear. Accountability grows out of humility and integrity. Blame will cause regression, just the opposite of what the person pointing the finger wanted. Why? Because everyone in the department now understands that if it can happen to poor Fred without warning or reasonable circumstances, it can happen to them. And then what? Loyalty is gone. Trust is gone. Communication is gone. Creativity and innovation are plowed under. Creativity and innovation can flourish only in an environment of safety and risk tolerance.

"Soon, top management is driving the staff from behind with a stick instead of pointing the way from the front. Blame is not a component of improvement, and that applies across the board, to marriages, families, businesses, schools, government, you name it. Accountability is a component of improvement because it seeks first to understand and learn.

"There is a learning element in accountability that is missing in blame. There is also an implicit understanding that whatever problem occurred, the people involved would under normal circumstances have produced excellent results. When results amount to something less than expected, accountable organizations want to understand what happened. What was the unanticipated factor that played into the failure?"

"I wish it worked that way."

"Trust me, it can. There is also a level of fairness in accountability that is missing in blame. After the audit is complete, someone might well lose his or her job, but it will be based in truth and carried out with respect. There's a message sent to staff under this process, too: 'I've been hired to do a job, to perform, and to be an asset to my group. This firm is not going to employ an unproductive workforce.' That's the message. And it's exactly the message the performers want to hear. I guarantee you that the performers in any organization are tired of carrying the nonperformers. Accountability enlivens the organization and boosts morale. Blame depresses the organization and crushes morale."

Jason sat silent, digesting the ideas.

"How about another example," Clara suggested.

"Okay."

"I coached Rachel's softball team some years ago. I learned some things about life I didn't know before. Softball. Who knew?"

Chemist. Mountaineer. Wife. Mother. Runner. Coach. Jason was mentally carving up the day and wondering when she slept.

"Let's say," she began, "you play right field on a baseball team. It's the bottom of the last inning and your team is up three to one. However, the opposing team has two men on base with two out. The sun is beginning to go down behind home plate directly in your line of vision, and you find yourself trying to shield the blinding light with your gloved hand because you've left your sunglasses in the dugout. A lefty hits a high fly ball right at you. This thing is way up in the air. With two out, the base runners are advancing and the hitter is running all the way. Then, to your horror, you lose the ball in the sun, can't see it at all. You hear a 'thump' and realize that the ball has landed a good twenty feet behind you. You chase the ball down as fast as you can and make a long throw to home, but you're too late. Three runs score and your team loses the game."

"Ouch."

"Your team certainly has you to blame for their loss, right?"

"No question. It might be a good idea to go straight to the car and get the heck out of there."

Clara chuckled. "That would be a good option if your team were a blaming organization, and it sounds as though blaming organizations are what you have experience with. However, if your team were an organization that believed in accountability, there would be some questions to ask, some information and learning to sift through."

Jason showed his confusion. "I made the mistake and lost the game. What is there to talk about?"

"Plenty. Let's take a closer look. Where's a left-handed hitter most likely going to hit it, what direction?" she asked.

"If he's a decent hitter, he's probably going to pull the ball. That means the ball is going to the right side of the field, first or second base, right, maybe center field."

"Good. So, your coach probably figured that out, wouldn't you think?"

"Yeah, I suppose. He'd have to be asleep not to."

"If he saw you out there in right field with a glove up in the air, trying to block the sun, and with no sunglasses, why didn't he stop the game and get a pair of glasses to you? I mean, come on, with a lefty at the plate, the chances are pretty good that a fly ball is going to you, isn't that right? Aren't those the little details a coach is supposed to be watching for?"

"I suppose so," he said.

"And where was the center fielder? Isn't he supposed to be backing you up on a fly ball hit to right? Where was he? The fact that you lost the ball in the sun and it dropped in behind you probably meant that the two base runners were going to score and the game would be tied. But if the center fielder had done his job, he surely could have gotten to the ball much sooner than you and would probably have stopped the hitter from scoring."

"Yeah, maybe."

"What about the second baseman?" she asked. "Shouldn't he have run out toward right field and placed himself in a cutoff position so you wouldn't have to make a throw all the way to the plate?

"We could even consider the pitcher. If he knew a strong lefty was at the plate who liked to pull the ball, and he knew there was a sun problem in right field, why didn't he concentrate on the outside of the plate and make the hitter go to the opposite field?"

"Never knew a pitcher who thought quite that rationally."

"Look, an accountable organization is going to look at the *whole* problem, at what happened, and they'll try to learn from it. They're not interested in placing blame. They're interested in being accountable, as a group, for their results. They want to wring the learning out of each circumstance. Suppose the coach had come to you after the game and said, 'Jason, you screwed up, but I'm partly responsible—I should have gotten a pair of glasses to you. I will not let that happen again. Also, we'll be working on backing each other up and hitting the cutoff man at our next practice.' How would that have made you feel?"

"I can't imagine a coach seeing through the disappointment of a loss clearly enough to say that, but if he could, wow. I'd never forget my glasses again. That's for darned sure."

"So," said Clara, "you're saying that his willingness to be accountable for his contribution to the problem and his desire to learn from it would motivate you to improve, is that it?"

"Absolutely. I'd walk through fire for a coach like that," he responded.

"It's not just about making you feel good and inspiring loyalty. The truth is, if the coach can help everyone see how they contributed to the problem, they all become more alert. If the other players are blaming you and not looking at their own contribution, the team continues to be 'I' centered, and not team-centered.

"On a great team, no player will ever say, 'Oh, that's his play.' He will always be looking at a situation and assessing what his contribution should be to the end result. He does not compartmentalize his performance or play."

"Where do I sign up?" asked Jason, giving her the thumbs-up sign. She smiled.

"Let's look at this from one more perspective. I have a friend, a very good friend, who's a spiritual person. She believes in a power higher than herself. She has a firm belief in God."

"Sounds like my parents," he said.

"Part of her belief is that she'll be held accountable for what she's done, that there will be a day of judgment, and unless she addresses her misbehaviors—she would call them 'sins'—the judgment is not going to be a pleasant experience. For years she beat herself up and blamed herself for not being the kind of person she wanted to be. She was always disappointed in her actions. She would get to the point of feeling nearly valueless—and this is one extraordinary woman. She was full of self-blame.

"Now remember, blame is one-sided. Blame looks only at the liabilities and ignores the assets, so it's easy to see how someone could begin to believe that they were bankrupt of value if that was all they saw in themselves."

Her eyes drifted, gathering the story.

"During a conversation a couple of years back when she was particularly low, I reminded her that her belief was that God would hold her accountable, not that He would blame her. She looked at me like I was nuts. I tried to explain the difference.

"Accountability has a learning component. Yes, perhaps she has made mistakes—debits, liabilities. But from those mistakes have come learning, wisdom, lessons that can be passed on to children, spouse, and friends. Learning that gave her a greater ability to relate to people who struggle, wisdom that comes only through a collaborative combination of learning, experience, and suffering—those are the credits, the assets.

"There are two columns on the human balance sheet. Blame says that my friend should be interested only in what she did. It ignores what she learned. Blame makes strong things weak because it sees only liabilities, sorrow, pain, shortcomings, mistakes, discouragement, fear, and so on. Accountability makes weak things strong because it sees not just the liabilities but also the assets: the learning, wisdom, temperance, and good that can come from bad choices.

"What is the point of an omniscient God wanting to fix blame? He knows everything. There's nothing she could confess that He doesn't know. So blame would be a complete waste of time, and the God she believes in has no time to waste time. The only possible point of a judgment is for *her* to learn something, to be accountable, to see assets and liabilities.

"She finally got it. Now, it isn't as though she's out there looking for ways to make mistakes. However, when mistakes are made, and they surely are, she consciously looks for the learning. How can she avoid doing this again? What did she learn about herself? What did she learn about human behavior? How might she help another who is suffering through the same bundle of circumstances? And learning, Jason, is a product of humility. This new perspective has changed her outlook about who she is and what she's here for. Life is beyond anyone's total control. The humility to know that with choice also comes disappointment allows us to overcome the bruises. Humility takes a thorn and turns it into a rose."

"I could use a few less thorns," Jason commented.

"True for all of us, I'm afraid. Look, humility allows me to realize that not all wisdom is in my school. Humility lies on the ragged edge between knowledge and ignorance, between what we know and what we don't know we don't know. Humility plows a fertile field ready to accept the seeds of change.

"For years science and society believed a flat earth to be the center of the universe. We were the chosen ones. We lived on the right side of the right planet—obviously, or we'd all have fallen off—a planet around which rotated all the heavens above. Oops. We discovered a round earth on which all 'sides' were habitable. And we found that instead of being the center of the universe, we were located in an obscure area of a small solar system that is a wisp of a spiral arm of a smallish galaxy in a massive universe—a discovery that did not go unpunished by those making the rules at the time. The only thing centered on us was us, along with a lifeless, colorless moon that fries in sunlight and freezes in the dark, which proved somewhat less than our expectation."

Both of them cast their eyes momentarily skyward.

"We humans," she said, "have a tendency to become intoxicated with our own importance. When science does discover the center of the universe, it's safe to say it will not be us. That's not to say that we should forget about taking care of ourselves. It does mean that humility is required to remember who we are.

"Humility will come to us all, either by circumstance or by conscience. Humility by circumstance is the devastating natural disaster we thought couldn't happen, or the one we thought we were prepared for. It's Mother Nature showing her supreme power over inconsequential man. It's a medical condition that sets us back. It's the loss of something we were dependent upon. It's the unexpected exposure of our shortcomings or misdeeds. It's the fall of a business or industry that seemed stalwart. It's the death of someone close and the realization of our own vulnerability. It's a divorce. It's the loss of a job or lack of promotion. It's a wayward child. It's anything that brings us down a few notches and makes us realize that perhaps we're not the invincible, independent agents of success we thought we were."

"Welcome to the human race," Jason offered.

"Indeed. Humility by conscience is the fundamental recognition of our dependence on someone or something else, an intense understanding that we are a very small part of a very large whole. It is this kind of humility that the axioms require. Humility by circumstance, on the other hand, is outside in and usually temporary, except in extreme situations such as ongoing starvation, disease, or a similar world crisis. We soon forget our vulnerability.

"Humility by conscience is inside out and usually long-term. It's an understanding that lodges in your soul and is unshakable. Inside out is better than outside in, but more difficult to accomplish because it involves choice."

Jason whistled softly, on the verge of being overwhelmed.

"I don't want you to misunderstand. Humility is not a willingness to be run over. It is not an act of surrendering to anyone or anything that comes along. It is not sheepish or spineless. Humility does not wither at conflict or keep silent in the face of evil.

"Carlos Castaneda said something I've always liked. To

paraphrase, he said that the humility of the warrior is not the humility of the beggar. The warrior lowers his head to no one, but at the same time, he doesn't permit anyone to lower his head to him. The beggar, on the other hand, falls to his knees at the drop of a hat and scrapes the floor for anyone he deems to be higher, but at the same time, he demands that someone lower than he is scrape the floor for him. Do you see the difference? One is based in a respect for all people. The other is based in fear. Big difference."

Chapter 26

THANK YOU

There are some," Clara said, "who may misunderstand the axioms. They may think of them as internal considerations—how they see and feel about the world around them. Although this is an important first step, it by no means defines the path. The real power of the axioms comes in their execution—in action! It is the doing, not just the thinking, that accelerates the axioms to full velocity. I want you to think deeply about that during our discussion: 'How do I act on these ideas? What should I be doing?' Do you understand, Jason?"

"I think so, or should I say 'I do.'"

"Good catch." She laughed. "Can we move to the third axiom?"

"Absolutely," Jason said.

"The third axiom is *gratitude.* Gratitude is an acknowledgment of the blessings in our lives and a commitment to live and be happy right now, today. Not to look back longingly on yesterday, and not to wait and focus forward on tomorrow. Far too many people overestimate the value of the things they don't have, while underestimating the value of the things they do. Don't make the mistake of believing you need something you don't have."

"Like I said, Clara, isn't that the American way?"

"Perhaps, but there's no lasting contentment down that path."

That, he knew, was true.

"Gratitude," she said, "brings an appreciation for what's ours. Gratitude stops or reduces the comparisons we make between others and ourselves, comparisons that are bound to build fences. Simple gratitude brings a simple peace. The antonyms of gratitude are conflict, pain, discouragement, and envy. Gratitude, like humility, recognizes that what we have is what we need. It provides us a realistic perspective. After all, when I compare my problems with the problems of the other six billion people on earth, do I really have it so bad? Do I have food to eat when I want? Do I have shelter overhead and a bed to sleep on? Am I warm in the winter? Do I have clean clothes to wear? Do I have shoes on my feet? Is education available to my children? Is high-quality medical care readily available? If your answer is yes to all of these, you're lucky. Very lucky. Billions of people cannot answer any of them in the affirmative."

"Intellectually," he responded, "I understand that I'm lucky, that I've won some kind of genetic lottery. But getting from lucky to grateful doesn't seem so easy. It's one thing to compare myself to a global population, one that I very seldom experience, and another to understand that I have lots to be grateful for given my personal circumstances and the environment I swim in every day."

"Great observation," Clara remarked. "Let me share something with you that has lately made the rounds in pop culture but is now finding root in science. It's difficult, if not impossible, to be angry or fearful or unhappy and grateful at the same moment. Certainly you can bounce back and forth, but you can't harbor both emotions in the same moment. You cannot at the same time shake a hand and deliver a blow. Now, frankly, I don't know if that's true for all emotion.

Perhaps it is. If it is, that fact doesn't make its practice any less effective. Gratitude pulls the plug on anger, and anger is responsible for a horde of bad choices and poor behavior."

"Hey, you're looking at the poster guy for anger. And I'm not proud of it."

"Perhaps that's true, but I've not seen it in you, Jason." She paused. "Anger is the great justifier—someone did something to me that was unjust, something that made me angry, which justifies my revenge. Once again: bad stimulus, bad response. Where does that loop stop? It stops when one party to the loop—and it only takes one—looks through the lens of compassion, humility, and gratitude and finds a third alternative, something other than fight or flight. I cannot emphasize it enough—most of our misery and virtually all of our happiness is found not in the stimulus, but in the response.

"Gratitude also requires that we live in the now. Being grateful does not include a wish to return to yesterday or a desire to have tomorrow get here as quickly as possible, for then, and only then, will I be happy. People who think that way find that yesterday is gone forever and the tomorrow they're looking for never arrives. The folks that practice gratitude turn lemons to lemonade. They are optimistic, but not in the traditional sense that they see the world through rose-colored glasses or are ignorant of the distress and turmoil around them. Not at all. Their sense of optimism is different. For them, optimism is embedded in the principle that the bigger the problem, the larger the learning. The bigger the challenge, the larger the opportunity. I suppose it is a variant of 'What doesn't kill me only makes me stronger.'"

"I have that posted on my desk somewhere, but for the wrong reasons, I think. How does that work in real life?"

"Let me give you an example," she offered. "Some years back my family and I were headed to Italy for a vacation. Our flight took us through Paris and a change of planes. As luck would have it, we arrived at De Gaulle late and missed our connection to Florence. You can imagine our thrill in finding that the next flight out was seven hours later. Great, we thought. Seven hours in the Paris airport. Seven long, wasted hours in the Air France lounge when we could be wandering the streets of Florence eating pistachio gelato.

"My husband wasn't thinking like the rest of us. He never does. He asked if anyone would care to see the Louvre, the Arc de Triomphe, the Champs-Élysées, maybe enjoy a baguette at a sidewalk café. It was as if someone found an unopened Christmas gift in July. We grabbed a cab to downtown and had a ball. We barnstormed Paris for five hours. My husband turned our misfortune into wonder because, where we saw problems, he saw opportunities. Some people just have the knack for that sort of thing. We went right to resentment. He went right to gratitude. We knew we were stuck. He knew that the heart of Paris was a short drive away."

"What a remarkable guy."

"He is. It was my husband, again, who motivated me to come to Silcox after my cancer diagnosis. You'll remember I told you that gratitude took the fear away. Once the fear was gone, I began to fight the cancer.

"Almost immediately after the diagnosis, when I was trapped in fear, he made a statement that irked me at the time because it seemed insensitive. He said, 'Cancer, one more mountain to climb. Go get 'em, Clara.' I wanted to smack him. I was simmering in feeling sorry for myself and he yanked me right out of that pan. I soon came to realize he was absolutely right. Cancer was one more challenge in a long line of challenges. Like I said, most of our happiness and misery lie not in the stimulus but in our response. The stimulus was cancer. I saw darkness. He saw light in the options, in the possible responses, and he pointed the way. I did the rest."

"You speak of cancer as if it was a blessing, Clara."

"Don't get me wrong," she responded. "I wouldn't wish cancer on anyone. But when that kind of stimulus plants itself on your doorstep, it can become a remarkable experience if you'll allow it. Or it can be horrifying. It was my choice. *My choice.* I can't very often control the stimulus, but I can certainly control my response."

"I'm not sure how I can control my response," he managed. "People do stupid things, annoying things. They make me angry. Isn't that just the way it is?"

"No, it isn't. People will always do stupid things, Jason. Heaven knows I've contributed my share. However, they don't make you angry. You choose to be angry. Maybe you think anger works for you. Maybe anger is your habitual response. Maybe you've come to believe intimidation is a good strategy—when you get really angry, people back off and give you what you want. Maybe you simply haven't realized or understood that there are other options.

"I want you to consider something that may be hard for you to swallow."

"Imagine that," he responded with a sly smile.

Clara cocked her head to the side and smiled back.

"I acknowledge that instances arise for each of us that may justify anger as a legitimate response. However, what if I told you that anger, in the vast majority of life's circumstances, is at its heart nothing more than selfishness? It is a unilateral emotion intended to serve your own selfish interests. You get angry because, fundamentally, you are not getting what you want. It's a terrible-two tantrum clothed in a cloak of adult legitimacy. But a tantrum by any other name . . .

"What if people began to understand that there are better strategies, better alternatives for coping with life's unexpected bumps, bruises, and disappointments? What if there are strategies that will work far better for them and those they influence, who generally are lined up against the wall preparing for the firing squad?"

"I don't buy it, Clara. Sorry. I remember getting really angry with Brian's soccer coach for his lack of playing time. The guy was nuts.

212

Never did understand Brian's potential. Really ticked me off and I let him know. My anger wasn't selfish. I was being an advocate for my son. Not a thing wrong with that."

Clara smiled.

"What?" he asked, defensively.

"The truth is staring you in the face and you still don't see."

Jason raised his arms in disbelief. "What truth?"

"Not once during your explanation of Brian's predicament did you mention what Brian wanted. Brian wasn't getting the playing time *you* wanted him to have. You weren't getting what you wanted, Jason. Did you ever really ask Brian what he wanted?"

"That's not fair," he responded.

"Why? Because it uncovers a painful truth? Look at you. You are so habitually in love with anger as a response, you can't imagine another alternative, and it scares you to death, doesn't it?"

Jason looked away without comment.

"Don't you dare retreat. You've got to find a new path. Yes, it's a little frightening if that's all you've known. But there are many other options."

She paused, backing off a little.

"I want you to think of it this way. There are these wonderful trails in the woods near my home. Miles of trails bordered by tall Doug fir, vine maple, ferns, really beautiful stuff. People have walked these trails for decades and, as a result, they are smooth and easily identifiable. Imagine that one of these trails leads to a blind curve covered with heavy undergrowth that ends abruptly and cascades over the edge of a ravine to a pile of rocks twenty feet below. However, because the trail is already cut and I know no other alternative, I continue to walk the trail and topple over the cliff, again and again. Good strategy?"

"Do I really need to answer the question?" he responded.

"No. There could be a hundred other ways to get to the other side of the ravine. The best alternative may even require breaking a new trail through brush and overgrown terrain. However, the trail is cut where it is, so I follow it.

"Your brain is just like that. You have neural pathways that are well worn from habitual decision making. Some may work great. Others, not so well. Anger, not working so well. There are many alternatives, any of which may require breaking a new trail. The more you use the new pathway, the more entrenched it becomes. Soon, the old pathway to anger will grow over, replaced by a strategy that is now clearly marked and much more effective, much more enjoyable."

"I can't even imagine what that might offer," he responded.

"Gratitude is the new trail, Jason. Doesn't matter if your problem is anger, fear, or hate. Gratitude may not be the only strategy that works, but it has proven its effectiveness time after time. It's what brought me to see cancer as a grand experiment in human endurance and the linchpin of some truly remarkable friendships."

"I'm afraid that would take more guts than I possess," he said.

"You have it in you, Jason. We all do. People who have never had cancer cannot possibly relate to those who have and their appreciation for the experience. It is beyond their understanding that gratitude is a large part of the journey. In those dim hours of treatment, gratitude became the greatest of virtues and the foundation of all others. 'Cancer survivor' doesn't begin to cut it. If you've survived cancer, in so many ways you are a better person than you were before the disease rampaged through your body and brought light to your mind.

"I'll never forget the day I returned home from my last chemo treatment. We turned into our neighborhood and the most sensationally unexpected vision appeared before me. All the trees along the street from the corner to our home were wrapped with pink ribbons of encouragement. You just can't imagine what that meant to me, not in a hundred years. From the loneliness of chemo to the arms

THANK YOU

of people I loved, and none of it would have happened without the cancer.

"And the result? I think I'm more compassionate now, more humble, and more grateful. I became extraordinarily thankful for what I had mistaken for small pieces of my life, things I'd taken for granted far too long. Have you ever noticed the structure of a leaf? The perfect arch of flower petals? Have you ever wondered why planets and stars are always round and their orbits always elliptical? Have you discovered how wonderful it is to sit quietly with someone you love, to simply listen to that person's heart beat? It is a symphony of silence. I began to see wonder everywhere. Absolutely everywhere. I learned that people are vastly more important than things."

Jason shrugged and shook his head.

"What's wrong?" she asked.

"Are you suggesting that it's going to take the prospect of death to teach me how to live?"

Her eyes twinkled as a moment passed between them.

"I really hope not, Jason. But life is habitual. You've got to find a way to break the destructive cycle. If not, you're doomed to a great mistake. Let's use the prospect of death for a moment. Not yours, but your son's. Picture yourself in the position of having a child die before you.

"What would you be willing to change about your life to bring him back? What would you give up? What would you start doing? Just about anything, right? Sometimes it's hard to find gratitude until you perceive a loss. You take your relationship with Brian for granted—that is, until you get a grip on the fact that he could be gone tomorrow. He's one heartbeat away from being only a memory. The question is, does the realization of that possibility increase your level of gratitude for your wonderful son? And let me assure you, Jason, it could happen. Trust me."

Jason nodded affirmatively. "I understand. And yes, it does

215

produce a broader sense of gratitude for the blessing of a son." He turned toward Clara with some concern.

"What is it?" she asked.

"Have you lost a son or daughter, Clara?"

"A story for another time, my friend."

Jason observed that Clara had been invaded by a sadness that pulled her countenance down like limbs heavy with midwinter snow. He was curious and concerned for her state of mind; however, she'd made herself clear. Not now.

She breathed deeply and collected herself.

"For me, the cancer and other experiences motivate me to express appreciation and gratitude often. I need to do better. To be appreciated is a universal craving. To withhold gratitude from someone is like buying a gift and failing to deliver it. Intention has no value in this regard; all that matters is an outward expression by word or action. Failing to understand that most of us have much to be grateful for is pure blindness, pure selfishness. It is ignorance at its worst."

Chapter 27

THE VOICE

Joe Walker had worked with Jason for thirteen years and been a thorn in his side for most of it.

Joe led the creative team at Northwest Design and Engineering, a Rembrandt with a palette board full of iron, glass, stone, and space. His ability to mix texture and structure created architecture that was masterful. Jason was the finance guy, following behind Joe with a financial analysis and budget—the artistic equivalent of spray paint and masking tape. There was a natural tension between them from the start, a tension grown out of the disparate soil between aesthetics and economics, creativity and profitability. Joe loved organic spaces, but they tended to be expensive to execute and difficult to build, which caused animosity between the design group and the money guys.

Initially, the discord was all business. However, it didn't take long for it to become personal. The public acclaim Jason received as a result of bringing projects in on time and under budget was a raindrop compared to the torrent of accolades thrown at the feet

217

of Joe Walker, and that soon began to consume Jason like a festering infection. Jason made a pile of money for the company, but Joe branded it, and Jason always wanted what he didn't have. He wanted the notoriety.

Jason had to admit that his displeasure with his colleague had little to do with legitimacy. It was not really a struggle over ideas, business decisions, concepts, or project management, but Jason framed it that way in an attempt to keep his personal dislike personal and his shallow activity discreet.

What made it worse was that Joe Walker was a great guy. Honest. Creatively consistent. Good with a team. Likable. But he was a right brain in a left-brain world, an artist among MBAs, a gazelle in a hungry pack of tongue-hanging hyenas. Jason disliked the credit Joe received through practicing a skill set Jason perceived as soft and certainly subjective. A number was a number, and usually it was easy to tell whether it was right or wrong. Creative design was a whole different matter—an indefinable quality that couldn't be perceived until large amounts of money had been consumed. Despite computerized modeling, the building had to be built before human eyes could really understand its beauty and functionality. It was a world Jason didn't understand, wasn't good at, and, as a result, didn't trust.

Given the tension, Jason went about making life as miserable for Joe as possible. Joe, of course, usually had no inkling of his tactics. Jason was practiced in the art of concealed sabotage; he knew how to plant explosives below the waterline.

Jason thought it ironic that while he was sitting on the south side of Hood and contemplating the symmetry of Mount Jefferson, Joe was bouncing off the inside of his skull. Amazing the paths the mind walks of its own accord. He wondered how compassion, humility, and gratitude might color Joe Walker in a different light. How could Jason alleviate suffering? Was there something to learn? What was he grateful for? Thoughts began to flood him.

Stop being a roadblock.

Stop lobbying for failure.

Stop talking ill of a good man.

Stop smiling at him face-to-face while stabbing him in the back.

Stop the sabotage.

Stop considering what I might get out of the project and start considering the team as a whole.

Could he learn something from Joe about design?

Were there truths about design that were just as legitimate as the truths behind his numbers?

Could he admit wrong?

Could he express appreciation to Joe, even after all the years of conflict?

Would Joe accept something from him that didn't contain acid as an ingredient?

Could he offer his help?

Could he place his colleague in front of himself and his own selfish interests?

Could he sit in an executive meeting and publicly praise Joe?

Jason understood that just because he was willing to try to respond differently didn't mean Joe would reciprocate. What then? Would he have the guts to continue, or would he revert back to the old Jason?

Who knew? However, Jason thought it remarkable that the simple exercise of looking at his colleague through new eyes changed his colleague. How was that possible? Another present to add to Clara's box of mystery.

"You're lost in thought," Clara said.

"Just thinking about work. You?"

"I was thinking about Tank Man," she said. "Remember Tank Man?"

"Tank Man?" he responded. "The guy who came out of nowhere

to stand in front of Chinese tanks at Beijing's Tiananmen Square. That guy? Late '80s, I think."

"That's him," she replied. "Alone, this guy stepped in front of a column of tanks sent into the square to stop government protestors. It was one day after clashes between military police and civilians resulted in what is known as the Tiananmen Square Massacre. Most of us remember the photographs.

"This unknown man, dark pants and white shirt, gripping bags in both hands, stepped in front of an unknown outcome. What we didn't see is just as remarkable. We didn't see him putting himself in position while the tanks were hundreds of feet away. He had time to think this through, and he did it anyway. A rifleman from one of the tanks could have fired a shot and killed the man, or they could simply have run him over. Even so, he stood there alone. When the tank attempted to go around him, he moved in front and blocked its path, even climbed up on the thing at one point."

"The guy was nuts," Jason offered.

"No. The guy was committed. He was going to stop the column or die trying. What do you think it took for him to respond like that? What could he have been thinking?"

"I can only guess, Clara. Maybe he'd just had enough. Maybe he knew that if those tanks reached the protestors, people were going to die. Maybe he had friends and relatives in the square. Perhaps something deep within this guy spoke to him, told him he must do something, that he couldn't just stand innocently by and watch the slaughter."

"What did he gain," she asked, "from putting himself between tons of weaponry and unarmed civilians? What was in it for him? Was he obligated to act like that?"

"I don't think that was even a consideration," Jason responded. "Perhaps he was obligated to himself, knowing that once prompted he could take the required action or pay for his inaction for the rest of his life. It's interesting. If he hadn't acted, Tank Man would mean nothing to us. No one would look at him and say, 'Well, you had a chance to play chicken with the tanks and didn't.' Not a soul on earth would have held him accountable, except himself."

"Why," she asked, "would he be accountable to himself?"

"Again, I'm guessing. I think he probably heard that voice, that quiet whisper: 'You must act!' 'You must do something!' 'You must stop this!' To this day, I don't believe we know his name. I think it was one of those moments, Clara, one of those rare occurrences when the right thing is done for the right reason, without regard for self, and in the face of overwhelming odds."

"I think you're right, Jason. The fourth axiom is the most diffi-cult because it may require self-denial. It demands action outside our comfort zone, and is dependent on our ability to listen and then act in a way that so often is not very convenient. This axiom is perhaps best described as a moral compass, sorely needed in a world that seems to wander without direction."

Jason grinned. "What is it? Voices? Listen to the voices? I believe I learned about that in a psychology class I took years ago, and it wasn't talked about as a virtue."

"Maybe it should have been," she responded. "The fourth axiom is *conscience*, or the ability to make moral choices. When I say *moral*, I don't mean it in the sense of some rigid morality. I mean *moral* in the sense that a voice inside you is attempting to communicate right and wrong. It's telling you 'I ought' or 'I ought not,' and you have the ability to follow its advice."

"A choice," he offered, to which she nodded.

"A choice that will end either in remorse or in integrity. A choice that will present itself in the form of a defining moment, small or large, in which a perceived sacrifice is required first before the payoff is unveiled."

Jason inclined his head in agreement.

"If I asked you what the most damaging social problem of our age is, how would you answer? Difficult question, I know."

Jason raised his eyebrows. "Wow. I'm not sure. I think we get lost in the symptoms and never treat the real cause. Crime; enormous power held in too few hands; diminished human potential through the use of drugs and lack of education; the breakup of marriages and families; environmental degradation; an unwillingness to understand other cultures; a lack of affordable health care; too many resources going toward the construction of weapons; the disrespect we show to the poor and the elderly. It's tough to pick just one."

She pointed toward him, excited now. "What if I told you that these issues and certainly our own personal problems all begin in the same way? These are human problems, all of them, manufactured by people, each of whom is a link in the causal chain. Every one of these problems has its genesis in the violation of conscience. Someone ran the roadblock his or her conscience had erected. The flags were ignored and people betrayed themselves. Some who came after followed their lead. Decisions were made at critical times and places.

"Someone made a conscious determination to put aside social good and, at significant public expense, follow profit instead. Someone decided that telling the truth was personally depreciative or financially unrewarding, so they lied instead. Someone with an appetite for power found truth unappealing, so they manufactured their own version of reality instead. Someone skipped school and did drugs instead. Someone ignored the promises they made to their spouse and had an affair instead. Someone realized it was hard to earn, so they began to steal instead. Someone wanted more money to buy the conveniences they desired, so both spouses got jobs, developed careers, worked long hours, and ignored their kids instead. Someone is fearful of befriending people who think and look different, so they hate, ignore, or mistrust them instead."

Jason's face was growing more pained with each example Clara gave.

"Isn't that human nature?" he asked.

"Give me a reason why it should be."

"I can't," he said.

"Precisely. Each of these begins with just one person violating his or her conscience, which leads to a collective violation. You do not act in a vacuum. It takes just one person to build a bridge of betrayal, and a swarm of others will follow him or her over it. Never exchange dignity for ease. The dignity you're selling will not be limited to your own.

"These and scores of other problems we cause for ourselves every day begin with the violation of conscience. Seldom is what we're running toward what we really want."

"How is that possible?"

"We run toward self-satisfaction, which eventually brings remorse. And we run away from self-sacrifice, which would eventually bring a sense of peace that is unimaginable to anyone who has not experienced it. It is the human condition: the path of least resistance. Making good choices takes practice and repetition, one right decision at a time. It's not an easy thing, even for those who seem so consistent in its application."

He could only shake his head.

"The good news is that, just as the betrayal of one conscience can lead to collective betrayal, one person's determination to follow his or her conscience and not succumb to personal or social pressures can lead to a collective following of conscience. History has proven that true over and over again. Never, ever believe that your influence is inconsequential. A small pebble dropped in the middle of a big pond makes waves."

She paused, giving him time to ponder.

"Conscience has such things as courage, truth, fairness,

responsibility, and justice as companions. Its opposites are evil, immorality, and falsehood. Everything in life is kinetic. Nothing is static. We are either progressing or regressing. A willful determination to follow your conscience leads to progression. A selfish decision to ignore it leads to regression. Every time! I challenge you to give me an example where this did not prove true in your life. Just one!"

"I'm thinking," he said.

"You'll think a long time," she smiled. "There are a number of definitions of conscience. Some believe it's the voice of God. Others believe it's the voice within. Some believe it's culturally ingrained and varies by location and circumstance. Some would prefer to limit any conversation about conscience to a discussion about moral cognitive neuroscience.

"Regardless, there is something we can all agree on. And I'll prove it by asking another question. What is your mother's birthday?"

"Beg your pardon?"

"You heard me, and you'd better know the answer, young man."

They both laughed.

"March third," he answered.

"And where was that information before I asked the question?"

"What do you mean, 'Where was that information?' I don't get the question."

"Well, did you have it on a slip of paper in your pocket? Did you reach up and pull it out of the sky? What?"

"It was in my head. Memorized."

"Yes, it was in your head, but not in the conscious part. You had no thought of your mother's birthday until I asked the question. Then, almost magically, it appeared to you. Your memory is stored in your subconscious mind. Your subconscious is the source of all memory, all learning, and all change. It is a vast resource that all of us carry around every day and take completely for granted. Your brain is the finest and most remarkable piece of organic architecture in the known universe. In it are stored all the experiences of your life.

"Our memory is wonderful. Our recall is terrible. Our conscious mind pales in comparison with our subconscious. However, we attempt to rule our world with our conscious mind—the puddle ruling the Pacific."

"A small puddle, in some cases," he said.

"True enough. From where do you think your conscience is obtaining its information? When your conscience is saying 'I ought' or 'I ought not,' where does it look to determine the right response?"

"Well, put that way," he answered, "I guess it's obvious. It looks in my subconscious mind."

"Exactly. It looks in this vast reservoir of wisdom and experience. What has gone well in the past? What's gone poorly? What brought joy and happiness? What brought sorrow and misery? What is right? What is wrong? It extracts your collective life experience, makes a determination for your continued benefit, and feeds it to you as a voice inside your head. And what do you do with the advice?"

Jason winced. "Too many times I ignore it. I do something else instead. Something I think will get me what I want sooner or in a greater degree."

"Exactly. You and I and everyone on the planet overrule this ocean of wisdom with the information gleaned from the puddle. Great idea, don't you think?"

"Doesn't appear to be so great," he responded.

"Our subconscious mind is the smartest thing we have going for us if its prompting is in harmony with the axioms. Shouldn't we give it the benefit of the doubt and go with it more often than we do? Wouldn't that be the prudent thing, the proven thing? Don't you think its advice would lead you to the right response?"

"Clara," he said, shaking his head, "that isn't easy to do."

"You won't recall me ever saying it would be easy."

"No, you didn't."

"Listen to me, Jason. It may not be easy, but you have it in you. You can do this. Give yourself a chance. Please let me help you. I was once way off course. Someone reached down and lifted me up. Let me repay the debt and do the same for you."

Chapter 28

WHO ARE YOU?

The wind was beginning to calm, five or ten miles per hour now, and for the first time all morning his jacket stopped flapping.

"These are the axioms, Jason: Compassion. Humility. Gratitude. Conscience. Four elegantly simple words that hold the collective power to produce a peace unknown to most of us. They are the foundation of authentic human expression. On these rest our own sense of worth, an overpowering influence for good, and the ability to accomplish much. You've got to find a way to make them yours, Jason, to embed them into your character like DNA is embedded in your chromosomes. They will make all the difference."

Clara reached for her pack and removed her first aid kit. Unzipping it, she pulled out a small mirror and held it up.

"What do you see, Jason?"

"I see me," he said. "I see myself."

"Are you sure?"

"I'm sure. It's me. It isn't Sophie. Thank goodness it isn't Jeff."

"Are you absolutely positive you see you, and not something else?"

Clara's questioning made him reconsider. "What am I supposed to see?"

"You do not see you, as strange as that may sound. You see an image of you, a symbol, a value of yourself. I want you to watch the mirror very carefully."

Clara gripped the sides of the mirror with both hands and applied pressure, putting a slight bend in the panel.

"I can distort this mirror. I can distort your image, this value of yourself. In fact, I can bend the mirror to the point where the value displayed has very little relation to the truth."

He watched the mirror as his face widened considerably, then narrowed again.

"If I distort it enough, it will break."

Jason nodded again. He'd been doing a lot of that lately.

"Now, you do exist. At least I hope you do. You are self-evident. What you look like has a certain truth. The image in the mirror is a belief or value, and I can distort that image to the point where it is no longer reflecting anything close to the truth. If I distort it enough, it breaks. The most accurate image reflected in a mirror is the one reflected off a *true* mirror, a mirror that is absolutely flat, without distortion.

"The best way to ensure that the mirror stays true is to frame it, to support it. I believe that if you frame your values and beliefs with the axioms—with compassion, humility, gratitude, and conscience— you'll build and support a reflection of the world, your relationships, your accomplishments, and yourself, that is more accurate than any other image."

Jason was visibly excited now. "These axioms sound interesting, and I appreciate their value, I really do. No one in their right mind is going to argue against the value of compassion, humility, gratitude, or conscience. But how do these ideas stand up in a world of aggression and competition? It's a dog-eat-dog world out there. You know that. You've been there."

"I do know that," Clara said. "You need to ask yourself a very serious question: What is the alternative? What does someone lacking the four axioms look like?"

Jason was praying she wasn't about to read his resume. "It's probably not so pretty," he said sheepishly.

"His problems are manifest in a variety of thoughts and behaviors, but in general, this person has no concern for reducing or eliminating suffering, which means he's so consumed by his own problems that he's blind to anyone else's. His pain is paramount—the only thing that matters. He has no interest in new learning because he knows it all already. He doesn't value the opinions or ideas of others. He discounts any inclination toward an acknowledgment that he may not be right every moment of every day, an attitude that crushes the creativity and innovation out of anyone within his scope of influence. His patience is as thin as his head is thick. He has no interest in the concept that there may be more than one right answer. *His* answer is the only one that matters. He has nothing to be grateful for—he believes he's earned everything he's got without any help from anyone. He thinks he stands on his own shoulders, a posture that causes him pain and is incapable of producing elevation."

"I know people like that," Jason said softly.

"He's one-dimensional," she continued. "He tends to read in narrow subject matter with which he's thoroughly familiar, extending his already impressive grasp on information that he then uses to intimidate his peers. He motivates and is motivated by fear and a scarcity mentality. After all, the pie is only so big, and he wants his share before it's gone. His pastures are never green; therefore, he shows gratitude to no one. He's never happy now. He'll only be happy 'when,' a state that never arrives. He generally attaches strings to a compliment or civility, expecting something in return—remember, he's looking for personal esteem from the outside in.

"He considers himself a nice person—after all, he sometimes does nice things for people—but he has no awareness of who he's really thinking about when he's considering himself a nice person. He's practiced in the art of expressing false innocence, which becomes acidic to anyone taken by it. He betrays his conscience at every turn, and, in the end, has his actions so disconnected from his values that he tramples any sense of integrity or self-worth. He's consistently inconsistent. He looks for acceptance and personal esteem in immediate gratification—what or who will get me what I want and need now? How will this make me look? How can I manipulate the circumstances to cover my mistakes or take credit for the work of others?"

Jason rolled his eyes. "I know lots of people like that, too."

"Let me be clear. There is rarely a person who is devoid of all the axioms all the time. Most of us use all the axioms sometimes, and a few use some of the axioms all the time. The challenge is to employ the axioms under pressure, when being rejected, when feeling attacked, when we're on the verge of anger, or when conflict arises. Our work is to always ask the question, 'How might this circumstance be transformed by compassion, humility, gratitude, and conscience?'"

"Tough work."

"It is. So, Jason, what would a person who is immersed in the axioms look like?"

"I'm not sure," he answered. "I tend to see them as someone, I don't know . . . soft?"

"I think you're way off."

"There's a first time for everything."

Clara laughed. "I like you, Jason. Where have you been all my life?"

"Oh, busy making myself miserable," he joked, but not really.

"I think," she continued, "the person who has adopted the axioms as his own and acts within them sees suffering in the world—not just in the media, but in people immediately around him—and is personally determined to reduce or eliminate it.

"He sees his problems from a perspective that may even turn them into blessings. He has a keen and abiding commitment to learning new things, realizing that learning is an ever-expanding awareness of his own ignorance. He reads widely and deeply, on a diversity of subjects. He values the opinions of others and has no hesitancy in admitting he might be wrong now and again. His attitude considers and applies new learning and breeds creativity and innovation.

"He's grateful for every day. He lives now. Not yesterday. Not tomorrow. He wrings out all he can from life. He understands the sacrifice of others and acknowledges good work whenever he sees it. He's a builder. He knows that finding new solutions to difficult problems is much harder than finding fault or making excuses for why something cannot be done. As a consequence, he values reasonable risk and is not at all afraid to fail. He has the audacity to create."

"Audacity?"

"That's exactly right. Most people just accept things. This guy doesn't. He motivates and is motivated by love and an attitude that there is plenty for all. He forgives easily and is quick to give credit and take blame. He follows his conscience. He walks the talk. He's demonstrated a consistent ability to make moral choices that may be, in the short run at least, detrimental to his own advancement, which only serves to draw people to him. His actions are integrated and consistent with his values. He has a deeply held notion of who he is, a quiet confidence that seems to instill trust and confidence in those who know him best. He's a follower who gets followed, and he generally carries more influence than he's comfortable with."

Her eyebrows rose, as if to check in with her audience. Jason nodded in return.

"Now, I ask you, who do you want to work with? Who do you

want to work for? From which of these do you want to purchase products, service, or advice? Which do you want to call a spouse? Which do you want to call a friend? Who do you want to vote for? Who would you choose as a parent? As a teacher or elected official?"

Clara softly pounded her gloved hand on the snow.

"Who in their right mind would want anything to do with the first? Even the person who *is* the first would choose the second! These axioms are not spineless. Just the opposite. It takes strength to produce these kinds of behaviors because they are driven from the inside out rather than the outside in.

"And," she continued, "remember this—the answer to any problem lies at a level lower than the level at which the problem occurred. All the personal esteem in the world isn't going to resolve the problems associated with a lack of integrity. Problems of integrity are based in inconsistency between behavior and beliefs."

Aaron came trudging toward them from below, pack buckled at waist and chest, helmet and gloves on, ice axe ready and strap secured. It was evident that he'd exhausted his desire for photographs and seemed irritated at the length of the rest.

"Do you think," he commented, "we can get moving now, or what?"

It wasn't so much a question as an order.

"I think Aaron's right," Clara said, without any hint of frustration or defensiveness. She bumped Jason's forearm with her left hand. "We'll continue this later."

She whistled like a pro and raised her voice.

"Let's get this crew moving. Jeff, Sophie, let's go. There's a view up top you don't want to miss."

Clara stood and walked back to her equipment, hands gently clapping to the beat of her footsteps. The climbers stored their cameras and returned water bottles to netted pockets. It was beginning to warm. The sun shone bright and clear in the eastern sky, casting a long shadow of each climber across the icy white-blue face to the west. They considered and adjusted their clothing, substituting light-weight "poly" gloves for the heavier expedition gloves.

"I'd like you all to wear glacier glasses from here on out," said Clara. "You'll burn your retinas up here before you know it, and that'll hurt like the devil. Everyone clip in; tighten the safety screw of your carabiner down good. From here on up I want you in the climb, not in your job, your marriage, your portfolio, or your troubles. Remember, this mountain will hurt you if you're not paying attention. Be aware of the rope in front of you. I don't want a bunch of slack. Everyone okay to go?"

All nodded that they were ready.

"Sophie?" Clara's tone and raised eyebrows spoke a thousand words.

Sophie gave two thumbs up. "Still a three and ready to run. Let's go get this thing."

"Good, good," Clara said. "Quite a girl, Sophie."

Clara slipped on dark glasses, flipped the rope aside, set her axe, and started up. The rest followed in turn.

Chapter 29

INTERNMENT

The angle of the mountain steepened considerably as the team made their way toward 10,000 feet and the Devil's Kitchen, a heated volcanic dome that emitted geothermal sulfur in sufficient amounts to knock a climber silly. It was a smell like burnt gunpowder and not easily filtered or forgotten. Jason considered it a stern reminder that they were climbing the back of a geologic monster. The smoke and sulfur had a source, and, frankly, he didn't really want to consider how far below his position the solid rock became flowing fire.

Steel Cliffs towered above the climbing route to the right, clothed in icy white. On the left were Illumination Rock and Castle Crags. Not wanting to expose the climbers to the sulfur any longer than necessary, Clara set a fast pace toward the Hogsback, a snow ridge several hundred feet high and the preferred route for climbers on the south side of Hood. The Hogsback continued to incline as they made a gradual traverse northeast toward the Pearly Gates, a rock formation encrusted in sculptured ice, the product of a howling wind.

Clara stopped the group near the top of the ridge.

"Everyone okay? I want you to check your harness and rope. Make sure you're secure. This next section is the steepest on the southern side, and a fall is dangerous. I want you to be careful, not fearful. Be smooth. Nice and slow; nice and steady. Place your axe. Take a step. This is not a race . . . Sophie."

"Hallelujah to that," Jeff announced from below.

"Just above us is the Bergschrund, at about 10,700 feet, the most dangerous feature on the south side. It's a huge crevasse, a product of the glacier pulling away from the steep head wall. Given where the Hogsback formed this year, we'll traverse it on the left. A hundred feet above the mouth of the crevasse is the Chute."

Clara pointed to a steep gully a couple of hundred feet above.

"The Chute leads up through the Pearly Gates, which straddle the route. Everyone see it? Then it's up the last summit ridge to the top at 11,240 feet. We do not want to pay a visit inside the Bergschrund. That's one nasty piece of mountain—take my word for it. It's deep, it's wide, and it hurts."

Every climber was nodding back at their guide.

"Now, everyone listen up. I'll say this now, and then again when we get to the top. The Bergschrund is only five hundred feet from the summit. Do not get careless after we arrive on top. This is a big mountain. If you unrope, I want you well back from the north cornice. A slip over the north edge will cast you into a thousand feet of free fall. And a slip to the south will probably dump you in the Bergschrund, but only after you've accelerated down the steep Chute for hundreds of feet. Not a pretty picture either way.

"Everyone clear? Jeff? I want you to have fun up there, but I also need you to have respect for the fact that you're standing at relatively high altitude just a few feet away from big trouble."

"I think," Jeff said soberly, "it's fair to say you have my attention."

"I don't want your attention," Clara responded, "I want your commitment. There will be no goofing off up there. Majesty, yes. Humility, yes. Wonder, yes. Photographs, hugs, handshakes, yes. Pranks, no. Too dangerous. I'm a mother hen up top. You get too far away, and I get anxious. Too many weird things can happen. And if you think it can't happen to you, let me be the first to say you're dead wrong."

"Nice choice of words," Jeff chimed in.

Jason was beginning to understand Clara. He thought of their earlier conversation and the difference between accountability and blame. Intuitively, he understood what Clara was trying to tell them. She didn't want them to fear the mountain, just to respect it a great deal. Big difference. Fear, he remembered, brought trouble. Not an ingredient you'd want to add in any measure at this altitude.

Clara had the group bunch together and, once again, checked their harnesses. "Now, let's get up there.

"Sophie, how's the shoulder? It'd be my honor to carry something for you. Really would."

"Thanks, Clara, but I feel great."

With that, they were climbing again.

They made a slow traverse to the left of the Bergschrund, staying well away from its mouth.

"No one ever fell in who didn't get close to the edge," Clara said.

Jason thought that was advice he needed to apply more often. Each climber was silent now, just the sound of his or her own footsteps, axe placement, and breathing. This was not the place to gaze wondrously at distant landscapes. As spectacular as the view was, safety was by far the largest concern. Clara had made that clear.

Jason recalled his dream of the night before and shivered.

A hundred feet above the giant crevasse they entered the Chute, which, on this day, was covered in rime ice, made of supercooled water droplets that freeze on impact with any object. Jason had considered himself in reasonable shape, having spent most of the winter in the gym preparing for Hood. However, the climbing was exhausting, much steeper than a typical stairway, and at nearly 11,000 feet, oxygen became a sought-after commodity; the law of supply and demand at work.

He knew he didn't dare turn and look at Sophie. She probably hadn't broken a sweat. Above him, Aaron appeared strong and determined, his steps choreographed in unison with Clara's. Jason had found a rhythm as well, even at this elevation: set the axe with his right hand resting on the axe head, left foot step up, breath, breath, reset the axe, right foot step up, breath, breath, reset the axe.

He remembered Clara's description, "a slow rise." Even with the exertion required at this height, the climbing was meditative, and Jason found he had to willfully keep his wits about him to avoid drifting off in thoughts that could get him hurt.

Just below the Pearly Gates, Clara stopped for a moment to take stock of her team.

"Everyone okay? Aaron, you're a rock. You haven't slowed a step all morning. Jason, you're doing great. Sophie, you look like you just stepped out of Silcox. And Jeff, look at you. Great determination."

Jeff shook his head, sweat pouring from his face. "Are we there yet?" he whimpered.

"I must admit," Sophie said, "that I've been riding piggyback on Jeff most of the way. Just look at him, poor fella."

"If I could catch ya, I'd kill ya," Jeff responded.

"Not much chance of that," Clara offered through a smile. "To the top, then. We'll slow it down a bit now and let you enjoy the short trip up this last ridge to the summit. Shouldn't be any problems the rest of the way, but let's remain careful."

It took just a few minutes to make their way up the last ridge. Clara stopped the group just before they reached the top.

"Everyone up here with me," she said. "We'll stand on top together."

Slowly they made their way to the summit, together. Five climbers, most of them novices, huddled on what seemed at that moment the top of the world. They stood, drinking in the view.

"Look at that," Clara said quietly. "Have you ever in your life seen anything like it?"

For the first time, Jason considered the word *breathtaking* to be wholly inadequate. To the north, 11,000 feet below them, ran the great Columbia River—a small snake viewed from this elevation. Mount Adams and Mount St. Helens loomed in the distance. To be outside and under your own power while looking down at those two great peaks was numbing. He had seen them from an airplane many times. But this was different.

Beyond St. Helens, Jason could see the enormous flanks of Rainier rising to over 14,000 feet. He was transfixed. As he made a slow turn to the west, the coast range came into view. Continuing his scan, he could see the Willamette Valley and, to the southeast, Jefferson, the Three Sisters, and Broken Top, all gleaming magnificently against a deep blue sky.

"I don't know what to say," Sophie offered, "other than thank you. This is just awesome, just . . ." She shook her head.

Clara smiled broadly.

"You've been in the mountains all your life, Sophie. How is this different?"

Sophie placed her left hand on top of her head, as if to extract the right words.

"I've spent all my time in the mountains under the influence of adrenaline. I went up them only to ski down as fast as I could. Up. Down. Up. Down. Going up was never the point. Going down was the thing. I rode a lift and bore the inconvenience just so I could fly to the bottom. Sure, you appreciate the mountain, its natural beauty, and its size. But this! This is something different. Very different."

Sophie turned slowly and took in the landscape two vertical miles below. With a voice that whispered in reverence, she continued. "This, Clara, is almost religious. This just became less of a climb and more of a pilgrimage. This is a church, as sacred a place as I've ever visited. And we are lucky enough to witness its visual sermon. This is tranquillity and laugh-out-loud wonder all in the same breath. I can't begin to describe it." Sophie reached for Clara's hand. "I understand something about why you climb mountains. Thank you, Clara. Really."

Clara pulled Sophie next to her and with her arm around her shoulder said, "My good friend, it has been my honor."

With Sophie still under her arm, Clara let them all know that, given the perfect weather and time of day, they could spend as much as an hour on top.

"Take some photographs, write in a journal, grab a snack, whatever you'd like to do. Make sure you stay hydrated. Enjoy your time here. We're in no great rush to start down. But, let me remind you to stay clear of the north cornice and watch your step. Remember, the Bergschrund lies just below us to the south, mouth wide open."

Aaron, who hadn't breathed a word since arriving on top, released the black plastic waist and chest buckles on his Gregory pack, swung it off his shoulders, and set it down in the snow. He removed a small digital camera from an outside pocket. Loosening the top draw cord, he pulled out a cardboard cylinder with white plastic end caps, about two feet long, from the main compartment.

"Clara, is it okay to leave this here while I walk around a bit?" Aaron asked.

"Sure, leave your pack there. No need carrying it around. But please stay away from the north cornice."

"Thanks," he said. "I will."

Jason noticed that Aaron seemed introspective, even polite, which was a twist.

All of the climbers went their separate ways for the moment. Jason found himself wishing Anna were with him. *She'd love this,* he thought. He wandered around for a few minutes, took some photographs, and noticed Aaron off to the east side of the summit, about twenty feet away, kneeling in the snow in front of what looked like a small flag. Jason was impressed with Aaron's devotion as he knelt there, nearly immobile, knees touching, thumbs and fingers of both hands pushed together and resting on his upper legs. Jason thought it unkind to be eavesdropping, but he couldn't pull himself away. This man who had seemed so cold and insensitive for the last two days was displaying behavior that didn't appear to fit with the selfish person Jason had judged him to be.

Jason shook himself and turned away, but Clara's voice was inside his head.

Either give him some privacy, or engage him face-to-face.

"You must be kidding," he said out loud to no one but himself.

Jason knew that audibly arguing with himself at age forty-four was not the way to win friends or influence people. But still, engage him face-to-face? On that his conscience was insistent. *How about another alternative? Another option?* he countered mentally. He was sure that Aaron would not welcome an interruption. Invading this moment—whatever it was—was not going to enamor Aaron to newfound friendship. Still, the voice was undeniable.

This is just great, really great, Jason thought. *Okay, Clara, this is for you.*

As nervous as he'd been in years, Jason made his way toward Aaron. A photograph here, one there. Examine the snow conditions for . . . absolutely no reason at all. Meticulously clean his spotless glasses. Unzip an outer pocket, stuff a hand inside expecting to find who knows what, pull the hand out and zip the pocket.

Just go talk to him, for Pete's sake. Her voice was in his head again.

Jason was close enough to recognize that the flag he'd seen earlier, which the breeze was now gently moving, was double-sided. On one face, a white flag with a red circle in the middle. Japanese. On the other, the Stars and Stripes. American. What do you say to that? *Hey, nice little multiple personality flag you got there, Aaron.* Yeah, right. However, he was beyond turning back. He'd traversed across the summit, albeit in a nonsensical serpentine path, and he was close enough to Aaron that to not say anything now would appear astoundingly absurd.

"Hey, Aaron, tell me about the flag," he blurted.

Real smooth, he thought immediately.

Aaron didn't move from his kneeling position.

"This flag is why I climbed this mountain," Aaron said. "You probably think that's foolish."

"Not at all," Jason replied. "We all have our reasons, none more or less reasonable than the next. It certainly isn't any more foolish than the reason I'm up here."

Aaron looked over his shoulder at Jason. "And why are you up here?" he asked.

"My life is miserable and I thought maybe the thin air would break up the concrete I have for brains."

The self-disclosure seemed to puncture Aaron's armor. He laughed.

After a moment's hesitation, Aaron asked, "What do you know about the internment of Japanese Americans during World War II?"

Jason knelt on one knee beside Aaron and raked in a handful of snow. "Not much, I'm sorry to say," he responded. "I know it's been widely denounced by more recent politicians. I know they were pulled from their communities during the war out of fear that they were helping the Japanese military plot and carry out a strike against the west coast of the United States. Beyond that, I really don't know a whole lot."

"I can tell you more than you'll want to hear. I know facts, figures, quotes, and details. This is my family history, which is something most important to me. And what's important gets attention."

"I understand," Jason responded. "Listen, Aaron, I don't want to disturb you, but I'd really like to know more, especially since it appears that you and your family were directly involved."

Again, a moment of hesitation. Then Aaron began.

"My father was born in Japan in 1916 and moved with his mother and father and one younger sister to the United States, to San Francisco, in 1931, in the middle of the Great Depression. Tough time to move to America. He was fifteen. He became a U.S. citizen and married my mother in 1935. He was nineteen and confident, she, sixteen and the most beautiful thing he'd ever seen.

"In a few short years the war in Europe began its rumblings. From 1939 through 1941, the FBI compiled an index of 'enemy aliens.' My parents' and grandparents' names were on that list. My father and grandfather operated a successful restaurant that had become a hangout for Japanese community leaders in San Francisco."

"Were they proven to have plotted against the U.S.?" Jason asked.

"Heavens, no," Aaron responded. "But they were Japanese. Period. The tragic attack on Pearl Harbor in December of 1941 that put the United States into the war was also the beginning of trouble for my family. This internment, as it's now called, consisted of the forced relocation of nearly 120,000 Japanese and Japanese Americans, half of whom were children and nearly 80 percent American citizens, from their homes in California, western Oregon, western Washington, and southern Arizona. It turned into one of the largest controlled migrations in history.

"In May of 1942, just five months after Pearl, General DeWitt, who was the appointed administrator for the newly created internment program, issued an order requiring all people of Japanese ancestry, whether citizens or not, to report to civilian assembly centers while the newly formed War Relocation Authority put the finishing touches on the permanent camps. These camps were built mostly on Native American reservations west of the Mississippi. No compensation was provided to the reservations. They weren't consulted, either. Those living on the reservations at the time took some consolation in knowing that at least they'd get the improvements made to their land—however, in the end, the buildings and well-tended gardens were bulldozed or sold by the government."

"Why in the world would they do that?"

"I don't know. Perhaps out of a desire to erase any physical evidence of an unfortunate set of decisions. Whatever the case, the internment, known as Executive Order 9066, was considered a military necessity at the time, and was meant to protect against domestic espionage and sabotage."

"Was there evidence of that?" Jason asked. "Inside the western United States, I mean?"

"No. None. But the war was heating up and so were the accusations and incriminations against Japanese. General DeWitt repeatedly told newspapers, 'A Jap's a Jap,' and testified to Congress about the fact that he didn't want any of us here, that we were a dangerous element, that there was no way to determine our loyalty. He even said that all of America must worry about the Japanese all the time until we were wiped off the map. You can imagine what fear and passion that stirred up in the hearts and minds of people in America.

"At that point, it didn't seem to matter that even J. Edgar Hoover opposed the internment and refuted General DeWitt's estimate. Hoover wrote a memo to Attorney General Francis Biddle about the fact that he'd investigated every complaint involving Japanese American complicity with the Japanese military and had not found one shred of evidence that substantiated the allegations."

"If I recall," Jason said, "Hoover was not really known for his openness with minorities. Are you telling me that a letter from the director of the FBI, who was one tough cookie, had no effect?"

"Apparently, because the evacuations began immediately and on very short notice. The internees had no idea where they were going.

Many families were forced to leave with just the clothes on their back. Officially, they were told they could bring only what they could personally carry. The U.S. government promised to store larger household items such as furniture, but only if boxed and labeled, which few had time for. The government refused to make any promises about the security of their personal assets.

"My parents lost nearly everything. My father walked away from his restaurant, which happened to be located in a building owned by another Japanese American who was interned, a building that was later sold for pennies on the dollar."

"He never got his restaurant back?" Jason asked.

"How do you get a restaurant back after being gone for nearly three years and, upon your return, finding that the building in which it operated is now occupied by someone else? How do you get a restaurant back when your clientele has been forcibly scattered from eastern Washington to Wyoming?"

"So where did your parents go? Where were they sent?"

"They were sent to Tule Lake, California, a camp with watchtowers, razor-wire fences, and armed guards with orders to shoot to kill. Tule Lake was reserved for Japanese who were particularly suspect, which included community leaders, teachers, and priests. Housing consisted of tar-paper–covered barracks of minimal construction, no plumbing or cooking facilities, and unpartitioned toilets, all of which met the terms of international law at the time but were personally humiliating for an already humble people. Some families were split up and sent to different camps, a particularly difficult hardship."

Jason's eyes were wide. "Your parents were forced to go to Tule Lake? They were given no other options?"

"All Japanese were given the option of moving inland and out of the restricted zone on the west coast. Fewer than 10 percent of them chose that option, overwhelmingly due to limited resources and mounting hostility from the rest of America.

"Finally, sometime in 1944, when Japan's military was on the run, the U.S. government began releasing people to return to the west coast. And in January 1945, the exclusion order was rescinded. Most were incarcerated just over two years, some up to four years.

"Many who were friends of my parents were forced through social intimidation to return to Japan. Some have argued that the Japanese Americans were, indeed, disloyal, and their return to Japanese soil was evidence of that fact. However, it must be remembered that they had already been labeled 'enemy aliens,' lost their businesses, had their livelihoods destroyed, and were forced to quickly sell homes and property for next to nothing before entering the camps."

"My gosh, Aaron," Jason managed.

"Many were wiped out financially and left with no other option than to return to extended family overseas. And to make matters worse, some who returned to Japan were conscripted into the Japanese army. Certainly there were a few who returned to Japan, and others living in the U.S., who probably held some allegiance to Japanese military interests, but the emphasis should be put on *few*, very few."

"What happened to your family?"

"Physically, they recovered. But emotionally, it was a shock, especially to my father, who believed America to be a land of freedom, justice, opportunity, and fair dealing. Our entire Japanese American culture was nearly destroyed due to a belief by a paranoid few that something might happen. We were found guilty by association, by the color of our skin. It was this gross violation of individual rights by a democratic government that my father couldn't fathom and, paradoxically, probably never would have experienced under the constitutional monarchy that rules Japan. And that crushed him for most of the rest of his life. He remained here, and in many ways he loved this place. He worked hard, paid taxes, earned a hard-won respect from his peers, and was outwardly positive to business and social contacts. But privately he would tell you that his boyish enthusiasm for this great country never returned. Never again did he trust the authority of the U.S. government, and he took any communication, whether local, congressional, or presidential, with a skeptical air and critical view."

"Unbelievable," said Jason.

"I remember my father telling me once," Aaron continued, "about a questionnaire that was distributed throughout the camps, asking for volunteers for the United States Army. He completed the questionnaire and accepted their invitation, on condition that his rights as an American citizen be restored. How, he asked me, could a government ask him to fight for the freedoms of those on foreign soils when that same government had stripped him of his?

"To this day, I'm not sure that was the right response. I just don't know. But I don't blame him. Not at all. Remarkably, many Japanese Americans did volunteer from the camps, including the famed 442nd Regimental Combat Team, which operated in Europe and was one of the most, if not *the* most, highly decorated unit in U.S. military history."

"Did your family return to San Francisco?" Jason asked.

"No, never did. They knew nothing would be there for them. After Tule Lake, they went directly to Portland. I was born there in 1950. Both my father and mother died there some years back."

"How did they recover from a hit like that; what did they do?"

"Well, some small amount of compensation was paid to them in 1948 as a result of their internment, and that got them on their feet, at least. Dad started a nursery and successfully operated that until just before his death. Some stepped forward and tried to right the wrong. During the war, when fear pulsed through the veins of America, Colorado Governor Ralph Carr was the only elected official to publicly denounce the incarceration and apologize for the internment, an act that cost him reelection. Just goes to show that common knowledge is commonly wrong.

"In '76, President Ford was really the first U.S. president to publicly call the internment wrong. In '80, President Carter established a commission to study the detention. President Reagan officially apologized in '88 and admitted that the relocation was based, in his words, on 'race prejudice, war hysteria, and a failure of political leadership.' Then, in '90, the U.S. government offered $20,000 in reparation to any surviving internee, approximately 60,000 in all. It was a lot of money and well appreciated, but it represented a small fraction of the value of assets lost and was disbursed forty-five years after the camps were closed. That's a long time for the collective conscience to take action. Money will never buy trust."

"You wonder," Jason said, "how this could happen. I mean, this is the land of the free and the home of the brave. Right?"

"It's all about people," Aaron replied. "This is the land of free people and the home of brave people, until fear and mistrust begin to corrupt our thinking. It's a little scary to know that, despite language in the Constitution commanding that no person shall be deprived of life, liberty, or property without due process of law, those safeguards were trampled in a military order called 9066.

"A couple of years ago I read the autobiography of Chief Justice Earl Warren, who happened to be a key proponent of internment and California's attorney general at the time. I've committed these words of his to memory: 'I have since deeply regretted the removal order and my own testimony advising it, because it was not in keeping with our American concept of freedom and the rights of citizens. Whenever I thought of the innocent little children who were torn from home, school, friends, and congenial surroundings, I was conscience-stricken.'

"So, Jason, this is a story of families being torn from their homes; businesses, livelihoods, and property lost; people sent to temporary assembly locations, then transported to permanent camps; housed in poor conditions with little health care and bad nutrition. What does that sound like to you?"

"Unbelievable. It sounds like your family went through hell," Jason replied.

"I wasn't talking about my family, or Japanese Americans. I was speaking of the millions of wonderful Jewish families who were subjected to unspeakable things during the war. Their suffering far exceeded ours, but it's difficult not to notice the similarities. Both sides did horrible things. Fear of a people brings the hatred of a people. Once fear and hate find their way into the collective conscience, awful things can be justified. Horrible things. Sometimes it takes a generation to pass before we are willing to shine a light and illuminate our wrongs. Justification, like uranium, has a long half-life. It poisons the people it comes in contact with.

"And I fear these mistakes are being made over and over again. We don't seem to learn the lessons of our fathers."

He paused, drawing a deep breath of perfect air.

"My biggest problem was that I let this be my problem. For years I walked around with a chip on my shoulder over this whole debacle. What did that get me? Nothing, discounting the ulcer and stress-related headaches. I've got to let the bitterness go. And this little flag, Japanese on one side, American on the other, planted on the highest point in this state, is my offering to my father and mother that I will not forget their courage, that I hold their efforts to survive and thrive in the highest esteem, and that I will move on. A photograph of this moment will hang in my home for as long as I live. Silly, I know, but there is an awful lot of emotion behind this little symbol."

"Certainly explains why you've been so anxious to get to the top of this mountain," Jason offered.

"It explains it, but doesn't justify it. I'm usually fairly laid back. But this got in me and I had to get it done. I'll need to apologize to the rest of the group, I'm afraid. I haven't been much of a team player, and I'm sorry about that."

"Understandable."

Kneeling, they both watched the small flag blow in a light summit breeze.

"Listen," said Jason, "I appreciate you being so forthcoming. You didn't have to tell me a thing, but you did. Thank you."

"Maybe I can return the favor sometime, help break up some of that concrete," Aaron responded.

"Maybe over rainbow trout and a fly rod on the Deschutes?" Jason suggested. "I'm sure you could teach me a thing or two."

"You got it. Let's get a date planned before we leave today."

"That'd be perfect. Thanks."

Chapter 30

CHANGE TO CHANGE

Jason stood, placed a hand briefly on Aaron's shoulder without speaking, and walked back toward the rest of the group. He reflected on the opinion he'd formed of Aaron before this conversation. How poorly he had judged him! Thankfully, his conscience had gotten the better of him and he had taken a chance and followed the voice, Clara's voice. In doing so, he'd discovered that he had misread Aaron's actions and attitude completely. He would have missed gaining a new friend and new understanding if he had let his fear get the best of him. "The puddle ruling the Pacific," Clara would say.

Clara had removed her pack and was sitting against it, enjoying a hot drink from a stainless steel thermos.

As Jason approached, Clara said, "This is the best restaurant in the city, don't you think? Up here, PB and J is a delicacy. Heck, a strong cup of tea is nectar of the gods with this view in front of you."

"No argument from me," Jason responded.

"So tell me," she asked him, "is it what you thought it would be?"

He cast his eyes out to the panorama before him.

"It is, and more. And it makes all the difference to have people here to share it with. All of us arriving on the summit at the same moment was an experience I won't forget."

He sat in the snow next to her, legs outstretched, feet crossed, arms and gloved hands supporting from behind. For a minute or two they both sat in silence, taking in a green and glorious landscape few would ever witness from this perspective.

"Clara, this entire trip has been really wonderful. The climb. This view—look at this view! The conversation. The time I've had to think about what I'm doing and how I'm doing it. Your patience. Your view of life. Your willingness to be open about some personal experiences. I'm guessing I'm neither the first nor the last to have this experience. Why me?"

"I don't know, maybe you made yourself available, left yourself open. You came up here looking for answers. It didn't take a mystic to read your face and understand that you were not a happy guy. I don't know if anything we've talked about will change that. That's up to you. But sometimes things just happen, usually for a reason we're not aware of.

"The question is, what will you do when you return to your everyday environment, to disagreements with Anna and soccer games and staff meetings full of personal rivalries and cutthroat competition? What then? The axioms sound good at 11,000 feet, but can you apply them at sea level? Are you willing to *be* the change you know you want? Or will you fall back into the 'old Jason' whom everyone expects to show up—and continue to be miserable?"

"You say 'old Jason' like I've put him aside already."

"Have you?" she asked.

"Doesn't sound like much of a choice," he said wistfully. "But change doesn't come easy."

"Change isn't easy for anyone. That's the rub. But, know this—to not apply what you've learned and believe to be true, to not execute on your values, is unacceptable. Those who have mastered an ability to change understand the principle behind change."

"That's an interesting thought," he answered. "For me, change usually looks like chaos just before it turns into failure. If there's a principle there, it's hidden under piles of turmoil and wasted effort. To change something—a behavior, for instance—is like trying to bench-press three hundred pounds. I can push like mad, but the bar goes nowhere. Ultimately, I stop trying. I see the bar and the weight. I know it's heavy. I know I've failed miserably before. So, why try it again? Why put myself through that?"

"So, you give up?"

"I can't lift three hundred pounds. Not in a million years. And no amount of positive psychology is going to change that."

"No, but you and I together can lift three hundred pounds. You and Anna can lift three hundred pounds. You and Brian and Jesse can lift the weight. You are not in this alone, my friend. That's your mistake. You believe you've been left to lift the weight yourself, left alone to change. You can lift some of the weight. Someone else, someone you trust, can lift the rest. Over time, you'll become stronger. One day, with practice, perhaps you'll be able to lift the entire weight yourself. But to try for the big lift alone, the very first time, knowing that it's beyond you, is setting yourself up for failure and discouragement. There are always other alternatives. Open your eyes.

"The question is not, 'How can I lift three hundred pounds alone?' Instead, try asking yourself, 'What resources do I have that could get this job done?' Maybe the answer is to get help, or to reduce the weight. Maybe the answer is to distribute the weight over several bars, or to lift it with a new technique. Find an alternative that leverages the true principle."

"So, what's the principle behind effective change?" he asked.

He could almost see the lesson forming in Clara's brain. "Let's say, for just a moment, that you are a rubber ball," she said.

"My family would love that," he said.

"Good. You've heard of Newton's Third Law—for every action there is an equal and opposite reaction? Another way to state it: There is opposition in all things. Would you agree with that?"

"Yeah, I think I would."

"Good, good. The sphere is a good representation for how we change, or attempt to change. Why? Because change affects the natural shape of our lives.

"The natural shape of your life can be represented by a sphere. The sphere can be traveling in any direction and at any velocity and still remain a perfect sphere—as long as direction and velocity remain constant. You could be going forward or back, up or down, fast or slow. You buy that?"

"I do."

"Okay. Now, let me ask you this. What happens to a perfectly round rubber ball when it's dropped from ten feet in the air and hits a concrete floor?"

"It bounces," Jason replied.

"Is that all?"

"I know you well enough by now to understand that when you ask, 'Is that all?' the answer is definitely no. However, I'm not sure what you're getting at."

Clara smiled.

"A rubber ball dropped from ten feet above ground is perfectly round—that is, until it makes contact with the floor. You buy *that?*"

"Absolutely."

"What happens when the ball makes contact with the floor? Sure, it bounces, but something happens before that. And what happens before the bounce is the key to its ability to bounce. It deforms. It compresses. It stores energy. At its lowest point, it is less round than oblong, having experienced downward and lateral stress. We could say that the stress of impact has changed its shape. Even a first grader experienced at kick-ball knows what's about to happen. It's going to bounce. The ball has stored the energy and is now ready to move in a new direction, different from before.

"I think it's fair to say that most of us understand this law and how it applies in the physical world—how it works on this rubber ball. It drops, hits a floor, deforms under stress, stores energy, and, finally, reacts—it moves in a new direction.

"So, what happens when a human being attempts to change?"

"Well, my personal experience is—not much," he answered.

"And the question is, why? Why not much? Change for the better rests on a principle. Maybe you're not happy with your fitness, how you feel. Maybe you're struggling with your marriage, or your career. You name it, the principle is the same. There is a law that directs our desire to change. This law applies equally to the ball and to people, namely, for every action, there is an equal and opposite reaction."

Jason's head was already nodding. "Can't wait to hear this one."

"Okay. Let's assume you want to lose some weight and get the old body in better shape—you want to look and feel better—the universal New Year's resolution, right? The health and fitness ball is in free fall and you want to change its direction. You've literally become a sphere. Now, remember, to change direction requires you to experience impact. Then you begin to feel stress and deformation. Deformation begins to store energy. And finally, thank heaven, you begin to move in the direction intended. You bounce."

"I've been accused of being a little off the wall from time to time," he admitted.

"Me too. For a person resolute about losing weight and getting in better cardiovascular shape, all the New Age diets can't get you past the simple fact that such an accomplishment is contingent on consuming fewer calories than you burn—eat less and exercise more. And what happens? If you eat less than you have in the past, you get hungry. Your body is going to rebel. And even though you may be consuming better fuel, having cut out half-pound hamburgers for lean beef and fresh vegetables, initially you're going to feel tired, just a bit off. You've changed fuel and upset your biochemistry.

"Now, combine a new diet with unaccustomed exercise, and the ball really begins to deform under stress. New physical demands result in a soreness you hadn't counted on. Pain is now semipermanent, coming only while breathing. You may feel you're making little progress. Just a week or so into this new lifestyle comes a critical time. Maybe you've lost a couple of pounds, but at what expense? You're tired, sore, hungry—fairly miserable. You thought you had resolved to change direction so you could feel better, but you're limping, starving, and more than a little cantankerous. What's worse, you've been exposed to people who relish the consumption of only fifteen hundred calories a day, look excruciatingly fantastic, and run like the wind."

"Been there, done that. I hate those people," Jason commented.

"So, you want to quit, don't you? You hurt, you're hungry, and you hate tofu. This isn't working the way you expected. Like I said, this is a critical time. You are at maximum stress and deformation. If—and it's a big if—you understand the law behind the process, and if you keep at it, you know you're about to experience a bounce, a change in direction. The stress begins to convert to vertical energy. You soon begin to enjoy a good sweat and the way it actually energizes you. You begin to realize that other problems in your life that you once considered Himalayan don't loom as large. Now that you are demanding more from your firming physique, you crave good food, healthy food, food that tastes great and provides an abundant source of energy. Maybe even tofu."

"I'd still hate tofu, trust me."

She laughed. "Making positive changes in your personal relationships will require the same commitment. The principle is identical. Improving your relationship with your spouse may first demand some soul-searching—coming to grips with dumb things you've said and done and acknowledging those mistakes out loud to your spouse. You may need to reallocate your time and priorities, which have gotten out of whack over years of neglect, in order to be together more. These changes may be painful initially. Only you can determine whether the new direction is worth the deformation that comes at the beginning of the process.

"A change of direction, whether physical or emotional, demands impact, stress, deformation, energy storage, and rebound. In fact, we need to come to the realization that if a change in behavior is our aim and our attempt to change does *not* produce the deformation, we're not on the right track. You do not jump out of an airplane and expect to gain altitude. There is a law governing the inevitable fall to earth, and to expect something else is foolish. There is a law governing a person's desire to change for the better, and to expect something else is equally foolish.

"Most of us give up too soon and go in search of a less difficult route. Unfortunately, what appears to be way easier is never the easier way. The sad thing is, we give up while we're on the launchpad. We're fueled and pointed in the right direction, engines are fired, smoke and flames are billowing, and just when we're about to break the grip of gravity—just when we're on the threshold of a new direction—we give up."

"Change," he said, "is a pain."

"But the pain is usually brief. I don't know how much fuel the space shuttle has available at liftoff, but I'm guessing that within a few minutes of launch it has burned a substantial portion. Imagine that: a seven-day mission, and most of its fuel is gone in a couple of minutes. Did you know that the shuttle is purposely held down, locked to the launchpad until its engines have developed the necessary thrust? Engines are ignited and they scream to be let loose, but the rocket is held there until ready.

"Can you imagine what it must be like to be an astronaut sitting on top of that thing when it lights up? Wow! Once airborne, it jettisons its external tanks, and soon it's in orbit doing about 25,000 miles per hour and using a relatively minor amount of fuel. I'd be very curious to compare the shuttle's velocity-to-fuel-burn ratio to clear the tower, a few hundred feet high, against the same ratio during one full orbit around the earth, which might be 50,000 miles or more, depending on the diameter of the orbit.

"I do know that the short launch burns far more fuel than a complete orbit. There is no sidestepping Mother Nature, either when launching a shuttle, getting in better shape, or improving a relationship with a spouse. There is some initial stress involved in changing the way we think and act."

"Not the least of which is a sore back," he said with a smirk.

"Your conscience may be equally sore when you begin considering what you've done. Change requires lots of initial energy. Most of us can't figure out quickly enough how to convert or associate pain into pleasure. We decide that change is too hard, that this much work is too much work. Maybe we thought change would be immediate and results spectacular, only to come face-to-face with an immutable law, so we shut the engines down before we get airborne.

"Don't forget, though—changing direction for the good initially adds *more* stress. And so our good intentions have no chance of success because we were never prepared for the journey. Our worthwhile resolution is shelved until next year when we again dust it off and hope it may have gotten easier with the passing of time. It never does. The law never goes away.

"What if, instead, we could learn to expect the deformation? What if we started into a desired change with the understanding that, for a short time, things *should* be difficult, but that they *will* begin to improve—how much more effective at change would we be? Soon, we would know, there will be a rebound, a bounce, and a change of direction that is worthwhile in every respect. We would come to understand that the person relishing fifteen hundred calories a day, who looks great and has indefinite endurance, is in orbit at full velocity. What if we could teach ourselves to relish the deformation? Imagine that: the pain as a sign that the principle is working, that our actions are producing the desired result and will soon accelerate us in the right direction."

"I think you're right," he said. "I'd be more successful if I could go into change with a preconceived mind-set that the initial effort required is much larger than the effort to maintain the change once it occurs. To jump, I've first got to bend."

"How would that help you?" she asked.

"Well, if I actually prepared for the deformation, if I expected that initial result . . . that would be a whole new world for me. I'm embarrassed to say that I'm usually looking for a way to completely avoid the deformation."

She smiled. "Seek pleasure, avoid pain?"

"Exactly. However, you're saying that the deformation is a principle, a law of change, unavoidable if I want to make any progress."

Clara looked every bit the proud teacher. "That's what I'm saying. Look, from this moment on, how will you think differently about you? How will you think differently about Anna? How will you treat her differently? How will you think and act differently toward Brian and Jesse? How will you act differently toward coworkers? How will you manage them differently? How will you handle yourself when your conscience is telling you to do a difficult thing, 'I ought' or 'I ought not'? How will you inject compassion, humility, gratitude, and conscience into a circumstance in which they were absent yesterday? Can you picture yourself applying just one of the axioms? Tomorrow, maybe two. The day after that, who knows what might happen?

"What do you value? What do you believe? How can you begin to act consistently with those beliefs? This isn't some pie-in-the-sky philosophy. To change requires change. I know that sounds inane.

However, to change the way you interact with people, to be better, *you* must change, you must be different, you must think differently, you must act differently.

"And what will be the consequences of those kinds of changes? Initially, people might wonder about your motivations. Who is this guy? Who kidnapped Jason? They may distrust you. When that happens, *do not* resort back to the old Jason. Realize now, before you start, that mistrust may be a part of the process—commit yourself to continuing. You know the principle. You know where you are headed. Things will be difficult at first. But it won't take others long to completely forget the old Jason. Why? Because people respond to truth. The axioms stir something in all of us. Don't be afraid of the change that is in you. And so, I ask again, how will you think and act differently?"

Jason thought for a moment. "Well, I . . ."

"No, no," Clara said. "I don't want you to tell me. I'm unimportant. I want you to tell yourself. I want you to have a discussion with *you* about how today will be different from yesterday, how tomorrow will be different from today. I want you to consciously consider those things you're committed to doing, and those things you're committed to not doing, under any circumstance. Even the finest gardens need weeding, Jason.

"You've survived your worst instincts so far, if only by a whisker. You've got to find a way to get the axioms involved in your decisions. It was Aristotle who said, 'The best tragedies are conflicts between a hero and his destiny.' We all have a hero in us, you, me, everyone, but will we find our destiny? You cannot continue to separate society collectively from yourself individually; one is a direct reflection of the other."

"Hang on a minute. What does that mean?"

Clara gazed at him, eyes wide. "I'm not here to spoon-feed you all the answers. Think! What do you think it means?"

"You cannot continue to separate . . . what was it?"

"You cannot continue to separate society collectively and yourself individually."

She stared at him silently, eyes still wide and full of expectation. Jason felt like a crab in a deep pot of water on a hot stove, and the temperature was rising fast.

"Are you saying that the way society is feeling and behaving is a direct reflection of me, whether I'm at peace or at war with myself?" he managed. "I've got to tell you, Clara, that's just downright scary."

"You're finally getting it. Is it really such a radical concept?" she asked. "Who makes the decisions about how we behave as a society?"

"People in positions of power," he answered.

"Yes, but they are people first. That's the whole deal. The decisions you make as a manager reflect who you are as a person. That's unavoidable. In turn, those decisions are going to directly affect the lives of people who work for you. There's no great shock in that, is there? That concept can be applied to families, governments, schools, corporations, churches, nonprofits, you name it.

"You've got to stop trying to fight your way to peace. There is a better way. To continue to behave in ways that have proven hazardous to your survival is to cooperate with chaos. It's time for you to decide to change, Jason. Right now. Your discussion with me is coming to an end. Your discussion with yourself is just beginning. Stop worrying so much about the security of tomorrow and start caring for people today. That is the path to progress."

"I think you're forgetting something," he said.

"What's that?"

"We've not yet talked about the last three virtues."

Clara reached over and patted his knee.

"Plenty of time for that later. Besides, you already know them. We should get our equipment together and head down to see what Phil has cooked up for us."

"What do you mean, I already know them?" he asked.

"They are already in you. They're in everyone. Just like this view," she gestured broadly at the world stretched before them, "is in you. It isn't so much you looking out at this view as it is the view reaching inside you and connecting to something true, something that resonates."

"I think this view is not something I want to walk away from."

"Once you see the axioms work in your life, you won't want to walk away from them, either. They produce unimaginable results."

They sat in silence, quietly enjoying the sun and the sights from the top of an 11,000-foot volcano draped in snow and ice. Jason removed his gloves, opened an outside zipper pocket on his fleece, and pulled out a Cliff Bar. To his left, he noticed Aaron slowly making his way across the summit and back toward the group. Jason opened the foil package, removed the bar, and broke it in half.

"Hey, Aaron, care for a piece?"

"Sure, thanks," Aaron responded, sitting in the snow next to Jason and Clara. Jason offered the other half to Clara.

"You, Clara?"

"No, thanks."

Jeff and Sophie made their way over from the western summit and huddled over a small digital camera, scrolling through photographs. Jason stood to get a look. One of the photographs was off the north side and included Adams and St. Helens.

"Wow," Jason commented, bringing his right hand to his heart.

He noticed something in his inside pocket and remembered— Jesse's note. He hadn't thought of it since putting it there before leaving the cabin. He unzipped his fleece midway, reached inside and unzipped the interior pocket where the note was stored, and pulled it out. He carefully unfolded the paper and read.

"Dad, I hope you find what you're looking for on top of that mountain. We all do. I'll be thinking of you. Love, Jesse."

Chapter 31

THE FLAG

J ason knelt over the small Japanese-American flag. He read Jesse's note again before folding it once and carefully rolling it around the straw-sized wooden flagpole Aaron had planted in the snow. Once wrapped, he secured it with a piece of masking tape he'd removed from his camera bag.

"I hope I find it too, Jesse," he whispered to himself.

He rested there for a minute or two, then rose and made his way back to the group, all silent for the first time since reaching the summit. He walked toward Aaron, still sitting beside Clara, looked him in the eye, and extended his hand. Aaron took Jason's hand and nodded appreciatively. Neither spoke.

Jason moved to his backpack and began prepping for the descent. He drank some water, repacked his camera, and made sure the pack's outside pockets were closed and straps were secure. Hoisting the pack to his right shoulder, he turned back toward the group and reached with his left hand for the other strap, and he saw Clara.

Dumbfounded, he stood there motionless and watched her, now

kneeling over the small Japanese-American flag, securing the small, measured piece of seedling around Jason's note with knotted twine. She stayed there just a moment, stood, and made her way back across the summit to Aaron. Once again, without a word, hands were extended and heads nodded. Clara then walked to her equipment and began to pack. Aaron remained there, sitting in the snow.

Jason couldn't remember ever feeling like this. Clara's act had an electric effect on the group that was powerful, and she hadn't said a word. Jeff and Sophie moved to their packs and began preparing to leave the summit, or so he thought.

Jeff approached him with a postcard in hand.

Whispering, he said, "Listen, Jason, do you think Aaron would mind if I folded this around the base of his flag?"

Jeff showed him the postcard. It was the one his wife, Cheryl, had purchased at the gift store inside Timberline Lodge before their climb. On the front was a spectacular photograph of the south side of Mount Hood. On the back, a short note: "Dad. You're the coolest father in the whole world and we're so proud of you—whether you get to the top or not. Come back safe. Hugs are waiting." The note was signed, "Your girls."

Jason smiled and wondered if Jeff knew how lucky he was. "I don't think he'd mind at all," he offered.

Jeff approached the flag, folded the postcard around its base, nose to the wind, and returned to shake hands with Aaron, who now sat hunched in the snow, legs slightly bent, elbows on knees, hands on the sides of his head. He gratefully acknowledged Jeff and covered his eyes with gloved hands.

Sophie was last. She appeared to take nothing with her to the flag; empty hands dangled at her side. Once there, she knelt, just as the others had, and stayed for a short moment. She stood and returned to Aaron.

Like the others, she offered her hand. Aaron took it with tears flowing.

"Aaron," she said, "I don't know what that flag means to you. I don't need to know. I have nothing with me that is worthy of your flag or the other gifts that have been placed there, nothing except my gratitude for being able to experience this, to climb with you, and Clara, Jeff, and Jason. So, that's my small offering. I know you didn't really want me here, but thanks for letting me come along. It meant a lot to me."

She placed her left hand over Aaron's while still clutching his right.

Sophie walked over to her equipment, where Clara was waiting with her backpack held at shoulder level.

"Don't want to strain that shoulder, now, do we?" Clara said through a big smile.

"Thanks," Sophie said, reaching through the shoulder straps one at a time.

"Cinch that thing up good. It'll want to move around more on the descent than it did on the climb up."

Clara helped Sophie get the pack adjusted and made sure it was comfortable before doing the same for herself.

"Okay, gang, everyone ready?"

"We're ready," Jason said.

The rest of them nodded. Jeff stepped over and pulled tight a loose pack strap on Aaron's top pocket.

"Let's go," Jeff bellowed. "I've got three women at the lodge who can't wait to get their hands on me."

"Love is blind," Sophie giggled.

"Remember, same order as ascent. Stay in the same path we broke on the way up and we'll be in good shape. Nice and slow. Use your axe, just like we practiced. Let's get clipped back into the rope. We'll short-rope again on the way down. Any questions?"

Jason approached Clara and whispered, "What you did back there was . . . amazing. I don't know what else to call it."

"What did I do?"

"The seedling, the flag, come on, Clara, who else thinks like that?"

"You do, Jason. I just followed you. Jeff and Sophie followed you. I have no idea why you wrapped the paper around the flag. I just knew it meant something to both you and Aaron. My conscience told me I should acknowledge it. So I did. That's all. You were the one responsible for what just happened up there, and you didn't even know it. The axioms will do that. They take you right out of yourself. You just got a small dose of their power. Think about that."

Clara smiled at Jason, winked, then turned to the rest of the group.

"Let's go home."

Chapter 32

THE HOLE

The team carefully picked their way along the short summit ridge and down between the twin towers called the Pearly Gates, quickening their pace to avoid being hit by falling ice. The weather was holding sunny with little wind, and the temperature felt well above freezing. They had all shed their outer jackets and were down to fleeces or long-sleeved T-shirts. Clara slowed the pace back to a gradual descent and entered the Chute above the Bergschrund Crevasse.

"Careful," Clara called back to the others. "No hurry. Concentrate on every step, every placement. Looking good, everyone. If you get uncomfortable for any reason, stop, and I'll help you through it. Sophie?"

"Feeling great."

"Good, good."

Clara made her way down the Chute to within forty feet of the lip of the Bergschrund. Here, their path veered to the west around the crevasse before swinging back onto the Hogsback.

"I'm going to stop here," Clara said. "I'd like you to descend to me and step off the opposite side of the Hogsback, out of our climbing path. Come on down to me."

Each climber descended to Clara and stepped to the side to avoid being struck if a climber above them lost his or her footing and fell. Jeff arrived last, stopping just above the group on the climbing route.

"You folks are so good it's scary," Clara commented. She removed her glasses and began to wipe the lenses with the bottom of her fleece. "We'll take a careful loop to the right, west around the crevasse. Once we're clear of the Bergschrund and down the Hogsback, you can glissade if you'd like. However, if you do, I'd like you to—"

Sophie saw it first and pointed, then Aaron.

"Jeff," Aaron yelled, "watch yourself, we've got ice—"

Jeff ducked in time to avoid the blow. The rest of them scattered.

Clara, however, was not so lucky. She started to turn away, but not before taking a chunk of ice the size of a softball hard to the face. The impact recoiled her head back and took her feet out from under her. She landed on her left side, head facing down the mountain like a rag doll, and began sliding.

Aaron jumped for her, grabbing her boots just above the ankles. He desperately tried to swing his crampons down the mountain and plant them in the snow to stop their slide, but Clara's weight and momentum combined with his own proved too much, and he slowed their pace only slightly.

Perhaps as a result of all his practice, Jeff immediately fell on the head of his ice axe, burying the pick deep in the snow while screaming to the rest of them, "Arrest! Now! Now! Now! Arrest!"

Jason and Sophie dove for the snow and planted their axes as firmly as they were capable.

Fifteen feet below him, Jason saw Aaron heaving at Clara while gaining momentum. He also saw his rope go tight. Jason felt like a weed being ripped from a sloping flower bed. Aaron and Clara pulled him out of his original position and launched him in the air. On impact, he fought for arrest again, putting all his weight on the head of the axe. He could see the snow and ice streaking by his pick, creating a wake on the upside in the form of a "V."

Jason looked up the mountain to see Sophie bracing for the inevitable shock, which came in a second. The rope above him went tight. Sophie screamed as she was pulled down the mountain, but she held her arrest position.

"Fight, Sophie, fight!" Jason yelled, still sliding himself. Jason turned to look down in time to see Aaron, still struggling while holding Clara, go over the lip of the Bergschrund and disappear, their free fall tugging at him and accelerating his descent. Jason put his head down and applied all the pressure he could summon to the head of his ice axe.

Above him he heard Sophie, "Jeff, stop . . ." she screamed.

Jason felt a big tug on the rope above him, and his slide began to slow. "Fight!" he yelled, jabbing the snow with the spiked toes of his crampons.

Everything went silent. Jeff had stopped their slide, stopped them all. *Unbelievable*, Jason thought. Jason looked down to see that he'd stopped about ten feet above the lip of the crevasse.

Aaron broke the silence.

"Clara! Clara! Can anyone hear me up there?" Then again, "Clara!"

Jason yelled, "We've got you, Aaron, hang on."

"Clara's hurt bad," said Aaron. "She's hanging below me from her harness and not moving. There's blood on her face."

"Hang on," groaned Jason. "Sophie, Jeff, you okay?"

"Clara's bleeding. We've got to get her out of there," Sophie yelled.

Jason looked up. "Sophie, listen to me, are you okay?"

"I think we're okay," she answered.

"I can't move an inch without losing the grip I have on this axe," Jeff answered. "I'm afraid if I move, we all go in."

"Why in heaven's name didn't I take crevasse rescue more seriously?" Jason whispered to himself. He silently considered their choices. The radio was in Clara's pack. Calling for help was not an option. Better to get gravity working for them.

"Okay, look," Jason yelled, "Jeff, you and I are going to have to stay facedown and dug in, crampons, axe, teeth, whatever it takes. Understand?"

"You got it," Jeff said, grunting through his exertion.

"Sophie, I need you to move down enough to put some slack in your harness, enough to get unroped, but before you do, make sure Jeff and I can hold our spot. Once unroped, I want you to move as quickly as you can down here to me and get the aluminum stake, extra rope, ice hammer, two carabiners, and both ascenders out of my pack. Move!"

"I'm not sure you and Jeff can hold the weight. Clara and Aaron are hanging in midair. If I unrope—"

"Sophie!" Jeff interrupted. "We've got no other choice. The three of us can't hold them for much longer than a few minutes. Sooner or later gravity will drag all of us to the bottom of that hole. We've got to get another rope down there—and now. You're the only one who can do it."

"He's right," Jason echoed. "We've got to move."

"Okay, okay. You two let me know when you think you're ready."

"Aaron, you there?" Jason asked.

"I'm here."

"Can you get your axe or crampons dug into anything in there, or are you too far away from the wall?"

"I'm too far out, maybe six feet away," yelled Aaron from inside the crevasse. "I'm no help to you. Listen, I heard what you have planned. I don't think you and Jeff can hold us. There's a snow bridge about twenty feet below me. If I clip out, I can climb down the rope a few feet and make a jump for the bridge. Then you'll only have Clara's weight to deal with. I think I can do it."

"No! Listen to me—you have no idea whether that bridge will hold you."

"I don't care if it holds me or not. We've got to get Clara out of here. She's bleeding bad. With me off the rope, the three of you can pull her up. I'm going to unclip."

"You stay where you are! Let us try this first. If it doesn't work, then we'll talk about other options."

Jason considered the fact that Aaron wasn't going to agree and would unclip anyway. How to keep him there? he wondered.

"Listen, we're going to need your help getting Clara up safely. If she's really hurt, we may hurt her more just yanking her to the surface. We need your help."

Nothing.

"Aaron?"

"I'm here. Get moving."

"We're on our way," Jason answered.

Jason clawed and scratched the snow below him, trying to dig himself into the mountain as much as possible while keeping his body weight on the axe head. Jeff did the same above him.

"Jeff," Jason yelled, "you set?"

"No, I'm not set, but it's as good as it's going to get. Let's get Sophie moving."

"On my way," Sophie responded.

Slowly, Sophie inched her way down until she had enough slack between her harness and the short-rope to get free.

"You guys okay?" she asked.

Jeff groaned under the pull of the rope, taut as a guitar string.

"Just hurry. Get to Jason. We can only hang on so long."

"You two hold on. I'm about there."

Seconds seemed like hours. Jason felt Sophie above him ripping open his pack.

"Rope, bar, carabiners, ascenders, where's the hammer? Jason, where's the hammer? Got it. Found it."

"Sophie," Jason said, "you've got to get around the crevasse fast. Get to the down-side. About twenty feet below the lip, drive the stake in the ice with the hammer. Make sure you drive it at an angle to the slope. Bury it until you only have two holes showing. Understand?"

"Got it," she responded. "What then?"

"Tie a loop in the rope about fifty feet from one end and attach one of your locking carabiners to the loop, then attach the carabiner to the lowest hole on the stake and screw it tight. You with me?"

"Got it."

"Aaron is about fifteen feet below me on our short-rope, so he shouldn't be in the crevasse very deep, maybe five to eight feet. I want you to carefully attach the ascenders to the rope about twenty-five feet from the loop. Make sure they're secure. Then go to the edge of the crevasse and lower the rope down to Aaron. Drop it in until the ascenders are right in front of him. This is important. Don't let Aaron clip out of his rope until he's made a new loop in the rescue rope and attached his harness. I don't want him in there without protection. Can you do all that?"

"Done."

"Okay. One more thing. After you've lowered the rope to Aaron, and before he puts any weight on it, you've got to get back to the stake and tie another loop in the rope about two feet behind the stake. Attach your second carabiner to the top hole in the stake, and then attach the second loop to that carabiner. Understand?"

"I'm way ahead of you. You want me to get downhill from the stake, tie another loop in the rope and attach my harness. You want to use my weight as leverage on the top of the stake to keep it from coming out of the ice when Aaron puts his weight on it."

"Go, now!" was his response.

Jason's hands and forearms began to shake under the load.

"Sophie, got to hurry," he mumbled, his face buried in the snow.

Jason kept his head down, but could hear Sophie's footsteps crunching in the snow beside him. She was moving far faster than safety would permit, almost a sprint. Sooner than humanly possible, he thought, he heard her banging on the top of the stake.

Go, Sophie, he said to himself.

With eyes closed and his whole body shaking from the strain, Jason could barely hear the communication between Sophie and Aaron.

"Sophie!" Jason yelled.

"Just about there," she screamed back. "You hang on, you hear me! Hang on! Just a moment more."

Jason felt himself move, just an inch, then another. He was being dragged in. "Jeff, I can't hold it," he warned.

Above him, Jeff let out a groan that sounded inhuman, but said nothing.

Jason's slide stopped. He realized that the rope had stretched but Jeff hadn't given up any ground.

How in the world? Jason thought.

He dug in again with everything he had.

"Got 'em," he heard Sophie say. "Aaron is off your rope. Only Clara now. Let's go, boys. Quit wasting time."

In seconds, Aaron climbed over the downhill lip of the crevasse. Once safe, he clipped out of the rope, but there was no celebrating. He went right back to the edge.

"Clara! Clara!" he yelled.

Nothing. She hung faceup, arms and legs extended, like a pile of cordwood twenty feet below, still bleeding from the face.

"Aaron, we've got to set up a belay for Clara up here next to Jeff. Can you do it?" Jason asked.

"Done," said Aaron.

Aaron jumped back downhill to Sophie's belay and nearly ripped the carabiners from the stake, then pulled the stake from the ice, grabbed the hammer, and was gone.

"Sophie, thank you," he said back over his shoulder. "Now, go to the edge and keep an eye on Clara."

Aaron quickly moved back around the crevasse opening and uphill past Jason.

"That fly-fishing trip on the Deschutes is on me, buddy, every year for the rest of my life." He pointed a finger at Jason and was gone.

Aaron climbed to a position just below Jeff, planted the tip of the stake in the snow, and pounded the top with the hammer until it was nearly buried. He quickly slipped two carabiners through the only hole showing above the snow.

"Jeff, you are one strong ox, you know that? You just saved my butt. Listen to me, we've got to get you and Jason a rest. Let's not drop Clara now, okay? I'm going to get hold of the rope just below you and pull like mad. I want you to unrope from your harness and loop the rope through these two carabiners. Understand?"

"Yeah," Jeff responded. "You want to set up a belay."

"Let's do it," Aaron said.

Aaron stepped below Jeff, sat in the snow beside the rope, and jammed the heels of his crampons into the surface.

"You ready?" Aaron asked Jeff.

"Go."

Aaron picked up the rope, still stretched tight with Clara's weight, and pulled as hard as he was physically able.

"Good man," Jeff said. "Hold it right there."

Jeff scrambled to unclip his harness and get the rope free. He jumped down a couple of feet to the stake and looped the end of the rope through the two 'biners, then quickly descended another ten feet, sat in the snow with his feet pointing up the mountain toward the stake, clipped the rope back into his harness, and pulled.

"Got it," Jeff said. "Let's get her outta there, now."

Jason had watched Aaron and Jeff set up the belay and was just getting to his feet when Sophie jumped up.

"We've got movement!" Sophie screamed. "She's moving."

Jason felt fire rush through him.

"Clara, we've got you. We've got you," Sophie yelled into the hole. "You'll be out of there in a minute."

"Sophie, tell her we've got a belay set up with Jeff at anchor, and we're going to pull her up."

Jason jumped twice and was at the uphill rim of the crevasse next to the rope. He couldn't see Clara from his angle, but he knew that the taut climbing rope, which was cutting into the lip of the crevasse, was evidence that she was still hanging free inside the Bergschrund.

"Sophie, you stay where you are," Jason said, "and watch Clara. Talk her through this. She's banged the heck out of her head and may be a little disoriented. You keep her focused. Let her know we've got her. She's not going any farther into that lousy hole."

Jason turned uphill. "Aaron, Jeff, you ready?"

"Let's go," Jeff responded.

"Jeff, you watch that stake, make sure it doesn't come out of the ice," Aaron said.

Jason climbed back from the edge a few feet, far enough back to get a good grip on the rope with his feet dug in below him.

"Clara," Sophie yelled, "we're about to start pulling you out. You ready down there?"

Clara didn't say a word but gave her the thumbs-up.

"Jason, you be careful," Aaron cautioned. "One slip and you're going in unprotected."

"Roger that. On the count of three: One. Two. Three."

They all hauled back on the rope.

"Again: One. Two. Three."

Another pull.

"Again."

After a dozen or so pulls, Sophie yelled out, "Hang on, guys, she's just about at the ice wall on the up-side of the crevasse. Clara, make sure your hands are free of the rope, okay?"

Again, Clara gave the thumbs-up.

"Let's go, but very slowly," Sophie instructed.

"Six inches at a time, and slowly," Jason yelled over his shoulder. "Let's not hurt her."

"Got it," said Aaron.

Jason again. "One. Two. Three."

And then, "Again."

"She's close, she's right there," Sophie yelled.

Jason, leaning back into the hill, still couldn't see her.

"One more pull," he said. "One. Two. Three."

Jason saw a black glove appear over the upper lip of the crevasse, then the other.

"We've got you, you're going to be okay, you hear me?"

He looked at Sophie, kneeling on the opposite side of the crevasse, tears streaking her cheeks.

Jason crawled to the edge on his hands and knees, grabbed ahold of the rope with his left hand, and reached over the edge for a grip on Clara's backpack with his right.

"Pull," Jason said.

Slowly, Clara was pulled from the Bergschrund.

"Let's keep Clara belayed," said Jason, "until we can check on her and move her around to the other side. I don't like her perched here on top of this thing, understand?"

"I've got her," Jeff answered.

"Aaron, I need your help down here."

"On my way," responded Aaron.

Clara was lying on her left side, facing uphill. Blood smattered her face, apparently the result of a broken nose. She had lacerations on her right cheek and her helmet was cracked between the crown and the right ear. Jason winced at the impact required to break the helmet.

Leaning forward and resting a hand on her shoulder, he whispered, "Clara, where are you hurt, can you tell me? What can I do? How can I help you?"

"You did well, friend," she whispered weakly.

"It was all of us. We all worked to get you out."

"Not . . . the Bergschrund."

His face spoke his confusion as their eyes locked.

"Summit," she said. "Your work . . . up top."

"What?" he asked.

She summoned all her capacity to explain. "The flag, Jason. Made all the difference." After a deep breath, she added quietly, "One favor?"

"Anything."

"Find your family," she said. Clara closed her eyes and smiled.

Chapter 33

THE ANSWER

The Salem-based Blackhawk helicopter of the 1042nd National Guard Medical Company hovered overhead in clear skies and light wind. Mark Palmer, lead member of a three-person team from Portland Mountain Rescue, carefully covered Clara to protect her from rotor wash. She'd been placed in a rescue basket, secured, and prepared for hoist to the aircraft above.

Jason knelt at her side, looking up at the helicopter with concern.

"You folks did an outstanding job here," Mark yelled over the roar of rotor blades and swirling snow. "I've seen climbing teams much more experienced than this one fail miserably at what the five of you were able to accomplish. Just to arrest the slide was heroic, but then to move quickly and decisively to rescue your teammates—well, I really don't know what to say. Really remarkable. Great job."

Jason leaned forward and said, "It had much more to do with the woman who hung on the end of that rope than you'll ever know."

"I know," responded Mark. "We all know. She's one of a kind."

Jason reached for Clara's gloved left hand, the right having been wrapped in a splint. "You take care. I'll visit you tomorrow."

"Thank you, Jason. You saved my life."

It occurred to him at that small moment that him saving Clara from the Bergschrund was far easier than Clara trying to save his battered character.

Mark Palmer patted Jason on the back.

"We need to get her aboard, Mr. Snow," he yelled over the roar of an engine struggling at elevation.

"Where is she going?" Jason asked.

"Emmanuel Hospital," Mark responded.

Jason turned his attention back to Clara.

"Clara, you're going to be okay. I need to let you go." He smiled. "Try not to give these good gentlemen a hard time, all right?"

Clara smiled, winked, and motioned for him to come closer. She reached up and grasped the collar of his jacket. "I will never let you go. Friends for good, you and me."

He looked at her eyes, clear and determined. Her simple statement sent shock waves through him. He couldn't speak. It occurred to him that the expression would have seemed childish coming from anyone other than Clara. The difference in her declaration, the reason he could accept it, was simple.

He knew she meant it.

Jason stepped back into the rotor wash as the hoist cable was attached to Clara's basket. He waved as she began the ascent to the helicopter. Phil Chambers had come most of the way up the mountain by snowcat as soon as he heard there'd been an accident at the Bergschrund and was at Clara's side throughout the helicopter rescue. Now, they both watched as Clara was ever so carefully loaded in the helicopter and secured aboard. The Blackhawk backed away from the mountain and, once clear of the slope, banked gracefully to its left and slowly disappeared into the western sky.

Aaron, Sophie, and Jeff had descended an hour before. Aaron had been checked by the rescue team for trauma he may have sustained when he went into the Bergschrund. He was pronounced injury free and was cleared to descend to the lodge on foot on condition that someone accompany him. Both Jeff and Sophie immediately volunteered, but only after they saw that the 1042nd medical team had landed at Timberline to load equipment. Jason, however, had refused to leave Clara. Not that there was anything he could do besides offer her moral support. He simply could not leave her there.

"If one of us must come off the mountain, we come off as a group." Clara's statement of the night before rang in his ears.

So he had stayed with her.

"You've done all you can," Phil said. "She's going to be fine. Let's get you down. Some food might be good."

"Does sound good," Jason said.

They were offered an easy descent in the snowcat but passed on it, knowing that the relatively easy climb down would do them both some good. They gathered their equipment, packed up, and began their descent to Silcox, 3,700 vertical feet below.

Jason was quickly lost in thought as they descended. *The summit,* he thought. *What happened up there that Clara was so enamored with?* Was it possible that something as simple and obscure as a flag, a note, a sprig of seedling, a postcard, and a sincere expression of gratitude had been what had bonded them together and allowed them to perform the rescue, even save themselves? He didn't know. If so, it would prove a startling revelation to a man whose view of teamwork was steeped in formal controls and backstabbing competition.

It was not difficult to see the irony in their common experience. He had initially misread Aaron as being selfish and self-centered, yet it was Aaron who dove for Clara when she began her slide toward the Bergschrund and fought for her all the way in. He remembered Aaron's impatience with Jeff and Sophie during their training on

Monday and the weakness he had thought they displayed: Jeff, too big, too slow, unable to self-arrest; Sophie, too hampered by an injured shoulder.

Aaron had thought neither of them should climb, and his influence had colored Jason's thinking. Yet, it was Jeff's strength and Sophie's speed that had anchored their hope of rescuing Clara. Each of them had done their part and used their natural gifts—gifts different from those of the others—for the good of the group. Each of their gifts had proved extraordinary at the moment it was needed. They might have all been dead had it not been for, well, all of them.

It took Jason and Phil just a couple of hours to descend to Silcox, glissading most of the way. Jason, whose eyes and ears were now open to the lessons around him, heard the pleasant whisper of Clara's voice. It took many hours and huge effort to reach the summit, but only a fraction of that time to descend, a fact that was true for both climbing and personal progression. Hard-fought elevation could be lost much faster than it was gained. It was time he started focusing on summits.

It was approaching 5:30 p.m. and, having eaten next to nothing since breakfast, Jason was famished. Phil invited him inside the hut, but Jason preferred the bench outside where he and Clara had sat and talked the evening before, some of her tracing still visible in the snow. Phil soon returned and handed him a plate with a hot toasted cheese sandwich, two of his homemade chocolate chip cookies, and a cup of hot chocolate, then took a seat on the bench next to him.

"You're not eating?" Jason asked.

"Not hungry," Phil responded. "Can I get you something more? There's lasagna left over from last night."

"This is plenty, thanks. You've been very nice."

They sat in silence for a few minutes, Jason finishing his plate and gulping the last swallow of cocoa.

"Will you come back to the mountain?" Phil asked. "Will you climb again?"

Jason thought for only a moment before answering, "I don't think you could keep me away. Even considering the accident, the experience was . . . I don't know. Things happened up there I never thought possible. You've climbed with Clara. The experience wasn't as rigorous physically as it was emotionally and intellectually, even spiritually. She comes at you from all sides. My pride tried to fend her off, but the defenses only lasted a short time. Before I realized it, she was inside."

Phil chuckled knowingly. "She has that irritating tendency," he said. "Clara's a mirror. She comes by, you look at her, you see yourself more clearly than ever, you don't like what you see, she turns and shows you the truth about what you could be, then she's gone, leaving you to figure out what to do next."

"That's exactly how I feel. Like she's shown me the truth—or part of it, at least—and now she's gone and I have no idea what to do next. I don't even know the last few pieces of the framework."

"No matter," said Phil. "She probably wouldn't have told you outright what they were anyway. Once, after a conversation that I clearly did not follow, I asked her to just tell me the darned answer. Forget all the philosophical abstraction. I wanted to know, specifically, what I should do. Do you know what she said? Talk about irritating. She said, 'You know, you think the answer is in the answer, but it isn't. The answer is in the journey to the answer. So, for me to tell you the answer eliminates the answer.'" Phil laughed out loud. "I thought about that for about three minutes, then my head exploded. She can really get to you."

"She just left you high and dry?"

"At the time I thought so. But looking back, I can see that she was absolutely right. I knew the sequence; she even gave it to me in a formula I could relate to. I was a high school physics teacher for years. Always questioning. Always insatiably curious. Always wanting to know the answer. One day on her way up the mountain just after our conversation, she stopped at Silcox and left me a note, taped it to one of the burners on the stove. The note said: 'Life is contained in one simple formula: $P=ABC^2$. I'll be back in a week. Good luck. When you understand it, you must do something with it. Think Albert. Your friend, Clara.' That was it. Isn't she great? Drove me nuts for a couple of days just figuring the thing out."

"Life is contained in . . . what did she say . . ." Jason asked.

"$P=ABC^2$," Phil answered, smiling.

"What does it mean?"

"I finally got it when I thought about her 'Think Albert' comment, as in Albert Einstein. His famous formula for the calculation of energy is $E=MC^2$. Energy (E) equals mass (M) times the speed of light squared, the universal constant (C). I finally realized that in Clara's formula, 'C' was a constant and represented something very important, something she felt I could always depend on. If you know Clara and how she thinks and acts, the constant could be only one thing."

"What is it?" Jason asked.

"You know what it is."

"I do?"

Jason considered carefully what he'd learned the last couple of days. "The axioms," he said. "Compassion. Humility. Gratitude. Conscience."

"Exactly. The axioms. That left me with P, A, and B. Once I got C, the rest was easy. P is Peace. A is Action. B is Beliefs. Peace is the product of action, beliefs, and the axioms, which she squared due to their radical importance. Not a bad formula for a chemist."

"Can life be relegated to a formula?" Jason asked. "Is it really that simple?"

"Of course not. I don't think that was her intention," Phil answered. "I think Clara was trying to find a way to enter my world and relate truth in a way I might understand. Her brilliance was in understanding how I viewed things, what I was interested in."

"What about all the other virtues?" Jason asked. "We talked about integrity and personal esteem. She mentioned that there were three others, but we never got to them."

"You know the answer to that, too," said Phil.

"I do?" said Jason, unconvinced.

"Think. Hear Clara's voice."

Jason thought for a moment.

"You choose," Jason began, "what you believe, what you value, and you choose how you act. Everything else is a consequence."

Phil smiled. "No need writing formulas for consequences, now, is there?" he asked.

"I suppose not," Jason responded. "But I'd like to know what the other virtues are, just the same."

"They're intuitive, like a ball dropping down a stairway. One naturally comes after the next. Bop, bop, bop," said Phil. "The hard part is in the formula, in overlaying the axioms onto your own set of beliefs and convictions, then acting consistently with that combination. It's simple intellectually, but the impact emotionally is enormous. Living with the axioms in your life is fundamental; it's at the core of human existence. Living without them is much less powerful. It's the difference between TNT and an atomic bomb. One is much more fundamental, much more powerful."

"I've suddenly developed about a hundred questions," Jason chimed in.

"Good. Keep them handy so you can grill Clara the next time you see her. As for me, I just know what these things can do. You don't have to know the intricacies of atomic physics to understand the power of an atom bomb. You see it, you understand. I don't know all the concepts and philosophy behind the framework, I really don't. But I'm here to tell you the axioms produce a power far beyond what seems believable. Does an atom appear capable of releasing the kind of energy we now know exists there? I'm telling you, you start applying the axioms, you better stand back and be ready for the energy release."

"Can you tell me a little about how they've worked for you?" asked Jason.

"I'll try," said Phil. "I'm embarrassed to say I listened to Clara talk about the axioms for several years, all the while thinking them to be interesting concepts but not something that applied to life as I knew it. You can't argue with the value of compassion, humility, gratitude, and conscience, but I couldn't figure out what to *do* with them, either. I couldn't conceptualize the whys or hows of her philosophy, which means I didn't adapt them. They sounded good, but that was it."

"So, what did you do?" Jason asked.

"Finally, the pain in my life increased enough to make me look at what I was doing, how I was thinking about life and the circumstances that kept recurring. I began to see the same circumstances but different people, which was a real shock because it forced me to consider that maybe the problem wasn't all those people. Maybe the problem was me. Son-of-a-gun if *I* wasn't the common denominator. I learned something about myself I didn't much care for. I disliked my life, what I'd become, and the influence I was having on those around me, but I had no real desire to change. The only thing I can liken it to that you might understand is to say that emotionally, I had lung cancer but continued to smoke two packs a day. Makes no sense, I know, but that's the way I was operating.

"I'd like to say that I walked out of the darkness and into the light on my own. But, unfortunately for me, it didn't happen that way. I was thrown out kicking and screaming. I think Clara would call it the difference between changing due to circumstances and changing due to your own conscience. It was definitely circumstances for me."

"I don't want to pry or be presumptuous," said Jason, "but I could sure use an example."

"I'll tell you what happened the first time I saw the power of these ideas. I sculpt, have since I was in high school. I love the combination of art and science that sculpting requires. Clay, heat, wax, chemicals responding to fire and changing color, bronze, just love everything about it.

"About a decade ago I began to successfully sell some of my stuff. Soon after, I was fortunate to hook up with a woman who was a gallery owner downtown. Eva was well respected, had been in the business a long time, and she liked my work. We formed a partnership. I would produce the art; she would market and sell the pieces and set up national and international distribution. Make no mistake, she was a fine artist herself and knew the difference between art and junk. I was really excited about the possibilities of selling sculpture all over the world, a real ego trip. I became less focused on the work and more focused on the selling of the work. Big mistake.

"The second batch of sculpture I brought her included seven pieces. The day after I delivered the work, I received a call from Eva. She wanted to meet for lunch—probably, I thought, to talk about our international success and how I might produce more product. Imagine my shock when she told me all seven pieces were substandard. None of them were salable. They lacked depth, emotion, and creativity. They were nice, but far from inspiring. She told me I needed to refocus on the art, to start again. Finally, she told me she had lost some confidence in my sculpting."

"She sounds pretty tough," Jason suggested.

"She was. I was devastated, angry, depressed, insulted, and ready to rethink our whole business relationship. She'd lost confidence in my sculpting! Can you believe she said that? I hardly slept that night. I took her condemnation not as a comment on my art but as a rejection of me. I rehearsed in my head the conversation I was ready to have that would end our collaboration. Enter Clara."

"Just in time," said Jason softly.

"I was at Silcox the next evening, getting ready to climb Hood the following day and trying to clear my head. Clara was there. She knew I was a little down and asked what was going on. I told her my sob story. She smiled. I got angry, defensive. When I calmed down, we talked. She asked me some questions that stood my whole experience on its head.

"How hard did I think it was for my partner to deliver that message? she asked. Surely Eva would have preferred to say that the work was outstanding and would sell easily. It would have been much more fun and delightfully more profitable for her if that had been the case, but it wasn't. Clara reminded me that I had collaborated with Eva in the first place because of her knowledge and experience—but when she used that knowledge and experience to criticize my work, suddenly she became less qualified in my eyes.

"Clara asked if I thought my partner had suffered as a result of having to tell me the work was unacceptable. Had I made her job more difficult? I had to admit that she probably had suffered and that my response had done nothing but add hardship. Clara asked me if the work was up to my standard, if I liked what I had produced.

"'Separate the product from your ego,' she said.

"Well, once I did, I had to admit that the batch was less about craft and more about quantity. Given that, she asked if I had learned anything. Had I learned about art? Had I learned about the production of art? Had I learned about my partner? Could I bring myself to appreciate her courage and honesty? Would I really want to be in business with someone lacking those qualities? Could I humble myself enough to see the learning?

"Clara asked if there was anything I could find to be grateful for in this situation. There were suddenly scores of things I was grateful for. Almost immediately, the anger was gone. I was no longer offended. Instead, I was much more willing to see what had really happened, and I was sorry for the strain I'd put my friend under. Given all of this, Clara asked me what my conscience was telling me to do."

Phil stopped and cleared his throat.

"I'm sorry. This seems like a simple thing, but it was a turning point for me, not just in my relationship with my business partner but also in so many others. I drove back to Portland that night. Couldn't wait any longer. My conscience was too insistent. I called Eva on the way down, told her I had to talk with her that night, but not to worry. I met her at the gallery. I'll never forget our conversation. I simply told her the truth: I was sorry I had put her in the situation where she'd had to come forward and deliver such a difficult message, that it must have caused her pain and heartache. I told her I was sorry I had disappointed her. I told her how grateful I was that she'd had the courage to tell me the truth and how much I had learned from her. Finally, I told her I was committed to regaining her confidence in my sculpting, but that I would understand if she preferred to go in a different direction.

"I just tried to see her through the axioms, that's all. Well, by the time I was done, she couldn't speak. She walked around her desk with tears streaking down her face and gave me a hug. We've been the finest of friends ever since. I would do anything for her, and I think it's safe to say she'd return the favor. Do you know what it means to have people like that in your life? And to think I was *this close* to ending it. Just makes me ill to consider what I might have done, and what I might have missed in the ensuing decade without her.

"The axioms turned my world around. They saved my relationship with one of the finest people I've ever known. And here's what's frightening about what happened between us: To this day, she claims that what I said to her that night has influenced her in ways I can't imagine. It boggles my mind, that it was me who had an impact on her. She claims to have recovered a relationship with a teenage daughter because of the example I set that night. I had no intention of an outcome anything close to that. None whatsoever. I simply looked at her through the axioms and saw her differently. She saw the truth of that and, in turn, she looked at her daughter differently and saw the truth of it again. Peace came to both of us."

"Quite a story," said Jason quietly.

"This was a time in my life when loneliness had descended on me, not because I was alone but because I had chosen to segregate myself from human connection. I was convinced that a close relationship would reveal my weaknesses, why I was undeserving of trust, why I was unlovable. The axioms cut through all of that and brought me back—to my wife, my kids, and my friends. Back to life. It was as though a veil was lifted from my eyes."

Phil stopped for a moment to take in the epic surroundings.

"Listen," he finally said, "what Clara has taught you is true. I don't know what else to say. These simple things bring peace. Why? Because people instinctively respond to truth when they see it. It is in all of us, every one. For some of us, it's buried a little deeper, and the crust is a little thicker, but it's there. Was the conversation I had with my partner that evening a little frightening? Certainly. I had no idea how she would respond. I opened myself up to truth. She could have rejected my approach. Did I have any second thoughts about meeting with her on my way back to Portland that evening? You bet. But my conscience wouldn't let go. Will every conversation turn out so well? Some haven't, but that's okay. I can look myself in the mirror each morning and know I did my best. There is peace in that mirror now. Didn't used to be. There's peace for you too. I promise."

Jason swallowed hard. "My wife and I . . ." He couldn't finish.

"You're in some trouble?" Phil asked.

Jason nodded.

"It only takes one small light to illuminate a dark room. Turn on the light. The answer to your problem is not in your wife. It's in you."

Chapter 34

DAVID

T hey sat in silence, looking south from Silcox down the mountain. Jason finally recovered his composure and broke the stillness.

"Tell me about the last few virtues."

"I'm not the one to teach you about the virtues," said Phil. "Like I said, I don't really understand the whys, I've just seen them work."

He sat quietly for a moment, then continued.

"It occurs to me that you may be under a false impression that someone who understands the undercurrent of life's choices as well as Clara does would be able to avoid self-imposed tragedy. But Clara was not always so aware. She's struggled too. She's seen pain and heartache just like the rest of us, which makes her even more remarkable. Now she harbors an intense responsibility to pass on what little she thinks she knows, to build a bridge so others might not have to swim the river like she did."

"I don't know what river she swam, but if it produces a Clara Schroeder, maybe we should all jump in."

"I'm afraid most of us wouldn't make it. The river she crossed was swift and cold. I'm guessing she didn't tell you about it, or you'd know what I was talking about."

"Are you talking about her cancer?"

"No. She would tell you that was minor by comparison."

"Can you tell me? I mean, without violating a confidence?"

Phil smiled. "Knowing what you know about Clara, what do you think?"

They both sat silently. Jason wondered what could have carved such a deep swath through Clara. She was resilient and balanced, not someone you'd expect to be thrown off by life's surprises.

"Clara has a son," Phil began. "His name is David. I've never met him, though I feel like I know him well. David is the older of Clara's two children. Rachel is two years younger. To hear Clara tell it, he was the finest little boy to have ever graced the twentieth century. For the first few years, David was his mother's son. Followed her everywhere. What boy wouldn't be awestruck? Clara was a talented chemist who was on the rise, climbed big mountains, had a big personality, and was tall and beautiful in a natural way.

"By the time David entered middle school, Clara was convinced he was the next boy wonder. He had the brains, but he was missing a dose of the ambition she thought was necessary for great accomplishment. She was determined to light a fire under him, to make him what she wanted him to be. That was when things began to go wrong."

"I can see this one coming," said Jason.

"She pushed him so hard he began feeling as though he would never be worthy of her respect. He just couldn't imagine meeting the standards she set. Instead of following Mom around, he turned away and looked in the opposite direction—he looked for someone who would accept him for who he thought he was.

"By the time David entered high school, he was on the outside, socially and emotionally. He'd gotten himself into some trouble and seemed proud of it. Clara took his behavior as a personal stain on her credibility and pushed him harder. She feared that other good moms and dads would look at David and wonder about her and her influence. Clara once told me she felt as though she was in a death spiral with David. Every action she took seemed to drive David in a direction opposite from the one she intended. Down they went.

"Her husband would occasionally point out her disagreeable tactics and the acid they produced. She would get bitterly defensive and cut off any further conversation—a sign, she now understands, that her husband had fed her the truth. At the time, she couldn't swallow it, and she choked on it instead.

"Toward the end of David's junior year in high school, something snapped inside Clara. Instead of pushing him as hard as she could, she simply gave up. She pretended not to care. She went into survival mode. She told me once that her whole focus was to get him through his senior year and out of the house. Just endure it. She tried to tell herself she didn't even care if David failed to graduate. Just get through this. He'd be gone soon.

"Rachel was a sophomore the year David was a senior. Clara saw her as someone with less inherent talent than David, but she had a focus that came naturally and produced outstanding grades with very little encouragement from Mom or Dad. Rachel is Dr. Schroeder today."

"And what happened to David?"

"Well, Clara's wish came true. One cold, rainy, Oregon-in-February morning, David didn't come down for school, which was not unusual. She left for work without checking on him. When she arrived home that evening, there was no sign of David. She went upstairs and entered his room for the first time in months and was shocked to find it spotless. A small sticky note was stuck to the front of his dresser. 'I'm gone and out of your hair. Don't look for me.' No signature. No angry retaliation for the way he'd been treated. Just 'I'm gone.' That was it.

"Surprisingly, she told me she felt very little. He was probably hanging out at a friend's house for a few days, she thought. A week went by, and nothing. Clara became very anxious. She began to check around, to make some phone calls. Nobody knew where David was. She wondered about the possibility of an eighteen-year-old high school senior disappearing without telling anyone, an accomplishment only someone with no friends could pull off. Impossible, she thought."

"I don't like where this is heading," said Jason, shaking his head.

"She was wrong. David was remarkable. He'd left town without a trace. Clara was numb to it. One evening, about three weeks after David disappeared, she was at an orchestra concert that Rachel was performing in. A young man came forward and, accompanied by a woman on piano, played a remarkable violin solo to close the concert. It was stunning, Clara said. An ovation followed. Afterward, a woman about Clara's age stepped from the bleachers, walked across the floor, and took this young violinist in her arms. Clara couldn't hear what she said, but saw her take the young man's face in her hands and smile a mother's smile."

Both men drew a deep breath.

"Something broke inside her that night. She ran from the hall, down the corridor, and out into the parking lot. She found herself on her knees, her head leaning against a car she didn't recognize. Five years of barricaded emotion came pouring out. Tears flowed.

"How ungrateful she'd been for the wondrous gift of a son. How much pain had she caused him? How cruel had she been? Why had she not once tried to see the world through his eyes? How arrogant had she been for demanding he conform to what she wanted him to be? All these years she had driven him with a whip, seldom making the effort to walk with him side by side.

"She asked me once what I thought she would give up to hug her son, to take his face in her hands and tell him how much she loved him. Anything. She would give up anything."

"But it was too late. He was gone. They reported him missing, but since he was eighteen and there was a note, nothing much could be done."

"I can't imagine . . ." said Jason softly.

"Not many of us could, I suppose. Clara hasn't seen him since. Thirteen years. She gets wind of where he might be every so often. She once heard that David had a daughter born out of wedlock. Imagine, Clara could have a granddaughter she may never see. She's looked for years for the child. Never found her. Clara has an adopted family of climbers, many of whom travel extensively. Several of us carry pictures of David and a copy of his birth certificate, and we keep a lookout. I see him in every homeless young man I pass. I no longer view these folks as society's castoffs, but as missing sons and lost daughters. *Is it him*, I wonder? I can't imagine how often Clara considers his where-abouts."

"Wow!"

A moment of quiet passed.

"I think it's fair to say this would crush most of us. It was crushing Clara. That year was bleak. Summer came and went with little light and less hope. December arrived with Clara feeling as though she had nothing to celebrate. Rachel gave her a letter for Christmas. Nothing else. Just a letter."

"Was her daughter bitter?" Jason asked. "Just a letter?"

"Clara would tell you the letter was everything. In it, Rachel told Clara how much she loved her, how grateful she was to have Clara as her mother, that she wouldn't choose anyone else in the world to fill that role. She told her she knew the last few years with David had been rough, and she knew her mom was crestfallen about David and feeling guilty that she'd ignored Rachel as a consequence.

"One line dug deep: 'You are my shining light and have allowed me to see a new and wondrous world through my own eyes. Whenever I have a difficult decision to make, I ask myself, what would Mom do? What would she see? I am a reflection of you, which is more than I ever thought myself capable of being.'

"Rachel told Clara that she'd looked up to her all her life, and would for the rest of it. She told Clara that she was a woman of grace, intellect, warmth, spirit, and possibility, that Clara had an influence for good on those around her that she was incapable of recognizing. She said that although she too missed David, he had made his own choices—not that Clara wasn't a party to the difficulty, but that he was free to choose. Maybe someday Clara would meet David again and he would see her for who she was—a mother who loved her son.

"This young daughter told her mother that she would always be there for her. Always. No matter what. If Clara was suffering, she always had someone to lean on, depend on, cry on, and talk with. Clara has shown me the letter. It ends with Rachel saying, 'I am your daughter. You are my mother. Forever. Come home. We'll dry David's tears together. I love you. Rachel.'"

Both men sat quietly for several minutes, the wind the only sound. Jason considered how much energy Clara had spent in emotional combat with David, probably at the exclusion of Rachel. Yet, even at her young age, Rachel was somehow able to see through all that, to look outside herself and see her mom as someone who was suffering. The daughter came to rescue the mother. Truly remarkable for someone her age. Who was he kidding? It was remarkable for someone his age.

Jason remembered the old homeless man he'd treated so brutally. Someone's lost son, he considered. Connected to that old man were perhaps a heartbroken mother and a desperate father. Jason had done nothing but increase that suffering, a notion for which he was now pitifully ashamed.

And Anna. What had he done to Anna? It occurred to him that life was too short for selfishness.

"Clara would tell you she was reborn that Christmas day, limited only in her ability to perceive her own capability and conceive a response to the circumstances of her life. And that response is her choice. Her daughter stepped forward with the axioms when Clara needed them most. Compassion. Humility. Gratitude. Conscience. Simple things, really, but they rekindled in Clara the majesty of life and human influence. I think Clara now sees every relationship as an opportunity to learn and grow. She's willing to risk rejection to gain connection."

"Looks to me like she has a lot of connections going for her."

"True. But you can appreciate her feeling like she has little time to waste. She sees suffering and responds openly without worrying about the potential pitfalls. Her philosophy has been tempered at high heat. The bridge she builds is sturdy and sound. She would like nothing more than to keep others from the river. But, at the end of the day, it's our choice. Bridge, or cold river."

Phil paused a moment, then asked, "The question is, Jason, which will you choose?"

Chapter 35
HOME

J ason pressed the black button on the key fob, disengaging the security system. He opened the double doors at the back of the
Suburban, swung his pack and ice axe off his shoulder, and
dropped them inside. He took off his fleece, unlaced his climbing
boots and pulled each one off with the toe of his opposite foot,
slipped on a pair of running shoes, and closed up the back end.
Climbing into the driver's seat, he checked his cell phone for mes-
sages. Nothing.

He guided the truck south out of the parking lot and began the
twisting drive down Timberline's access road toward Government
Camp. Ponderosa pine appeared thick below the tree line as he drove
in and out of shadows, dirty snow still dotting the north-facing em-
bankments.

He'd not been on the road long when he was startled by something coming at him. Flashing headlights.

"What does this guy want?" he said to himself.

He shot past the black Volvo wagon before it dawned on him.

Anna. That was Anna's car. Red brake lights appeared in his rearview mirror and dust boiled up—it *was* Anna, and she was pulling over.

Jason jumped on the brakes and pulled the big Suburban to the shoulder in a skidding stop. He yanked the handle to the driver's door, quickly pushed it open, and jumped out. Brian was already on a dead run toward him, Jesse and Anna behind. He ran up the hill and met Brian in midstride; the kid nearly knocked him over.

"Dad, we heard. You okay?"

"I'm fine, Brian. Thanks."

Jesse grabbed him by the neck, tears streaming down her face, neither of them able to speak. Anna stopped a few feet away, watching.

Jesse released her grip and waved a sheet of paper at her father. "We stopped by the cabin on the way up for binoculars," she gasped, "and found this note on your desk upstairs. I love you, Dad." Jesse kissed him on the cheek and hugged him again.

"I love you too, Jesse."

At that moment, Jason considered all he'd accomplished—money, status, title, all of it—and it all paled when compared to hearing his daughter say "I love you." Clara was right: people mattered most. These three people, Anna, Brian, and Jesse, mattered most. But the note Anna had left in the cabin was still gnawing at him, and he silently considered the sickening possibility that they were through.

Anna walked forward tentatively. "Mountain Rescue called early this afternoon. They said there'd been an accident high on the mountain at the Bergschrund, and your group was involved. They didn't know what happened or who was hurt, but the initial report was that two people went into the crevasse."

Her voice cracked with emotion. "You scared us to death. I thought maybe we'd lost you."

He reached for her and they embraced. He could feel her weeping. It had been months, maybe years, since a hug had meant anything of value.

"I'm okay, Anna, I'm okay."

The family stood along a narrow stretch of two-lane mountain road for the next few minutes. Few words were said, but there was comfort in the fact that they were together again.

"Let's go home," Jason said.

"Brian, will you and Jesse drive the Volvo?" Jason asked. "I'd like to ride with Mom. Do you mind?"

"Sure, Dad. We'll follow you," Brian answered.

Anna placed the keys in Brian's hand. Jesse came to Jason and hugged him one last time.

"Thank you, Dad," she said, "for the best birthday present I've ever received."

"You mean the note?"

"No. For you, Dad. Just you."

Chapter 36

BREAK

J ason slept fitfully. He awoke once again to the illumination of his clock radio: 5:52 a.m. Despite the short night on Monday and an exhausting day on the mountain, his brain would not disengage. He finally gave up the fight, rolled out of bed, slipped on his sandals and terry-cloth robe, and quietly descended the stairs to the kitchen. He made a cup of hot chocolate, something he always found soothing, then wandered outside to fetch the paper.

Back in the house, he hoisted the hot chocolate and folded himself into a favorite chair, put his feet up on an ottoman, and scanned the headlines.

The front page consisted of the usual: missile attacks, suicide bombs, trouble between the city of Portland and Oregon Health Sciences University stemming from cost overruns on an aerial tram.

On the bottom right, however, one column in width, was a story of interest: *Novice Climbers Beat the Bergschrund on Mount Hood.*

Jason sat forward.

"A group of Mount Hood climbers, five in all, four of them

novices, extracted themselves from the infamous Bergschrund Crevasse yesterday in a self-rescue hailed 'brilliant' by members of Portland Mountain Rescue. Clara Schroeder, an experienced mountaineer and guide for Cascade Mountain Guides, and Aaron Nakashima of Bend fell into the crevasse, located at the 10,700-foot elevation on Mount Hood's south side, after having summited the 11,240-foot peak. It is reported that Schroeder was hit by ice fall, knocking her unconscious and precipitating a slide toward the Bergschrund. Nakashima, in an effort to stop Schroeder's slide, was dragged into the crevasse with Schroeder. Jeff Glendale of Portland, Sophie Frederickson, a University of Oregon student, and Jason Snow of Portland worked to rescue the two climbers. Schroeder was transported by a Blackhawk helicopter from the 1042nd Oregon National Guard Medical Company to Emmanuel Hospital and Medical Center, where she is listed in stable condition. The other four climbers, including Nakashima, walked off the mountain under their own power and were uninjured. Mark Palmer of Portland Mountain Rescue, who directed the emergency medical response and airlift, called the rescue 'heroic.' Phil Chambers, a well-known mountain guide and close friend of Ms. Schroeder's, was also on the scene, but declined comment."

He read the article several times, and then at 6:45 a.m. began making coffee. Anna's alarm would go off at 7:00 a.m., and he wanted to have a fresh pot waiting when she came down. He couldn't remember the last time he'd extended himself for her, even for something as simple as coffee, and he found an unexpected pleasure in it.

"Couldn't sleep?" she asked when she arrived a few minutes later.

"No, not much," he responded. "Take a look at this." He poured her a cup of steaming coffee with one hand and slid the newspaper in front of her with the other.

After reading the article, Anna asked, "How did the five of you pull this off? This guy from Portland Mountain Rescue called what you did 'heroic.' What really happened up there?"

"Clara happened. I don't know what else to say. She's remarkable."

"How is she remarkable?" Anna asked.

"She turned me inside out for two days, Anna. Made me see things in ways I've never considered."

Anna frowned. "Look, I want you to know that I'm glad you're off Hood and not hurt," she said. "You gave us a scare. But do you really think two days on a mountain and a chance meeting with an extraordinary woman is going to change things? Between us? Is that what you see happening here?"

"You don't think that's possible?" he asked defensively.

"I don't. Too much history, Jason. You've been absent from our marriage for too long."

He could feel the old Jason rushing to the surface and didn't like it, but combating forty-plus years of habitual stupidity was a war he had no experience fighting.

"Are you kidding me?" he heard himself say. "I haven't been *absent*. Dinners, movies, ball games, school concerts—I've run my tail off for this family. How can you say I've been absent? My work pays for the coffee you're drinking. Remember that."

Anna began to get angry but managed to collect herself.

"I'm grateful for your work and your financial support," she said, "but you're emotionally gone, Jason. You're a ghost, a vision without much substance. I can't remember the last time you and I had a decent conversation about something important, other than your work, of course."

"What's wrong with my work?" he asked incredulously.

"Nothing is wrong with your work. I just never thought you'd be married to it instead of to me. I'm at a point in life when it's time for me to consider the future. Brian and Jesse are out of the house in just a couple of years. You and I will be all that's left, and I must tell you that's a frightening thought.

"What are we going to do when it's just the two of us, just you and me? Are we going to be one of those couples who divide their miserable life together in two: yours spent at work and on the golf course, mine volunteering at various charities and working part-time, maybe California Pizza Kitchen with girlfriends and the mall in the evenings? Is that what you think I want, Jason?"

Anna's demeanor was glacial, and it scared him.

"Neither you nor I want to be trapped for the rest of our lives," she said. "You must admit you're as miserable as I am. It's time we made some hard choices."

"I can't believe this," was all he could think to say. He felt like he was on a speeding train and couldn't get off.

Anna took a sip of coffee.

"Let me be absolutely honest with you," she said. "I don't trust you. I don't believe you are willing to put in the effort required to change yourself or our marriage. Be honest with yourself. Do you really see that happening? Do you really think that's possible, given our history?"

Anna paused, and then continued, "I'm not willing to lay my heart on the chopping block one more time and watch you cleave it in two again. I don't believe you have the tools that allow you to see when you're hurting those closest to you."

He was getting a full dose of the pressure cooker of change and wondered if it was possible to outlast the heat of the moment. Clara had warned him about how hard it would be. He needed her wisdom now more than ever.

"So, no more chances?" he blurted out. "That's it? Are you really going to do this to the kids?"

Jason noticed tears rolling down Anna's face. Her eyes were wide, her mouth set square with resolution.

Anna stood straight and folded her hands together on the granite counter. "I can't be with you anymore, Jason. I can't. I'm at the end of the road. If I trust you one more time and you disappoint me, I may never again be able to trust myself or my own judgment. I'll wonder for the rest of my life how I could have been so stupid. You've not only wrecked this marriage, you're close to wrecking me, too. Let's get out while we both have something left of ourselves."

Her comment shoved a blade through his heart. Finally, he began to hear Clara and remember. He tried to breathe, to calm himself. His marriage was on the line, and he knew that what was said during the next few minutes might decide its fate forever. He needed to find a way through Anna's defenses—ironically, defenses he'd taught her to construct. He had to strip away all the crust that for so many years had hidden him from her.

Jason reached for her hand and said, "Please Anna, will you sit with me for a minute?"

Anna moved slowly toward a stool at the kitchen bar next to Jason, approaching him like a snake handler approaching a basket full of cobras.

He considered where he might begin.

"Anna, there are some things I want you to know and understand. I am the cause of your problems and heartaches, not that that notion will be revolutionary. I just want you to know that I know. I know I've been less than the man you'd hoped I would be. I know you're frustrated, angry, and discouraged about the way things have turned out. I know that the way I've acted would lead you to believe that you are not a priority for me, that, in fact, you are well down the list. I know I've caused untold suffering for you, and I imagine that most of that suffering has been cried out in the stillness of lonely hours when I was not there to wrap my arms around you and tell you things would be okay.

"I know I've been a callous husband, unloving at times. I lost myself, Anna. I feel like a man who for years has been wandering in deep woods, and who only now is getting a glimpse of a clearing ahead.

"I understand your unwillingness to believe that I might change. There's nothing in my past that would allow a glimmer of hope in that regard. And I don't blame you at all for not trusting me. I haven't earned your trust. I've done things you couldn't imagine and kept most of them from you, hoping you wouldn't find out or see the shame and disgust in my eyes. It's time you heard them, Anna, time you found out what kind of man you've been living with all these years."

"You've had an affair?" Anna asked. "Are you seeing another woman?"

"No, but that's about the only mistake I haven't made."

"Then what are you telling me? What are these things I can't imagine?"

"A discussion for another time. Right now, I want you to know that I still love you. I'll always love you. We were soul mates once, years ago. Whether we can be again, I'm not sure. You are a constant example to me of patience, goodness, and compassion, even in the face of my torment.

"Whatever happens, I'll be grateful to you for the rest of my life. Brian and Jesse have the finest of mothers. You've been a remarkable wife, more than a man like me should ever expect. If we don't make it, Anna, I want you to walk away knowing you did all you could. The failure that our marriage has become was not your fault. I understand that a relationship is a two-way street, but there's far more bad traffic on my side of the road than yours.

"I'm so sorry, Anna. I've taken you for granted. I've used your goodness against you, taken pleasure in that, even. What kind of man does that to the one person on earth he owes everything to?"

Anna sat speechless, looking down at the counter.

Jason paused, willing himself a sense of control.

"Anna, if a divorce is what you want, I won't stand in your way. I'll make you a promise: There will be no fight, no tug-of-war over assets, children, or egos. I'll give you what you want. I'm at your mercy. You've suffered enough at my hand. If you want me gone tomorrow morning, I'll pack my things and quietly exit your life. No sense in making this any tougher than it already is. It's your choice, Anna."

Anna sat in stunned silence at the revelations that had laid him wide open. But her next statement revealed that she had been burned too many times before.

"Words are nice, Jason, but your actions are the signature of your real intent. I'm not ready to spend the rest of my life with a man I can't trust."

She gasped for breath, as if she didn't quite believe this day had finally come. Gently she took his hand and struggled on. "Jason, listen to me. I love you. You are the father of my children. We are wrapped together, you and I, and will be for the rest of our lives. I've thought so much about us over the last months, especially when you were on that mountain. There are some great memories, things I'll cherish all my life, but are those memories enough to make up for the heartache and the distance between us now?"

Jason looked at his wife of twenty-one years, tears rolling down her face in a sadness not even he recognized.

"I don't know, Jason," she said, trying to catch a breath. "I need time to think. I need time alone."

He sat motionless. Stunned. She pulled her hand away and wiped her face, stood slowly, and walked from the room without another word.

Chapter 37

INTO THE DARK

He found himself alone, driving east on Sunset Highway, through the Vista Ridge Tunnel, north onto the 405, past the Pearl District, and east over the Fremont Bridge, the Willamette River translucent below. Jason exited to the right and down a short off-ramp to a stop sign. He accelerated across the intersection and into Emmanuel's medical campus. Among evergreens, rhododendrons, green lawn, and gardens, Jason found a parking spot in a concrete garage next to the main entry.

Thoughts of Jesse's note folded around him. Part of him wished he had it with him now, and part felt some sense of peace knowing it was waving gently at elevation, a reminder he could always look to there on the top of Hood.

He recalled the words of the short note: "Dad, I hope you find what you're looking for on top of that mountain. We all do. I'll be thinking of you. Love, Jesse."

He walked through automatic doors and found the information desk.

"Schroeder," he said. "Clara Schroeder?" He listened to the directions and rode the elevator to the third floor.

When the doors opened, he exited and took a few turns before noticing a crowd of people standing around the nurses' station forty feet beyond. Phil Chambers chatted with two men and a woman, all unknown to Jason.

Jason approached. Phil stood when he saw him. "Jason," he said warmly.

They shook hands like old friends, understanding in their eyes.

"Meet my wife, Julianne. Julianne, Jason Snow. Jason was on the mountain yesterday with Clara."

"Such an honor to meet you," she said. "I've heard so much about you. Clara's talked about you all morning, and she is not a woman easily impressed." Julianne smiled, her handshake as firm as her husband's.

How long had it been since anyone had felt it an honor to meet him? He considered that now, at this moment, he would happily give up any such accolade just to have Anna back.

He shook himself back to the present. "Pleasure meeting you too, Julianne." Jason scanned the hallway, where fifteen or so folks were quietly gathered in whispered conversation. "Who are all these people, Phil?" he asked.

"These are people who, over the years, have been adopted into Clara's extended family. Some are climbers. Some are former coworkers. Some are neighbors. Some are running buddies."

Phil pointed across the hall.

"That guy over there does her dry cleaning. That woman works at a café near Clara's old office—however, you'd be shocked to learn what she accomplishes in her spare time. They come from all walks of life. Rich and poor. Educated and less educated. They are all ordinary people who've done extraordinary things as a result of their association with Clara. Dear friends, every one of them."

"Quite a group of people," Jason said, a sadness in the fine texture of his voice. He understood the melancholy, the result of his thoughts of Anna. Emily Dickinson was right, he thought: Parting is all we need of hell. But there was something else, something unexpected that wrenched him—some dull awakening of the prospect that if it were Jason in the bed instead of Clara, no one would really care.

"Quite a woman," Phil responded.

They stood musing for a moment. Then, with a look of concern, Phil reached for Jason's upper arm and pulled him aside. "You okay, Jason?" he asked. "Clara's going to be fine. No need to worry. She'll be out of the hospital this afternoon and good as new."

"I'm fine, really. Just a little tired," Jason responded. "Phil, I'd like to see Clara for just a moment. You think I could say hello? Maybe sit by her bedside and see how she's doing?"

"She'd be very disappointed if you didn't. The nurses are a little riled with the crowd, so let's go to the end of the hallway and circle back around. Follow me."

Jason followed Phil to room 3873.

Phil stopped as they arrived at the door. "I'll leave you to talk with Clara."

They shook hands.

"Thanks Phil, for everything."

"It was my great pleasure," Phil responded. "I'm not sure I'll see you again today. Julianne and I are about to leave."

He stopped and looked away, then back at Jason.

"Listen, don't make yourself a stranger. Come see us soon. We can use men like you on the mountain. Clara needs men like you on the mountain. We'll see if we can make the next climb a little less eventful."

"You'll see me again," Jason responded. They smiled, and Phil waved good-bye as he walked away.

Jason Snow stood on the threshold alone, pondering the circumstances that had brought him to this place at this moment. Time clicked by in a two-count rhythm between despair and hope.

Gently, he pushed open the heavy door and stepped into the dark.

SOME PERSONAL THOUGHTS

Many if not all of us have people inside that are unknown, identities that are hidden due to a fear of rejection or misunderstanding, or simply because we do not really know ourselves. We put on the cloak of social acceptability for public appearance and carefully cover our true nature. Yet, our ability to do good in its most sincere and effective form is founded in our being true to who we are. That path must begin in love, with compassion its outward expression. I've been lucky. Life experience, family, and good friends have stripped away the false clothing of public acceptability and uncovered, to some degree at least, who I am.

I was born an only child, an Rh factor baby, in November 1957, in Sacramento, California, but soon moved back to my parents' generational birthplace just west of Portland, Oregon, where I've spent nearly all my life. I was blessed with a mother and father who loved me and were committed to my well-being. It was there that I met Val—while in junior high school, I'm somewhat embarrassed to admit—and married her some years later. We've been married thirty-one years and it's gone by in a blink. It was there that our two children, Nick and Lauren, from whom I've learned more than I've taught, were born and raised. It is there where remarkable friends, whom I miss, still reside.

The years have proven that the book of my life was written by serendipity. I have worked in construction, watered a golf course by night, been a ski instructor, owned a couple of companies, consulted, and worked in both small and large organizations. The only constants have been a dangerous sense of pure curiosity, a desire to create, impatience in my lack of progress, and very supportive family and friends. I've always been a writer, but shied away from the profession for fear of starvation. It's only been in later years, when my concern for feeding my family was supported by other means, that writing became a necessity, nearly unavoidable.

Writing and publishing a book takes a community. First and foremost, this book would not have seen the light of day were it not for the involvement of Tracey Snoyer, who pushed, dragged, inspired, critiqued, and supported *Snow Rising* since the first sentence was put on paper. Tracey was the first to understand. She's a member of my tribe and I'll be grateful for her friendship for the rest of my life. Patti Rokus, my nonbiological sister, was there from the beginning too, an early reader who always had well-considered counsel.

A couple of years ago we moved our home to an elevated bench above the Great Salt Lake, with the stunning Wasatch Mountains literally in our backyard. Serendipity once again imprinted its hand on my life. *Snow Rising* found its way to Jen Hogge, who saw something in the manuscript I didn't, then to Ron Millett (in the Philippines, no less), who provided the first dose of professional encouragement, and finally to Emily Watts (editor) and Chris Schoebinger (product director) and others at Shadow Mountain Publishing. My experience with them has been positive beyond any reasonable expectation, and their patience remarkable. However, I'm as surprised as anyone that "author" is now part of my biography.

I'll admit I'm a private man. *Snow Rising* will tell you more about me than I'm comfortable with. I'm partially revealed in both Jason and Clara, and life's lessons have sometimes come hard and left craters of regret. I'm hoping the Clara inside me is overcoming Jason's stupidity, that I'm pointed in the right direction. *Snow Rising* is not autobiographical, but it had its germination in personal experience and careful observation.

It's only now, looking back, that I can say that things happen for reasons unknowable at the time. Our life's work, then, is to be curious enough to discover the unknowable things, to surrender to the enchantment of living. Any acquaintance I have with joy, the essence of life, comes through an application of truth, which has stripped away the false clothing of accumulation. When all else failed, I returned to the fundamentals. *Snow Rising* is about those fundamentals.

We all have stories. Someday, perhaps, you and I can share a hot chocolate and you can tell me your story. I'd like that.

All my best,

Matt

I BELIEVE

I believe we are not in need of more influence, but more influence for good.

I believe in the inherent goodness of man. I believe we have an individual obligation to build, lift, inspire, and cultivate that goodness in ourselves and in others.

I believe that we possess a natural, imbedded appreciation for a small set of fundamental human axioms that, when witnessed, stir something in us that some have described as truth.

I believe that this truth is not dependent upon any particular philosophy or theology; however, any belief system that is dispossessed of these fundamental axioms is a false belief system, and it will ultimately bring sorrow to the individual and dis-integration to the organization.

I believe that life, like so many other remarkable systems around us, is a sequence that begins in choice and ends in consequence.

I believe human beings are capable of more than most of us

can imagine. I believe in the vast reservoir of unrealized human potential.

I believe that compassion overcomes hate, humility overcomes
pride, gratitude overcomes pain, and conscience overcomes evil.

I believe in the power of belief.

PRACTICES

Some Practices in Support of the Axioms: Compassion, Humility, Gratitude, and Conscience

1. Make a conscious decision to widen your circle of friends. Develop a new extended family. Invite someone new over for dinner. Find out as much about these new people as you possibly can.

2. Develop an exquisite sense of curiosity. This world we live in is remarkable. Open your eyes and see.

3. Volunteer at a children's hospital.

4. Volunteer as a reader at any local hospital.

5. Volunteer at a homeless rescue mission, particularly at a time other than Christmas or Thanksgiving.

6. Begin carrying sack lunches with you in your car to hand out to those asking for help. Make no judgments.

7. Take a class on a subject you've never studied.

8. If you have formal authority (as a parent, manager, or teacher, for example), lead discussions with questions and avoid making

P R A C T I C E S

immediate statements of opinion. Learn to speak last during group discussions where opinion and diversity of thought are valued. Encourage new dialogue.

9. Post the code CHGC (Compassion, Humility, Gratitude, Conscience) on your fridge or mirror as a reminder of true north.

10. Spend one hour a month as a mentor in a local public school.

11. Have your family adopt an underfunded charity. Do what you can. Don't worry that it's not enough. Start somewhere.

12. Begin to ask yourself: "If I apply compassion, humility, gratitude, and conscience to this problem, what alternatives might appear that I couldn't identify before?"

13. Begin valuing people more and processes less.

14. Be more aware of people and their needs.

15. "Stop Doing" lists may prove to be as important as "To Do" lists. Make a "Stop Doing" list.

16. Hold yourself accountable for a change you want to make in your life. Report to only yourself. No one else. Keep the process confidential.

17. Send or deliver a handwritten thank-you note to someone once a week for a minimum of three months. It cannot be e-mailed, blogged, typed, recorded, or phoned.

18. Commit to making an individual effort (not governed or organized by any group) to alleviate the suffering of one person you do not know.

19. Be kind—especially to those who don't deserve it.

20. Give sincere compliments freely.

21. Follow through on promises. Don't make promises you can't keep.

22. Begin to ask yourself: "If I applied compassion, humility, and gratitude to this problem, would my conscience drive me to take a different action?"

23. Do something—anything—that benefits someone—anyone—outside your family.

24. Take blame; give credit.

25. Be slow to accuse or take offense and quick to forgive.

26. Befriend someone outside your normal social circle, preferably someone whose life view is different from your own. Learn about what makes them tick. Ask questions. Why do they see the world the way they do? Climb into their skin. What is their life experience? This is not a debate. This is a learning opportunity—for both of you. Begin a dialogue. I'm not suggesting you adopt their lifestyle. I am suggesting you may want to broaden your outlook. Remember, understanding is the beginning of peace. What are you afraid of?

27. Write a note of condolence to someone in despair, but wait a month—wait until virtually everyone has forgotten the trauma and left the person alone. Let the person know that even with the passing of time, it's all right to mourn and to feel bad.

28. Begin to do small things that allow you to overcome your fear of telling those around you how much they really mean to you. People mourn at funerals partly because their chance to communicate is lost. Do not wait. Give them the gift now. If you wait, your chance may be lost.

29. Start right now, *right now*, to repair a damaged relationship. Be the one who steps up first. Do it now. Do not wait. If the reciprocal response is less than positive, try again.

30. Stop wishing idly that others had a better life. Do something. Work for it in whatever way you can.

31. Start a journal and commit yourself to regular entries—once per day, once per week, once per month—something, anything. Be absolutely honest with yourself in your writing.

32. Determine to say to people the nice things you think—deliver the gift.

33. Live in a state of delayed gratification. Give yourself an

obstacle to get through first before acquiring a much-desired prize. It will prove all the sweeter.

34. Apologize now to a family member, a friend, or a coworker for whatever stupid thing you've said or done. Don't assume that time has dulled the memory of the offended. Do it now.

35. Try a week without TV. Notice the changes in your interactions, your thoughts, and your choices.

36. Stop making decisions and taking action based on "what is right by me." Start making decisions and taking action based on "what is right." The latter may be slightly more inconvenient.

37. Volunteer to pack food at the local food bank.

38. Get trained as a hospice volunteer.

39. Do something that scares you to death (rock climb, sing in a choir, volunteer to teach or speak publicly, write a short story and submit it for publication, skydive). Do it now. Overcome yourself.

40. Take stock of your poor habits. Make a list. Show it to no one. Eliminate them one by one. Replace them with something personally and collectively meaningful. Write, paint, sculpt, return to school, exercise, read, cook, build something, volunteer, sing in a choir, learn to play an instrument, garden . . .

41. Do something anonymously to make the day for someone else.

42. Take no action that violates your internal sense of integrity. Stick to your guns. Follow your conscience in applying compassion, humility, and gratitude.

43. Develop your capacity for stillness. Find at least fifteen minutes a day to be alone, without being bombarded with cell phones, e-mail, computer games, newspapers, magazines, i-Pods, TV, treadmills, CDs, bills. Just you and your own mind. Be still. Imagine that.

44. Guard carefully the reputation you acquire with yourself.

45. Trust before you are trusted. If you get burned, trust before you are trusted.

46. Spend a day volunteering at a children's cancer hospital. Be

prepared: It may change your outlook on life. Go with family or a friend if possible.

47. Plan a day hike through an area within reasonable distance of your home that you've never seen. Take a camera. Print, sign, frame, and hang your favorite photograph.

48. Read a book that is well outside your normal areas of interest. Discuss the book with someone you trust. Stretch a little.

49. Begin now, right now, to do the one thing you've thought you should do for a long time, but this time, begin the action with a commitment to compassion, humility, gratitude, and conscience.

50. As a family, anonymously do yard work for a neighbor who is out of town. Swear everyone to secrecy.

51. Learn something new every single day: about a person (living or dead), an event (current or historical), an area of study, a new discipline (art, music, or the like), yourself. Take a class. Start living.

52. Volunteer as a driver for Meals on Wheels.

53. Volunteer to read in an elder care home.

54. Learn to be grateful for today. Appreciate how lucky you are, regardless of your problems. Measure your problems against those of six billion others and dare to consider that yours may not be that significant. Take a breath. Things have a way of working out.

55. Stop and pick up garbage along a roadway or walking path.

56. Stop being afraid of showing deeply felt human emotion. It's what makes us . . . human!

57. Never, ever attempt to motivate people through fear, guilt, control, or coercion. It may produce short-term results, but long-term effects include reduced effectiveness, resentment, conflict, and dis-integration. Find another way through compassion, humility, gratitude, and conscience. Remember: He who must state his authority to win an argument or to motivate—has none.

58. Begin to consider carefully how you can make decisions at home and at work that may not appear to advance your position,

status, or career, but will advance the position, status, or career of people around you.

59. Do some research about deceased family members. Where and when were they born? Where did they die? What did they do that might be notable? Did they leave behind journals or letters? What drove them? Include other family members in the search if possible.

60. Begin writing a journal specifically for future grandchildren and great-grandchildren. What do you want them to learn? Consider the way you are living. If you knew you were setting a pattern for future generations, what, if anything, would you want to change about yourself? How would you do it?

❄   ❄   ❄

The above list is by no means exhaustive. Make your own list of activities that support the axioms. If your circumstances allow, develop the list with family or friends. Put activities on your calendar so you'll find time to do them.

Do these things without expectation of something in return.

Do them as a family if possible and if your situation allows. If you are single, do them alone or with a friend. However, do not, repeat, *do not* let life's inevitable excuses become a barrier to action.

No one can do all of the activities suggested. But everyone can participate in at least one. Start now. Keep it simple. Don't wait. Stop the justifications.

Learn to ask and act on four simple questions:
• How can I alleviate suffering?
• What can I learn?
• What am I grateful for?
• What is my conscience telling me to do?

Remember: Life is a sequence that begins in choice and ends in consequence. Here's to choosing well.

BIBLIOGRAPHY

Bailey, Tim. Clackamas County Sheriff Criminalist. "Final Report on Mt. Hood Climbing Accident." *Traditional Mountaineering.* Traditionalmountaineering.org/Report_Hood_Bergschrund.htm.

Broom, Jack, and Steve Bovey. "Pointing Fingers in the Mount Hood Tragedy." *The Seattle Times,* July 25, 1986, A-1.

"Cascade Range Summary, Mt. Hood, Oregon." *United States Geologic Survey (USGS).* http://vulcan.wr.usgs.gov/Volcanoes/Hood/summary_mount_hood.html, and http://vulcan.wr.usgs.gov/Volcanoes/Hood/framework.html.

Castenada, Carlos. *Tales of Power.* Simon & Schuster, 1974.

Coffin, William Sloane. *Credo.* Westminster John Knox Press, 2004, 7.

"Description: Mount St. Helens Volcano, Washington." *United States Geologic Survey (USGS).* http://vulcan.wr.usgs.gov/Volcanoes/MSH/description_msh.html.

Dickinson, Emily. "My Life Closed Twice Before Its Close." *Poems by Emily Dickinson.* Third Series. 1896.

Feynman, Richard P. *Six Easy Pieces.* Penguin Books, 1995, 2.

Fuller, Richard, Edgar Mortimer Levy, and Sylvanus Dryden Phelps. *The Baptist Praise Book.* A.S. Barnes and Company, 1872, 260.

Heath, Malcolm. *Aristotle, Poetics.* Penguin Books, 1996.

Ihenacho, David Asonye. "Nigeria Corruption, The Press and the Government." *Nigeriaworld,* October 26, 2003.

"IMSCO Proposal / Report: Towards An African Solution." International Multicultural Shared Cultural Organization (IMSCO), a United Nations NGO, May 4, 2005. Request of the United Nations Secretary-General Kofi Annan for his report: In Larger Freedom. Document #001/ IMSCO-MDG/2005.

"Japanese American Internment." *Wikipedia.* http://en.wikipedia.org/wiki/Japanese_American_internment.

King, Martin Luther, Jr. "Tribute to Mahatma Gandhi." 1958.

Kouzes, James M., and Posner, Barry Z. *The Leadership Challenge,* third edition. Jossey-Bass / John Wiley & Sons, Inc., 2002, 393–94.

Lawrence, J. M. "How African Governments Gobble Aid." June 24, 2005. www.sluggerotoole.com./archives/2005/06/not_northern_ir.php.

"Mount St. Helens." *Wikipedia.* http://en.wikipedia.org/wiki/Mount_St._Helens.

"Mount St. Helens National Volcanic Monument." *United States Department of Agriculture.* http://www.fs.fed.us/gpnf/mshnvm/.

Peters, Ed, editor. *Mountaineering: The Freedom of the Hills,* fourth edition. The Mountaineers, 1982.

Prabhu and Rao, editors. *Mind of Mahatma Gandhi,* third edition. Navajivan Publishing House, 1968, 440.

"The Cascadia Subduction Zone." *The Pacific Northwest Seismograph Network.* http://www.pnsn.org/HAZARDS/CASCADIA/cascadia_zone.html.

"Timberline, the Real Deal." RLK and Company. www.timberlinelodge.com.

Warren, Earl. *The Memoirs of Chief Justice Earl Warren.* Rowman & Littlefield Publishers, Inc., 2001.

When you make it back from the summit, we invite you to join the ongoing discussion at www.snowrising.com. There you can contact the author, share your own observations, download a reading guide (perfect for book groups), and learn about upcoming author signings and how to schedule an author presentation.

Jason Snow's story continues in the sequel to *Snow Rising*, coming fall 2011. Watch for updates at www.snowrising.com.